T0043105

THE LOST
LETTERS
of
AISLING

ALSO BY CYNTHIA ELLINGSEN

Marriage Matters

The Whole Package

The Lighthouse Keeper (a Starlight Cove novel)

The Winemaker's Secret (a Starlight Cove novel)

A Bittersweet Surprise (a Starlight Cove novel)

The Choice I Made

When We Were Sisters

A Play for Revenge (a Starlight Cove novel)

THE LOST LETTERS

of

AISLING

A NOVEL

CYNTHIA ELLINGSEN

LAKE UNION
PUBLISHING

This is a work of fiction. Names, characters, organizations, places, events, and incidents are either products of the author's imagination or are used fictitiously. Otherwise, any resemblance to actual persons, living or dead, is purely coincidental.

Text copyright © 2024 by Cynthia Ellingsen
All rights reserved.

No part of this book may be reproduced, or stored in a retrieval system, or transmitted in any form or by any means, electronic, mechanical, photocopying, recording, or otherwise, without express written permission of the publisher.

Published by Lake Union Publishing, Seattle

www.apub.com

Amazon, the Amazon logo, and Lake Union Publishing are trademarks of Amazon. com, Inc., or its affiliates.

ISBN-13: 9781662513664 (paperback)
ISBN-13: 9781662513657 (digital)

Cover design by Caroline Teagle Johnson
Cover image: © Aastels / Shutterstock; © Abigail Miles / ArcAngel; © David Lichtneker / ArcAngel

Printed in the United States of America

To Ryan, Hudson, and Hazel. With love, always.

Chapter One

My mother nudged me as the motorcar sputtered to a stop.

"Evie, wake up," she whispered.

I'd fallen asleep against her, something I hadn't done since I was a child, lulled by the soft fur of her coat against my cheek and the glamour of her rose-scented perfume. Sitting up, I stared out the window, entranced by the magnitude of the hotel. It was completely made up of brick and stretched the length of a full city block, and its windows were surrounded by carved stone.

Our motorcar had pulled beneath a brightly lit overhang at the entrance, where doormen stood with the same authority as armed guards, regal in burgundy uniforms adorned with gold tassels and polished brass buttons. Well-dressed couples strolled arm in arm, and the anxiety I'd felt about traveling from our small town to Dublin faded away.

I rubbed my eyes and adjusted my dress, relieved that falling asleep on my mother had not invited a sharp rebuke. My goal was to stay out of the way, focus on my studies, and not cause a bit of trouble for my parents. They often traveled due to the nature of my father's position, and I was lucky to have been included on this trip. We had spent the week at my great-aunt's home in Wexford, with the famed Declee Hotel in Dublin as our final stop. I wanted to stay out of the way because I didn't want my parents to regret their decision to bring me or, worse, find a reason to send me back home.

A smartly dressed valet opened the car door, and my father stepped out first before extending his hand to my mother. They turned to admire the hotel, talking quietly to one another, and the valet offered me his hand. I gave him a brief nod, unsure whether it would be proper to accept, then fumbled my way out of the car on my own.

The air was warm and damp, smelling of petrol and the faded scent of hops: so different from the fresh sea air of home, where petrol was in shortage and the villagers managed on cart and foot.

I had just tucked a loose strand of hair beneath my hat when I noticed a girl who looked near to my age, fourteen, leaning against the wall and watching our arrival. Her strawberry blonde hair was pinned in soft waves beneath a forest green pillbox hat, perfectly matched to a pair of leather gloves, a green leather purse, and a navy-and-green-plaid houndstooth dress. The sophistication of her clothing and bright-red lipstick enthralled me, as I was not yet allowed to paint my face.

"Evie." My mother turned to me. "Stay close."

The girl's eyes met mine, and a smirk tugged at her mouth. My cheeks flushed as I followed my parents to the grand front entrance.

"Welcome, sir." The hotel porter greeted my father with equal parts gusto and respect. His burgundy uniform was impeccable, several steps up from those worn by the American soldiers who had questioned us at the blockade leading into the city.

Lights gleamed from above when we walked in. The bustle of people left me standing closer to my mother than I should have, and she nearly tripped. Quickly, I moved back.

A porter led us to a lift, then down a hallway to a wooden door with a deeply carved brass handle. With a flourish, he opened it and handed the key to my father.

The crystal chandelier blazed in both the entryway and above the couch in the sitting room, illuminating a fireplace, two sitting chairs, and a small library of leather-clad books. Small floral bouquets decorated each table.

My mother stopped short, and I nearly bumped into her again.

"Oranges," she said, clasping her hands.

The hotel porter nodded. "Small luxuries require large discretion."

There were two in a crystal fruit bowl, neatly nestled between brightly colored apples.

"The true forbidden fruit." My father tossed her one with a wink. "Confess that to the vicar."

"Brendan," she scolded, but she held the orange tight.

Even with my father's ability to bypass rations, I hadn't tasted the sweet citrus or seen its bright skin in my Christmas packages in years. It felt odd to find it like this, as if someone had left their best pearls on the table.

My father shook the porter's hand, a banknote passing between them like a breath. "Thank you, sir," he told the man.

The door shut quietly as he left.

"This is perfect." My mother brushed her hand over my father's cheek. "Exactly what was needed."

During the Emergency, which continued to drag on regardless of rumors that the end was in sight, our house had never been without sugar, tea, or food. My father's work with the government had helped him bypass the thin offerings of our ration books. Yet the general lack still forced my parents to conserve. My mother, always so pampered with her hand-tailored dresses and dainty shoes, had finally started to break.

The decision to stay at the Declee was made the night she burst into tears when our cook served yet another dark, lifeless loaf of bread alongside farmhouse stew. My father decided we should take a trip that would include a brief stay with her aunt at the halfway point, as Dublin was three hundred kilometers away. Then, he promised, we'd spend a week at the hotel.

"What about the petrol?" my mother asked. "There will be questions."

"There will not. I'll take several meetings while we're there," my father said, and that was that.

The thing my mother talked about the most on our drive from Wexford to Dublin was not the time we'd spent with her aunt but the meals we would have. This was even as our motorcar passed by a crumbling tenement with a stoop full of people so dirty and thin that they nearly looked like children. Perhaps they were. The thought made me feel guilty to be here, surrounded by such luxury.

I walked over to the window and pressed my nose against the glass. We were high up, the valet as tiny as a toy motorcar set down below. I felt a small thrill at this glimpse into the real world.

The state of emergency in Ireland had started six years ago, at the beginning of World War II, as our country sat watch in neutrality. Everyone felt the endless shortages, the rations, and a subtle fear that the world would burn. It was often rumored the Germans would attack Ireland, but in the past few days, word had been spreading that Europe was near to victory. My village in County Cork had been quiet through it all, though, making the threats feel like something in the distance.

I pressed my hand against the shining pane of glass while looking down over Dublin. It felt the same here, really, in this fortress of a hotel. I could watch the world from behind the glass and pull the curtain if its ferocity frightened me.

I was lucky. I knew that much.

∾

Once the porter had delivered our luggage, my mother insisted on attending a late lunch. As we headed across the lush carpet in the lobby that led to the restaurant, there was a sudden shout and commotion by the door. My father pulled my mother close, his face tight.

"It's over," someone cried. "The Germans have surrendered!"

My mother's eyes widened, and she gripped my hand. The sudden crackle of the radio boomed as a member of the front desk staff turned up the BBC. A man's voice announced that Victory in Europe would be celebrated the following day.

Everything happened at once. Men hugged each other, women cheered, and some people prayed. A small child, no more than five and dressed in ruffles, started to cry, probably at the noise and confusion. A man spun me around, giving me a hearty kiss on the cheek that made my entire body flush with embarrassment.

Everyone was laughing and hugging. My mother cried happy tears, and my breath felt tight and shallow. I didn't know quite what to think, say, or do.

"Let's eat," my father said. "Then we'll celebrate."

The news had spread to the dining room. The hotel guests milled about, talking and laughing, while the maître d' handed out small glasses of whiskey to the men.

Lunch was rich and plentiful, but I became bored when the meal ended and my parents kept talking with everyone around us. My father ordered a bottle of whiskey for the crowd and began telling tall tales of his travels. He became louder with each sip, discussing the threat of the Germans to Irish soil.

I tugged on my mother's sleeve the moment I had an opportunity. She turned to me, her face full of impatience at the interruption.

"My stomach hurts," I said. "May I go back to the room?"

I wasn't used to the rich food, and each time I thought of the heavy cream sauce, the urge to lie down became stronger.

"Of course." She seemed relieved. "You'll need someone to take you." She looked around the room and gestured for a woman who worked at the hotel to come over. Handing her a coin, she instructed, "Please see to it that she is returned to room 424."

"Aye," the woman said, accepting the tip and gesturing at me to follow.

The chaos in the lobby had died down, but the undercurrent of excitement remained. The woman nodded when we reached the lift and then headed back to the restaurant. I hesitated, surprised she hadn't planned to escort me the whole way.

"Thank you," I called, but she didn't look back.

It was expected that I'd go up to the room and rest. This turn of events had given me an opportunity, as it would be much more interesting to take in the sights and sounds of this new city. My parents preferred to be the center of any celebration, so they wouldn't be back soon. What would it hurt if I took a moment on my own?

I hesitated, resting my hand on the patterned wallpaper. My parents would be furious if they found out, but I'd be back to the room before they'd even left lunch. I could picture my father drinking there all afternoon and then the two of them staying out.

Perhaps not, as my mother would want to change for dinner and dancing. The mood in the air was strange, though. Now that something had ended, I felt the possibility of so many new beginnings.

I stepped into the bustle of the lobby and headed for the entrance of the hotel. The doorman didn't bat an eye, and relief swept through me. Perhaps what I was doing was not so wrong.

Outside, I watched the motorcars come and go. The sidewalks were becoming crowded as the news spread and people took to the streets to celebrate. As women dressed like my mother arrived at the hotel, some with diamonds glinting at their throats, the men called out greetings and congratulations. The asphalt was damp from a brief rain. It was cool, and I shivered slightly, tugging at my thin sleeves.

"Here," a sweet voice said.

The same girl I'd noticed when we arrived had come back outside, and she handed me a soft cashmere cloak. Deep green, matching the stripes in her houndstooth dress. She still wore the green hat but had taken off the gloves. Her cheeks were round, and when she smiled, her front-right tooth was crooked in the most charming way.

Linking her arm in mine, she said, "I've been waiting for someone to explore with. Come on."

The next thing I knew, we were on the streets of Dublin, walking along with the crowd.

"Wait," I said. "I can't—"

Her bright-green eyes evaluated me. "You're not allowed?"

I hesitated and looked around. Crowds of people were out and about, talking with urgency and good cheer. Small children and well-dressed women mingled with the crowds of men, and I felt the sense that everyone was coming together. No, I was not allowed, but this was something special, something I wanted a part in, and the fact that this girl was here with me made me feel safe and brave enough to do it.

"It won't hurt," I said, smiling back at her. "I'm Evie."

"I'm Harding. You're here with your parents?" The girl blew a small bubble. I stared, impressed that she had chewing gum. "I saw you arrive."

I nodded. "Yes, you?"

We had made it to the end of the block, and instead of answering, Harding moved forward with purpose. I followed, my breath coming at a quick pace. Now that we'd turned a corner, the people began to look a little rougher, and I tightened my grip on her arm.

"We should go back."

"Never go back," she said, cheerfully. "Always move forward."

The words gave me a jolt of courage, and I repeated them to myself as we pressed on through the crowd.

"There's something going on at the college," she explained. "I'd like to see. They were talking about it at the hotel."

We turned another corner, and suddenly the street was full. I stopped and stared. Elbows bumped into me, while chanting and cheers rang out all around. A blond-haired boy waved a large tricolor flag, shouting, "You've come a long way!" Those around him joined in the chant, while a nearby man with a violin played something I didn't recognize. A group of older women in worn dresses danced together, smiles lighting up their faces.

"This is incredible." Harding spread her arms wide, her face bright as the sun.

Someone jostled me, stepping on my foot. "Yes," I said, fighting off the pain.

Harding pushed us deeper into the crowd, then pulled me up onto a large stone platform that held a lamppost in place. It felt safer to stand up above the crowd, and for a moment, I had the space to look around. I saw people milling about and, in the distance, the university.

Harding sat down and pulled out a glass bottle from her handbag. Coca-Cola. My eyes widened as she opened it, hid it in a green glove, and passed it to me.

I had never seen Coca-Cola in real life, only in advertisements. My parents had spoken of it from their travels, but it was not available in Ireland. Yet here was this girl acting like it was as common as water.

"Cheers," she said.

"Where did you get this?" I breathed, feeling the weight of it in my hand.

"The soldiers at the repair base can get it." She grinned. "I have a friend who knows how to trade."

Slowly, I brought the bottle to my lips. The sweet, warm liquid fizzed in my mouth and throat, making me cough but instantly filling me with an inexplicable joy. How had this happened? Less than an hour earlier, I'd been paralyzed with boredom, listening to my parents talk about a world that had nothing to do with me, and now, I was in the center of it with one of the most beautiful people I had ever seen.

"Can you believe the Emergency is over?" I asked.

"Things won't change," she said with a scoff. "Not for some time."

"That's what my father says," I told her. "He works in the government, alongside the Electricity Supply Board. He has to travel often, so he learns what's happening abroad."

It was a privilege that my father was high up in the government and, to be frank, impressive. I wanted to impress this girl.

"Lucky for him." Her voice wasn't tinged with admiration but bitterness. "Does his position provide you extra benefits from the Department of Supplies?"

"I couldn't speak to that," I said, repeating the line my parents had told me to use if anyone asked.

It was true that our family was not required to stay within the petrol limits, and the stores sometimes looked the other way when Cook brought our ration book to be stamped. But my father had seen to it that Kislee, our village, received the necessary farming equipment to provide tillage of the land that kept so many in our area from starvation.

Harding frowned. "I'll bet he took what he could while the rest of us ate old potatoes, if anything at all. Tell your father that he's a coward for hiding out at the Declee instead of dealing with the damage. This country claims to be neutral. It's not neutrality—it's cowardice because no one wanted to take a stand and get involved. The ones who have will be persecuted for it, mark my words."

It had never occurred to me to think of my father that way. His parents were shopkeepers, and he had built his fortune from nothing. I'd always thought of him as heroic, and the idea that this girl wanted to challenge me on that made my cheeks burn.

"My father is an honorable man," I told her.

"No one is honorable when forced to choose between doing what's right and helping the people that they love." Her eyes flashed. "Most of Ireland has not been given a choice. Our government, including those in it like your father, would have been perfectly content to watch this country starve, and starve we did."

"That's not true," I said. "There are famines and shortages. The government is doing its best to keep us all from starving. My father brought assistance to our village. He has sacrificed his rations to—"

"You didn't say 'our rations.'"

I blinked. "I don't understand."

"You didn't say he sacrificed 'our' rations." Her gaze held mine. "He never worried his family would go hungry, and good on him. Well done. If given a choice, I'd do the same. I only ask that you understand that few people experienced the same luxury."

The judgment on her face filled me with rage. Quickly, I got to my feet.

"I should return," I told her.

"Don't bother with anger if someone speaks their mind." She shielded her eyes from the sun. "Listen to the words spoken, then make your own opinion, and say it."

I'd never been told to make my own opinion, let alone share it.

Her green eyes looked amused. "Do you even know how to get back?"

She had me there, but I was not about to admit it. Reluctantly, I sat back down. I took another drink of Coca-Cola, and she stretched out her stockinged legs in the sun.

"Where do you live?" she asked.

I didn't answer at first, to let her know I was still mad about what she'd said. She raised an eyebrow.

"Kislee," I said. "It's on the coast, near Kinsale."

"It's beautiful there, isn't it?"

"It's dull," I said, and she laughed. "My town is very small, and my parents are always away."

"How many people are in the schoolhouse?" she asked.

"Oh, I . . ."

There was a schoolhouse, a cute one that most of the locals attended, but my parents had sent me to boarding school once I'd passed primary, to receive a proper education. I didn't really want to tell her that, considering she'd seemed irritated to learn that my father had privileges that most people did not.

On the other hand, she had chewing gum and a Coca-Cola, so I doubted she knew poverty, even if she spoke of it. Besides, I no longer cared if I impressed her. If this girl was going to like me, I wanted her to like me for me.

I squared my shoulders and looked her in the eye. "Boarding school."

Once again, she laughed. Her back teeth were stained, probably from Coca-Cola.

"I could tell that about you," she said. "It's the way that you speak."

"How do I speak?" I demanded.

"Formal. Hoity." Her eyes shone. "I adore it. I adored you on sight, and I just know that we will be the best of friends." She leaned in. "Have you ever said a bad word?"

I couldn't tell if she was having a laugh at my expense. "Once," I admitted. "I stubbed my toe, nearly broke it, and it hurt so bad that I did say something. However, I will never tell you what it is."

"Feck, I was hoping." A sudden roar from the crowd made Harding jump. We both turned to look. Several flags had been hoisted up on the roof of the university, but not the tricolor.

"What are they doing?" I demanded.

"Celebrating the ones who fought." Harding's voice was grim. She scrambled to her feet. "Those bastards. Everyone is here to celebrate, yet the uni kids think it's right to turn on their own land?" Leaning forward, she shouted, "Ireland was kept out of the United Nations, and we weren't allowed to fight! Show some respect for your homeland!"

Her eyes were wild, and I wondered at this girl, bold enough to shout that into a crowd.

The majority seemed to feel the same as Harding, because as the tricolor was unrolled last, and hoisted up to appear on the bottom, the crowd let out an angry roar.

"The Trinity students are going to cause a riot," Harding said.

For the first time, concern crossed her face as she considered our position up on the small platform. No one paid us any mind. Everyone watched the men at the front trying to storm the fence and get to the greens of the college. A lanky man with dirty-blond hair rattled the metal gate, then started to climb it. A guard hit him with something, and he dropped down.

As we watched, the tricolor burst into flames.

"Why would they do that?" I gasped.

"Our neutrality. Like we had a choice."

I drew in a sharp breath, and Harding muttered, "We should get out of here." She surveyed the crowd and gasped, "What are *they* doing, then?"

I turned to look. Next to us, a small group of teenage boys held up a Union Jack flag while singing "God Save the Queen" at the top of their lungs. To their left, some rough-looking sailors approached.

"Traitor," one shouted, before bringing back his enormous arm and smashing it against the face of the boy leading the song.

There was the sick sound of flesh meeting bone as the crowd lurched toward the fight. The sailors were twice their size, but the teenage boys were faster. I watched as one came up behind and boxed a sailor in the ears. Fists were flying, and I stared in horror before my legs were knocked out from under me. I fell onto the hard platform, cutting my knee, as a group scrambled up for a better view.

"Watch it, lassie." A man with a deep sneer crushed my hand with his foot as he climbed up. I cried out in anguish.

Harding grabbed my arm just as I got pushed off the platform, practically twisting my ankle in the fall. There were people all around, cheering for the Irish sailors.

Feeling sick, I cradled my hand. It ached like my knee, but elbows and noise were everywhere as the crush of people moved forward, and their fury seemed to spread. Out of the corner of my eye, I spotted the angry lines of a swastika, followed by a thunder of rage.

"The world has gone mad, and we're in the epicenter," Harding said, grabbing my arm. "Follow me."

People were pushing from all sides, and I felt too frightened to move.

"Come on." Her hair had fallen from its pins, and her face was flushed. "We have to get out of here, eh?"

I watched my feet as they moved, heart pounding with the rhythm of my steps. The sun beat down, and it smelled like sweat and asphalt. Everywhere I looked, mouths were twisted in celebration or rage; it was hard to tell the difference. I clung tight to Harding, wincing as an elbow hit my face and desperate to make it back to the safety of the hotel.

"Where you going?" A man smelling strongly of whiskey yanked Harding to him. He kissed her on the lips, his hands traveling to her backside as I watched, stunned.

"Stop!" I pulled at his hairy arm. His hand shot out, striking me across the cheek.

Harding kicked him hard in the shins. He stood there weaving, then started to move toward her again. I grabbed his ankles and shoved, making him lose his footing and fall to the ground. Before he could get up, I kicked him once in the side and pulled Harding away.

We ran to the hotel, tears hot on my face and the taste of iron in my mouth. The drunk followed us, stumbling and clutching his side.

I needed to stop to catch my breath, but Harding ushered me to the front doors.

"Keep your head down," she ordered. "Go!"

The doorman didn't seem to notice my bloodied, swollen face, and the moment we were back in, Harding led me to a heavy door off the lobby. It took us to a stairwell and a series of hallways. I followed at a rapid pace, more worried about the man following us than where we might be going or how we'd get back. Finally, she pulled me into a small, dim room and shut the door.

A single bulb hung overhead, illuminating the closet lined with shelves of perfectly ironed and folded napkins, tablecloths, and serving towels.

"What is this place?" I asked, trying to catch my breath.

"The linen closet." She sank to the floor. Letting out a breath, she leaned forward and winced. "Evie."

My entire body was shaking, and I wondered if that man was still outside somewhere, waiting to attack the both of us.

"Here." She took a white napkin from the shelf and pressed it gently against my cheek. "You need ice. Stay here, don't move."

Harding peeked out of the closet, then darted out. I sat in silence, knees drawn to my chest, my body shaking with terror. At a sound outside the door, I sat up straight. It was only a room service cart squeaking past, and moments later, the handle rattled.

It was Harding, holding a small block of ice. Water dripped from her flushed hand, and she put the ice inside the napkin.

"Where did you get that?" I asked.

"The icebox, of course." She pressed it gently against my cheek. The chill dulled the pain, and I let out a slow breath. "How is that?"

"Good." I pulled back the white napkin. It was stained with blood. Reaching for a clean one, I rewrapped the ice and pressed it back to my face, leaning my aching head against the wall.

Harding's green eyes studied me. "You're sugar on the outside and gunpowder underneath. Thanks for saving me."

It hurt to smile, but I did it anyway. "Anytime."

Chapter Two

Chicago, present day

The sudden nip in the air meant the snowstorm lurking on the weather radar might actually happen. It was late March, technically spring, but Chicago didn't always play by the rules. I knew better than to step out of my brownstone without a heavy coat and at least three layers, especially this late in the evening.

My grandmother would be proud I was prepared. She grew up in Ireland and, as a result, still carried a raincoat every time the sky had even a hint of a cloud. The thought served as a reminder that she'd called a few days ago and I needed to call her back, but things had been so busy I hadn't had the time.

My phone buzzed.

Need me to grab anything?

Tia. Friend of the year, business partner of the year, human of the year. Every year, without exception, ever since we'd met in a biology lab during undergrad.

I texted back: No, just get there. Can't wait to open it.

I'd gotten a notification that the FedEx envelope we'd been waiting for had been delivered to the office ten minutes ago. I immediately canceled my meal delivery and called Tia, and we both headed back in.

It might have been nine o'clock on a Tuesday night, but that envelope held news that couldn't wait until morning.

The door jingled as I rushed into the corner deli, smiling at the sweet old Russian man behind the counter, the one who liked to slip extra homemade caramels into my bag and tell me that his daughter needed to stop painting her nails black.

Quick as the wind, I selected a bouquet of wildflowers, a bottle of champagne, and two ham sandwiches. The man threw in a few fresh chocolate chip cookies, and with a chorus of thanks, I was on my way.

The cookies were still warm when I arrived at the building where we rented shared office space. It was a sleek facility with medical capabilities that was a huge step-up, thanks to a grant we'd been awarded from the local university. Tia and I co-owned an independent business, but we'd sought out every bit of assistance we could find to get the necessary funding to bring our antiaging serum to the market. Because there was not a person on the planet opposed to glorifying youth and beauty, we'd made it to this point.

"Hi, Barry." I handed the security guy at the front desk one of the cookies. He had a son, engaged and planning a wedding. There were times I got the impression he thought I should've been doing the same. "Is there a letter for me?"

Handing me the envelope, he bit into the cookie with a smile. "Rainey, this cookie is just like the ones my mama used to make."

I smiled back and headed up. The green light to begin production on our serum practically glowed through the FedEx package. The paperwork would declare it free from contaminants and safe for the market. It was hard to believe that after years of work, we'd finally reached this milestone.

I set up the flowers and poured the champagne into coffee mugs. The office door beeped open, and I blasted "Ode to Victory" from my phone.

Tia and her tight black curls bounced into the room, her arms overhead in victory. Tortoiseshell glasses faithfully magnified her dark eyes, which gleamed in excitement.

"My hands are shaking," she cried. They were not shaking, not even a tremor, but I was right there with her. "We did it!"

Our victory dance was full of high fives and ridiculous moves. Laughing, we collapsed into the chairs at the conference table. Once we'd caught our breath, I passed her a sandwich, and she put her hand to her heart.

"Ham and cheese?" We'd lived on them during grad school. "You're brilliant."

"You are." I handed her a mug of champagne. "Cheers." The sharp sound of the ceramic echoed as we clinked mugs. "To years of blood, sweat, and tears. Thank you for all that you've put into this. I'm proud of us."

We took a drink and dug into our food. It was an unspoken rule that eating took precedence over everything. We'd once been in the middle of a fight about grant funding when our Thai delivery showed up. I'd been in tears, but we tabled the discussion until we'd eaten every bite of pad thai.

"Everything's lined up with production," I reported. "This is all we need. This serum is going to change lives for the better, in spite of what my mother might say."

My mother was on my side in all things, but she'd questioned my decision to go into the beauty sect.

"With your intelligence," she argued, "you should be trying to cure cancer."

She was only saying that because back in the day, I'd had a goal of doing research to develop a pain-free skin cancer cream. But when I graduated from college, practically every medical lab was on a hiring freeze. When Tia suggested I partner with her, I was quick to accept.

Besides, we knew our limitations. Curing cancer was not going to happen for either of us. Figuring out how to eliminate fine lines by boosting collagen production at a surface level? That, I could do.

"The timing is perfect." Tia picked up a piece of avocado and popped it into her mouth. "You know how my dad has been really putting on the pressure to show some results?"

Tia liked to joke that, now that we'd both turned thirty, we'd missed the window for the 30 Under 30 list, and as a result, her father's interest in her entrepreneurial spirit had waned.

"Well, here they are," I said, tapping the envelope. "I think we should dip the first bottle of facial serum in gold and give it to him."

"Yeah." Tia laughed, then looked down at the table. "I need to tell you something. I did go to an interview to appease him."

I paused. "Oh."

Tia's father had funded every aspect of her life, including her lakeview apartment on the Chicago Gold Coast, not to mention the majority of our business. That came with a price—specifically, a voice in her career choices. Still, the fact that she'd gone to an interview surprised me.

"How was it?" I asked.

"Interesting." She folded her napkin. "Their resources were impressive. They had labs for days. You would have loved it."

"It would be a different world," I admitted.

One where I didn't have to wake up at 6:00 a.m. to wait tables so I could afford to be an entrepreneur. Even though Tia and I owned the company, we barely made enough to pay ourselves, so I'd started waiting tables on the side two weeks after opening the business. I would have preferred to moonlight at a lab, but Tia's father didn't want us doing anything that could be a conflict of interest. Ironic, considering.

"Well, it's all there if we want it." She took another bite of her sandwich. "They offered me the job yesterday. Senior product development scientist."

The sandwich went dry in my mouth.

"I'm not doing it." She nudged me with her foot. "It was tempting, though. It was a huge salary, and the potential research opportunities were incredible. I think I just got ner—"

My cell phone rang from its place on the table. My mother.

"Do you need to grab it?" Tia asked.

"No." I sent her to voice mail. "The last three times we talked, she spent most of the time complaining about some guy who keeps putting signs up in the break room without the proper punctuation. It can wait."

My mother was a tenured professor at a well-respected university in Pittsburgh. She was smart and progressive, and I was typically entertained by her take on the world, but at the moment, I just wanted to relish in our victory.

"Let's open it." I reached for the envelope. "We've waited long—"

The phone rang again. It seemed louder, more insistent.

Tia squinted at it. "Still your mom."

Picking it up, I said, "Hey, I'm at work. What's up?" Silence. "Mom, are you okay?"

"Yes." Her voice was tight. Not her typical abruptness, but I could tell she was upset. "I'm at the hospital," she said. "It's your grandmother, Rainey. I don't think she's going to make it."

∽

Ice pelted the window of my apartment at a steady rate, its frosted patterns shifting and twinkling in the warmth of the streetlamp below. The digital clock blinked 1:15 a.m. next to my stack of journals, my water bottle, and a box of tissues. My white down comforter was pulled tight around me, soft as a pair of worn flannel pajamas.

The ice had shown up the second I was back at my brownstone, the envelope unopened, trying to book a flight to Pittsburgh. Everything was grounded until morning. I'd managed to get a ticket for the first plane out at 6:00 a.m., but I had no idea if it would actually take off.

The uncertainty made it impossible to sleep, along with the worry that if I did sleep, my alarm might fail. Not to mention the anxiety about my grandmother.

I'd always had a special bond with her. Even though my parents made plenty of time for me, my grandmother was the one who took care of me after school. She taught me how to play the piano, knit, crochet, and play poker. She listened when I cried about boys, taught me the importance of forging my own path, and would be the first person in my thank-you speech if I ever won the Nobel Prize.

The fact that I hadn't seen her in six months was inexcusable. Yes, I'd been trying to manage the business and all the complications that came with that, but she was ninety-three. She'd been there for each milestone in my life—every birthday, science fair, and graduation—and I should have been there for her.

I was frustrated to think that I'd let work guide everything, especially now that Tia had admitted to interviewing for a job. I'd always thought her dedication to the company matched mine. Yes, she'd gone to the interview to appease her father, but she'd been impressed. I could tell. It made me nervous, because if we quit now, it would be five years wasted, with nothing to show for it but my first gray hairs.

Rolling over in bed, I reached for my phone and texted her.

You up?

It wasn't uncommon for Tia to stay up half the night, puzzling out a problem or bingeing on game shows. *Jeopardy!* was her favorite.

Sure enough, she called right away.

"Can't sleep." The familiarity of her voice comforted me. "Any news?"

"It's pneumonia." My mother had updated me once I'd booked my flight. "The hospital wants to intubate, but my grandmother won't do it, so they're in a standoff, and she's trying to survive on an antibiotic drip. My mom thinks my grandmother is waiting until I get there."

"I'm so sorry, Rainey," Tia said.

"Me too." I stared at the patches of ice on the window. Every time a snowflake melted, it rolled down the window like a tear. "We should probably take a look at the approval now and map out the steps, so you can get things in motion while I'm out."

We'd decided to wait to open the FedEx envelope until I'd gotten everything set to go home. Now, it sat there on my dresser, waiting.

"Let's do it," she said. "I want to know it's official."

"Agreed." I slid out of bed, the floor like ice on my feet. No matter how much the old heaters in my apartment clanked and hissed, my small studio never really managed to get warm.

After tugging off the thin cardboard strip, I pulled out a sheaf of papers and felt a glimmer of excitement, in spite of it all.

"Here we go . . ."

My heart sank when I read the first two sentences.

> We regret to inform you that your request for market approval has been denied. The levels showed elevated levels of dangerous metals that . . .

"Read it!" Tia's voice rang out on the other end. "I'm so excited!"

"Um . . ." I reread the passage to myself, in complete disbelief.

How was this possible? We'd done everything right. Tested extensively in our lab and other labs. Our research showed the serum was ready, but according to this, it wasn't.

The implications steamrolled through my brain. We couldn't go to market. Our product had failed.

This can't be right.

It couldn't be. We'd known, without a doubt, that the serum was where it needed to be. Something must have happened in transit. The packaging, the temperature during travel . . . something. It was just a matter of figuring it out, and I didn't want to panic Tia in the process.

I couldn't tell her the serum had failed and then take off, when all I needed was some time to fix the situation. Especially since her father wanted her to step back from the business. This type of news could prompt him to put an end to everything, and I couldn't leave her to handle that battle alone.

"Rainey?" Tia said. "Did you open it?"

I paused. Everything had a solution. Science appealed to me for that very reason. With the right information, it was possible to fix almost anything.

I slid the paper back into the envelope. "Sorry. It's not the approval."

"What do you mean?" I could imagine her sliding her glasses onto the top of her head and blinking, a tic she had when puzzling something out. "It was from their corporate office."

"It's just some notice that they're delayed and will get it to us in a few months." I was surprised at how smooth my voice sounded, how easy it was to lie. "I can't believe I bought champagne for this."

"A few months?" Tia sounded outraged. "Rainey, that can't happen. We'll lose our grant funding. Did they give a date?"

"It's not months," I said, clicking my tongue like I was reading it. "It's weeks. May twenty-ninth."

That would give me plenty of time to figure out what had happened.

"Oh." She let out a breath. "Still, not ideal."

"No," I agreed. "But manageable."

Using that as a marker would give me time to be there for my grandmother, research solutions, and turn this thing around. I didn't want to lie to my best friend—I'd never lied to her—but I had to fight for the company.

"Is your flight still on?" she asked.

I checked it again. "So far . . ."

"Well, have a safe trip." She sounded tired. "Keep me posted."

We hung up, and I lay in bed, my body hot with shame. I couldn't believe that, as a grown woman, I'd allowed fear to push me so far from my moral compass, but at the same time, I knew our product was ready. I just needed the time to prove it without worrying that her father would shut everything down.

"Life will try to take things from you, to see how strong you are," my grandmother liked to say. "Don't let it. Find what you want, take it with two hands, and don't let go."

I felt a sudden urgency to get to her before it was too late. I tossed back the blankets, bundled up, and grabbed my suitcase. The door banged shut behind me as I rushed into the hallway.

Hang tight, Grandma. Please, don't let go.

Chapter Three

Ireland, 1949

"Evie, you must focus." My tutor's lips were tight, the area around the mole on her cheek flushed. "A girl of eighteen years of age should not find it so difficult to be still. When your father returns, we will both lose our free time if you cannot adequately sing the praises of Yeats."

I sighed, stretching my neck from side to side. I had been sitting in the parlor for two hours, reading the laments of the Irish poets. It was hopelessly dull, other than one or two lines I'd stumbled across that did in fact make me think of birds, flowers, and, yes, love.

The weather was unusually warm and bright for April, making it impossible to concentrate. I'd much rather spend time outdoors, walking through the tall grass of the bluff and catching the sea breeze. Or having a glimpse of Sullivan, the shopkeepers' son.

I'd known him since I was young, and only recently had his shoulders seemed to broaden, and his eyes now got a certain twinkle when he saw me. I'd started to look forward to seeing him at his parents' shop because of these things. In addition, he made a point of offering me peppermints from the candy counter. His mother would smile at him, saying things like, "That's enough, you little Romeo; she doesn't need your attention." He'd pretend to be embarrassed, but the second she looked away, he would give me a cute smile.

Lately, that smile had spent more time in my thoughts than it should have, and it was much more engaging than my studies.

"Your father will expect perfection," Fedelma told me. "Otherwise, why is he paying me?"

It was true, but I was not due to attend university until the fall. Besides, my parents wouldn't be back from Argentina for another month. Those details alone should have bought me a reprieve.

There was a muffled commotion in the main foyer, and with a look of concern, Fedelma got to her feet. The Emergency had passed, but it often seemed that, four years later, people still started at any small sound, worried the fighting would start back up again.

"What is it?" I asked, hoping the disruption would get me out of this room.

Seamus, our butler, appeared in the doorway. Normally stoic and dismissive, he, too, seemed flustered. "There is a visitor. I fear your father has accepted company and has forgotten to give us due warning." He turned on his heel and left the room, calling, "We must meet in the main yard to welcome them."

The idea that someone had come to stay was intriguing but, yes, upsetting if we were not prepared. Was I meant to entertain a stranger on my own? My parents had always been present, and I was unsure what would be required. Not to mention the fact that I often felt tongue-tied at the prospect of speaking with someone new.

"There must be some sort of mistake." I pushed back the draperies to get a better look. "My parents certainly would have told me."

Squinting in the suddenly bright light, I spotted a black motorcar sitting in the drive. Its driver stood by the back door. There were still few cars on the road, due to maintenance issues and petrol shortages, so whoever it was had to be important.

"What should I do?" I felt as frightened as Fedelma looked.

"Fix your hair." She guided me to the large mirror surrounded by brass leaves that decorated the wall. "It's too late to change."

In the mirror, my freckled cheeks looked flushed, and several curls had slipped down from my chignon to frame my face. I liked that look, but when I didn't make a move to put the loose strands in their place, Fedelma did it for me. She swiftly tucked and pinned them as our house staff rushed past in a flurry of chatter and worry.

Sweeping a cursory glance over me, she nodded. "You must greet them. Invite them in."

The moment I stepped outside, unsure what to say or do, the driver snapped open the back car door. There was a hush among the servants as a glamorous young woman with bright-red hair slowly exited. She shielded her eyes against the sun and looked up at the house, and my heart skipped with recognition.

The last time I'd seen her, we were hiding in the linen closet at the Declee, with blood dripping down my face. It was the single most exciting day I'd ever experienced.

"Harding," I whispered. Then, louder, I cried, "Harding!"

I rushed forward, smoothing my thin nylon dress and wishing I'd bothered to put on something finer that morning. I couldn't believe that she'd come, that she'd found me. I'd told her my name and village but had never heard from her by post, and with no way to reach her, I'd accepted that our friendship had been a moment in time. Now, I wanted to cry with joy at the sight of her.

I pulled her into a tight embrace. She smelled fresh, like powder and notes of bergamot. Her frame felt thin but strong, and an image of the way she'd kicked that man the night of the riot ran through my mind, as it had so often over the past few years.

My head was still filled with frightened memories, but at the same time, that experience had been more exhilarating than anything. Harding had been so brave, so powerful, and since then, I'd wished so many times to be more like her.

She rested her hands on my shoulders and smiled. "I found you."

Much like the first time we met, she wore Victory Red lipstick, but now, her skin shimmered beneath a thin layer of face powder.

Brow pencil gave her doe-eyed look a touch of mystery, and I suddenly felt shy.

Dropping her hands, she fanned herself with a pale-pink glove and looked up at the house. "I was on my way to visit my aunt. The thought alone bores me to tears. The moment the sea started to shine from the train window, I asked if we were anywhere near your village. When the conductor said we were, I decided to disembark and commission a driver."

That must have cost her a fortune.

"I do hope you've come to stay," I told her, even though I wasn't sure my parents would allow it.

They'd welcome anyone from my former boarding school, but Harding would be forbidden if they knew she was the reason I was out in Dublin that afternoon.

"Would you like me to?" she asked.

"I'd love you to," I admitted. "However, it's more boring here than your aunt's house could ever be."

"Impossible." She grinned, showing that crooked front tooth. "I'll send word to my aunt."

Spending time with her would be well worth the risk that my parents wouldn't approve. Turning to Seamus, I said, "Please prepare a room for my dear friend."

Harding linked her arm in mine, then led me up the steps to my house.

"I will require a bath and some lunch," she said. "Then you must introduce me to every corner of your scrumptious little town."

Seamus rushed past us and opened the front door.

The entryway was impressive, even to me, with its white-and-black marble floors and enormous portraits of our family. Harding took in the high-arched ceilings and striking chandelier, then gave a low whistle.

"This takes the breath away." There was a hint of awe in her tone. "Well done."

I beamed at her. "Welcome to Aisling."

~

The moment Harding was settled in to her room, Fedelma grabbed me by the arm and practically dragged me downstairs.

In the parlor, she clicked the door shut and crossed her arms, staring me down. "You are not prepared to entertain a guest." Her voice was as sour as cabbage. "What will your parents think when they learn of this?"

I straightened my spine, determined not to be cowed. Fedelma scolded me often, and back when I was younger, she'd bruised my knuckles daily with her wooden ruler. I didn't think she would do such a thing now, as she was no longer my governess. Still, she did have the power to make Harding leave, unless I could come up with something, and quick.

"Fedelma, she attended boarding school with me and often promised to visit." I prayed that Harding would go along with the ruse. "It would be a great offense if we sent her away, especially after the use of petrol her visit required."

The Emergency was over, but the rationing was not. Petrol was hard to come by, and it wasn't just anyone who could afford to commission a motorcar. Fedelma knew as much, and she crossed her arms more tightly while staring me down.

"I understand you're concerned that I can't adequately host." I dabbed my damp forehead with a handkerchief. "However, my guest will require little more than I do." I sat up straight as an idea hit. "Fedelma, why don't you take a week away from my studies and spend time with your family instead? I know that you've longed to be with your sister, and you deserve to see your niece."

Fedelma's sister had given birth just three months back and, shortly after, received word that her husband had been killed in a farming accident. Fedelma had not taken time away to be with her family, but I knew it was something she wanted to do.

At my offer, she frowned and adjusted the sleeves of her dress. "I cannot. The house staff would have questions."

Through the open window, I could hear the chattering of the birds and smell the vibrant scent of the gorse. It would be such a pity to continue to spend every moment of the spring in this dim, dull parlor.

"The staff has no idea about the arrangements my parents have made with you." I kept my voice low. "I could even send you off with a basket of food from the kitchen and a wrapped parcel of chocolates."

Chocolate was a delicacy, as it was often scarce. It would be worth losing it for the week of freedom I'd gain.

Fedelma pressed her lips together. "What if your parents return early?"

I almost had her.

"Then I'll tell them you'd fallen ill." I took her hands. "Fedelma, you've served me so well for years. You deserve to take this time."

Finally, she softened like butter. "This is too kind of you, miss. I've wanted to meet my niece for months now, and my sister's having such a hard time. I do thank you."

I blushed. "Oh, I'm not going to pretend to be some sort of a hero. However, this arrangement works out perfectly for the both of us, doesn't it?"

We smiled at each other. It felt so good to think that for once, I was in charge of my life, instead of letting each moment be dictated by somebody else.

~

Once Harding was refreshed, we headed out for the walk I'd longed for since that morning. It was a perfect afternoon. The sun was bright against the green grass, and the longer blades nearly glowed as the wind blew through them. We walked along the edge of the cliff, considering the white froth of the water crashing against the edge, and the near blackness of the sea.

Harding stared out at it with her arms folded tight. "It's so clean here. Such a difference from the filth of Dublin."

Dublin had smelled, I remembered that. It was tinged with hops and sulfur, not to mention all the people. Here, everything was fresh dew and moss.

"You've been back?" I asked. "Since that night?"

"Where do you think I live?" She glanced at me and continued walking.

I had so many questions, but I didn't want to be intrusive. Dublin must have felt a long way off, especially since she'd traveled alone.

Our walk was silent, other than the wind blowing against our faces and the grass brushing against my legs. The soft feeling of the blades was something I'd never taken the time to consider, until I watched Harding pushing the grass out of her way with every step.

"We can walk in the road," I suggested. "It might be easier for you."

"This is fine." Harding lifted her face to the sun. "I'm grateful I found you. This time with my aunt would've been excruciating. I promise I won't be a bother to you. I love art, you see, and plan to spend many hours of the day off with my paints and brushes."

I brightened. "I've planned to learn. Could I come with you?"

Harding chewed her lip. "It's a solitary thing. I'm not my best unless I have the chance to wander and let the day lead me where it may. Surely, you understand?"

"Yes, of course," I said, impressed.

What a marvelous thing to have such a talent. People often complimented my piano playing, but I'd longed to have a skill with something lasting to show for it.

While we walked, I considered the wonder that was Harding McGovern. Everything about her was mysterious, and so interesting. I hoped she would enjoy Kislee. The town itself had little to offer, with only the milliner, a tailor, a dry goods shop, and a pub, but Kinsale was only an hour's cart ride away. Perhaps it could also inspire her art.

I stopped walking and held out my hands. Harding took them without hesitation, and her pretty eyes settled on mine.

"I am delighted that you are here," I said. "You may roam our town as you see fit, and find inspiration where you will. I admire you so, Harding. I'm delighted you came to stay."

Instead of smiling back, her expression clouded.

"What is it?" I said.

"Evie, how honest with you can I be?"

"Please, speak your mind," I said, worried I'd somehow offended her.

Harding blinked as hair whipped around her face. "That night in Dublin, I felt like I'd found a dear friend; then, moments later, you were lost."

The relief that she felt the same made my breath catch. "Yes."

My parents had searched frantically for me when the riots began. The moment we emerged from the linen closet and into the lobby, my father whisked me away in the motorcar, straight back to Wexford. My parents had not given me a chance to say goodbye, and I'd often wondered if that was the reason Harding had not written.

"I've wanted to find you for years," Harding said. "However, my parents . . ."

Her eyes filled with tears. Perhaps her parents had been as angry with her as mine had been with me.

I put my hand on her arm. "What is it?"

"My parents died. A few months back. It was a sailing accident, and my parents and the crew died in frigid waters." She sniffed and gave a firm nod. "There, I said it. Got it out of the way. I, Harding Keelin McGovern, am an orphan. It sounds so incredibly Dickens, doesn't it? Quite pathetic."

It didn't sound pathetic at all.

"Oh, Harding," I breathed. "I'm so sorry."

There had been so many times during my life when I'd worried the same fate would befall me. My parents were always traveling, and although I didn't believe it to be dangerous, my mother had confided there was always some level of risk. The worry had been much more intense when I was younger, but now I considered the reality from a detached standpoint: the need to visit the solicitor, go through the appropriate time of mourning, and, of course, then being without them.

That feeling was not all that unfamiliar, as I had spent much of my life at school or in the care of the household staff, but those times reconciled with the truth that they would soon be back. My mother and her perfume as sweet as mulled spice, and my father with his robust laugh and intelligent gaze. Losing them would be hard.

"I'm so sorry for your loss," I told Harding, and she gave a brave nod.

"Thank you." She held up her hands. "I do not intend to be dreary—"

"Don't pretend for me." My voice was sharper than I intended. "We are to be the best of friends, and that doesn't require pretense."

"I feel the same." She let out a breath. "I do hope you'll be patient with me. I must determine how to build an entirely new life without them. They left me with connections and money, so that's made my survival quite simple, but in order to feel like a respectable girl, I must pretend I have someone watching out for me at all times, and nobody is watching out for me."

"Not your aunt?" I said, and she paused.

"My aunt is busy with her own life. I told you I was going to her house, and that's true; however, she is not there. I would have been there alone."

"It's like that for me," I said. "My parents are away quite often. There's a bit of freedom in that, but—"

She gave an eager nod. "Freedom is exciting, in some ways, but it can be frightening. It's like the sky." She gestured at the endless gray space. "It can be easy to lose yourself in it."

The way she spoke engaged me more than the poems I'd been forced to read that morning.

"Where would you go if the sky was yours?" I noticed a sprig of green with a yellow flower that had attached itself to my sleeve.

Plucking it off, I rolled it between my fingers. The buttery petals of the furze rubbed against my fingers, leaving a golden stain.

"America." She shrugged. "My aunt plans to take me there in the fall. The opportunity there is incredible for young women. Secretly, I plan to stay and live a life of exploration. I simply do not see the point in getting married and spending the next twenty years of my life turning out children to care for, or being unable to accept a job because I'm a wife. I want adventure, and now, I'm free to take it as it comes."

"America." The idea of traveling all that way sounded exciting. "That's quite brave."

"It will be," she said. "I don't have adequate funds to remain there yet, as my parents' estate needs to be settled. It'll take time, but I cannot stay in this country for long. It's been torn apart. The Emergency has ended, and yet, discontent bleeds on." She made a face. "I'm on the side of survival. Marriage would trap me here, and I want no part of that."

The sun was hot on my face, and I pulled on my bonnet. "I know you don't mean to marry, but your heart might have other ideas."

I thought again of Sullivan. I wasn't in love with him, or even all that interested in getting married, but I'd always enjoyed his company, ever since we were little kids.

"What will you do?" Harding asked.

"University."

"I see." There was a hint of disdain in her voice.

"You don't like school?" I said, surprised. She seemed too intelligent to be disinterested in learning.

Harding ran her hands over the tips of the grass. "University does not teach a thing about what's actually happening, about the people who are starving and the danger facing us all. It won't teach me anything I can't learn on my own."

I didn't understand what she meant. The Emergency was long past. Yes, there were still some minor inconveniences, but things were nothing like they were with the threat of the Germans looming over us.

"Will you still leave for America if the estate isn't settled?" I asked.

"It will be."

The idea that I'd lose her so soon filled me with disappointment. She linked her arm in mine.

"You must visit," she said. "Trust me, once you hear how much fun I'm having, you won't have much interest in wasting your life here."

I looked out over the vast sea, trying to imagine what could be beyond.

My future wasn't something I'd spent much time considering, as my parents dictated where I would go and what I would do. For the first time, it occurred to me that it might be possible to have a voice in my plans.

Chapter Four

Pittsburgh, present day

Making it home felt like trying to run through deep drifts of snow. There was a delay when the plane was deiced on the tarmac. A delay bringing the jet bridge out when we landed. Then my phone's battery gave out, so it took extra time to get a rideshare, and there was another delay in traffic on the way to the hospital. Finally, I arrived, praying I'd made it in time.

I checked in at the front. My grandmother was no longer in ICU but had been moved to a room.

"Is it a hospice room?" I asked.

The attendant checked her notes. "No. It's regular."

The news let me take in a proper breath for the first time since my mother had first called. I stopped at the bathroom to rinse off my face and brush my teeth before rolling my small suitcase to the elevator. The hallways were bright white and seemed dreamlike after my sleepless night.

My mother set down her book when I walked in and held me tight. The hug made me brave enough to look over at the bed. My grandmother was asleep, with her mouth wide open. She looked twice as thin as usual, her skin stretched tight across high cheekbones, but her color was good. She wore her favorite nightie, the one made of Irish linen.

Nodding at it, I said, "I'm glad she's wearing that."

My mother peered over her reading glasses. "The nurses tried to make her put on a hospital gown, but you know how that went."

I smiled and pulled my sweater tight. The hospital room was freezing but smelled good, like the coffee my mother was drinking, and something clean, most likely disinfectant.

"It's good to see you," I told her.

My mother looked older, with a deeper tone of silver in her hair. I had to really think about when I'd last seen her. Thanksgiving. Tia and I had had a grant deadline two days after Christmas, so I'd stayed in Chicago in December to celebrate Hannukah with her family instead.

"How is Grandma doing?" I asked.

"Hard to tell." My mother sat back down, and I pulled over a chair of my own. "It's too early to get our hopes up, but the nurses seem to think she's turned a corner."

My pulse quickened. "I hoped that was the case, since she's not in hospice."

"It's not a guarantee." My mother glanced at the machine posting the vitals. "Her fever went down, though, and the antibiotics have everything under control."

My relief, coupled with the race to get here, made me feel light-headed. "So, she's not dying?"

"Well, we're all dying." My mother pinched her lips the way she did when she thought she'd said something clever. "However, your grandmother might get the dignity to do it at home, one night when we don't expect it, so as to give us a good fright in the morning."

I almost expected my grandmother to open her eyes and start laughing.

"That's such good news," I said.

"I'm cautious in my optimism. Her cough is horrendous."

I wanted to hold my grandmother's hand but didn't, for fear I'd wake her.

"Do you want to rest?" my mother said. "You look exhausted."

I knew I should be strong enough to power through with an espresso and some conversation, but I really hadn't slept at all. Besides, I didn't know if I had it in me to share details about my life, especially if my mother asked about the business. She'd supported my aspirations, but I knew she'd prefer to see me with a steady job in a research lab.

"I'm exhausted," I admitted.

My mother went to the small hospital closet, standing on her toes to reach the shelf. She might have aged, but she looked as strong as ever. Tennis put my mother through college, and she'd continued to play, which had kept her young and fit, even in her sixties. I'd made my way through college on a swimming scholarship, but I'd barely seen a pool since graduation.

My mother handed me a pillow and a blanket. "Use that chair for a bed. It kicks out and lays flat."

The pale-blue vinyl chair wasn't exactly comfortable, but it was better than the seat on the plane. I closed my eyes. It felt strange to sleep in a hospital room instead of my apartment, not to mention having my family nearby.

It was a sense of being stuck in limbo, experiencing life as it had been before I'd become a grown-up. I pulled the rough hospital blanket up to my chin, my eyes trained on my grandmother's chest. The beep of the heart monitor kept time with the rhythm of her breath.

~

I was still at my grandmother's bedside a week later, but this time, we were at her house. My grandmother lived right down the road from my mother, in a suburb close to the university where my mother worked.

Back when my grandfather died and my parents were still married, they invited my grandmother to move in with them. She'd refused but had bought a house on the same block, which made it easy for me to drop by, long past the days when I needed to be there after school.

My grandmother and I had spent so much time together after my grandfather's death. She loved riding her bike, so we'd explore after I got out of school and see where the afternoon would take us. My favorite memory was the night we'd stumbled across the opening of an opera downtown, and my grandmother decided to buy us tickets. We parked our bikes outside, bought fancy dresses at a thrift shop down the road, and joined the well-heeled crowd.

Later in life, my mother told me that period of time had meant the world to my grandmother.

"She was so lonely once she retired and was without your grandfather," my mother recalled. "You gave her a reason to embrace life again."

Now, I looked out the window to fight back the emotion. Our neighbor was out shoveling the late-afternoon snow, and the metal shovel pinged against the ground. I knew he'd shovel my grandmother's driveway next. The neighbors had all known me since I was little, and I'd already clocked in at least two hours of small talk and reassurance that my grandmother was fine, and no, we really weren't in need of a casserole.

Getting to my feet, I rubbed the crick in my neck. I'd spent much of the week when my grandmother slept with my eyes glued to the computer, trying to figure out what had caused the serum to fail. I hadn't found a thing in our records, and at this point, I was certain our sample had become contaminated in transit. Before I could file for an appeal, though, I needed to coordinate the evidence, and come clean with Tia.

I had broken her trust, but surely she would understand. I'd been upset about my grandmother and unprepared to see negative results. In short, I'd panicked, which had to be a forgivable offense.

Unfortunately, Tia wasn't the only one with a voice in our business. If her father found out what I'd done, it could cause a major problem, because he hadn't wanted me to be a part of things from the start.

The first time I met him was at a dinner following graduation, at a country club out in a suburb of Chicago. The club required women to wear a dress to dinner, but Tia had forgotten to tell me, so I'd worn a skirt and blouse. I could tell he wasn't impressed. Then I made the mistake of correcting him at dinner.

It happened at a large table full of academics. Everyone was discussing an article in the Sunday paper about AI in medicine. Tia's father was quoting it nearly verbatim, so I assumed he wouldn't mind if I corrected a part that he'd remembered wrong.

When I did, Tia nearly choked on her water. She nudged me hard under the table, and I stopped talking. Her father continued to butcher the facts, but then he made a point of repeatedly asking me if he'd gotten it right. From that night on, he called me a "spitfire," but it wasn't a compliment.

It might be simple to tell Tia I'd panicked the night that my grandmother had fallen ill, but it could cause a serious problem with her father. I had to wait, so I could fix the whole mess without her father finding out first.

My grandmother's eyes fluttered open. "Rainey?" she said. "Is—"

The words were cut short by a thick, racking cough that echoed through the room. Quickly, I kneeled next to her.

"How are you doing?" I asked.

She took my hand, staring straight ahead. We stayed that way, her brittle skin resting in mine, the thick diamond ring leaving a delicate imprint, until her eyes became unfocused. My body tensed. Then her chest moved up and down, and I breathed in a small sigh of relief.

My grandmother's voice was strong and firm. "Take me home."

I gave her hand a gentle squeeze. There had been moments when the medication had left her confused. The confusion upset my mother, but I'd researched my grandmother's medications, and confusion was an expected side effect, so I wasn't too concerned.

"You are home," I said. "Get some rest, and I'll be right here beside you."

She rubbed her face. "I need the letters."

I glanced at the bedside table to see if my mother had been reading something to her. My grandmother's eyesight had faded with age, and she could no longer read independently. I didn't see a book on the table, other than the Bible she'd brought from Ireland. I held it up. "Did you want me to read this?"

"The letters." My grandmother struggled to sit and then swung her legs to the edge of the bed. Her nightgown billowed in white around thin legs covered in varicose veins.

"I'll find them," I said. "You rest." My grandmother had been up and about in the last day or so, but even trips to the bathroom made her tired.

"Rainey, I need to go to Aisling." She gripped my hand, hard. "I've made a terrible mistake. I need to go home." Her eyes were wild, and I felt her forehead. It wasn't hot.

"We'll figure it out." This sudden sense of urgency was new, and I was starting to get concerned. "Rest for now, and we'll figure it out in the morning."

My grandmother's eyes met mine. "Promise you'll take me."

"Sure."

In the morning, she might not even remember that she'd asked.

My grandmother gave a little nod and lay back down, as if relieved. I helped her get back to her pillow and tucked the blanket tight around her.

"It's going to be all right," I said, kissing her on the forehead.

Within moments, she was asleep. I tiptoed out of the room to find my mother.

My mom was down in the study with a cup of Earl Grey tea that peppered the room with its spicy scent. Outside the window, dusk had started to fall.

"Would you like some tea?" she asked, without looking up from her computer. She was reviewing work from her students, which is how she spent a lot of her time.

"No." I took a seat on the antique love seat. "Grandma was confused when she woke up. It's probably the medicine, but she said she wanted to go home. To Aisling. Is that where she grew up in Ireland?"

"No, she was from a village on the southern coast. Did she say anything else?"

"No." I considered the pictures on the wall of the study. They were of my mother and my grandparents, but there wasn't one picture here or anywhere else of Ireland. My grandmother couldn't hide her brogue, but she'd never told us a thing about her life back home.

"I don't like it that she won't talk about where she's from," I said. "I've asked her a hundred times, and she's always changed the subject. There was that one time where I really pushed it because I wanted to write that report for history class or geography or something—remember that?—and she actually got up and left dinner."

My mother winced. "I remember."

I'd pressed my grandmother in between bites of salmon. She'd tried to change the topic a few times, but when I kept at her, she'd daintily folded her napkin and set it gently by her plate. Then she walked out the front door and slammed it so hard that the mirror on the wall shook.

I hadn't asked her about Ireland since.

"I'd like to know more about her past while we still have the time," I said. "It's always seemed strange that she won't talk about it."

My mother closed her computer. "She talked about it some. Little things. But it's not really that strange that she wouldn't." My mother slid her reading glasses up on her head. "Your grandmother grew up during the war, which was a painful time for a lot of people."

"Ireland was neutral, though."

"Ireland was endlessly complicated. The poverty was horrible, not to mention the fighting between those who wanted to be independent and those who supported British rule. Ireland might have been neutral during the war, but many of their people were starving. There was no money, food was in short supply in many regions, and the rations lasted until the midfifties. Not to mention the fact that the men who fought on the side of Britain were shunned after the war. Oh, and they never said 'war.' They called it the 'Emergency.' It was a terrible time, full of heartbreak and ruin."

"I can see why she might not want to talk about that," I said. "At the same time, it's a pretty big piece of the past to leave behind."

"Her parents died, too," my mother added. "Right around then."

"During the war?" I asked.

"After, I think."

I took out my phone. "What was the name of her town?"

"Kislee. It's in County Cork."

I hesitated. "Which is . . . ?"

My mother put on her glasses on and took a look. "The bottom-right-hand side of the map, next to the ocean and the Celtic Sea. Her village was relatively close to Kinsale. County Cork is stunning in pictures. So green, of course, but it has mountains, the water, and one of the biggest cities in Ireland."

"And the Blarney Stone."

My mother gave me a faint smile. "Sounds like you've familiarized yourself with Ireland as well in spite of your grandmother's lack of interest."

"I mean . . ." I shrugged. "It's Ireland. Am I supposed to pretend like it's not there?"

My mother didn't respond. Once I'd looked up Kislee, I scrolled through the pictures, enchanted by the bright-green grass and the gorgeous deep blue of the sea.

"It's stunning," I told her. "There are problems everywhere. Why would she leave?"

"Beauty doesn't always show what's below the surface. Isn't that the theme of all fairy tales?" My mother hovered next to the couch, peering over my shoulder.

The main street in Kislee was as quaint as a film, complete with small pubs, grocery stores, and storefronts. Towering hills surrounded the small village, and I even saw pictures of people riding in horse-drawn carts. It was rustic and just the type of place I'd love to visit.

My mother took a seat beside me on the couch. "It's been difficult for me, too, to not know what her life in Ireland was like. I became obsessed with Ireland when I was a teenager, but eventually, I accepted the fact that she didn't care to discuss it. What's the place she mentioned again?"

"Aisling," I said, typing it in. "It means 'dream,' apparently."

A long list of options popped up, so I tried again, partnering it with "Kislee." The Aisling in Kislee was a bed-and-breakfast that looked like it had been a stone manor by the sea. It was covered by English ivy, with large windows and several rooms.

"That's pretty." I showed it to her. "Did she stay there or something?"

My mother hesitated. "Maybe? She never went back, not once she'd moved to America, so perhaps when she was young."

I studied the photo a moment longer, then clicked on the "About Us" section.

"Mom . . ." I could hardly believe what I was reading. "Unless I'm missing something, this used to be her home."

Chapter Five

Ireland, 1949

I sat in the parlor, sipping a cup of hot tea while I waited for Harding to join me. Tea was typically my favorite afternoon treat, but I was so nervous to speak to her about what was on my mind that I could hardly taste it.

Three months had passed in a breath with her at Aisling. It was as if she'd been there forever, and we focused on simple pursuits when we were together. We'd fallen into a comfortable routine of walks, reading by the sea, and laughing about anything and everything that amused us.

Poor Seamus was on the front lines. Harding found him hilarious and secretly mimicked his voice, posture, and sour attitude with perfection. Even though we only joked in private, sometimes when he was around, I'd think of something Harding had said and nearly burst out laughing.

I'd also taken her to the candy store, where she'd noticed Sullivan right away.

Once we'd left, she sang, "Evie, that boy in there only has eyes for you. He can't look away. Seems you might have the same problem."

I had thought my interest in him was well hidden. Instead, Harding had given it attention, which made me blush.

"How's the peppermint?" she asked.

I broke it in two and handed half to her.

She tasted it and smiled at me. "Sweet on the lips. Just like a kiss."

During our time together, I'd learned Harding was passionate about politics, and she often talked about the Emergency. When I asked how she knew so much about it, she gave me a baffled look. "I read." She led me to my father's library and plucked a short-story collection off the shelf. "Try this one," she'd said, handing it to me.

The next few nights, I immersed myself in heart-wrenching stories about Ireland and the conflicts on our land. The words stayed in my head. One night, I woke up with my sheets drenched in sweat, and I realized that I'd been dreaming of bombs dropping, explosions filling the sky, and the crash of glass. These ideas were still fresh in my mind, and I regretted reading those stories. I didn't want to face all the things that made the world unpredictable, the events that had caused so many others pain.

When I'd said as much, Harding scolded me. "You must be aware of the world around you. To understand the threads that bind us all together."

We also spent time with innocent pursuits. Helping out at the church and schoolhouse, entertaining the local children, and having tea with an occasional primary school friend. Of course, Harding liked to keep life interesting, and one night, she convinced me to go to the pub the next town over to have a drink in the snug, the hidden room where no one would see us.

I was sick from whiskey for the next two days, but in the moment, sneaking into the secret room to share a drink with her—something I would never have tried on my own—felt daring and incredibly grown-up. We'd talked and danced to the music we could hear through the wall, and at the end of it all, I couldn't even walk out of the pub.

Some friends of hers, men I'd never met before, took us back to my house. I knew it was improper and that I should have been frightened, but I kept to myself and stared up at the stars as the wagon brought us safely back home.

The men had been kind, just like so many of the people Harding had befriended during her short time in town. It felt as if she knew everyone, perhaps because she spent so much time out wandering or because she was unconcerned with our social hierarchy. She had ties everywhere. I was proud to have introduced such a sunny being into the fabric of our town.

True to her word, Harding had also spent much of her time away from the house to paint. She was a perfectionist with her art and refused to show me any of it. I was so curious, but I didn't press her because I knew she'd share it in her own time. Unfortunately, that time was about to come to a rather abrupt end.

My parents were scheduled to come home in two days. Seamus had been lit with purpose, bustling through the house to make sure the preparations were perfect. Weary of his enthusiasm, I'd nearly asked if he'd scheduled a marching band. I wanted to see my parents, but not if they would take issue with Harding's presence in their home.

I had opened up to Harding about so many things, but I'd avoided talking to her about my mother and father. Mainly because of her reaction the day we'd met in Dublin, when I'd told her of my father's work with the government, but also because Harding no longer had parents. I certainly didn't want to tell her that mine wouldn't welcome her with open arms.

"Hello, hello," Harding called, stepping into the parlor. "Oh, that tea looks divine." She poured herself a cup, then flopped into a chair. "I've been out and about all day long, and I'm simply famished. Shall we ring Seamus for sandwiches?"

"Yes, of course," I said.

I'd been fine with the soda bread, but I'd always told Harding that my house was her house. I felt so guilty to think that this sentiment could change.

Seamus accepted her request with a slightly dour look. Once he'd left, Harding settled in to the chair with her tea and spread the skirts of her sleek, floral dress out to look like a fan. The wooden trunk she'd traveled with had been full of such enticing pieces, and she never hesitated to visit our local tailor to update them or to allow me to try them on.

"Evie, I know that you wanted to speak to me about something." The room was hot, and the late-July heat forced the flies to move more slowly than usual. "Before you do, I must tell you what's been on my mind, as it's troubled me for a few days now. I'm afraid it will upset you."

"What is it?" I asked.

Harding set down her teacup. "With your parents' return, it's time for me to make an exit."

The clock that clicked on the mantel seemed to go silent, along with the bird that chirped outside. My hand, I realized, had planted itself on my heart.

"Leave?" I managed to say. "You said you were going in the fall."

"I don't mean to America. I couldn't bear to leave town before seeing you off. I mean Aisling."

It was as if Harding had sensed what I was about to tell her. That was her way, and it had made our friendship so easy.

"Oh," I said.

"Yes." She adjusted her skirts. "Earlier this week, Seamus informed me I would be asked to vacate the premises once your parents returned. I was taken aback, of course, but instantly made the proper arrangements. I think he'll be happy to have me gone."

My mouth dropped open. "That boils my blood." I couldn't believe Seamus had been so presumptuous. "He shouldn't have spoken for me."

Harding grinned. "Why do you think I sent him to make me a sandwich?"

I snorted, practically laughing out loud.

"It's fine," she said after taking an enthusiastic drink of tea. "It didn't bother me. What would bother me is upsetting your parents, so

I let a room in town for the next few weeks, over the livery stables. That way, I'll still be here until it's time for you to leave."

The livery stables belonged to the Hannigan family. The family was respectable and kind, but it would be difficult to get there, to still be able to see Harding every day.

"Then where will you go?" I asked.

"My aunt's house." She smiled. "Then America."

"I respect your decision," I said. "However, I do regret it. I wish you'd stay here."

She gave me a knowing look. "Evie, you called me in to ask me to leave."

"No, I . . ." I lowered my voice. "I was going to ask you to continue with the story that we attended boarding school together."

Harding's eyes widened. "From what I've heard, your parents would have been a bit more complicated to fool."

The fact that she understood that, and had made other accommodations without making me ask, made me breathe a deep sigh of relief. It was one thing to lie to my parents once, but quite another to keep up the farce, day after day. Now, I wouldn't have to resort to that deception, and Harding could remain in town without bother. It was just that we wouldn't be together.

Seamus returned with a plate of small sandwiches. He delivered them without a smile or a word.

Once he left, I said, "I'll speak with him."

She rolled her eyes. "Don't. He's a sour old thing. No need to have him turn over in his pickle jar."

Once we'd eaten, Harding got to her feet and flashed one of her magnetic smiles. "Care to take a walk along the moor? We could stop for some penny candy after."

I smiled at her. "Sounds delicious."

⁓

We had reached the edge of the hillside when Harding turned to me with a mischievous look in her eye. "I was talking with some people about the swimming hole. Shall we try it?"

Immediately, my mouth went dry. Harding was often up for adventure, and each time she convinced me to try something new, the world somehow felt bigger. Yet my parents had forbidden me from using the swimming hole under any circumstance.

It was in an area where a winding path led down behind the cliff walls to a bright-blue pool of water that was connected to the sea through a small pathway in the rock. The pool was dangerous because of its deceptive stillness. The tide and the wind could turn it deadly in an instant.

"I'm not allowed," I told Harding. Before she could protest, I added, "The locals know it's unsafe. I'd question the scruples of the friend who encouraged you to try it."

"Indeed." Harding raised her eyebrows. "I'm still interested. You don't have to go. I only ask that you stand watch in the event that you need to call for help."

Even though I didn't want Harding to take the risk, it would be impossible to talk her out of it. So I led her down the pathway, feeling adventurous and a little bit proud that I knew how to get there. In truth, the swimming hole was something I'd wanted to try my entire life, but I had been too scared to do so.

Once we'd made it past the jagged rocks of the hill, I admired the tranquil blue water. The pool was large, nearly nine meters across, with a small waterfall that trickled down from the upper rocks.

"I'm properly chuffed," Harding said before stripping off her dress. If she felt shy to stand in her underclothes, it didn't show, because she was too busy beaming at the water.

The wind had picked up, but the surface was still. Turning to me, she said, "Well, what are you waiting for?"

My mouth dropped open to protest, but at the same time, the question rang in my ear.

What *was* I waiting for?

I had wanted to do this my entire life. No one was here, it was a beautiful day, and I was hot. What would it hurt for me to step into the water, if only for a brief moment? Still, the fact that my parents had explicitly instructed me not to left me feeling lost.

"I don't care to," I lied.

"Of course you do." Harding pulled up my dress, and reluctantly, I helped her take it off over my head, followed by my shoes. My teeth started chattering, and I said, "What if we're killed? Or injured? Or—"

"What if we have the time of our lives?" she asked. "Come on."

Grabbing my hand, she led me to the edge. It would be an easy jump, only a short distance down, and there were several footholds to get back up on dry land, but my legs still trembled.

"Harding, I—"

"One, two—" I tried to pull my hand away, but it was too late. Harding heaved me toward the edge with her, shouting, "Three!"

Our bodies crashed through the water, its icy cold cutting into my bones and weighing down my undergarments. I broke the surface, full of fury, until I saw the joy in Harding's face.

Her eyes were as green as the trees, and water ran down her pale skin. She looked young and more luminous than ever.

"Isn't this splendid?" she cried.

I had taken the leap. The rules had been broken. There was nothing to do but revel in it.

Flipping onto my back, I floated across the water, enjoying the simple freedom of the burn of the sun in my eyes.

The walk along the moor warmed our chilled bodies. A storm was coming, and the sea was whipped into a white froth that crashed up and over the rocks, rising like steam against the edge of the cliffs. It made me nervous, wondering what could have happened if the weather had hit while we were swimming, but it was a wasteful thought. My hair was damp, my heart full.

The idea of seeing Sullivan at the candy shop put an extra speed in my step. I'd have loved to confide in him how we'd spent the afternoon, but I dared not. Halfway up the path, Harding came to an abrupt stop.

"What is it?" I asked, then noticed someone approaching in the distance.

It wasn't uncommon to see people we didn't know out on the moor. There was a shipping port a few towns over, and visitors would eventually make their way to our town, so I wasn't sure why Harding's body suddenly seemed tense.

The man was getting closer, and he was stocky, with black hair and a thunderous expression. He looked like he might have spent his morning in the pub, which actually could mean trouble.

"Stay here," Harding said, in a low tone. "I'll find out what he wants."

Squaring her shoulders, she marched across the grass.

I hung back and debated what to do. We were a five-minute walk away from town but as isolated as could be.

I couldn't see Harding's face as she approached him, but by the movement in her hands and shoulders, she was animated. Finally, she handed him something and he turned, heading back the way he'd come. She watched him for a moment and then waved at me.

The sun peeked through the clouds on her walk back, and she shielded her eyes. "He's headed to Stone Grove," she called, once she was close. "Got turned around."

"What did you give him?" I asked.

She frowned. "Oh, he dropped his hat."

It was possible that she'd caught his hat in midair and I hadn't noticed, but I suspected the true story was that she'd given him a few coins. Harding had such a good heart.

"You're dear," I said, linking my arm in hers. "I'll miss having you at home."

Her face relaxed into a bright smile. "Then let's leave for America. Today. Forget uni—you don't need it. We could have wild adventures."

Before I met her, I never would have considered it. Now, I could only regret that I didn't have a choice in the matter.

"I will visit," I promised. "One day."

"Don't marry Sullivan if you ever plan to leave this place," she warned. "The moment you do that, you'll be stuck here forever."

My cheeks colored. I liked the way that Sullivan smiled at me, and I liked laughing with him, but I didn't plan to marry him.

We walked in silence for a moment; then I said, "If you don't want me to marry him, why do you always ask to go get candy?"

"Because." She winked. "You like peppermints."

We stepped off the grass and onto the main street, calling out greetings and waving at friends every few steps. It was busy with everyone out and about while the rain held off.

Our little town was typical of so many, with most of the stone houses close enough to make conversation but far enough apart to care for the stock. The pub was at one end of the street and the school at the other, with O'Leary's Dry Goods Shop right in the middle.

I checked my reflection in the glass as we walked. I looked pretty, but nothing like Harding. She was a beauty, with her long hair and natural curls. There was something about her, a certain spice, which made me question if Sullivan could become more interested in her than in me.

Through the window of the shop, I spotted him leaning against the counter, looking bored out of his mind. He'd once told me that he wanted to be a train conductor, but his father had grand plans for him to manage the store. I wondered if he'd accepted the idea of spending the rest of his life in a state of monotony. Harding was speaking with someone, so I signaled to her that I was going to head inside.

The bells jingled as I walked in, and he brightened. His nose had more freckles than I remembered, and it looked like he'd been in the sun.

"Top of the afternoon, Evie," he said, smiling.

"Hi," I said. "I think I've seen about everyone in town today. It's been a nice walk. The rain's held off."

"I hope the rain's not waiting for you to walk home." He leaned on the counter, showcasing his strong, tanned forearms. "Your father's due back soon?"

"Yes, this week."

"Good. My mother is hoping he'll bring news of a change in the rations."

It had been four years since the end of the Emergency, and the people of Ireland were still required to use their ration books. Issues such as a lack of fertilizer or farm equipment had affected the food supply, along with heavy rains or freezes. It would be much better if the rations could be a thing of the past, but they continued to drag down the joy in our future, as the leaders fought against the risk of another famine. It was something I hadn't understood in detail until Harding pushed me to learn more about it.

The door opened, ringing the leather strap of bells. Sullivan's smile dimmed as Harding strolled in.

"Hello, hello," she called.

"Hello, Harding."

Sullivan became busy with some things behind the counter as we browsed. Harding and I took our time selecting candy from the penny jar. When it was time to pay, she slipped me some coins and walked over to the door, giving me another moment to talk with Sullivan.

"Well, enjoy the afternoon," he said. "I look out the window on a day like this and wish I was outside." He slid our choices into a brown paper bag. "We should go on a walk one afternoon. May I call on you?"

My cheeks burned at the offer. I wondered what my parents would say at the idea of me spending time with a shopkeeper's son. My grandfather would have looked at his family as equals, but my family had risen above that. Such things mattered little to me, but I knew my mother would have plenty to say on the topic. It would be wise to take this opportunity before my parents thought to make it forbidden.

"Yes, that would be lovely," I said.

This time, Sullivan looked right at me when he smiled. It made me a bit breathless to think that I hadn't read him wrong; he was, in fact, interested in me.

"You'll like these," he said, adding a few butterscotch pieces to the bag.

"Oh, I didn't ask for—"

"It's on the house." He dropped my coins into the register. Looking over at Harding, he seemed to note that she wasn't listening, and quietly, he said, "Evie, you must be careful with her."

"Sorry?" I asked.

Harding held an almanac, absently flipping through its pages while watching out the front window.

Sullivan hesitated, then said, "This is a conversation for another time."

Harding turned to us then, her smile too bright. "Shall we go?"

Sullivan handed me our bag, and Harding looped her arm in mine. The bells on the door jingled a farewell as she led me out.

Then she stopped walking to call back, "I've already told her not to marry you."

I nudged her sharply with my elbow. It wasn't like her to be rude.

Outside, I looked up at the sky. The clouds were thick again, and we'd need our raincoats before we made it home. I walked in silence, barely tasting the piece of candy Harding handed me.

"Don't be cross," she said. "He needs to know it's not an option. It's only fair."

"To whom?" I demanded.

"Him."

I rolled my eyes. "I haven't decided what I'm going to do in life."

"Exactly." Her gaze was steady. "Until you know, do not waste time on promises you do not intend to keep."

~

That night, I sat in Harding's room and allowed her to plait my hair and pin it up. I never enjoyed the process when Fedelma did it, but Harding made it fun.

Once we'd finished, she studied my reflection in the handheld mirror. "You didn't like what I said about Sullivan this afternoon."

"No matter," I said.

Sullivan wasn't much on my mind. Instead, I was thinking of how lonely I'd be once Harding was gone. We sat on her bed, the two of us dressed in our evening gowns, with our hair done as if we were headed to a grand ball.

"I need to share something." Harding ran her thumb along the stitching in the quilt. "Since I'm moving later this week and we won't have nights such as this."

The thought pained me as I pictured all the times we'd talked until the moon was high.

"This time with you has served as a balm to my soul. I have never met someone so willing to let me be myself. There's no judgment from you. I felt it in Dublin, and I've felt it here. I think of you as a sister, Evie. The sister I never had."

My eyes filled with tears. "I feel the same."

Harding nodded. "I've told you so much about how you need to be bold, to speak up, to know your own mind. However, in the midst of that, I've begun to think about how a butterfly grows in a cocoon." She smiled at me. "Don't be in a hurry. I've . . ." She looked down at her hands. "There have been times I've taken shortcuts, and if I could do it all again, I wouldn't. I'd be me, without apology. Do what will bring you joy, but don't rush. It takes time to know everything that you are and all that you can do. I can already see that you will do a lot. I see that about you."

Later that night, as I drifted off to sleep, the words rang in my ears. Never in my life had I thought I could do much of anything, other than what was expected of me. The idea that I could do more left me considering possibilities far beyond what typically shaped my dreams.

Chapter Six

The next morning, my mother and I waited by my grandmother's bed-side, coffee in hand. I was so full of questions by the time her eyes fluttered open.

"Good morning." My mother set down the mug and reached for her hand. "How are you feeling?"

"Better." My grandmother stretched before letting out a racking cough that left her looking tired and frustrated. She turned to me. "Did you pack up?"

My mother and I looked at each other.

I pulled out my phone. In the "About Us" section of the website for Aisling, one of the lines had read: *This majestic home was first constructed by Brendan Campbell, a prominent leader in Kislee, as a seaside sanctuary for his wife, Alannah, and daughter, Evie.*

"Is this where you wanted to go?" I held out my phone. "It's a bed-and-breakfast now, but it's called Aisling."

My grandmother's facial expression softened. "Yes, that's it."

"Mom, was this your home?" my mother asked.

"Let me see it again, please," my grandmother said.

I handed her the phone. She lay on her side, scrolling through the pictures. It had always impressed me that she was so proficient with technology. There were times I still struggled to turn on the cable.

My grandmother set the phone on the bedside table and cleared her throat. "I think I'm dying," she said as matter-of-factly as if discussing the weather. "I need to go back before that happens."

My mother tensed. "Go back to the hospital?"

"To Ireland. I'd like to give him the letters," she said, coughing. "It's time."

"Who? What letters?" my mother asked, taking a seat on the edge of the bed.

My grandmother patted her hand. "I don't wish to discuss that."

My mother and I looked at each other. Perhaps the letters were some sort of final will that she needed to get to her lawyer. That could be done electronically, though.

"You no longer have any financial interests there, do you?" my mother asked, as if reading my mind. "Are you still connected to Aisling?"

The bed-and-breakfast website said that Aisling had been sold years ago, but perhaps the money from the sale was still sitting there with a solicitor, left behind.

"No." My grandmother pushed her body into a sitting position before indicating we should open the yellow brocade curtains. I did, then watched her stare in fascination at the dust swirling through the room like snow. It was possible that the medication was still affecting her, which would explain this sudden whim to return to a place she wanted nothing to do with.

"I'd like to read the letters one last time before I die," she said. "I'd like to share them." Her voice was so quiet that I barely heard this last part, but I thought she said, "He needs to know what he meant to me."

My mother looked at me in surprise. *What?* she mouthed.

I shrugged, feeling uncomfortable.

My grandparents had been married for fifty years before my grandfather passed away. I'd seen pictures and old videos of the anniversary party they'd held at a banquet room, where they served steak and mashed potatoes before dancing the night away. My grandfather had held her close, and I'd decided I'd only get married if it was with some-one who loved me like that. It was hard to believe that my grandmother might have held a flame in her heart for someone other than my grand-father, but anything was possible.

"Rainey, I'd like you to come with me," my grandmother said. "To Ireland."

My mother stiffened. "Mom—"

My grandmother looked at me. Her brown eyes had become cloudy with time, but her gaze was strong and steady. "I will go alone if I have to, but I'd like to go with you."

"Let's talk about this another—"

"It has to be you," she insisted. "It would be too much for your mother."

"Grandma, you need to rest." My voice was firm. "Let's revisit this later today, okay?"

My grandmother waved her hand, as if frustrated, then leaned back against the pillow. Her eyes drifted shut almost immediately.

My mother lifted her chin. "Excuse me," she said, and she left the room.

I found her in the hallway, next to the window table with the fake orchid.

I kept my voice low. "You okay?"

Her eyes blazed. "I have spent a lifetime wanting to know what happened in Ireland. I wanted to see her home, see where she was raised. She refused to take me."

"I know," I said. "I think—"

"Now that she wants to go, I'm not invited? It would be too hard on me? I'm not fragile, Rainey."

"You're invited," I said. "I think she just figured you wouldn't take her, so she decided to focus on the sucker in the room."

Even though my grandmother and I had always had a special bond, she and my mother were close as well. But my mother was known to take her time when it came to things like planning a trip or making a big purchase. My grandmother probably thought I wouldn't overcomplicate things.

My mother shook her head. "She's not well enough to go to Ireland. It's . . ." She leaned against the wall, and I realized she had dark circles under her eyes. "It's too complicated." We stood in silence. "She's never asked for anything like this. She's never even talked about it."

"I know," I said. "It could be the medicine—"

"No, I mean . . ." My mother thrust out her chin. "She's spent her life running from whatever is back there. The fact that she wants to face it now must be a sign that she needs to do it."

"What are you saying?" I asked.

My mother let out a breath, her eyes rimmed in red. "It's the final thing she wants in life. I love her, and I guess . . . I'd be grateful if you'd give it to her."

"You want her to go?" I said, surprised.

"No." She shook her head. "But I don't want to hold her back."

I considered the logistics. I didn't need to return to Chicago quite yet. I could continue to work remotely and petition for an appeal. Besides, I'd been so panicked at the idea that my grandmother was going to die. If I rushed right back to Chicago without spending any real time with her, how would that be different from losing her altogether? I could call her, sure, but the opportunity to be with her again, maybe for the last time, was right in front of me.

"Okay," I said, slowly. "If she's still talking about it tomorrow, it's something to really consider."

My mother nodded and then wiped some dust off the ledge of the window.

"We'd have to wait until that cough is healed and get her cleared by the doctor, regardless."

"Does she even have a passport?" I asked.

Did I? Yes. From a trip to France in college, so it wouldn't be expired. It was probably still in my old bedroom.

"She has a passport from that conference we went to in Italy."

"So yours is good, too," I said.

My mother sighed. "I can't go. It's almost the end of the school year. The only thing that would excuse me would be bereavement."

"Wouldn't this count?" I asked.

"I doubt it." My mother avoided my eyes. "On top of that, I'm heading up three end-of-the-year projects. It would be a mess for me to leave."

Frustration built to think that my mother would be willing to stay behind. Yes, her work was important, but this could be the end of her mother's life.

"Mom, I'm sure she'd want you there," I insisted. "This is your chance to learn her history. Besides, it's not a good idea for me to go alone. Even if she recovers enough to make the trip, she could relapse, and she hasn't even been back in seventy years. It could be hard on her, mentally."

"I'd like to be there," my mother said. "But I can't."

I couldn't believe my mother was being so selfish. I opened my mouth to say as much but stopped when I saw the look in her eyes. She wasn't being selfish. She was scared.

"Maybe you'll change your mind," I said, careful to keep my voice gentle. "It's still possible it's the medication talking, anyway."

My mother nodded. "If nothing changes, though, you'll . . ."

"Let's wait and see."

The next morning, my grandmother only wanted to talk about Aisling. This time, she was even more insistent, nearly booking a flight for herself until my mother convinced her to wait.

It took two weeks from the time my grandmother had been released from the hospital to get her well enough to meet with her general practitioner to discuss our plan.

During that time, I split my worry about my grandmother with work, spending every spare second gathering evidence to prove the serum had been contaminated in transit. The breakthrough came when I discovered the shipping company we'd used had some prior incident reports that backed my theory, which would nearly guarantee an appeal.

Since there was a strong chance I was going to Ireland, I decided to tell Tia everything once I was back in Chicago. I didn't like lying to her, but given the timeline, it would all work out. I'd return with a solution instead of a problem.

We met with my grandmother's doctor in his office, and his expression grew more concerned with every word. He checked her vitals, listened to her chest, and frowned.

"You don't think she's doing well?" my mother said.

"No, she is," he said. "She's fully recovered."

My grandmother nodded. "See?"

"However, I don't think I can approve of this idea." The doctor sat back and folded his hands. "If the pneumonia doesn't resurface and kill her, she could get a blood clot from her time on the plane."

"So, she shouldn't go?" my mother asked.

"I do not see it as a risk that she should take."

"Excuse me," my grandmother said. "'She' is sitting right here, and her ears work just fine. You, sir, just said I'm fully recovered. I'm perfectly capable of deciding the risks I do and do not want to take. I also have a passport, so unless you plan to personally go to the airport and take the wheels and wings off that plane, there's little you can do to stop me."

The doctor shook his head. "Seems like you're back to your old self, then," he said, and he made some notes in his chart.

My grandmother turned to me. "Rainey, are you coming with me?" Her eyes were bright and hopeful.

I considered what she'd said about risk. It was a risk to take my grandmother to another country when her health could take a turn. Was it one I was willing to take?

The answer came quickly.

Yes.

I'd made a mistake and I knew it, spending so much time wrapped up in work, away from the people I loved. I wanted to fix that while I still had the chance.

Taking her hand, I said, "Looks like we're going to Ireland."

～

It was foggy when we landed in Dublin, so we couldn't see much from the window of the plane or the rideshare van on the way out of the airport. My grandmother did well on the flight but dozed off in the van, and I was quick to join her. I blinked open my eyes nearly an hour and a half later, with a crick in my neck, to the cheerful sound of the driver singing.

"Good morning to you, then," he said, spotting me in the rearview mirror. "We're nearly there. Ten minutes."

The scenery had changed. The landscape looked like a sculpture carved into stone, frosted with moss and vegetation, stretching up and rolling beside us. In the distance was the sea. Bright blue and shocking, really, in its vibrancy.

This was the Ireland I had seen pictures of and had imagined, and now, I watched as my grandmother pressed her hand to the window, as though peering at a mirage.

"What do you think?" I asked.

She seemed bewildered. "I don't know."

I bit my lip. The doctor had been bullied into giving her a clean bill of health, but it was a long flight. It left my feet swollen, my mouth dry, and my head foggy, so I could only imagine what my grandmother was going through. It scared me to think we were on the other side of the ocean, with no easy way to get back home.

Before I could respond, she said, "You know, I stopped letting myself think about all the things that made Ireland beautiful. Now that I'm here, it's like a dream. I know you're worried about me, Rainey. Don't be. I'd have come, with or without you."

It was a relief to hear it.

I took her hand. "Well, then. Welcome home."

∽

The roads got bumpier as the van exited the motorway. My grandmother stayed silent, watching out the window as we passed through the small village I'd studied in the pictures. When we pulled up to the sprawling stone house that had once been her family home, she let out a sharp breath.

"It looks exactly the same."

The house was covered in trimmed English ivy that covered the front like a well-planned green cloak, showcasing bright, shining paned windows. Two gas lamps were lit at the entryway, and a cheerful sign hung next to the front door. In careful, black script traced in gold it read: *Aisling.*

The grandeur of the house startled me. It had looked lovely in the pictures online but didn't seem quite as large as this, or maybe it was that the pictures underplayed the water view in the background.

It was surprising to discover my grandmother's childhood home was so striking. For the first time, I understood she had grown up rich.

It wasn't something that had occurred to me before. I'd always assumed she'd fled Ireland in search of a better life. Maybe that part was true, but based on this place, money wasn't a part of that.

It also occurred to me that the sale of the home must have brought in a fortune. My grandparents had always been comfortable, but I'd assumed that their money came from my grandfather's work as a banker. Perhaps there was more to the story.

"You lived in this house?" I asked, wondering if I'd misunderstood. "It's where you grew up?"

"Yes." Suddenly, she looked pale. "I . . ."

"Let's get out," I said, quickly. "Get some fresh air."

The driver helped us both out of the van. Her color came back, and we stood in silence, taking deep breaths of the sea air and staring up at the house.

"Welcome!" A woman with a dimpled smile stepped onto the front porch, waving. "I'm Nora." She came out to greet us and indicated our driver should put our luggage on the porch.

"It's so nice to finally meet you," I said, shaking her hand.

Nora and I had spent nearly an hour on the phone when I'd called to book a room. I'd explained to her my grandmother's history, as well as my concerns. She was so eager to have my grandmother come stay that she'd practically given us the room for free, only charging us the cost of food and taxes.

For some reason, I'd expected her to be my mother's age. Instead, she barely looked older than me. Her pale-blonde hair was styled in one of those flouncy bobs, and she wore her green sheath dress with a pair of cozy-looking sneakers.

I had the impulse to hug her but didn't. My grandmother, on the other hand, did not hold back.

"Nora, your kindness has meant the world to us," my grandmother said, kissing her on both cheeks. "Since you live in my old house, I'm going to think of you as family."

Nora beamed at her. "I think it's so special that you've come. Would you like to see what we've done with the place?"

The three of us walked together up a cobblestone path, and I helped my grandmother manage a short series of steps that led under a covered front awning. She seemed eager, as if the nerves in the van had drifted away like the whitecaps on the sea.

"Now, I don't know how involved you were with the sale," Nora said, "but your family sold this to an older couple who lived here happily for several generations. Their children put it on the market about ten years ago, and it's been a joy for me ever since."

My grandmother smiled. "I'm so glad it's been in good hands."

Nora opened the front door. "Does this bring back some memories?"

The entryway stretched up two floors, with a grand staircase in the center and two large windows with an incredible view of the water. Modern light fixtures hung at three levels like birds in flight, and I stared at it all in wonder.

"This is beautiful. Does it look the same?" I asked my grandmother.

"Not a bit," she said. "I saw that on the website, though." Her eyes were bright, and she kept looking around. "What did you do with the chandelier?"

Nora's face broke into a smile. "I hoped you'd ask! Look, I got this out for you, just this afternoon." Inside the drawer of an antique decorative table, Nora had stored a shining piece of crystal. Handing it to my grandmother, she said, "That chandelier was a work of art, but the wiring gave out and couldn't be fixed, so we had to take it down. I held on to the crystals to make jewelry."

My grandmother held the diamond-like sculpture up to the light. "It's hard to believe I'm touching this. I'd have given anything to hold one of these when I was a child."

"Full circle," Nora chirped, then stuck out her arms. "Look. That just gave me the chills. Now, follow me. There's more that might look familiar."

Nora took us to the main room, to the right of the entryway. It stretched all the way to the back of the house, and its walls were painted a deep forest green. There was a large stone fireplace next to a collection of chairs and a cozy-looking couch, as well as an entire wall of wooden shelves stuffed with books organized by color. The windows were multipaned and large, displaying views of a cheerful flower garden, a small fountain, and a grass court where a group of guests played croquet.

"This door opens into the garden." Nora gave a little grunt as she slid it to the side to let in the fresh sea air. "Do you remember this door?"

"I most certainly do," my grandmother said. "I pinched my finger in there a number of times, growing up."

"Well, I've continued your legacy," Nora said. "I should probably get it replaced, but it would be impossible to find one like this, with the small square windows. The glass is ancient and perfect."

"Just like me," my grandmother said, and we all laughed.

It was a good sign that my grandmother was being glib, but I did wonder what she really felt, seeing her home transformed in such a way. It had been strange for me to see the changes in my house when I came back home after college. It threw me to discover that my memories lived on in a completely different setting than the one looking right back at me.

"Do you have photographs?" I asked Nora. "Of the original house?"

My grandmother, to my knowledge, did not. It was possible they were tucked away up in the attic somewhere, but I doubted it. She tended to be tidy, with each corner of her house perfectly organized. She'd once told my mother that the lack of clutter would be her inheritance, which had sent them both into peals of laughter. The thought of the two of them together made me wish my mother had come with us.

"Oh, I have pictures," Nora said, with a cheerful smile. "I photographed the heck out of this place before the remodel. I also have an entire trunk of things that belonged to your family that I plan to have my husband pick up tomorrow."

My grandmother went still. "What sort of trunk? Wooden?" She started to cough, and even though I winced, it sounded much better than even a few days ago.

"I believe so," Nora said. "Yes, it's wooden. I'm sure of it."

"Did it have any papers?" I asked.

"Possibly?" Nora clicked her tongue, thinking. "There was a photo album, and some paintings, from what I can remember. It's in storage, but we can see what's in there tomorrow."

My grandmother looked out over the backyard, her gaze on a small building next to the woods. "It's really beautiful here."

Nora nodded. "I don't know how you could ever leave."

"I had no choice." My grandmother turned away from the window. "That's what I believed back then. I thought it was much too dangerous for me to stay."

Her words surprised me, but Nora just nodded. I could tell she was used to listening, waiting to see if the person she was speaking to would say more. When my grandmother didn't, Nora said, "Well, the flight here can be long and sometimes exhausting. Let's get you to your room to rest. Would you like me to bring up a spot of tea, or would you prefer supper from the pub?"

"I'd like to rest," my grandmother said, taking it all in as we walked.

Nora led us to an elevator and upstairs, down another long hallway. She stopped at the door at the end of the hall, and my grandmother moved to open the one across from it.

"It's over here," Nora said, gently.

My grandmother's brow wrinkled, her hand resting on the knob. It was as if she'd just realized the room wouldn't be the one where she'd grown up. It hadn't occurred to me to warn her.

The corner room had plenty of light from two large windows with airy pale-blue curtains that complemented the Irish chain-patterned quilts on the beds. There was a small stone hearth to the left of the southernmost window, and the small table in the sitting room overlooked a flower garden bright with roses and wildflowers.

I looked to my grandmother for approval. "Do you like it?" She had walked over to the window by the fireplace, her hand pressed up against the glass.

When she didn't answer, I told Nora, "She's hard of hearing when her back is to you. I'm sure this is a lot to take in."

Nora gave me an understanding look. "I'll leave you in peace, then. Oh, here." She handed me a guest folder. "You'll need this information. Wi-Fi password, places to dine. I recommend the pub immensely. It's excellent for food, and it's only a quick walk down the road. Please ring if you need anything at all."

"Thank you," I said. "I'm truly grateful to you for this time here."

Nora smiled at me. "We're happy to be having you."

Once she left, I stood in silence at the window with my grandmother. "If this is too strange for you, I get it. You tell me when it's time to go. I can get us on the next flight."

That said, I doubted a healthy ninety-three-year-old could do a back-to-back international flight, not to mention someone who had just recovered from pneumonia.

"No, we're here." Her voice sounded tired. "I'm proud of myself, Rainey. It took me too long to find the courage, but it feels right and good to breathe the air I was breathing when I was born. It is confusing that Aisling no longer belongs to my family," she admitted, settling into a chair. "But I spent seventy years of my life away from here. How could I expect it to remain the same? Time waits for no one."

"Your bedroom was across the hall, I take it?" I asked.

"Yes." She looked around the room. "However, I always wanted to spend time in here. It was our most glamourous guest room, you see. When a dear friend of mine visited, she lived here for quite some time. There were so many happy memories within these walls." She stood up. "I think I need to rest."

Once I'd helped my grandmother get settled in to bed, she peered at me from out of the pillows. "Getting old isn't as terrible as they tell you. The chance to come here and see it all with different eyes . . ." She looked around the room. "I hope being here can chase some of these bad memories away."

"Yes," I said, curious as to what she meant. "I hope that it will."

I opened the window to let in the sea breeze, wanting to hide the emotion on my face. It was unsettling to see my grandmother so vulnerable, while not knowing what had caused her so much pain. The breeze was cool, and when I turned to tuck the quilt more tightly around her, she was already asleep.

Chapter Seven

Ireland, 1949

My parents arrived home with much fanfare. Seamus called upon me to dress for their arrival and meet them in the driveway along with him and the cook, Mary. There were a couple of false alarms where Seamus saw dust blowing up the lane and assumed it was them, so I stood waiting for several minutes before heading back inside.

I had not scolded Seamus about what he'd said to Harding because I expected that, if I didn't make trouble for him, he wouldn't make trouble for me.

"I'm pleased you planned this," I told him, the third time we waited in the drive.

He gave me a pert nod, then stood at attention, his posture as perfect as a peacock's. My parents' motorcar bounced over the cobblestones, and I rubbed my palms on the skirt of my dress, wishing I didn't feel so nervous to see my family. I shouldn't have felt nervous. They were my parents. Yet I barely knew them, not even as well as I knew my tutor, and certainly not as well as I knew Harding.

They stepped out of the car, blinking in the sun. It had been nearly three months since they'd been gone, and they both looked different, somehow. My father's hair had grown longer, and there was a shiny shape to it. His clothes also seemed more relaxed. My mother was the opposite, with shorter hair and deeper tension around her eyes.

My mother greeted Seamus and the cook first, then embraced me, holding me tight.

"My dear, dear girl." Her warm lips kissed me on the forehead as I breathed in the scent of her exotic perfume. My mother never returned smelling the same. "Evie, you have become a young woman."

Perhaps she thought that because Harding had taught me new and interesting ways to style my hair or because I'd started to smudge an incredibly discreet amount of shadow into my eyebrows. Either way, the remark made me stand taller.

"Welcome home," I said.

My father headed for the front steps. Then, as though remembering he had a daughter, he said, "My darling Evie," and he gave me a kiss on the top of my head. Turning to Seamus, he said, "I must review my correspondence. I'll require a briefing on town affairs in thirty minutes."

My mother watched him go, her expression unreadable.

"Shall we head inside?" she asked, turning back to me.

They had arrived back in time for dinner, and I looked forward to hearing all about their adventures over the succulent fish the cook had spent the day preparing. Once inside, though, my mother gave my arm a gentle squeeze. "It's wonderful to see you, my darling. I have quite the headache, however, so I must get to bed." Turning to Seamus, she said, "Please send the tea to my room."

The dismissal stung, and I wondered if Seamus and Mary had noticed that my parents had no interest in seeing me.

I had looked forward to spending time with my mother and had hoped to share the same closeness that Harding and I had experienced all summer, but that was not her way. My mother had never expressed much of an interest in me, and I'd accepted that. Now that I'd spent time with Harding, though, I understood that it was possible to share a home with people eager to hear what I had to say.

For the first time, I felt cheated to understand my parents would have invested more time and energy talking with the O'Learys up at their dry goods shop than they'd bothered to spend in discourse with me.

~

The next day, I returned to town for a dress-fitting appointment at the tailor's. My entire wardrobe for university had been planned by my mother several months back. The dresses were ready, and the tailor needed me to stand like a statue to make the finishing touches.

My reflection startled me. I looked much more grown up in this finery, like someone ready to take on the world. I half wished we could have been closer to the window on the chance Sullivan might walk by and notice.

"These dresses are lovely," Mrs. Marris said through the pins in her mouth. "I do believe your mother will be so pleased. When's she back this time, then?"

"Last night," I said. "She'll adore them."

"Ah, uni will be a grand adventure for you." Mrs. Marris's round face was wistful. "There was a time I'd dreamed of going, but . . ." She gave a little laugh as she glanced around the shop. "Enjoy the time while you have it. You will learn so much."

I gave a perfunctory nod, but at the same time I felt pained to imagine the next few years of my life spent behind a desk. Especially when there was little expectation from my father that I'd actually use that education to obtain a job. The whole thing felt like such a farce.

Melancholy weighed on me after I said goodbye to Mrs. Marris. Rain clouds had grayed up the sky, matching my mood. I could already imagine the wet and cold sweeping through the fabric of my clothes, in spite of my raincoat. The chill I'd feel before sitting in front of the fire, breathing in the faded scent of the woodsmoke.

I was in no hurry to return home, in spite of the threat of rain. Instead, I decided to visit Harding and began to gather a bouquet of wildflowers for her on the way. I'd just turned onto the lane that led to the smaller houses and stables when I spotted Sullivan, walking along. He was eating an apple with sure bites, and when he spotted me, he came to a halt.

"Hello." His blue eyes were clear. "Didn't think I'd see you out."

"Yes, I had business with the tailor." Social niceties complete, I said, "Sullivan, what did you mean? When you spoke about Harding?"

He looked around, as though fearing someone might overhear.

"Walk with me." His voice was low. "There's much to say."

"How intriguing." I gave him a slight smile, but this time he didn't smile back.

He was silent as we walked down the lane. The scent of gorse was heavy in the air. Grass as tall as my torso waved around us.

Sullivan's parents' house was a light-blue two-story a few streets over, and I feared we'd make it there before he told me what was on his mind. Two of the village children ran past, one clutching a small wooden airplane, before he finally stopped and turned to me.

"I know you care for Harding." His freckled face was lined with concern. "Do you know she's involved with things that you should have no part in?"

My cheeks colored. Perhaps someone had seen Harding and me that night at the pub or at the watering hole. If Sullivan had heard about it, my parents would, too.

"Like what?" I asked carefully, running my hands over the tips of the grass.

He took a bite of apple. "Harding brought an element to this town that we'd managed to avoid. Now that it's here, we don't know what to do about it."

"You're making no sense."

"Evie, she's involved in black market trade."

I almost laughed out loud. The black market trade was made up of dodgy people. Criminals. Not respectable young women like Harding.

"It's most likely the reason she chose to come here," he said. "Harding needed an introduction into this area, from a respectable family. Now, she's deeply ingrained and—"

"This is truly insulting," I said. "Harding came here to visit me because she's my friend. You're not the type of person I thought you were, to say these—"

"I saw her, Evie! Two villages over. She was selling goods."

The clouds rolled overhead, and I put my hands into my coat pockets, unsure what to say.

"How do you know there wasn't a simple explanation?" I demanded. "Did you ask?"

"I know because I have friends there." Sullivan's face was full of apology. "My parents suspected it because Harding began taking our business away the moment she arrived, and my friends confirmed it. She has access to everything. Lipstick is hard to come by. She has it in abundance. Stockings for women. Tobacco for the men. Sometimes, even whiskey."

"How is that a crime?" I said. "You're not speaking of rations."

"She's done it with rations, too." He shrugged. "Luxuries are difficult to get. Without coal and petrol in abundance, trains run slow and lorries aren't on the road, and when they are, if they break down, the garages aren't open to fix them. So, getting these things frequently when we cannot do the same means she has a contact at the shipyard."

I stared at Sullivan in disbelief. "That can't be possible." The idea of Harding spending time at the shipyard and gathering up a bunch of goods to sell was ridiculous. "Where on earth would she put these things, to start?" He began to answer, but I said, "Besides, her parents left her plenty of money. She doesn't need—"

"It's not always about need. People want money. Even if they don't need it." His tone turned gentle. "Evie, if your father catches wind of this, he'll bring it to the Garda. Have her thrown in jail."

"For what?" I demanded.

"The rations are still a law."

"Sullivan, how is this any different from what my father does?" I pressed him. "He helps this entire town bypass rations."

On more than one occasion, my father had seen to it that our town received extra shipments of tea or, on one Christmas, chocolate. Sullivan's parents worked with him to ensure that certain products weren't stamped "Christmas Week." I had considered the practice noble, rather than dishonest, but maybe it wasn't.

"Your father helps us provide those things to the people at normal prices," Sullivan explained. "Not marked up beyond recognition, at numbers so steep that he's pocketing a profit. This thing Harding is doing, it's not right."

The righteous tilt of his chin infuriated me. Rules were rules. It was hypocritical for Sullivan to think otherwise.

"I don't know that any of us have a clear picture of what's right anymore," I said. "Considering we've spent years simply trying to hang on, I don't see the need to look for trouble in someone like Harding. There's difficulty enough in this world, don't you think?"

"Evie, this isn't looking for trouble. It's here." Sullivan pitched his apple core into the grass. "I don't think you should see her anymore."

The sheer audacity stunned me into silence. It also gave me a glimpse into marriage. The reason Harding wanted no part of it.

I crossed my arms. "Sullivan O'Leary, you don't have any say in who I am friends with."

"Evie, I care for you and your safety. The people Harding deals with are dangerous. My parents, even during our darkest times—the moments there was not a drop of soup for our table—wouldn't have gone near this sort of thing."

"I'll talk to her," I said. "Find out if there's any truth behind this."

"Don't mention I was the bearer of the news. I worry that if you do . . ."

His voice trailed off.

I crossed my arms. "What?"

"I've come to care for you, Evie." His eyes were frank. "I don't want Harding to turn you against me."

I was flattered, but also annoyed. "I have my own mind."

"Yes, I can see that," he said, with a grin. "Harding has her own army, though. There are people in County Cork who benefit greatly from the things that she's doing. I don't want any trouble. Especially for you."

I stood silent, thinking it through. Harding had protected me during the riot in Dublin. She'd pulled me away from danger and brought me to safety. Sullivan must have misinterpreted whatever he'd heard, because it didn't add up with the person I knew.

"Harding is my friend," I told him. "I don't know who is telling you these things, but I can assure you, they're lies."

"I hope you're right," Sullivan said. "For all our sakes."

Turning on my heel, I headed back toward the house, hands shaking. I couldn't visit Harding with this on my mind. She would know something was bothering me in an instant.

The rain began to fall, and I pulled up my hood, blinking as it still blew into my face. I didn't believe that she was involved in the things Sullivan had suggested. She'd been a guest in my home, and we'd spent practically every moment together, other than the hours she went off to paint and explore.

I stopped walking.

Harding had never once shown me her artwork. I'd asked countless times, and she'd made excuses, but more than that, I'd never seen evidence of her work at all. No stacks of papers, smudges of paint on her fingernails, or even supplies, come to think of it. I'd assumed it was all in the black bag she carried when she left, but considering what Sullivan had just said, I wasn't certain of anything at all.

Pulling my hood close, I renewed my stride. It was hard to believe that Harding would do anything illegal, but she often spoke of injustice and unfairness. She'd inspired me to speak up about the same.

If Harding was part of the black market, then it would be to bring a sense of equity to the community. To provide access. At the same time, it scared me to think she could be involved with dodgy people. The danger could come back on my family and me.

I hoped I wasn't involved in something that I shouldn't be, simply by virtue of being her friend.

Chapter Eight

Ireland, present day

The quiet walk to the pub to get my grandmother some dinner was one that I welcomed. It was late afternoon, and the sun was bright, with rain clouds far off in the distance. The air had a sweet coconut smell that reminded me of a tropical vacation.

It was the gorse, I decided, the yellow flowers that speckled the landscaping along the front path. Its unique scent, along with the endless sky and fresh air, gave me a sense of peace I so desperately needed.

Bright green surrounded me on all sides, particularly on the hills in the distance. There, it turned into something deeper and darker, peppering the sides with vegetation. There were sheep—or maybe cows—along the hillside, and taking it all in felt like stepping back in time.

That illusion was upheld as I got closer to town, the long country grass brushing against my legs from the edge of the road. The pub that Nora had recommended looked cute, but first, I took a few minutes to walk down the main street to explore.

The buildings were side by side, as many as five in a row, all two-storied, with a business on the bottom and living quarters on the top. Each cluster of buildings was separated by a gap. The colorful storefronts with living quarters above were full of charm, and I took an endless number of pictures.

Relishing the aroma of freshly baked bread, I wondered if the store-fronts had been in business back when my grandmother was young, or if the town had been built up over the years. Most places looked established but not ancient, so most likely, the town had grown.

I passed two bakeries, three pubs, a clothier, a seamstress, a cobbler, an apothecary, and a bookshop. There were several other small businesses, but they didn't seem that interesting, probably handling things like insurance or travel. I did walk up to a real estate office and browse the home prices in the photographs in the window. A couple of incredibly tiny cottages were available for a little over €115,000, and I wondered what it would be like to swap out rent in Chicago for a romantic cottage by the sea.

Turning back, I went to the pub Nora had recommended. It was adorable on the outside, with flower boxes and a few bicycles parked in the rack giving it a down-home feel. When I walked in, daylight disappeared and I blinked, allowing my eyes to adjust.

The faint scent of whiskey, coupled with smoke from the fireplace, made it as cozy as a hot toddy, as did the low murmured chatter and laughter of the guests.

Wooden booths lined the walls, and smaller wooden tables were situated throughout the room. In the back was a long bar, complete with wooden barstools. A soccer match played low on a television in the corner above a small, empty platform for live music.

I didn't see a hostess anywhere, and it seemed as though everyone else had already settled in with a pint of Guinness and a hearty bowl of soup, so I walked up to the bar. The bartender smiled and wiped off the one spot left at the counter, gesturing for me to come and take a seat. He looked about my mother's age, with ruddy skin and freckles that matched his brown cap.

When I pulled out a barstool, several of the men turned to glance at me. Most of them were old-timers, the sort who looked like they came to the pub to get coffee in the morning and then never left. It was possible some would remember my grandmother, but maybe not. So much time had passed since she'd lived here.

The jet lag was starting to set in, so an Irish coffee seemed like the best solution. The bartender took my order without a word, then set off to collect some payments and crack a few jokes. He worked his way back to me with the drink, then leaned on the counter as if settling in for a chat.

"You American?" he asked with a kind smile.

"What gave me away?" I asked.

He winked. "The cabbage soup is good today, but you're going to be liking the fish and chips. Maybe the roast."

I wondered which would be the best choice for my grandmother. Probably the soup, even though I didn't care for the smell of cabbage.

"I'll need it to go, please," I said. "Fish and chips, and a bowl of the soup. Probably some bread, if you have it."

He chuckled as if I'd said something funny and wrote it all on a slip of paper before turning it in to the kitchen. Returning, he said, "What brought you to Ireland? Will we be seeing your pretty face for long?"

It was the type of comment I'd have stonewalled back in Chicago, but I didn't mind it here, maybe because the man seemed so endearing.

"My grandmother," I said. "She grew up here and isn't doing so well, so she wanted to come back one last time."

"What's her name?" he asked. "I grew up with all of them old women telling me what to do."

"Evie Campbell. Well, it was Evie Campbell."

The man's hands, which had been busy starting a drink, went still. "Evie's come back, then."

"Yes." I was delighted. "You really know her?"

"My father, Sullivan, he was a good friend of hers." The man finished making the drink and went to the other end of the bar.

I'd hoped he'd want to reminisce, but he probably didn't have anything else to say. I wanted to ask if his father was still alive, because if he and my grandmother had been close, she would certainly want to visit with him.

I sipped on the Irish coffee while I waited for the food and considered the crowd. It seemed to be a decent mix of tourists and locals. A few families with children were at the tables, and a wide range of people in the booths along the wall: rough-looking men who could've been from the shipping boats, an incredibly attractive guy with dark hair who was sitting alone, and a group of older women who struck me as well-dressed tourists.

The bartender returned with my food in a bag and set it down, tapping the counter. "Tell Evie that Sullivan O'Leary sends his regards."

Before I could ask more about his father, someone summoned him back down the bar.

"Thank you," I called. "I will."

Even though I wasn't sure about the tipping process, I left a few extra euros on the counter for him before heading for the front door.

I was just about to push it open when an older man who looked rough and wiry blocked my way. "You're Evie's granddaughter?"

"Yes." There was something aggressive in the way he was looking at me, something that I didn't like.

"You people be having a lot of nerve to be showing your face here."

This man must have been drunk and was mistaking me for someone else. I held up my hands.

"I think you must have the wrong person." I tried to move past him to the door, but he reached out as if to grab my arm.

Back in Chicago, Tia had insisted we take self-defense classes. I'd felt ridiculous at the time, but I must have learned the moves, because my arm shot right out and blocked him. He looked surprised, and then he chuckled.

"You're just like her," he said, his mouth twisting with the effort to not slur his words. "Thinking you're some sort of vigilante, but when it all falls apart, you run away."

"I'm sorry." Deliberately, I made my voice a little louder. "I think you've had too much to drink."

The attractive man I'd noticed earlier looked over. Frowning, he watched, with a questioning look. I didn't need his help, not yet, but I wanted someone to pay attention.

"Evie Campbell is a coward," the man at the door said, his breath sour. "She was a thief. They came looking for the money. Did she tell you that?"

"That's enough, Jimmy." The bartender had come out from behind the bar. "We're all going to be letting the past be the past, agreed?"

I gave a firm nod. "You gentlemen have a good night."

I was stepping out the door and onto the cobblestone sidewalk when Jimmy shouted, "Tell Evie she's the reason her parents are dead!"

Turning, I stared at him. The light in the bar was dim, but for the first time, I noticed he had a scar across his eyebrow, and a hateful look on his face.

"That's enough, Jimmy," the bartender warned.

"No, no, Mac." He pushed the bartender's hand off himself. "She said she didn't know, so I'm going to tell her."

The whole pub was watching now, silent. The handsome man who had been sitting alone was on his feet, as though unsure what to do.

"Evie left her parents wondering about everything from her safety to her sanity. Until—"

"Don't," the bartender said.

"Until what?" I demanded.

Jimmy spat in the dirt on the ground in front of me. "Until they were murdered."

Chapter Nine

It took me most of the day to ease my mind about the worries that Sullivan had presented. The summer day stretched dully in front of me, and I could only sit in silence in my room for so long. Finally, I decided that I must talk to Harding.

The walk along the path reminded me of the conversation that morning with Sullivan, the way he bit into that apple without a care in the world while saying such terrible things. It made me regret the time I'd spent thinking of his freckles and bright-blue eyes. Brought on by boredom, surely. He'd leave my thoughts once I attended university, and his absence would be a welcome relief.

The stables had the strong scent of manure in the heat, and I wrinkled my nose, hoping that the smell did not travel to Harding's room. Rickety wooden steps led up and over the barn, and I followed them to a wooden door painted white and gave it three firm knocks.

There was silence, and I had a brief moment of worry that I'd come to the wrong place altogether. Then footsteps crossed the floor, and the door was flung open. The familiar sight of Harding's mischievous face pushed away the concerns that had plagued me for the past few hours. I embraced her and set down the picnic basket I'd brought.

Eagerly, she took my hands. "Come see." Her voice was filled with delight. "I just finished decorating in hopes that you'd arrive."

The room she had let stretched out over the top of the barn, giving her a huge amount of space. It had a small bed with a simple quilt and pillow, a dressing area with a looking glass and Harding's trunk, as well as two comfortable chairs and a small table. The four open, wooden windows afforded a view all the way into town.

"This is lovely," I said.

It was, in spite of the smell of the stable. I liked the ability to look out, to take in the small structures in our town and gaze at the sea. I could even see my house, if I looked from just the right angle.

"Could you see me coming?" I asked.

Harding laughed. "I was busy reading, so I wasn't paying any attention at all. I could, though. Isn't this wonderful? It's like a watchtower, and I get to guard Kislee."

The fact that she felt such affection for our town gave me mixed emotions. On one hand, I was overjoyed to think she felt a part of things, but it also hurt to think that people had said such things about her.

"What'll you do for food here?" I asked.

She grinned. "Come to your house, of course. My stay here's only for a few weeks, until you're about to head off to university. I'll also take my dinner in the pub."

I took a seat in one of the wooden chairs, staring out at the view. "I need to speak to you of something," I said. "Can we be heard up here?"

Harding shook her head. "No one's in the stables during the day. Only early mornings and evenings. What is it? Your parents are home now, I heard."

"Yes, you must meet them." I took a breath. "So someone brought something to my attention that concerned me. I'm angry about it, to be quite frank, and not at you."

Harding's face lost its expression. "What is it?"

I explained what Sullivan had said, and she listened, smiling slightly here and there.

"Do you think this is true?" she asked.

"No," I said. "Not at all."

I'd given it a lot of thought since my conversation with Sullivan. I'd never once seen any goods stored at my home, and I was in her room all the time. Even though the room at the stable was enormous, there were nothing here, either, piled up like in a stockroom. The more I thought about it, the more I realized the very idea of it all was ludicrous.

She fiddled with a button on her dress. "Perhaps I've done wrong. I've made many friends here, and if someone needed something and I heard of someone else who had it, I was more than happy to help connect those two people."

"There's nothing wrong with that," I said.

One of the most admirable things about Harding was her ability to help others. I'd seen her bring stew to a sick neighbor, give Fedelma a bouquet of wildflowers, and slip penny candy to the kids in the village. She certainly did not deserve to be punished for that.

Harding nodded. "Then I'm as frustrated as you are to hear that kind actions have cast suspicion on my name. Most of all, I'm sorry to hear it's caused you to worry."

I reached out and held her hands. "My primary concern's your safety. The person who told me made me fear something could happen to you."

Harding waved her hand. "Fear is the greatest weapon people use to get you to do what they want. It can be a powerful thing."

We sat in silence. Then her face brightened. "I've come across a deck of playing cards," she said, pulling them out of her trunk. "Would you like me to teach you how to play gin rummy?"

Joy filled me. I had been so distressed by what Sullivan had said and how Harding would react, but she had made the conversation as gentle as the wind. Everything Harding did made my life more fun, and I was grateful for each moment I got to spend with her.

"Deal me in," I said, quoting a novel I'd recently read.

Harding raised her eyebrows. "A card shark, eh?"

We both laughed, the sound echoing in the empty room.

❧

Two days later, my parents decided to travel to Dublin to visit friends of my father's. My mother was rushed, trying to get out the door while giving last-minute instructions to Seamus regarding their return.

"You will be back soon?" I asked her. "We've barely had a chance to speak."

My mother kissed my cheek. "I know, darling. We will, once we return."

"How long will you be gone?" I repeated.

"Two weeks, perhaps three." She lowered her voice. "There have been rumors of unrest, and your father wants to ensure he has the proper information to disseminate to our village."

"Unrest in Northern Ireland?" I asked. "Does it have to do with the Republic of Ireland Act?"

Harding had often spoken of the injustice that part of our country was ruled by the monarch, and the changes this separation would bring.

For the first time since she'd come home, my mother really looked at me. I could see her evaluating whether I was capable of understanding what she had to say.

"Yes," she said. "There are still protests in response, as there are people in this country who wanted it under Irish rule and people who wanted the opposite."

"Which side do you think is right?" I asked.

My father walked into the room. "We must leave."

My mother nodded at me. "I'll be interested in speaking with you further upon my return."

It was the warmest, most accepting moment I'd shared with my mother in years. I was surprised that the way to get her engagement was to talk of politics, as I did not realize she was interested.

I planned to ask Harding about it all so that I could learn more. She was full of knowledge because she read the papers whenever she could find one, and had opinions about what was right, what was wrong, and what needed to be fixed. I didn't plan to parrot back her ideas, but I did want to better understand what was happening at the moment so I could have an intelligent conversation with my mother.

If that was the way to get through to her, then I was willing to do it.

～

Harding and I fell into a delightful pattern of spending each day together above the livery stable, until it got so hot that it became unbearable. Then we would walk along the moor.

Friday morning, Fedelma returned to give me a review prior to university, since I'd be leaving in a couple of weeks. I was frustrated to not make it to Harding's until late in the afternoon. I rushed up the stairs with my picnic basket and knocked on the door. She didn't answer. Frustrated, I assumed that she must be out, and I decided to wait for her.

When I walked in, I stopped short to see that her trunk had been turned over, her clothing strewed all around. I froze at the sight of blood on the floor.

"Harding," I called. "Harding!" My voice grew more frantic, and I looked all around the room just to be certain that she was not there.

I ran down the stairs, practically falling in my haste.

"Harding!" I shouted, and heard a low groan from the stables.

I rushed forward, into the barn. It was silent. The stall door at the end was open, and straw spilled out into the aisle.

"Hello?" I whispered.

A low moan answered me. I rushed forward and stopped at the sight of her crumpled up in the hay. Her dress was ripped, blood on her legs, and her right eye nearly swollen shut. Sickness washed through me.

"What happened?" I cried, falling down next to her.

Her hand was limp, her pulse barely there.

"I'm fetching the doctor," I said.

"No!" She tried to grab my hand. "I'll be ruined. Please."

It was then that I understood. She had become a fallen woman, through no choice of her own.

"Who?" I whispered.

Harding didn't answer, instead staring straight ahead. Her body shook with small convulsions, and I found a horse blanket covered in hair. After laying it over her, I fetched water from the well outside and made her drink. She lay back on the ground, blood trickling down her cheek.

"I'll be right back," I said.

"No." The word formed on her lips, but she closed her eyes.

I didn't know where to go or what to do, and my mind went straight to Sullivan. He'd already told me that he was concerned about Harding, and I knew he was someone who would help, someone I could trust. He would either be at home or at the store. His house was closer, so I ran there first.

My hands shook as I banged on the door. I didn't know how hurt Harding was or whether or not we were in any further danger. What if whoever had done this to her planned to come back?

Sullivan opened the door right away. Seeing my panic, he said, "What is it? What's happened?"

Once I'd explained, he grabbed his gun and a medical kit. Together, we ran toward the barn. Sullivan stood guard at the door as I washed Harding's beaten body, applying iodine to her cuts and bandages to stop the bleeding. She stared straight ahead, a blank look in her eyes.

"You will come stay with me," I told her. "You can no longer stay alone."

She didn't reply.

"Sullivan," I cried, and he rushed forward.

He listened to her breath and nodded. "She's okay," he said. "I'll carry her."

We took the back route to my house, through the woods. Harding was limp in his arms, and I held tightly to her hand. I pushed open the back door. The kitchen was empty. I hesitated, as I could not chance the servants seeing her like this.

"The gardener's cottage," I decided. "It's vacant."

Sullivan nodded and carried her across the lawn. The gardener's cottage was back by the woods, and it had locks on the doors.

Sullivan laid her gently in bed as she stared straight ahead.

When we stepped outside, hot tears rolled down my cheeks.

"Who could've done such a thing?" he asked, crouching on the ground. He tugged at the grass, unable to meet my eyes. "It needs to be reported."

"It can't," I said. "She'll be a fallen woman."

Sullivan shook his head. I knew he thought this had happened because of the things he'd warned me about, but I still didn't believe that. One of the shipping men passing through the pubs must have caught wind that she was staying alone. My heart burned with shame that I'd allowed her to take that risk, all because I hadn't been brave enough to face my parents.

"I'll stay out here with her." I looked at him. "You mustn't tell anyone about this."

"No." His eyes met mine. "You have my word."

We looked at each other for a long moment. I was grateful for him, as well as for his quick assistance.

"Thank you," I said, and he nodded.

I went inside and locked the door tightly behind me. It would be a long night, listening for every snapped tree branch or the sound of wheels on the road, whether it be a horse cart or an automobile.

Harding was staring at the ceiling now, with tears rolling down her cheeks. I sat next to her bed and took her hand.

"You're safe here," I told her. "Nothing will happen to you."

Even as I said the words, I wondered if they were a lie.

Chapter Ten

Ireland, present day

Murdered?

The words rang in my ear. I took off down the road, determined to get back to the bed-and-breakfast. Surely, there was some mistake. It was impossible that my grandmother's parents had been killed. She would have told us that.

But would she have, though?

My grandmother had refused to speak about her time here, and she'd said that it took courage for her to come back. That man had called her a thief. I knew that was impossible, but there had to be some story there.

The wind picked up, and the storm clouds that had seemed so far off were now gathering overhead. It was about a ten-minute walk back, and I picked up the pace, wishing I'd thought to grab one of the raincoats Nora kept on the hooks by the front door.

Someone shouted behind me. I started walking faster, my breath coming quick. People had been out on the street when I'd left the pub, but this stretch to the bed-and-breakfast was away from everything.

The person shouted again, and I turned, bracing myself to face good ol' Jimmy. I was startled to instead see the man from the booth, the attractive one with the dark eyes. He jogged up, his curly brown hair falling over his forehead.

"Hey, I'm sorry. Jimmy's an idiot." He held up a raincoat. "It's about to pour. Where are you headed?"

"Aisling," I said.

"I'd be happy to walk with you," he said. "This wasn't a good welcome to Ireland, but Jimmy's always fired up about something."

"You know him?" I said, but of course he did. Every person around here, unless they were a tourist, had to know everyone else. It was too small a town not to.

"Unfortunately." He walked next to me with long strides, the musk in his cologne pleasant in the humid air. "That guy can't remember to pay electric, but he could tell you—in detail—each of our transgressions, without breaking a sweat or losing his balance on the barstool." The guy gave me a commiserating smile and held out his hand. "I'm Grady."

"Rainey."

I knew that I should feel a little nervous about walking alone in another country with a stranger, but I didn't. The way Grady looked at me seemed protective, not flirtatious, even back when we were in the pub. Thunder rumbled off in the distance, and within moments, a large raindrop fell right onto my forehead.

Grady tossed me his coat. "Here. You're going to need this."

"No, it's yours," I said, startled at the kindness.

"Nah, I'm used to the rain." He lifted his head up and caught a drop or two in his mouth, as though to prove it.

"We can share," I said, lifting up the coat like a blanket so he could fit under it, too.

He hesitated, but seconds later, the rain started pelting down, and he ducked under with me. It was a tight squeeze, and I could smell the wet wool of his sweater and that enticing cologne. The moment almost felt romantic, except that we kept knocking into each other's feet every few steps. We ran down the road and up the path to Aisling.

There, we stopped beneath the covered awning, and he lowered the coat, shaking it out. Rain poured down off the porch like a waterfall. It bounced off the cobblestones, reflecting in the light from the gas lamps.

"Thank you," I said. "I appreciate you walking me back."

Now that we were looking right at each other, I noticed his eyes were captivating, a greenish gray with full lashes and heavy dark eyebrows. He also had the perfect amount of dark stubble on his cheeks and a rugged way about him that made me want to go back to the part where I could smell his cologne. He gave me a slight smile, and I flushed, worried he knew what I'd been thinking.

"Anytime," he said.

I turned to head inside, and he followed. I paused. Right before I opened my mouth to ask if he was staying there, too, Nora rounded the corner with a plate of cookies.

"Your first rain," she sang. "I'll get you a towel. And I see you've met my brother."

Her brother. It was indeed a small town, and in this case, I didn't mind. If Grady was family, there was a good chance I'd see him again.

He hung up the raincoat and took off his wet boots, revealing a pair of thick red-and-blue-striped wool socks. The socks made him a little less intimidating, which was a nice reprieve, since he had me feeling a bit flushed. The reprieve was brief, because next he took off his damp sweater, which pulled up his white T-shirt, revealing some seriously impressive abs. I looked away, pretending to be interested in the view of the rain out the window.

Nora walked back in. "Towels," she said, handing us both one. The towel was thick and warm. I wondered if she kept a collection of them on a radiator somewhere.

"Thank you," I said, rubbing the water off my arms.

"Of course." Nora headed back down the hall, calling, "Grady, wrap it up. My guest needs to get some rest."

Grady, who had been busy towel-drying his hair, winked at me.

It hit me that he had the perfect combination of good looks and self-effacing charm, not to mention that accent. He probably enchanted a new tourist every week. Perhaps a little distance would be wise.

"It was nice to meet you," I said. "Thanks again for the raincoat."

"Not that it did a bit of good," he said.

I smiled and gathered up the food I'd ordered from the pub.

"Before you go, I do want to tell you this," he said. "There's one thing we're not good at in Ireland, and that's keeping our mouths shut, but Jimmy had no business speaking to you in that way."

I paused at the bottom of the stairs. "Is it true? What he said?"

Grady shrugged. "I don't know. I wasn't around back then."

"My family doesn't know anything about my grandmother's life here." Running my hand over the smooth grain of the railing, I added, "I just got here, and within a few hours, two big bombshells have already gone off. I'm a little worried about what else I'm going to find."

"Sleep on it, then," he said in that charming lilt. "Your worries will always be there, waiting for you in the morning. Better to greet them with a clear head."

I headed up the stairs, the scene at the pub replaying in my mind. I was tired all the way down to my bones, but nervous energy pulsed through me.

They were murdered.

The idea left me with so many questions, and I wasn't sure whom to ask. My grandmother was the obvious choice, but I was doubtful she'd tell the truth, even if I did ask.

When I walked into the room, my grandmother was awake but still in bed, staring up at the ceiling.

I held up the bags. "You hungry? I wasn't sure what to get you," I said, setting her food on the table at the back window. I hoped the soup wouldn't be too heavy for her stomach. It immediately filled the room with the aroma of cabbage and boiled bacon, and her eyes lit up.

"That smells wonderful."

I had never been a fan of cabbage—its smell made me think of sour things—but my grandmother seemed delighted. She ate more than she had in weeks, and even smeared more butter onto her bread.

Even though I wanted to dive into our family history, to better understand if there was any truth behind what I'd heard, it didn't feel like the right time. She was quiet as she ate, I was exhausted, and I didn't want to get into anything that might upset her.

Instead, I focused on my fish and chips. The fish was crunchy and salty, perfect with the side of vinegar.

"Let's get some sleep," I said, once we'd eaten. "It's going to take some time to adjust to their clock, but we might as well do our best to get started. I'll start searching for the letters in the morning."

"Rainey, it's wonderful of you to be here with me." She fiddled with the cross around her neck. "You must have so many questions."

"I do, but they'll be there in the morning."

Once she'd settled back into bed, I gave her a firm kiss on the forehead. "I did meet a friend of a friend of yours at the pub tonight," I said. "The bartender's father was a guy named Sullivan. Do you remember him?"

My grandmother's eyebrows went up. "I never forgot him."

I paused. "Would you . . . want to see him? His son seemed really nice."

"I'm sure he is." My grandmother yawned. "Goodness, I'm tired. Cabbage isn't something you'd expect to dream about, but I just might."

Deliberately, she pulled the quilt close and settled in to the pillows, shutting her eyes.

I wondered if her friendship with Sullivan had not ended well. Maybe I could ask his son about it, but at another time.

Even though my grandmother was already snoring, I was wide awake. It would be the middle of the afternoon back home. Still, I got into bed and pulled up the sheets.

I needed to try to get on their clock, to rest and have a clear head. That would help me make a good decision on how much to share with my grandmother about what had been said at the pub and find the courage to ask how much of it, exactly, was true.

~

My phone rang just as I'd drifted off to sleep. Mom.

"Hold on," I said into the phone.

I grabbed a robe and headed down the main steps, hoping not to bump into anyone. The lobby was empty and it was dark out, so I slipped outside. The outline of the cliffs against the night sky was gorgeous, and the weather was now cool but perfect.

Pulling the robe tightly around me, I brushed the water off one of the chairs from the rain and took a seat. "Hi."

"How's it going?" my mother asked.

It was quiet in the background, and I pictured her in her office at the university. I wondered if that man she'd liked to complain about had left any more signs in the break room, although that conversation had gone by the wayside weeks ago, when my grandmother had first gotten sick.

"I don't know," I said. "It's strange to be here. The house is so grand and . . ." I hesitated, not wanting to tell her what had happened at the pub. "I have so many questions about why she would give this up. Her family was a big deal in town."

"In what way?" my mother asked.

"I'm not sure yet, but Aisling is a palace. The pictures don't do it justice." I considered the way my grandmother cradled that piece of crystal from the chandelier. She'd put it on her bedside table, probably to see while she drifted off to sleep. "Something pretty awful must have happened to drive her away. You really should talk to your department and take your vacation time. Grandma needs you here."

"I don't think that's the best idea."

"Mom," I said, "this was her life. You really should see it."

"Rainey . . ." Her tone was cautious. "You're my daughter, so I hesitate to tell you this."

Considering I'd just been told my great-grandparents were murdered, I wasn't exactly in the market for more bad news.

"What?" I said.

"I don't want you to think I'm this awful person for not coming there. Your grandmother and I are close in a lot of ways. That took effort, though. She wasn't the best mother."

I sat up, putting my feet into the wet grass. "What do you mean?"

"Your grandmother wasn't around. When I was young, Helpful Heart took up her time. Everyone in the city needed her. She was there for them, but not for me."

My grandmother had founded an organization to help young, unwed mothers, and she had changed so many lives. I hadn't realized my mother felt it was at her expense.

"It was hard for both of you, I imagine," I said. "I don't even have kids, but the business takes up all my time."

"It's hard to be a working mother," she agreed. "But I managed to make time for you."

I thought back to my childhood. I liked seeing my mother achieve big things. It showed me that I could do the same.

"I think that her job was just different," my mother said. "There were all these people who needed her, and, in the process, she forgot I needed her, too. We've worked through it," she said, quickly. "I feel bad even telling you. It's just that, to have her tell me that she didn't want me in Ireland . . . it brought back some old, unwelcome feelings."

I didn't know what to say. My mother had set boundaries when it came to what she'd share about my father and the divorce. I didn't know why she thought I wanted to hear about her problems with my grandmother.

"I'm telling you," she said, as if reading my mind, "so you understand why I'm not there. She said she doesn't want me there, so I'm not going to come."

"*Mom.*" This was ridiculous. "She was on medication. She wants you here."

"Did she say that?" my mother asked.

I stared up at the sky. The clouds from earlier had cleared out, and I focused on the light of the moon. It was hard to hear this, and I couldn't help but think my mother was making a huge mistake.

"I love your grandmother, Rainey," my mother said. "I'd do anything for her. So I'm going to respect her wishes. Speaking of, I do need to get back. Call me soon, okay? Love you."

"Love you, too."

I hung up and sat back in the chair. The silhouette of the sea was etched against the horizon, and I tried to pattern my breath with the roll of the waves. The past few hours had been too much. My heart ached for my mother, my grandmother, and all the pain of the past.

I needed sleep, to clear my head, so that this wouldn't feel so overwhelming. I was used to being able to fix things, to finding solutions. Not this, though. Was there really a way to fix the past?

I headed inside, my feet cold in the grass, and my text alert chimed. Tia.

Do you have time to talk?

It would be such a relief to share some of these feelings. Typically, Tia and I talked multiple times a day, but we'd barely spoken since I'd left Chicago. I wanted to call her, but it didn't seem fair to ask her to listen to my problems when I planned to keep up a lie.

I texted back:

Just got to Ireland! Let's try tomorrow.

I headed inside, depressed. The pressure of everyday life was still here, even though I was in another country, living another existence altogether.

What was it that Grady had said—the things that we worry about would still be there, waiting for us in the morning?

I feared my jar of worries was about to get more complicated than it ever had before.

Chapter Eleven

Ireland, 1949

I telegrammed my parents about having Harding stay, planning to keep her hidden so the house staff wouldn't figure out what had happened:

MY DEAR FRIEND HAS RETURNED FOR A VISIT. WOULD IT BE ACCEPTABLE TO WELCOME HER?

They sent their approval, appeasing Seamus. I stayed in the gardener's cottage with Harding. I brought her meals and slept in the bed with her, hoping that my presence would offer protection as well as comfort, while knowing full well I could offer neither.

She refused to speak of what had happened. The moment she was well enough to get out of bed, she insisted on doing all the things we'd enjoyed together, such as playing cards and reading. We could not go on walks because her face had not yet healed, and we couldn't have people asking questions. Sullivan said no one had seen us the day we'd carried her through the woods, so the whole thing could remain quiet.

The attack had left Harding fragile and nervous, two things that she wouldn't admit to.

"What will you do?" I asked one night when we had settled in to bed. "Will you still go to America?"

It was evening, and, although not quite dark, the birds had fallen quiet, and the bugs were singing their song. Harding had not been sleeping well, and I looked over to see her lying there, her eyes wide open.

"Yes. Soon." Her voice was firm. "I will not let anyone take that away from me." She turned to face me, propping her chin on her elbow. Her eyes looked almost black in the darkness. "I should have left this place a long time ago."

"I'm glad that you stayed," I told her.

Harding hesitated. "There are some things about me that you should know." She got out of bed and shut the windows. Sitting on the bed, she wrung her hands. "It's important that you understand that the things I have done were for the purpose of building a life for myself. I . . ." She wrapped the quilt tightly around her hand. "I took it too far. There were people that . . ." She faltered and then fell silent.

"You have nothing to fear here," I said, quietly. "There is no judgment."

"I'm worried that it would be dangerous for you to have too much information," she whispered. "To know too much about me and the crimes I've committed."

The shadows on the wall seemed to grow longer, and I felt a sudden, crawling sensation in my stomach.

"You must be honest with me. Please."

She let out a breath. "Evie, I'm part of a black market ring that steals goods from the import docks. I have a contact within the Mercantile Marine who helped me resell them to families in need. So I wasn't only doing this for personal gain, but I did make a small fortune from stolen goods."

I stared at her. "Oh."

"Yes." Harding gave a firm nod.

My neck started to feel hot, thinking about how firmly I'd fought Sullivan on this issue. I'd been so sure Harding would never do that. Now, a million little moments clicked into place.

The wide variety of people she knew. The man on the bluff who seemed threatening and out of place in our safe town. The little luxuries she'd always had, from the moment we'd first met.

"Please, say something," she pleaded.

I studied her face. The bright purple of the bruise on her eye made me think of a wildflower twisted in the weeds. She reached her hand forward, and I hesitated before taking it.

The idea that Harding had done these things shocked me, and I didn't know if I could accept it so easily. The rations were in place to avoid shortages and profiteering, to give everyone a fair chance to have the food and supplies necessary for basic living. It wasn't right that she'd used the situation for personal gain, especially after speaking so harshly about others who did the same.

"I don't understand how you could do that," I said. "You say families in need, but I'm certain those families had the money to give you in exchange for what you brought to them. So, you allowed the rich to have access to everything, but the poor had to live off what they were allotted?"

Harding drew her hand back. "Surely, you hear your words? We met at the *Declee*, Evie. Your parents took you to that hotel because they wanted a fine meal instead of yet another menu presented by the Department of Supplies."

"You were there, too," I said. "If memory serves."

She laughed, her crooked tooth flashing. "Did you actually think I was a guest there?"

Time seemed to skip as I remembered the first time I saw her, standing out front, daintily pulling on those green leather gloves.

"You weren't?" I said.

"No." Harding went quiet, then she said, "I did business there. Met prospects. Hid out in the linen closet when I needed a rest, then went right back to it. I've worked hard. To be quite frank, if I had not benefited, someone else would have in my place."

I couldn't believe what I was hearing. My entire perception of Harding was wrong. I'd assumed her background was like mine, but now, I had no idea who she was.

"I see you're upset, but think it through, Evie. Is anyone truly pure? Consider the glimmer man. Everyone in Ireland feared him."

Back during the Emergency, the glimmer man was tasked with guarding the small amount of gas that was not to be used—not even the smallest glint—outside designated cooking hours. Our cook often turned the stove on anyway to keep a kettle boiling in the event my mother wanted a spontaneous cup of tea. Cook wasn't concerned about getting caught, as our village was small and word spread in an instant if a stranger was in town; everyone watched for the man tasked with guarding the gas.

However, once when my parents were out of town, the glimmer man arrived without warning. It was by grace, Fedelma said later, that the forbidden flame was out and the stovetop cool. Otherwise, we would have lost our gas supply for quite some time.

I considered Harding. "I don't know what that has to do with anything."

"Well, why would you fear him if you followed the rules?" she said. "Everyone feared him. So everyone broke the rules. You see?"

I shook my head and got to my feet, pacing the room.

"Please don't be angry," Harding said. "I simply wanted you to know the truth. I did take advantage of some people, but I also ensured certain families did not starve. That's the truth I see when I close my eyes at night and the reason I don't feel bad for the money I made."

"What about this, then?" I demanded, gesturing at her bruised eye. It looked so painful in the evening light. "Do you regret that?"

She twisted the blanket with her free hand. "Life is full of risk, I suppose. You have to choose the ones you are willing to take."

The cabin had become hot with the windows closed, and I sank back down on the bed. I felt too sad to move, too frustrated to look at her. It was all wrong. The things she had done, and what had happened to her.

"Do the authorities know?" I asked. "About you?"

Her body tensed. "You wouldn't tell them."

"No," I said, offended. "I'm sorry you think that I would."

I'd asked because she was staying at my home. It would be one thing for my parents to learn that I'd lied about having a friend from boarding school here but quite another if my guest was apprehended for an actual crime.

"I know that it's hard to put trust in me after this, Evie." Harding lay back on the pillows. She looked so young, and the sorrow in her face seemed etched into her skin. "It comes with culpability for you. I don't know that telling you was the right choice."

"Why did you tell me, then?" I demanded.

She'd spoken to my concern, that I was putting my family at risk for shame, or worse. I didn't want to live in fear, in a constant state of worry that someone would come for me the way they had with Harding. For the first time, the plan to leave for university in a week felt like a relief.

"I don't want to lie to you anymore," she said. "I want you to understand the truth about me. I did it to make money to live a good life in America. The problem is that the money is hidden, and I can't access it without getting caught. So it sits there. Perhaps someone's already found it and taken it; I don't know. I would like to have it. I've earned it, in so many ways."

"What do you mean 'without getting caught'?" I said. "I want to know what level of danger you're still in. Will the Garda come and arrest you?"

"I'm not worried about the Garda," she said. "If anything, I'm worried because I did not pay my partners their fair share. They were disgusting, dishonest human beings, and to be quite frank, I thought they'd be too dumb to figure it out. Turns out, I was wrong. I'll pay them back. It's the only way for them to set me free. But Evie, I couldn't bear to lose you over this."

I couldn't bear to lose her, either.

I'd told her I wouldn't judge her. That I'd stand by her side. I had failed her in the first promise, but I could live up to the second one.

"Then I think you should see it through," I said, quietly.

The realization that I was going to try to accept the situation seemed to settle around her like a warm blanket. Clearing her throat, she looked away.

"How would I do that, then?" she asked.

"Get the money, pay them back, and all will be well," I said. "Won't it?"

"I'd like to think so," she said. "I have to get the money from its hiding spot. I have little idea how to get what's left to America without getting caught."

"Smuggle it in," I suggested.

Her eyes widened. "That's bold, then. How?"

"I don't know. You're the one with contacts at the shipyard."

"Those are the last people I'd want to tell about this," she said, laughing. "It would be gone in an instant."

I thought for a moment. I could think of few ways to get goods onto a boat without having them checked. Let alone money. However, I'd just finished reading a novel about a band of robbers who hid their jewels under false bottoms in crates.

"Your trunk," I said. "We could build a false bottom."

She turned to me, her face bright. "That's a great idea, but I don't know that the money would fit." She tapped her fingers against the quilt. "It's something to think about."

If the money wouldn't fit, there had to be quite a bit of it.

"How much are we talking about?" I asked.

"Enough to last a lifetime. That's all I'll say."

"Why, that's . . ." I got to my feet, trying to comprehend it.

No wonder she was frightened. The sum had to be huge.

My shoulders tensed. "Where is this money?"

What if it was in my home? Hidden beneath the floorboards, putting us all at risk.

"Hidden away where no one can find it."

"Not here, though, right?" I asked.

"Of course not." She laughed, then got serious. "When the time comes, I plan to disappear. I will be in touch, but I want you to know this now, in case there's a night where I need to run."

I shook my head in disbelief. How naive to think we'd be safe in a small house with a tiny lock on the door. It made me wish that my father was still here to protect us. He wouldn't, though. He would send her straight to the authorities.

"Do you think we're in danger now?" My voice was barely a whisper.

"I'm always in danger," she told me. "Not you."

I took a seat in a wooden chair, my stomach tied in knots.

I didn't want to dwell on her attack or the circumstances that had led us here, but it would be foolish to assume that now, everything would be all right. The attack was a rebuke or, perhaps, a warning. Someone wanted her to pay for her sins.

I wanted her to find a way to America, as soon as possible.

When it came time for me to attend university, I was relieved to get away from the immediate fear but filled with anxiety at the thought of saying goodbye to Harding. Ten days had passed since her attack, and the bruises had faded, but the brutality of it all had not. There was a hesitancy in the way she moved, the way she carried herself, that hadn't been there before. My thoughts were not on whether or not I'd enjoy my time at school; my thoughts were on the fact that I did not want to be separated from her. When it was time for her to take the train to her aunt's house, we clung to each other, weeping, as we said our final goodbyes.

I cried myself to sleep that night, scared for her. I'd never loved anyone the way I'd loved Harding. I'd adjusted what I was willing to accept, and how much I was willing to forgive, when she'd finally shown me who she really was. I didn't know how I felt about it all, but in spite of everything, I still cared for her like a sister.

It was so hard to let her go, and a huge part of me wished I was brave enough to join her in America, but it would be impossible without any idea how to survive on my own. This had been a season in my life, and I needed to accept that time wouldn't stop, regardless of whether or not I'd recognized its value as it passed me by.

The next morning, Seamus loaded a trunk made by Sullivan into the back of the wagon that would take Fedelma and me to the train station. She was set to escort me on the train the short trip to University College Cork, to my room and my new life. She would stay for a week. I couldn't help but wish that my mother was the one doing this with me instead.

Sullivan came to say goodbye. He had served as a kind and watchful friend. I was still mesmerized by the handsome cut of his jaw and the twinkle in his eye, but I knew that once I left, the possibility of our lives intertwining would end. By his rueful look, I could tell he felt the same.

"It's been a pleasure seeing you this summer," he said.

The words meant so much more, and I knew it. "You too."

I eased into the back of the motorcar, the leather hot against my back. The driver began our journey to the train station, and as I turned to watch Aisling fade in the distance, my eyes filled with tears.

"It can be hard to let go of your childhood," Fedelma said.

I nodded, but I wasn't crying because I was leaving my childhood behind. I was crying because I was saying goodbye to a summer that had left me struggling to figure out what was right and wrong, and the type of person I wanted to be.

∿

The gray skies of February were as dull as my studies. The only subject that kept my interest was political science, as I often heard Harding's voice in my head, emphasizing or debating the points made in the classroom. I held my books close, careful not to slip on the path as I walked from the main school building to my lodging. It would be one thing to have snow, like we had in January. The frost allowed the women in my dormitory to enjoy a fun afternoon of sledding on the hill, but the weather now chilled me to the bone.

Walking into the lobby, I checked my cubby, hoping for a telegram from my parents or Harding. I had heard from her twice, right when I had started school, but then I had not heard from her again. I prayed it meant she'd made it safely to America.

The girls I had met at university were interesting to talk with, and we spent a lot of time together during our studies, but I didn't care for them the way I did for Harding. I missed her point of view, her bravery, and the way that being around her had made me feel. Like I still had something special to contribute to the world and that I had a responsibility to figure it out.

It worried me that I hadn't heard from her. I was scared for her safety but also terrified that, like those years after we'd met in Dublin, she would go silent and cease to be a part of my life.

Letting out a sigh, I was turning to head toward the hallway to my room when a sweet voice said, "Goodness, I have missed seeing that face."

My heart leaped. Harding sat in a chair near the entrance, covered up by a large coat, her smile as bright as the sun. I rushed forward to hug her, but she didn't jump to her feet. Instead, she rose slowly, allowing the coat to fall back. I took in a sharp breath. My eyes met hers, and she nodded, a grim expression on her face.

Harding was with child.

∾

We walked through the cold to a nearby pub. The thick, greasy scent of boxty hung thick in the air. I ordered the fish and chips, and Harding settled on a simple stew. The pub was crowded with university students and local workers, much louder and busier than the one back at home. Harding wore a fake wedding band on her left hand, and I gave it a questioning look.

"For protection," she said, quietly.

"Oh."

I didn't know what else to say.

We sat in silence, my cheeks flaming. The door to the pub opened, and I was grateful for the sudden rush of cold air.

"It's good to see you," Harding said. "I missed you."

"Yes," I said. "You too."

We kept up stilted small talk until the food arrived. She took a few bites before pushing it away.

"May we speak of it?" she asked with her typical frankness.

I nodded but avoided her eyes.

"You do understand that this is a result of what happened in the barn, yes? That this was not my choice?"

It took me a moment to understand. Once the words had sunk in, I was overcome with shame. "No," I whispered. "Oh, Harding."

"Don't." Her voice was sharp, but when I reached for her hand, she didn't push it away.

Letting out a breath, she said, "I began to feel ill shortly after I arrived at my aunt's house. I was able to hide it in the beginning. She's the one that I was supposed to spend the summer with, and the one who had scheduled a year abroad in America. I had fully intended to join her, but once it became clear to me what had happened, I had no choice but to hide it until she left, for fear of being sent to the Magdalene laundries."

I put my hand to my mouth. "Would she do that?"

"Of course." Harding's mouth tightened. "She would most certainly see me in need of reform."

Fedelma had threatened me with such when I was a child. The laundries were institutions where ill-behaved girls were sent to work, away from their families and the outside world. The very idea terrified me, and I worked extra hard to be good. Then, once, when my mother was home, I spilled a glass of milk and begged her not to send me. My mother was properly horrified that Fedelma had made such a threat, and it was never mentioned in our house again.

"Did your aunt suspect anything?" I asked, focusing on the brass button on the sleeve of my coat.

"No. I was very careful, and she was none the wiser. I saw her off in October."

"What will you do now?" I asked.

Harding's hands shook as she smeared butter on the bread. "Hide at her house until the child is born. I have also been very careful to keep my condition from those in the village, because I do not want word to get back to her or anyone else." She set down the piece of bread. "I do apologize that I've been out of touch. I've been adjusting to the situation and finding acceptance."

It was quite a thing to accept.

"Where will you place the child?" I asked.

"I . . ." For the first time since I'd met her, Harding looked lost. "I will keep it."

I sat back in my chair. "What?" It was baffling she'd consider such a thing. "You can't. Will you marry?"

Without a husband, Harding would be shunned. It would be impossible for her to find a match in her condition. That is, unless she already had some sort of arrangement in place.

"Why would I take a husband?" She ate her stew in silence. Then she said, "Evie, my parents were terrible people. Traitors to this country, loyalists. Pious and pure, yet willing to let their neighbor starve in the name of the crown. I did not have a choice in who raised me. I do have a choice in who raises my child." Her voice was firm. "This is my child, regardless of the circumstance."

My eyes stung. "It will be so hard."

"Everything is, though, isn't it? I still plan to leave when I can. For America."

Harding sat stoic and strong, her mouth set and determined. In spite of my misgivings, I admired her.

"I think you are very brave," I said. "But I've always thought that."

"I'm a coward." She flicked a small crumb off the table. "I came here today because, Evie, I need your help. I'd like you to be with me when the baby is born."

"Of course," I said. "We'll let a room nearby. I can't leave campus at night, but I can be there whenever I do not have class, or whenever you need me."

"I don't have the means to stay in town." She lowered her voice and leaned forward. "I have not been able to access my money. I could not risk it like this. I must stay at my aunt's house, but it is only an hour by train. I was hoping that you could come up on the weekends."

The idea of traveling alone sounded unsafe.

"What if I just came to stay with you now?" I said.

Harding hesitated. "You can't. You have school."

Yes, but I'd leave for her. I had no interest in attending. It was something that I was doing because I did not dare stand up to my parents, and the days were a constant test in drudgery.

"My parents will be in Buenos Aires until school is out," I said. "They wouldn't know."

I wouldn't be allowed to leave, though. The woman at the front desk and the dormitory monitor were very firm on our times and curfews, as were our professors. I couldn't just disappear, or my parents would be informed within the day.

"We must be clever about it," I said, slowly. "My parents would need to request my presence back home. One of the girls on my floor left because someone in her family fell ill."

Harding brightened. "We could send a telegram."

"That's what I was thinking, but it wouldn't work," I said. "The university would reply back, and Seamus would hear of it. He'd send word to my parents immediately."

Harding smiled. "Not if he never received the telegram. Colin owes me." Colin ran the telegraph service back in our village. "He would hold the message."

I didn't want to lie to my parents, but if anything happened to Harding, I'd never forgive myself. I'd heard Fedelma speaking with one of the other servants back when her sister was pregnant. Fedelma had lived in fear of her sister experiencing complications, and I didn't want Harding to be alone in case such a thing happened.

"Let's wait a few months," she said. "Not because I feel I'd be robbing you of some grand education, but because I'll need you when my child is born. I have no idea how to take care of a baby, and to be quite frank, the idea of giving birth terrifies me. Perhaps you could come at the end of March?"

I fiddled with my napkin. If we waited, it would be much less likely I'd get caught. My parents were not the type to do a surprise visit, but we were not that far from my home. If business called them near Cork, I'd like to think they would stop by to see me.

"We'll plan for the beginning of April," I agreed. "Perhaps Colin can hold my transcript this summer as well, as it will show my absence. I can return briefly to finish my exams and close out the year."

Harding studied me. "Are you sure you want to do this?" When I nodded, she looked down at her hands. "I've done so much wrong in my life, Evie. Sometimes, I think you must be an angel sent to watch over me. I don't understand how someone so good has accepted someone like me."

I was devoted to Harding because she encouraged me to ask questions, to speak my mind, and to be bold. She had taught me that it was possible to take my own path and shape my world into what I wanted it to be, a thought I'd never considered before meeting her. My feelings were hard to put into words, so I kept it simple.

"Because you're my sister," I told her. "The one I'd always hoped to have."

Her eyes filled with tears. "Now look what you've done," she said, wiping at them. "I really thought I'd be alone in this."

"You will never be alone," I promised. "I will be right by your side."

Chapter Twelve

Ireland, present day

The next morning, I requested that breakfast be served in the room. Nora brought up two plates full of scrambled eggs, beans, well-done sausage, and a potato galette with sundried tomatoes.

"Look at this breakfast." My grandmother was delighted. I helped her settle in at the table, and she dug right in. "Nora, did you make this?"

Nora blushed prettily. "I did."

My grandmother nodded. "We had a cook here when I grew up. I woke up anticipating breakfast this morning but didn't dare to dream it would be like this. I haven't had white pudding in years."

I must have looked confused because Nora winked at me. "The sausage."

"Oh, got it." I smiled. "Well, someone's happy."

"She does seem properly chuffed," she said.

I walked Nora to the hallway. Once we were there, I lowered my voice. "Hey, do you mind if I talk to you for a second? This is probably bad timing, considering you are a bed-and-breakfast and it's currently breakfast, but . . ."

She laughed. "The food's on the warmer and hardly anyone's awake. What's up?"

"Well, I had some questions for you about something I heard last night."

Nora nodded, wiping her hands on her apron. "Grady told me there was some trouble down at the pub."

That saved me from having to explain it.

"Yes," I said. "It sort of showed me that there are so many pieces of our family history that I don't know. I think I told you on the phone that my grandmother has always been close-lipped about her time here. If you do know the story or rumor or whatever, I'd like to hear it. Later," I said, quickly. "Whenever it's convenient."

"Because stories of murder should be centered around convenience," Nora said, which made me like her even more. "Well, I was going to have my husband pick up the trunk from the storage unit, but he got called in to deliver a baby, so perhaps you and Grady could go out to get it. He could tell you what he knows on the drive. Unless you and your grandmother have something planned."

My grandmother needed to rest. I could take her out later to see the town if she was up for it.

"I'd like for her to rest this morning," I said. "If the letters aren't in the trunk, we'll have to start looking for them."

Nora cocked her head. "Letters?"

I explained, and Nora put her hand to her chest. "Well, they probably *are* in there. Goodness, if you'd told me over the phone from the States, I could have found them, made a copy, and sent them your way. Saved you a trip. Easy."

We both laughed, because of course, none of this was easy.

"Let me call Grady. I'll ring up to let you know what time to be ready."

"Thank you," I said.

Back in the room, I poured myself a cup of coffee. It was so rich that the aroma alone nearly gave me the caffeine boost I needed to survive.

"How is it?" I asked my grandmother.

"It's so interesting to have these flavors back in my mouth again, after so many years," she said. "There have been moments where I had dreams that I was eating something in particular from here, like this one apple cake our cook used to make. I never thought I'd get to taste these things again." She set down her fork and gave me a long look. "Are you happy in Chicago?"

The question was so far from apple cake that I didn't know how to respond. It wasn't something I thought about much. My days were too busy. I typically woke up at 6:00 a.m. to wait tables before heading into the office at ten. Then I spent the rest of the day there, grabbing dinner around eight before falling into bed and doing it all over again.

"Yes," I lied. "I think my life will get easier once the business is successful, but it's been pretty busy for the past few years."

"It goes by quick," my grandmother said. "Don't forget to leave time for the things that really matter."

"What things are those?" I asked, giving her a wry smile.

I fully expected her to say marriage, or falling in love, but instead she said, "The things that make you happy."

It had been a long time since I'd even considered what those things were. Live music was one of them, cooking was another. Time in nature, which made me wince, considering I spent every second of my life indoors. It was all too much to dive into at the moment, so I held up my cup of coffee.

"This makes me happy, being here with you," I said.

"Good," she said. "Life goes faster than you'd expect. Keep making a point to do the things that make you happy, Rainey. If I die today, I will rest in peace knowing I explained that to you."

I knew she was kidding by the twinkle in her eye.

"You're not going to die today," I said, with a groan. "We still have a list of things to do before that, and one of them is to find you some apple cake."

My grandmother got to her feet. "Do you mind helping me get dressed, then? You've just given me the will to hang on for one more day."

～

Grady came to pick me up at eleven o'clock, looking inviting in a deep-green button-up shirt, worn jeans, and leather boots.

It was perfect timing. My grandmother and I had spent the morning strolling the grounds. She showed me where she used to walk along the moor, the place she'd carved her initials into a tree, and her favorite path to sneak down to the sea. She'd settled in for a nap right before Grady stopped by.

"I appreciate you doing this," I said. "I'm happy to buy you lunch."

"It will be fun," he said. "Nothing like searching through old family artifacts. Maybe we'll end up finding one of those lost paintings—you know, like how people buy them at a rubbish sale, only to discover they're worth millions?"

His carefree spirit was so attractive. It made the task at hand seem a little less daunting.

"Did Nora tell you what we were looking for?" I said, and he shook his head. "Letters." I shrugged. "I don't know who they are to or from or what, but that's what we're looking for."

"Intriguing," he said.

We went out to the driveway, where there was a motorbike parked in the roundabout.

"Where's your car?" I asked, looking around.

"I could grab one if you'd like, but then it would be a jammer."

"I don't know what that means," I said, shielding my eyes from the sun. He grinned. "Stolen."

"Yeah, the motorbike's good," I said, and he handed me a helmet.

I'd never been on a motorcycle or any type of two-wheeled motorized transportation in my life, but I climbed on after him.

"Wait," I said as he moved to rev the engine. "How can we bring a trunk back on this? 'Trunk' means 'trunk' here, right? Not, like, 'smallish box'?"

Grady laughed. "The owner of the storage unit has a lorry. She'll let me borrow it." The bike rumbled, shaking my whole body, and he called, "Hang on."

I looked for some handlebars to grab on to and then realized he meant hang on to him.

The next thing I knew, we were flying across the Irish countryside. It was like something out of a movie, circling the edge of the coast and looking out over the sea with the mountains climbing up above us. I stared at the scenery in awe, wondering why I had never done anything like this before.

I guess it was because I had always been too busy trying to survive. My grandmother's words about doing things that made me happy rang in my ears, and I held on to Grady a little more tightly. This qualified. There was no question about that.

Maybe because Grady had talked about discovering an old painting, I had imagined that the storage unit would be some dusty place over-loaded with old junk. Instead, we pulled up the drive in front of a sleek modern building next to a public park. My legs still shook slightly as I got off the bike and followed him up to the front desk.

A young woman working on a computer brightened to see him and rushed out to give him a hug. I wondered if this was his wife or girlfriend and hoped that she wouldn't mind that I'd spent the last forty-five minutes holding him tight, while trying to not give over to fantasies about some quick overseas fling.

"It's still fine to use Siobhan's lorry?" he asked once the two had caught up.

"Yes, if you bring it back in one piece."

Grady gave her his charming smile. "When have you known me to be anything other than slow, safe, and controlled?"

She rolled her eyes and handed him a set of keys.

"Good luck," she told me.

I had a feeling she wasn't talking about the truck.

The storage unit was neat, tidy, and well lit. Grady knew exactly where to go and led me past a bunch of furniture and well-categorized boxes to the trunk that had once belonged to my grandmother.

"Here it is." He crossed his arms, a move that emphasized his broad shoulders. "Do you have any idea what's in there?"

"No." The curiosity of it all had my pulse racing. "Do you care if I take a peek before we move it?"

"That's why we're here." He settled in to one of the antique chairs, adjusting the sleeves of his shirt. "I'm interested to see what you find."

I appreciated that he was willing to hang back and wait without trying to beat me to it or invade my space or be a part of something that really didn't belong to him. The word that kept coming to mind with him was "respectful," and I realized that I'd be much more interested in dating if the men I met acted a bit more like him.

I sat down on the cool stone floor of the storage unit, lifted the brass latch, and opened the lid. The inside of the trunk smelled like old paper and cedar. There was quite a bit inside: a small jewelry box, several books, some ledgers, a photo album, and, sure enough, a stack of hand-written letters, tied with a piece of red string. The letters were tagged with a small Post-it that read, *Found in remodel in East bedroom wall.*

Carefully, I opened the plastic bag to be sure that the letters had something to do with my grandmother and that this wasn't just a stack of old papers. Sure enough, I recognized her handwriting right away.

"Look at this," I called to Grady.

I showed him the letter on the top through the plastic bag they were stored in. The first words were "My precious darling."

"Love letters," I said. "I haven't even read them yet, and I already have the chills. Look at the date."

He peered over my shoulder, close enough for me to feel his body heat. "Decades ago. Sounds familiar, since I can't remember the last time I wrote a love letter."

I had a feeling that this guy could not only write a love letter; he'd probably written one last week.

"Oh, wait," he said, and a smile spread across his face. "I do remember, actually. It was in primary, for Aoife O'Malley of the bows and blonde curls. I spelled 'marry' wrong, so she thought I wanted her to help declare my love for Mary Murphy of the sour face and tight braids."

I laughed. "That was your last love letter?"

"Tragic, I know."

We looked at each other for a minute. Then I held up the letters. "Do you care if I take a little bit of time to look through these? Or do you have to get back?"

Nora had promised to check on my grandmother every hour and bring her lunch, as well as anything else she might need.

"You have me as long as you need me."

I sat on the floor, next to the trunk. He settled in on the ground as well, leaning back against the wall and closing his eyes as if taking a rest.

"My grandmother can't see well enough to read anymore," I explained, and he opened his eyes. "I want to read through them before I read them to her. I need to know what I'm walking into."

I didn't want to be in the middle of reading the letters to my grandmother, only to find out they were written to English royalty or something.

"If there's something in Gaelic and you need a translation, let me know." He stretched. "It would be a shame for you to not be understanding it when someone says 'I love you.'"

Hearing those words in his Irish brogue made my cheeks burn.

"Thanks," I said. "I'll let you know."

My eyes fell on his hiking boots. The boots were a dark, worn leather, hand stitched around the edges and incredibly European. It was a little disorienting to think that, only a day ago, I had started my day on the other side of the ocean. It already felt like I'd been here much longer than I had.

I opened the plastic bag and pulled out the first few letters, careful with the old and delicate paper, hoping they wouldn't crumble right there in my hands. The paper itself was simple, a perfunctory sheet with my grandmother's ornate handwriting.

My breath caught as I read the first line:

My precious darling . . .

I checked the dates. They were out of order, and I probably needed to fix that, in case there was some sort of beginning, middle, and end. They were also a little confusing, as they were written in a different format from that used in the US.

"I'm embarrassed to say that I already need your help." I passed the stack to Grady. "Can you help put these in order, earliest to latest?"

It wouldn't take much brain power to sort them out, but Grady could do it without thinking. Sure enough, he had the whole stack categorized in an instant, then returned them to me.

Leaning his head back against the wall, he closed his eyes again.

Silently, I began to read:

> My precious darling,
> There are moments when I wonder what it is you see when you look at me. So different from her, in every way. Yet, when I'm with you, the song that you put into my spirit makes me feel so alive. I'd sing it to the hills, the sea, and the skies. I love you!
> The rays of sun fall into your eyes divine and my heart warms to watch them shine. You, my precious, precious darling—I am so thankful you are mine.

It was hard to imagine my grandmother trying her hand at poetry, as she wasn't particularly sentimental, but it just showed how in love she was. I was interested to discover who this man was who'd brought up such feelings in her, and I kept reading.

> My precious darling,
> I'm stunned that anything can be as beautiful as the green of your eyes. The way you watch me as you put

on the hat I knit for you—only laughing a little!—as I stared, in awe of everything about you.

Each moment together gives me hope that my life will be grand, full of laughter, love, and these moments of wondrous surprise. Yet I'm so full of life with you that it's the smallest moments that make my heart leap—laughing, dancing, cooking for you . . . so simple. Isn't that what love is?

Time, it will march on, but please, tell me you will always be like this here with me, holding my hand, forever.

"This is fascinating," I mused, and Grady opened his eyes.

"What's fascinating?" he said. "The fact that I was almost asleep or . . . ?"

"Sorry," I said. "Should I get you a pillow? A blanket?"

He came over to sit by me. The proximity of him made me lose my concentration, and I had to think about what I'd been about to say.

"I'm just so curious about who this guy is. My grandmother was married for, like, fifty years. I had no idea she had some lost love."

He studied me. "She didn't tell you who it was?"

His tone made me wonder if somehow, this was going to be one of the things that everyone in the village knew about, and I only needed to ask.

"Do you know?" I felt disappointed when he shook his head. "I'm wondering if the man she wrote these letters to went to America with her," I said. "Otherwise, I don't see any reason that she would run away."

"What reason did she give for going to America?" he asked.

"She hasn't told me or my mother. She's always kept it close to her chest. It's surprising to me that the place she ran from is the place she wanted to return to at the end of her life."

"Maybe she feels like she has unfinished business. Something brought her here."

"Supposedly, these letters," I said.

I went back to reading.

> My precious darling,
> Sometimes I feel as if the world is nothing but drudgery and impossibilities. Things I will not do. Challenges I cannot face. Times when I realize that I'm not brave, and never will be.
> These are the moments I turn to you. Your heart beating so steady, like the tick of a clock. Your love, it's healing me. Letting me forget all that went before.
> This life is so fleeting. These moments where I fret and fear, the only thing that matters is you by my side. I whisper the words that I hope you hear in your dreams: I will love you, forever.

"There's something wrong in this one," I said before moving on to the next. "Like she's scared, or something."

> My precious darling,
> You are a part of my heart, a part of my soul. This morning, you whispered, "I love you," and I couldn't help it, I broke down and cried, thinking of my parents, and how they want to keep us apart.
> I can't imagine a time without you, and if one should ever come, I want to think back to this. The fireplace on. You next to me, your green eyes steady on mine. A book resting between us.
> How is it possible that two people, so different, could be brought together like this, the stars overhead, the sea crashing below, surrounded with nothing but hope for the future?
> Days like these, I rock in this chair, thinking of how empty my life would be without you.

"She mentions her parents in this one," I mused. "They don't approve of this relationship."

I'd just been about to dive into the next one when Grady said, "You hungry? There's a pub that's the best of them all right down the road, and I can go grab us something."

Even though my body clock was off, my watch read noon.

"That would be great." I started to dig into my purse for some money, but he waved me off.

"It's on me," he said. "What would you like?"

I didn't have the foggiest idea what would be a typical thing to eat for lunch, so I said, "Surprise me. Last night I had fish and chips. I'm not big on cabbage or things that smell like cabbage."

He indicated the letters. "Still good?"

"Yes," I said. "They're charming. They definitely read like they're from another time."

He headed out. I set down the stack and took in a deep breath, trying to center myself. It might've been the jet lag or maybe I was hungry and hadn't noticed, but the letters were making me feel sad.

They were so sentimental, and so full of love. It made me wonder if I'd ever feel that way about anyone.

I'd thought I'd been in love once, in college, but I was so caught up in my studies that I took him for granted, and he moved on. I had cared about him, no question, and I wished I could have done a better job of showing it. Still, when I thought of true love, I hoped it would feel a little more like what I was reading, or like my grandparents dancing that night at their anniversary.

Picking up the letters, I flipped through a few of the pages, wondering who they'd been written to. What had compelled my grandmother to travel across the ocean to reread them, when she'd already shared a lifetime of love with my grandfather? It was all so confusing, and as I settled back in to read, I hoped the answer wouldn't lead me to heartbreak.

Chapter Thirteen

Ireland, 1950

The main room in the house that belonged to Harding's aunt was dark. Outside, the air was humid with the faded scent of rain and moss. The fresh, bright feeling of new life, of spring. Harding and I had spent the evening in our chairs by the fire, talking, but now, we had settled in to a comfortable silence.

Harding was the centerpiece of the room, with her fully round body and feet resting on the needlepoint-covered stool. She looked strong, tender, and determined. I admired her immensely for not being bitter and, instead, awaiting this child with an open mind.

"Will you read to me?" she asked.

I reached for the chain on the lamp on the table. It made a lovely metallic clicking sound, and I never tired of the sudden burst of light that illuminated the room. We'd been through the bookshelves from top to bottom in the six weeks since I'd arrived and had read everything that looked interesting.

When I got up to look for something new, I found a book in the back that we hadn't read yet. It had fallen sideways behind the others. Stretching my fingers to get it, I pulled it out.

The cover was of faded red leather embossed with gold, entitled *Children's Tales*.

"This is perfect," I said, holding it up.

"That looks lovely." Harding pulled her quilt closer and stared into the embers.

I opened the book, reading the handwritten name in the upper corner. *Grace Delany.* It was written in childish print and dated December 1904. Perhaps the book had been given to her as a Christmas present.

"Is this your aunt?" I asked, showing her the name.

"Yes." Harding closed her eyes, indicating she was too tired to talk.

I started to read, entranced by the lyrical stories and beautiful drawings. Suddenly, Harding let out a sharp gasp.

"Harding?" I said, glancing over at her.

Her eyes looked haunted. I slid my train ticket into the book; we'd been using it as a bookmark.

"Tell me what's wrong," I said. "Is it time?"

"I think so," she whispered.

Gently, I took her hand and led her to the bed, where she sank down and buried her head in the pillow. Her shoulders shook in a silent sob. I laid the back of my hand on her forehead, like Fedelma had done so many times before for me. Her temperature felt normal.

I knelt down, resting my hands on her shoulders. "Do not be afraid. I will fetch the doctor."

"Evie." Turning, she stared up at me with a tearstained face. "What if I cannot love this child?"

The fear made me wince. It would be easier, really, if she would let this baby belong to someone else. She wouldn't have to give up the rest of her life or face judgment at every turn. Even so, it was not my decision to make.

Taking her hand, I said, "Your heart will guide you. You do not have to be afraid."

Tears slid down her cheeks, and then her face contorted in pain.

"Let me get the doctor," I said, quickly. "Breathe."

~

I ran into the village as fast as I could. With each step, I imagined Harding further in pain, scared and alone. I banged on the door of the doctor's house.

His wife answered, and once I'd passed on the message, she nodded. "Boil water, gather some rags, and return home to care for her. He will be there shortly."

I ran back to the house. Harding's eyes were wide and panicked, her skin pale. Sweat rolled down her cheeks, and she groaned.

"Please, is the doctor behind you?" she begged.

I went to the window, legs trembling, but I pretended to be calm. "Not yet. He's on his way and has given me some tasks."

I threw another log on the fire, along with a kettle of water. Briskly, I adjusted the pillows and blankets, then gave her my hand to grip tight. I had never seen a baby born, but I had witnessed the birth of horses and sheep.

Harding had never seen a birth and had admitted during one of our evening talks that it was the unknown that scared her. I did my best to describe what I'd seen but had no way to understand how it would feel. Harding was panting as she gripped the bedsheets, clutching her abdomen. My stomach turned; I was unsure whether she was in danger or if this was how it should be.

I held her hand tight, gave her something to bite down on, and kept rushing out to the main room to check in the front window for the doctor. Would he ever come? As the minutes passed, I became frightened that I'd have to handle this on my own.

The bedsheets became soaked and sour, smelling of fear, sweat, and the water that had come before. The tendrils around Harding's forehead were damp, and I brushed them back, whispering words meant to soothe as her body writhed, fighting to escape the pain.

The moment I thought she couldn't take it anymore, a car door slammed and the doctor burst in. It had started to rain. He stepped forward with his black bag, his coat and gray hair damp.

I hung back, waiting for instructions.

"Bring me several towels." He laid out sharp metallic instruments. Resting his hand on her forehead and then her stomach, he nodded. "It should be soon."

The words were comforting, and Harding's eyes met mine. She managed a brave grimace before the next wave of pain hit her. I sank onto the floor next to the bed, wanting to bury my head in my hands but forcing myself to stay strong.

I braced as she gripped my hand with all her might.

It could've been a few minutes or an hour when a cry different from hers rang out through the room. The doctor held a wriggling, red mass of flesh attached with a shiny silver cord. I took in a sharp breath at the realization that there was another life with us, and my eyes filled with tears.

The doctor handed Harding the baby, and she closed her eyes as its mouth took her breast. The picture in the firelight was so beautiful that the terror from the past few hours washed away.

The doctor stood in silence. Then he said, "I know your aunt well. She did not mention you would need assistance."

Quickly, I stepped forward. "Her aunt knows nothing of this. Quite frankly, she wouldn't approve of the marriage. Harding's husband is stationed overseas with the British armed forces."

The doctor glanced at Harding, and she gave a resolute nod. "I do intend to tell her. It must come from me, though."

"If she has any hope of receiving her blessing," I added.

The doctor frowned. "I will not speak of it. However, I quite doubt she will ever approve of that. To be perfectly frank, I do not."

"I understand," Harding said, ducking her head.

The doctor became all business. He lectured Harding on what to do with the child, handled the remainder, and told me to clean up the bedsheets.

"I'll be by tomorrow," he said when I fumbled with Harding's coin purse, which she had prepared. "I will check on the child and collect payment then."

"Thank you," I told him, and he gave a sharp nod.

Three of us remained in the room as his taillights headed down the road. Harding and I looked at each other and then at this red, beautiful creature resting in her arms.

I will protect him with every ounce of my being, I thought.

I lay down next to them on the bed, and I barely slept a wink that night.

～

The tiny little red body, with an even tinier birthmark on the back of his arm. The wrinkled face. The hands and feet that didn't quite know what to do.

Joy filled me each time I looked at him, as I realized that we were responsible for this human. The one thing that I hadn't factored in was the fragility of his little life. That he would be so small.

Harding had spent the last nine months with him growing inside her body, acclimating to the idea of him. In some ways—and perhaps this revealed a level of naivete I did not know I had—I had pictured the baby as a young child. A boy, yes, wearing socks pulled up his calves, shorts, and a collared shirt, while chasing after a ball. To see that he was simply a tiny little thing was surprising to me. I'd tell Harding, one day, and we'd share a laugh, but for now, her focus was on resting, healing, and caring for her son.

The next morning, she said, "Sit down. Here, you must hold him. Let him feel you. Attach to you."

The moment the small weight settled in my hands, my body went soft. The feeling of his skin was like nothing else, and I breathed in his yeasty, sweet scent. His body was nearly weightless, but his warmth was heavy, and I could feel each little beat of his heart, scampering forward into his dreams.

It was the first time I had ever held a baby, and all I could do was stare at him. His eyes cracked open briefly, unfocused, before closing again to go to sleep.

"What will you call him?" I asked.

"Alby."

"Hello, sweet Alby," I said, gently touching his small fingers. "We love you."

Harding watched us, and from her place in the bed, she said, "I need to speak to you about something that is quite complicated."

My chest tightened. I knew what she would say. It would be impossible to keep this child, so she'd decided to turn it over to the orphanage. I feared that in spite of the tenderness she'd demonstrated, the situation was getting the better of her.

Harding reached out her hands. I hesitated, then passed him over. She gently kissed his head, and he snuggled in to nurse.

"Evie, I'm still a target," she said, leaning back against the pillows. "Until I get that money and pay my partners what I owe them, I will continue to have a target on my back. I do intend to settle my debts as soon as I can be away from Alby to do so, but I fear that even then, I will still be in danger. You and I need to put a plan into place. I need your word that you will care for him if anything happens to me."

I drew back. "What?"

Harding was no longer a part of the trade. She'd told me her involvement had ended the moment she was attacked, and I had assumed she'd handled her debt in the time we were apart.

"I thought you'd taken care of all that," I said, horrified. "You told me that all was well."

"I never said it was over." She kissed Alby's head, looking so removed from the terrors we spoke of. "It will be well. I assured my partners I'd pay them back, with interest, and I still have time to do that. It's not as though anyone is after me right now. At least, I don't believe that to be the case."

The cottage had felt like such a cozy respite, a comfortable escape. My skin crawled to think it might be the opposite, that I could awaken at any time to a knife at my throat, someone demanding answers I could not give.

"This has to end," I said. "My father will help you. I'll insist. He would—"

"No," she said. "He deals with people who are honest and forthright. The men that I need to avoid are neither of those things."

"He could have them arrested," I said.

"It's more complicated than that." She pulled Alby close. "I will pay my debts, but I'm worried they will still want more. Everyone knows of the money I've made, that it's still hidden. I will be safe once it's in America, and I will take passage as soon as my son is hearty enough to make it through the journey."

The risk of illness needed to pass by, but more than that, Harding was worried about food. If her milk lapsed while at sea, it would be difficult to get Alby the necessary nutrition. Once he was bigger, these issues would be nothing of great concern.

"My son," Harding said, repeating the words with wonder. "In the midst of this darkness, saying that makes all of this seem so much brighter." She touched his small fingers and smiled at me. "I love him, Evie. With all my heart."

Letting out a sigh, she pulled the bedsheets close around them. "I do feel safe here, yet we cannot stay forever. You'll need to return home, or your parents will learn that you have not been at university. Colin has held all communication, but I think they'd notice if you didn't show up this summer, right?"

I wasn't entirely certain of that, but she had a point. However, I was not about to let the two people I cared about the most struggle to survive on their own.

"If I have to go back, you'll join me until you can leave," I said. "You'll stay at my house with Alby. I will speak to my parents, and we can hide out in the gardener's cottage, as we did before."

"The scandal is too great. Besides, someone would find out. It would be impossible to hide him there."

"Then what will you do?" I demanded.

She hesitated. "I don't know."

The brightness in her eyes spilled down her cheeks. I clasped her hand, cold in spite of the heat of the fire. Her fingers were strong, her grip firm.

Alby finished eating, and his head rested against her body, contented. Harding watched him closely, as if memorizing every moment. Then her face crumpled in silent agony.

"I don't know what to do," she whispered.

I wished I had an answer, but it felt like there was nowhere to go from here.

~

An idea struck me a few days later. Harding was asleep as I held Alby. I awaited eagerly for her to awaken, and once she did, I passed him to her before sharing it.

"To be clear, you are not afraid to be seen out in the world, right?" I asked. "It's allowing Alby to be seen with you that is making you feel scared. That it would put him at risk?"

Harding rubbed her eyes and took a drink of water. "Yes."

"If Alby is the issue, we will pretend he does not belong to you."

She looked baffled, and I held up my hand. "The one thing that university was good for, perhaps, is this: I learned that an incredible number of children have been abandoned. Fathered by soldiers, only to be left behind. So what if we pretend that I found Alby by the side of the road? We would already have it planned that you were coming to stay with me for the summer. No one would know any better."

Harding considered the idea. Then she began to nod. "You would have to tell everyone that you found him, though—make up a big story so that people would talk. Have plans to send him away."

"Then you could . . ."

Harding nodded. "Take him to America." She hesitated. "It might work."

"It will work if we do it right." My skin tingled at the possibility. "I don't need to return for three more weeks. We have plenty of time to solve it by then."

I didn't like the idea of lying to every single person I loved, but I could ask for forgiveness later. For now, my priority was to help Harding so that she could find safe passage from a life that had ceased to be her own.

Chapter Fourteen

Ireland, present day

Grady strolled back into the storage unit with a brown paper bag in hand and triumph on his face.

"Victory," he said. "I got—" He stopped, suddenly. "Wait. Did you do something different with your hair?"

Ever since we'd arrived, I'd had it pulled back in a ponytail. It was easy to travel with, and it stayed out of my face. I'd pulled it down while reading, and the loose waves had tumbled out around my shoulders.

"It's a mess," I said, starting to put it back up.

"No, it's lovely." Grady took a step forward, and I looked at him. "I mean, put it up if you'd like, but it's truly lovely."

He set down the bag of food and sat down next to me. "How are the letters, then?"

"Well . . ." I wondered if he could tell I'd been crying.

"Not good?"

"Well, I do think it ended rather badly."

I put the pages away into the plastic bag, still reeling from what I'd read. I'd made my way through all of them, and once they ended, I felt like I'd gone through a breakup. Two of the letters were written after the guy she loved had left, which was especially painful. She'd mourned his loss and spoke about him being taken from her.

"That's tough," he said. "Especially to think that all these years later, heartbreak still sounds the same."

His ring finger was empty, so he wasn't married. I wondered what type of heartbreak he'd experienced.

Grady started to pull the containers out of the bag, the heavenly aromas filling the storage unit. Then he paused and got to his feet.

"Come on," he said. "I have a much better idea."

~

Grady led me out to the park I'd noticed when we'd pulled in. It had gotten surprisingly busy and was full of people cruising the bike path, having picnics, and playing with their dogs. The grass was as green as ever.

We found a picnic area with a wooden table. A small brook bubbled nearby, and the whole thing was so picture perfect that I felt like I was in a drawing from a fairy tale. He pulled out the food containers and set them on the table.

"It smells great," I said, taking a seat.

I opened mine to discover a large bowl of stew, with substantial cuts of beef, whole carrots, and sliced potatoes. A piece of bread was in the partition next to it, slathered with thick Irish butter. It smelled delicious, like a warm house in the winter.

Grady lifted his spoon. "Here's to perfection."

Truer words were never spoken. The stew was so full of flavor: a perfect blend of meat, vegetables, and garlic, not to mention Guinness and red wine.

"Wow," I said. "I didn't expect a gourmet meal at a picnic."

We ate in companionable silence as the bees hummed past and the birds sang in the trees around us. It was so nice to be outside in the fresh air. I slipped off my flats and slid my feet into the grass, reveling in the decadence of it all.

When was the last time I'd taken the time to eat lunch outdoors? I knew of so many picturesque views and perfect dining spots in Chicago, both near parks and by the water, but I never took the time to use them. I spent my time tucked into my office, in the labs, because a moment like this didn't seem as important as it felt right now.

"Nora told me you wanted to talk about the pub," he said. "The thing Jimmy was saying."

"Yes," I said. "I mean . . . murder? My family knows nothing about it."

Grady took a bite of bread. "I can only tell you what I've heard, but I wasn't around then, of course. Supposedly, your grandmother's parents were killed right outside of town. They were returning home from Argentina, where her father did a lot of work. He was important to the town. Had a big government job in electricity planning but also helped people get what they needed, bypass rations, that sort of thing. There were a lot of farms that failed at that time because it was hard to get fertilizer, but not around here." He took a few bites of his stew. "I think—maybe because your grandmother had gone to America and that was still fresh gossip—the narrative was that their deaths were somehow her fault. There was a rumor that . . ." He hesitated.

"Tell me," I said. "Please."

"That she stole some money. The people who came to get it back killed her parents for revenge."

"What?" I said, setting my water bottle down with a thud.

That was impossible. My grandmother was one of the most honest people I'd ever met. I could think of plenty of times when people hadn't wanted to hear the truth, but she was honest to a fault and didn't hold back. Unless it was about her own personal history, of course.

"That can't be true," I said. "Do people really believe that? She'd be devastated."

"Whether it's true or not, people in the village were angry at her because of all that happened after her parents died," Grady said. "So many villagers ended up losing their farms because her father was this benefactor of sorts who had somehow kept everyone in business, and they blamed her when he wasn't around. I don't see how that's fair, but people wanted somebody to blame, and she was the only one left."

I took a bite of bread. Maybe because of the topic, it felt comforting. It was one of the best things I'd ever eaten, still warm, with a hard crust and soft center.

"I wonder if she came back," I said. "When she heard they'd died."

We'd always believed that my grandmother had never returned to Ireland, but considering she didn't speak of that time at all, it was possible that she had, and we didn't know about it.

"From what I understand, she wasn't in contact with the solicitor's office until a few years after her parents died. I doubt she knew about it until long after the fact. Aisling went to the market soon after."

It must have been so hard on her, to learn of the death of her parents from the other side of the world. I wondered what had happened to make her want to leave in the first place. Maybe her parents had tried to prevent her from being with the mystery man from the letters.

Grady studied me. "You okay?"

"Yes," I said. "I'm just thinking about how little I know her. I've always accepted the idea that there was a part of her life that we didn't discuss. Now that I'm surrounded by stories I've never heard, I think it's strange that my mother never pushed to find the answers. Why would she accept the fact that she would never get to really know her mother and leave it at that? I've tried to ask about Ireland many times, in many different ways, but I could only take it so far."

"You've lost me," he said.

I tried to piece together my thoughts. "I've always felt that, with a grandmother, there's a line you don't cross, you know? A level of respect that should be maintained, so I never asked questions beyond what felt appropriate. But my mother should have, because that's her *mother*. With your mother, it's fair game to ask those questions."

"Why?" he said.

"Because your mother is your mother. She's been there from the beginning, and she'll be there at the end."

He shrugged. "Not everyone's mother is like that. Mine was, but I've known plenty of lads who weren't close with their mum."

"Their relationship was more complicated than I assumed, I guess," I said. "Which is strange to me because they lived on the same street, bought each other matching coffee mugs, and even shared shoes. They simply didn't talk about this. It's such a big part of my grandmother's life, though. I don't understand why my mother didn't push harder."

"Maybe she was respecting your grandmother's wishes."

"Yes. I suppose but . . ." I fiddled with a piece of the crust. "Maybe I've got it all wrong. How close can you really be with someone if you're not willing to show who you really are?"

Even as I said it, I thought of the lie I'd told Tia. I still felt guilty, but the situation was something completely different. I'd only lied to her because I was confident I could fix things, and I planned to come clean once it was resolved.

It was a moment; it didn't define who I was. But what would Grady think of me if I told him?

"I think the things that we hide from others are more about a fear of being honest with ourselves," he said. "The world wants us to be perfect, and when we're not, it can be hard to admit that."

I took a drink of the sparkling water he'd gotten for me and considered what he'd said. The guilt I'd felt since I'd lied to Tia was self-inflicted. I doubted Grady would judge me as harshly as I'd judged myself.

"I do wish my mother was here," I said. "This means so much to me, to be here with my grandmother, but I think it would mean even more to my mother."

"You're here in proxy, right? So it's your responsibility to share what you're seeing so that your mother can decide whether to get on a plane."

"She can't, though," I said. "She thinks my grandmother doesn't want her here, and on top of that, she has to work. It's the end of the school year, and . . ."

"It's also the end of her mother's life, isn't it?"

"It's so hard to tell," I said. "My grandmother keeps cracking jokes about it all. She took the last cookie on that plate in the entryway and wouldn't split it with me because, quote, she 'could die tomorrow.'"

Grady laughed. "I like your grandmother."

"She's fun." I set down my spoon. "She could return to the States and live another five or ten years. Or . . ." I looked out over the beauty of the landscape. "Maybe she plans to die here. I don't know."

"Your mother's accepted both outcomes?" he asked.

I brushed some crumbs off the table. "Good question. Either way, I'm afraid it will be harder for her to learn my grandmother has all these secrets she didn't share."

"Some things are hard to face up to," Grady said. "Maybe it just took time, and now, your grandmother's ready to face them."

"Well, when you're ninety-three, you're living on borrowed time," I said. "Cutting it close, don't you think?"

"Maybe she works well under pressure." Grady scooped up the last bits of his stew. "I bet she had a hard time with the idea that her parents were killed after she'd left."

I nodded. "Like, if she'd been here, maybe it wouldn't have happened. Even if it had nothing to do with her."

"Are you going to bring it up?" he asked.

"Not yet. We came here for love letters, apparently, so there's no need to muck it up with murder."

Grady nodded. "Words to live by."

We packed up lunch and headed out to find the truck. Now that I'd had some food and sunshine, it would be easier to look at the letters again.

I held tight to one that was close to the bottom:

> Life continues to roll forward, my darling, as sure as the sea. You have taught me so many things. To be quick to love. Easy to laugh. Most of all, to understand that the only true fear is that we might never have the opportunity to experience true love. You, dear one, need not be afraid. I do love you, with all my heart, and I always will.

Chapter Fifteen

Ireland, 1950

My mother stared at me, wide eyed. "You found . . . a child?"

I had walked into the foyer, surprised at the sight of my home after such a long absence. The small house that belonged to Harding's aunt had been my world for the past three months. Now, I was as awed by our entryway as Harding had been when she first arrived.

Fumbling with the blanket, I opened it to show my mother. "Doesn't it break your heart?"

Alby was two months old. He opened his eyes and reached out his hand, clenching it in the air. My mother stared at him in confusion, and then her eyes swept over my body as if to ascertain that the child was not mine. Once that was settled, she moved in closer to peer at him.

"Goodness," she whispered. "Who would have done such a thing?"

I was shaking inside, but more with the fear that my parents would insist on sending Alby to an orphanage. Harding and I had agreed that if my parents moved in that direction, I'd have no choice but to tell them the truth.

"We have to get him care," my mother said, as if reading my thoughts. "Report this to the Garda."

"Of course," I agreed. "We will tell them, but I won't allow this child to go to an orphanage. He'll stay with me."

The sweet, yeasty scent of Alby wafted up to me. The top of his head was covered with soft fuzz, and it took everything in me to not lean down and kiss it. Instead, as I adjusted him in my arms, I pretended to nearly drop him.

My mother quickly grabbed hold. "Darling, you can't hold him like that. It's like this." Once he was safely nestled back in my arms, she shook her head. "We cannot keep him for long. He needs to be with his mother."

"His mother left him by the side of the road," I said. "I don't think he needs to be with her at all after that, but if we find her, I suppose we'll have no choice."

My mother studied him. "He was really by the road?"

"Under a tree."

My distress was genuine. Risking this farce had pained me greatly. It required me to convince the driver to pull over at the right time, in the right village, so that I could notice Alby. Harding was nearby, keeping watch, but so many things could have gone wrong that my body didn't stop trembling for at least an hour afterward, when Alby was with me in the back seat, with Harding following far enough behind to keep from being spotted.

Now, my mother reached forward and gently touched his face. Alby opened one eye and then let out a little yawn. She took a step back.

"We will need to find a way to feed him. I will find out if there's a nursemaid in the village."

I pretended to think. "What about Fedelma's sister? Her husband was killed in a farming accident, and she needs income. If she had a child last year, would she still be . . . ?"

I knew full well Mona was still nursing, because Fedelma often complained that her sister nursed her children until they were practically grown.

"I'll send for her," my mother said. "I'm sure it would be meaningful for her family to obtain a wage. In the meantime, we must get him some water and have him examined by the doctor. Your father will have much to say about this, but with his permission, we will keep the child until we know more."

I managed to swallow, in spite of the lump in my throat. "Good." He gripped my finger with his palm. It was one of my favorite games to play with him, the thing that entertained him the most.

"What shall we call him?" my mother said.

I pulled the note we'd prepared out of my purse with my free hand. It was folded, creased, and smeared with the slightest touch of dirt to make it convincing that he'd been outdoors.

Please care for my Alby.

I held it up and showed it to her.

"Here," I said. "I think his name is Alby."

~

I spent so much time with him in my arms, singing him songs and reading to him, and my mother seemed baffled by it all. I think she'd expected me to leave his care to the servants. One afternoon, she walked into the library to discover me sitting in the darkness, and put her hand to her chest.

"What on earth are you doing?" she demanded.

The heavy curtains kept the room cool and protected the wooden shelves full of books, so they often remained closed, but she walked over and threw them open, scattering dust in the rays of sun.

"Well, we *were* doing shadow puppets." I held up the torch and shined it at the wall. "He was particularly interested in the butterfly."

It was the only shadow I could get quite right, perhaps with the exception of the spider.

My mother took a seat next to us on the couch. "I'd like to hold the child."

This was new. I had few memories of her holding me when I was young. I hesitated before passing him to her.

Alby was still tiny, and she held him carefully. Fedelma's sister had agreed to be his wet nurse during the day, and the doctor had advised us on how we could provide supplements for him during the night, using sugar-sweetened cow's milk. Of course, that wouldn't be necessary once Harding arrived.

My mother played with his feet for a moment, then said, "I never knew you were interested in children."

"I'm not." I turned off the torch and leaned back against the soft upholstery of the couch. "There is something about this little one that has taken my heart, though."

"I can see why." She seemed preoccupied with the peach fuzz on his head, then said, "Young men won't be nearly enchanted by a woman weighed down with a child, in spite of how it all came to be."

I nearly laughed out loud. "*What* young men?"

"Sullivan."

My mother's words felt like a test, and I didn't quite know what to say. The fact that she would ask these questions at all meant she and my father had recently discussed my future, a thought that made me uneasy.

I cared for Sullivan, but my parents wouldn't consider him a true contender. He was the only person in town who knew the truth about what had happened with Harding, though, and I had no doubt he would keep the secret about Alby once he pieced it together. Sullivan was handsome, kind, and trustworthy, but would it be fair to bring him into all this?

Besides, if I married Sullivan, my role would be the wife of the village shopkeeper. Everything I did would be contained to this town. I'd raise Sullivan's children, host dinners, and wait for my life to begin.

I might have accepted that prior to meeting Harding, but now, I understood that the world had a lot more to offer than what was put right in front of me.

"Sullivan has been a true friend," I told my mother. "However, I'm not concerned with enchanting him."

"I imagine he's already enchanted," she said. "Evie, it's important to have someone by your side. I'd like for you to start thinking in that direction. The world continues to be complicated, and I'd like to know that you have someone looking out for you."

My conversations with Harding, along with my time at university, had taught me so much about the problems Ireland had faced and was still facing. Rumors of rebellions. Endless threats. It often felt as if the trouble would never end, but I did not see marriage as a solution to any of those issues. If anything, as Harding had once said, my life would cease to be my own.

Now that I'd witnessed the pain of childbirth, it was not something I planned to rush toward. I also hadn't determined whether I wanted to have a career. Women had opportunities now that they didn't have when my mother was young, and I wasn't certain yet what path I wanted my life to take. But I did know now that I didn't want someone to choose that path for me.

Squaring my shoulders, I said, "If and when I choose to have someone by my side, it will not be because I'm looking for a caretaker."

My mother frowned. "I'm not suggesting that. You are a young, educated woman. The possibilities for you are endless. It may be tempting to settle for what's easy, but I expect you to do something of value."

So she must have heard that Sullivan and I had become close last summer. This conversation was a warning. I could get close, but not too close.

Alby began to fuss.

My mother got to her feet and handed him back to me. "We should find Mona. I imagine the child is hungry."

I followed my mother out of the library, speaking to Alby in soothing tones. Mona came out of the kitchen, drying her hands on an apron, and whisked him away. It gave me a small pang to see him go, and I could only imagine what was going through his head. Harding would arrive in two days. Considering it was difficult for me to be separated from him even for short moments, I knew it must have been agony for the two of them.

~

Harding arrived with a bright smile and a fashionable dress, playing the role of my old boarding school friend with perfection. My parents welcomed her with many questions, delighted to hear that she'd enjoyed her stay the summer before and, of course, her time at boarding school with me.

When Mona walked in with Alby, my shoulders tensed, but Harding barely blinked. She peered down her nose at him as if he were a strange species of bird and declined to hold him when I offered.

"I don't know a thing about babies." She pushed up the sleeves of her dress. "I also fear he wouldn't be a good accessory for this dress."

My mother laughed, and the two of them spoke about gardening. I was so relieved to see Harding had won over my mother that I didn't dare calculate the number of lies quickly adding up.

My parents had given us permission to stay in the gardener's cottage, as we'd planned, to allow us some form of independence. I think my parents also approved because it would mean silence in the house. Alby wasn't a good sleeper, and I'd been awake with him often, pacing in the main hall at all hours of the night.

The moment Harding and I closed the cottage door, away from the eyes of my parents and the house staff, she pulled Alby to her breast and silently wept. I rested my hand on her shoulder as she fed him, understanding full well the pain the separation had brought.

"Are you okay?" I asked, quietly.

She squeezed her eyes tight against the tears.

The windows to the cottage were open due to the heat. There was little we could say for fear of being detected, but it was stunning to me how easily our story had been believed.

That sense of relief was put to the test a few days later, when Harding and I were playing with Alby in the grass on the side of the house. Perry, the main Garda in Kislee and the next village over, pulled up in his motorcar. Even though Perry was in charge of enforcing the laws, he sometimes shared whiskey with my father, so I'd never feared him. But Harding shrank back at the sight of him making his way to the front door with a bedraggled couple.

"They're here for Alby," she whispered.

"What?" I nearly strained my neck, trying to get a better look. "No, that couldn't . . ."

Harding let out a strangled sound as she pulled her son close. "I didn't even consider people might come forward to try and claim him as their own. They want a free boy, an extra hand on their farm."

"Go to the cottage," I told her. "Stay there, and if there's any reason to run, I'll find a way to make a loud sound, and you can sneak out through the woods."

Harding gave a grim nod and then swiftly walked across the lawn.

I rushed inside and through the back, to find my father looking incredibly annoyed, probably to have two people with dirt under their nails standing in his front door.

"Ah yes." He gave me a stern look. "Evie, the parents have been located. Please gather the child and his things."

"Excuse me, sir." I had been taught to speak to my father with respect and reverence, even though I felt like screaming. "We cannot simply give Alby away to any stranger who shows up at our front door." Turning to Perry, who had a face full of freckles that reminded me of Sullivan, I said, "I do hope that it's fair of me to ask them to describe exactly what the child was wearing and where they left him?"

The couple, who had been standing there in silence, exchanged glances. Finally, the man took a step forward.

"Ma'am, I don't mean to cause a bother, so I'd like to have my son and to go on my way." Gesturing toward his wife, he said, "She's not going to remember what she dressed him in, so there's no need for all of this."

"Could you be so kind as to tell me his name?" I asked.

"Alby," the man said.

My father must have spoken it before I'd arrived. Even though my stomach felt sick, I said, "Could I trouble you to spell his name?"

The man curled his lip. "You think I don't have an education because I spend my time toiling the land?"

Perry stepped forward. "I don't think it's necessary for him to—"

My father crossed his arms. "I do think my daughter makes a good point. He'd know how to spell the name of his son."

Perry sighed. "Let's have it, then."

"A-L-B-E-E," the man said.

"Excuse me," I said, feeling quite breathless. "I'll be back in just a moment."

The man looked triumphant, and his wife had an ugly smirk on her face.

I banged into the cottage, and Harding jumped. "Are they gone?"

"Not yet," I said, and I grabbed the dirt-smudged note that I'd hidden in the children's fairy tale book, alongside my bookmark. Racing back across the lawn, I caught my breath and smoothed my hair before walking back into the main room.

I handed the note to Perry and said, "I do believe there's been some mistake. I hope that this kind couple finds their son, but we don't have the child they're looking for."

Perry's face colored, and he shot a look at the man, who stuttered about the need to keep looking. He and his wife turned and were ushered out the front door. Perry returned to offer his apologies to my father, and I stepped forward.

"It's important for you to know that the baby was found with a very particular item of clothing on that no one would forget about," I told him. "Certainly, they should be able to describe it."

"Tell me what it is to save us the trouble next time," he said, pulling out a notebook and a pencil.

My father put his hand on my shoulder. "Go ahead."

"Typical baby clothes, but he also wore a pair of yellow knitted socks. They're unique. He has a small red mark on the back of his arm."

Perry made a note of it, then nodded at me. "Good day."

My father saw him out. When he returned, he considered me with something bordering on respect. "That was impressive," he said. "How did you know they were lying?"

I smoothed the skirt of my summer dress, hoping my hands weren't visibly shaking, even though I was shaken up inside. "Harding and I saw them walking up to the house. They looked like two people moving toward an opportunity rather than parents worried about a child. In addition, the clothing the baby was found in was quite clean, and their clothing was not, so I felt something was off."

"Well done," my father said, nodding. "Well done."

On the walk back to the cottage, my cheeks colored with the thought that I'd earned my father's praise for something that was a complete fabrication, especially since I rarely earned his regard. I let out a pent-up breath before walking back into the comforting smell of woodsmoke that was particular to the cottage. Harding was seated in the rocking chair, holding Alby close.

"Are they gone?" she asked.

When I nodded, she sat in silence for a long moment. Then she let out a string of profanities that made my cheeks color, ending it with, "You would have to be the scum on the bottom of someone's shoe to step forward and try and claim a child that was not your own!" She let out an angry breath. "How are we going to make sure this doesn't happen again?"

"It might," I said. "If it does, we will just do exactly what I did this time. I will ask for a description of what he was wearing."

"What if someone gets it right?" Harding whispered while chewing on her fingernails. She'd been so confident from the moment I'd met her, but not about this. The thought of losing Alby must have weighed on her each moment, and I fought to find the right words to give her comfort.

"They won't," I said. "It's impossible. The most important detail is that he was wearing the pair of yellow socks you'd knitted. No one could pull that out of thin air."

Harding threw her arms around me in relief, and I held her tight. The idea that someone had tried to take Alby was frightening. If I'd had to reveal to my parents that I'd lied to them, everything would have changed in an instant. We had to be careful, and we couldn't get caught.

~

With time, our days and nights became more relaxed: people had stopped coming forward to make a claim on a child who was not theirs to get an extra farmhand, and my parents accepted the idea that we would foster Alby for the remaining two months of summer.

One night at dinner, my father said, "You will return to university. I want to be clear about that."

"Yes, of course," I said. "If the mother doesn't come forward, Alby will go to the orphanage in the fall."

My parents looked at each other, and my mother gave a slight nod.

Harding took a bite of soup. "He'll really be here the whole summer?" she complained.

"This child is helpless, Harding. I'd like to offer him love and support, as long as I have the chance."

"You're a better person than I am," she mumbled, and my mother hid a smile.

The only one who knew the reality of the situation was Sullivan. He came to visit a week after Harding arrived, a brown-paper-wrapped parcel in his hands. Harding and I had been playing croquet on the back lawn while Alby slept in a wickerwork cradle.

"I heard you had a young one," he said.

Our eyes met briefly, and he gave me a quick nod, as if to acknowledge that we had nothing to fear from him. I nodded back, grateful for the kindness.

Sullivan had become even more broad in the shoulders and handsome around his eyes. More and more, I'd started to entertain the possibility that perhaps, all that I needed was right here, in this village, in my town. I could marry Sullivan, and he would understand my purpose in visiting America.

"It's so nice to see my two favorite ladies," he said. "And now, my favorite little boy." He dropped to his haunches, waving at Alby. "I brought you a present."

He started to hand the gift-wrapped package to Harding, but quick as lightning, she passed it to me.

"Evie is the baby lover," she said, loudly. "I'll let her be in charge."

Sullivan nodded. The three of us sat in the shade with the baby. The grass on the lawn was bright green, and beyond the bluff, the sea was a deep blue. Clouds dotted the sky, fresh and light, and a gentle breeze wafted the scent of grass and flowers. I memorized the moment, enjoying every second of sitting with the three people in the world who knew me the most. Then I unwrapped the brown paper.

"Sullivan," I breathed. "This is wonderful."

He had gifted Alby a small toy soldier doll made of cloth, perfectly detailed in every way, and a small silver-plated rattle that must have set him back at least a week's wages.

I didn't dare look at Harding for fear we'd start to cry. Instead, I brought the toy soldier to Alby and held it over him to see if he'd be interested. He was drowsy, his eyes only half-opened, but when he saw the doll, his face split into a smile. After wiggling it around for a moment, I placed it on his chest for him to hold and snuggle with.

"This isn't the summer the two of you expected," Sullivan said.

"No." I looked at Alby. "Yet it will definitely be the best summer of our lives."

Chapter Sixteen

Ireland, present day

The drive from the storage unit in a truck was just as scenic as the drive to the storage unit on Grady's motorbike, which he said he'd retrieve later today. The truck had to be from the eighties, with rough shocks, but we rolled down the windows, and I felt my hair whipping around my face. I hung my arm out the window, the sun warming it, and drank in the incredible scenery.

We saw a lot of cattle, but we also spotted sheep up on the hillside. I'd seen them on the way and wondered why so many had colors painted into their wool.

"Is someone vandalizing the sheep?" I pointed at one of the flocks. Some were pink and others blue. "Or is it to identify gender or something? To start the dyeing process before you sheer them?"

"Strong guesses, all of them," he said with a smile. "It's a way to identify the flock. The different colors keep them straight, because without keeping the sheep enclosed, they naturally mix together. Then it's hard to tell what sheep belongs to what flock."

"Huh." I gazed out at them, noticing a few different colors.

"They're registered, counted . . . it's big business, sheep. Not as much as it used to be, but it's still important to the economy. In areas where people can't have an ag farm because the land isn't good enough, they can still raise sheep."

Grady squinted in the sun and reached in his shirt pocket for a pair of sunglasses. They were aviators, mirrored, and he looked so attractive in them that I forgot all about the sheep. Instead, I kept sneaking looks at him, wishing the ride would never end.

Once we'd arrived at Aisling, he backed the truck right up to the front porch, loaded the trunk on a dolly, and wheeled it up the ramp. We walked together to the elevator and then to my room.

My grandmother wasn't there, and for a second, it felt a little intimate having Grady standing next to my bed. His eyes met mine, and I had a feeling he was thinking the same thing.

"Well, thanks for your help," I said. "It was nice of you to spend your day doing that."

He shrugged. "Nothing like a picnic in a park with a pretty girl."

He probably didn't mean much by it, but I still blushed.

Nora was in the hall when we walked down the stairs. "How did it go?"

"We found them." I held up the plastic bag. "They were in the trunk, labeled from the remodel. I'm so glad the workers didn't throw them out."

"Me too. I made it clear to the workers to set aside anything they found. Now, I can't take credit for the other items in the trunk. They were kept by the family who bought the property from your grandmother. I think they said they'd tried to communicate with her, but she never came to pick them up, so they left them when they moved."

"Where is she?" I asked. "I'm excited to have her take a look at these."

Nora led me to the back window and pointed at the lawn. "I set her up out there a couple of hours ago, and she has not wanted to come back in. Her appetite is good—I got her some more cabbage stew from the pub—but most important, her spirits are high."

"Thank you," I said. "You're very good at your job."

"Oh, I don't think of it as a job. I think of it as a joy."

It had been quite some time since I'd thought in those terms about my job back in Chicago. Tia and I had started the business because we were passionate about science and discovering new things, but this year, her father had really pushed us to focus on bringing the product to market. I looked forward to getting past all that and spending more time in the lab.

Nora bustled off, and Grady, who had left to load up the dolly, came back in. I was glad to see him, because I'd figured he'd just left without saying goodbye.

"I hope your grandmother enjoys the letters."

"Thanks again for your help today," I said.

He gave my shoulder a gentle squeeze. "I'll be seeing you."

I walked him out to the porch, noting the easy way he moved. When he got to the truck, he turned back and smiled again before getting behind the wheel.

It had been a good day. I hadn't spent that much time with a guy in ages, and I appreciated his perspective. That fact alone was probably what made me blush each time his eyes met mine, but I was already hoping for another chance to see him again.

Letting out a breath, I headed back to the lawn.

"Hi," I said, kneeling next to my grandmother's chair. "Did you have a good day?"

"It was like time travel." Her faded eyes were bright. "Out here, it looks the same, smells the same, and even the bugs sound the same. I'm the only thing that's different. Well, and them, of course." She indicated the handful of people out on the lawn, some playing croquet and others sitting beneath a gazebo, reading. "It's as if strangers invaded my home," she whispered, "but if I turn my head and look out at the water, they disappear. I actually used to do that a lot when I was younger, because my parents would have houseguests for weeks at a time." She patted my hands. "Did you find them?"

"Yes." I presented her with the bag of letters. "If these are them."

My grandmother pulled one out. Her face softened, and she handed them to me. "Yes. Will you—"

"Of course."

She leaned back against the chair, closed her eyes, and waited. I settled in to the grass and began to read.

~

For the first few letters, my grandmother sat back and listened. I couldn't tell if she was affected by them at all. Perhaps she regretted coming all this way to hear them. Then, as I continued to read, I realized she was listening intently, and beginning to get upset.

There were moments when she twisted the sleeve of her shirt, shook her head, and, once, put her hand to her chest as if in pain. After I'd finished the seventh letter, I set it in the stack and said, "You doing okay?"

My grandmother started, as though surprised to hear my voice in the present time. Resting her hand on her face, she said, "I didn't know it would feel like this."

"What do you mean?" I asked.

"Time heals. That's what we're told. Forgiveness heals." She lifted her palms. "I was so sure time would give me perspective, but the hurt is still there. The anger."

"The love?" I dared to ask, and she closed her eyes tight.

"Yes," she said, softly. "There is most certainly the love."

I sat with the weight of the letters in my lap. The sea was blue in the distance, the wind painting the air with the smell of coconut from the gorse. My grandmother's shoulders were hunched, and it hit me that one day, long after she was gone, I'd want to step back into this moment with her.

"Grandma," I said, and she looked at me. "Thank you for bringing me here to do this with you. For letting me in."

"You're welcome. I haven't done that, really. It's been hard on your mother that I've never talked much about my life." She gave a slight cough and reached for the limoncello water sitting by her chair. "I kept thinking that I would."

I waited to see if she'd say more. When she didn't, I said, "Would you like me to keep reading?"

She stared out at the water. "Perhaps two more. I'm tired, Rainey. I didn't expect this to make me feel so tired."

I took out the next one and began to read. It was a happier one, and a series of emotions passed over my grandmother's face. Delight, wistfulness, then tears. I handed her a napkin, and she dabbed at her eyes.

Once I'd read both, she motioned for me to keep going. "I need to hear them. I want to hear them all."

I kept reading, deep into the afternoon, after everyone had already headed off for cocktails or dinner. I reached the last letter and realized we were the only two left on the lawn.

"This is it," I warned, holding it up.

Carefully, she wiped her nose. "Yes. I know."

> My precious darling,
> You don't start loving someone because it will last forever. You love someone because, despite the fear that one day it will end, you are unable to do anything else.
> Now that you are gone, my heart is empty. You've been taken from me, but you will always be a part of me. My love for you will live on in every breath, and I hope you know that I will never stop thinking of you.
> I love you, my darling. Always.

My grandmother stared out at the water. Her eyes were bright.

I hoped that the idea of slipping back through time could help her now. That, as she stared out to the sea, her mind could go to another place. One where she could go back to such pure joy, her arms holding tight to the man she had once loved.

Chapter Seventeen

I was on my way to the dry goods shop when I happened upon Sullivan. He was halfway down the path that led to my house, dressed in a button-up shirt and carrying a bouquet of wildflowers. I stopped suddenly, confused.

He took off his cap and smiled at me. "Hello, Evie."

"What are you doing out here?" I asked. "Shouldn't you be working?"

I'd been on my way to see him. Well, I was headed to purchase some items at the store, but I'd been looking forward to admiring all those freckles sprinkled across his nose like cinnamon sugar.

Sullivan gave a sharp nod. "I have the day off, and I came out here to see if you would be interested in walking with me." The words came out of his mouth as though they'd been rehearsed, and I squeezed my hands tightly as I considered my answer.

He wanted to walk with me. Did I want to walk with Sullivan? It scared me to take that next step, especially given the way I'd felt about him that day he'd brought Alby gifts. We'd been friends for so long, but I didn't know that I was ready to make promises that I might not keep.

Lately, I'd been thinking about what I wanted to do with my life. My connection with Alby had left me thinking about actual orphans. The children who had been abandoned due to the lack of resources or the shame brought upon their mothers. Surely, there must be a way to help them? It wasn't something I'd be able to do in a place as small as this, but it was a new thought, one that had started to take shape somewhere in the back of my mind.

Evidently noting my hesitation, Sullivan said, "Things are changing in our lives. I know that. I'm not asking you for more—not now, at least. I'd just like to walk with you." My cheeks flushed, and he handed me the bouquet of flowers. "These are for you."

"Thank you." I held them tight, then said, "Where shall we walk to?"

It all felt so formal. Different from running up to greet one another when we were kids.

"Do you still have an interest in butterflies?" he asked.

A smile tugged at the corners of my mouth. "Of course."

~

Sullivan led me a few farms over—toward a newer property that I was not familiar with—and gave me a big smile as something sweet wafted our way. It was lovely, and I'd smelled it before but couldn't place it.

"What is that?" I asked.

"Come see," he said, leading me down the path and around the corner. There, I stopped in surprise. The entire field was planted with lavender.

I'd smelled it before, because it was in one of my mother's perfumes, and the scent had always appealed to me. Closing my eyes, I took in a deep breath. When I opened them, Sullivan was watching me as though entranced.

We looked at each other for a long moment before he cleared his throat. "My parents gave me this plot of land to do what I wanted," he said, and he walked toward the endless display of rough purple flowers. "It didn't feel right to do much other than crops for some time, but now, there's enough food to go around, at least around here. I'd plow this land right up if anyone needed me to, but for now, I think this is wonderful."

"It is," I said. "I'm mesmerized."

He smiled at me. "We have that in common, then."

My cheeks went hot, and I turned my attention to a bright-orange butterfly, then a yellow one, then white. They were everywhere, and I stopped walking, to stand and watch as they darted around us amid the steady hum of the bees.

"What do you plan to do with the lavender?" I asked.

"Sell it in the store," he said. "As a home fragrance or decoration. With time, I do think it will draw an interest. If not, I think it's certainly something to feast the eyes on, don't you?"

He held out his finger, and a butterfly landed on it. "Come here," he said. "Hold out your hand."

Cautiously, I moved toward him, and the butterfly crawled onto my finger. I'd never thought to catch one before, and I stared at its delicate body in wonder. The wings were fragile, but its legs seemed so strong. With a flutter, it flew away.

Sullivan and I spent nearly an hour walking through the lavender fields, catching butterflies and telling stories. Finally, we sat next to the field under a tree, and he handed me a piece of peppermint.

"Things are better with Harding now?" he asked.

"You tell me," I said.

"She hasn't been involved for some time. Did she tell you that?"

I nodded. The peppermint was cool in my mouth.

"She's a great girl, Evie. The way she loves her child." He looked at me. "I want you to know that I feel that way."

Our eyes met, and he gave a slight nod.

"Thank you," I said, quietly.

I was grateful that he'd accepted Harding. More than that, it meant everything that he knew that it mattered.

Getting to my feet, I said, "Well, this was a delightful day, Sullivan O'Leary."

His fingers brushed against mine for the briefest of moments, and my pulse skipped.

Holding my gaze, he said, "I hope we can have many more, just like it."

~

That evening, something was on Harding's mind. Perhaps it was the time I'd spent with Sullivan, but I wouldn't speak to that unless she brought it up. She'd seemed lost in thought for most of the day, and then, once an evening rain shower cooled the night, she shut the windows of the cottage. Alby was finally sleeping soundly in his cradle, and she beckoned for me to join her at the kitchen table.

"We need to discuss two things." Her gaze was frank. "One, I need to know that, if something should happen to me, you will find the money I've set aside. It's for Alby."

My shoulders tensed. "Harding, nothing's going to happen to you."

"Yes, I know that." Her eyes looked tired. Alby had not been sleeping, and she'd been awake with him all hours. "Yet, if something did happen, I need your word that my efforts have not gone to waste. I want to provide a good future for him."

"I don't . . ." The tension in my shoulders became heavy.

I looked around the room. The candles were lit, creating a yellow halo of light that made me feel warm and connected to Harding, in spite of the dark shadows in the unlit corners of the room.

"The money is a burden, Harding," I said. "It's what's forced you to hide. I don't want to hide."

"No one will know that you have it," she said. "You have no idea where it is now, and I'm not going to tell you. That way, you can say with the utmost confidence that you don't know, if someone were to ask."

The very idea made me shudder. I could imagine that the type of person who would ask wouldn't be someone I'd want anything to do with.

"However," she said, "I'll leave the answer somewhere for you. It won't be simple to find, but you will be able to figure it out, if you look hard enough."

I wasn't so confident, but I nodded. Truly, there was only so much I dared to know.

"What if the people who want it have tracked you here?" I looked toward the windows. Outside, the branches of the trees stretched up toward the sky like weary bones.

"I'm sure several people know exactly where I am." She laid her hand over mine. "It will not put you at risk. No one will bother me while others are around. It would do them no good. Thanks to you and your family, I feel safe here."

I swallowed over the lump in my throat.

It had been easy to pretend that there was no risk other than Alby, but I couldn't help wondering what would happen if the people who wanted her money came to our home, wielding weapons and demanding it. Logically, I knew that wouldn't happen. The Garda would step in, and those people would be arrested, just as they would if they tried to rob anyone in the village. Still, the idea made me nervous.

I fiddled with the pink and white wildflowers Sullivan had given me, brushing a small speck from the Queen Anne's lace.

"The other thing I need to speak to you about is a bit more difficult." Harding put her hand to her forehead and looked over to the crib where Alby soundly slept. "You and I spoke before about how, if anything were to happen to me, you would care for Alby. That you would watch over him."

I nodded. "Yes."

"I didn't mean that you would be sure he made it safely to an orphanage. I meant that I want you to raise him as your own. As your child."

"Harding, this type of talk is scaring me," I said, getting to my feet. "Look, if you feel you're in danger here, we'll leave; we'll run. We won't stay here if someone could take you from me. We'll run and hide instead."

Alby let out a small sound, and we both looked over at him. He looked so small and fragile in the dim light.

"Evie, it's a simple thing." She sounded impatient. "Tell me you'll keep him safe."

"I cannot." My fear was that if I spoke the words out loud, the idea that something would happen to her would come true. "I refuse to say yes to the idea that something would hurt you."

"Then you're not the friend that I thought you were."

With sure steps, she got up from the table, scooped the baby from his crib, and left the cottage. I watched as she stalked across the lawn, standing on the bluff as she looked out over the sea. Probably wishing she were away from here. From this. From me.

I wanted to offer comfort, but my fear of losing her was too great. I couldn't picture a world without Harding in it. Tears streaming down my face, I lay in bed facing the wall, the darkness of the night as quiet as a tomb.

~

Harding refused to speak to me the next morning. It angered me that her frustration had interfered with the idyllic life we'd been living. The silent glances, the stubborn shape of her shoulders, and the sense that I had somehow done her wrong.

Finally, after lunch, when Alby was down for his nap, I said, "We cannot go on like this. I love Alby as if he were my own. I simply cannot bear the idea that anything could happen to you. Surely, you know that."

Harding was sitting by the window, knitting another pair of socks. Setting them down, she regarded me. "I'm afraid, Evie. Every day, my stomach is twisted in the deepest, darkest sense of fear. If I don't know he will be cared for, all I can think is, 'What will he do if I'm gone?'"

Even though it hurt to imagine a world without Harding, I realized it was hurting her more to think that her child could be on his own.

"I understand," I said, quietly. "Then I swear on my life that I will protect your child until my dying day."

Her eyes filled with tears. "You give me your word?"

"Yes." I gripped her hand tight. "I give you my word. He will be my son."

~

The weeks passed, and we settled in to a joyful routine. Breakfast in the main house, playtime with Alby, followed by a feeding, then a nap. While he rested, Harding and I would spend our time practicing piano, talking, or reading the paper, before he woke for more play, followed by lunch.

During the afternoon, we stayed out on the back lawn. We only took walks along the moor when Sullivan was free to join us, and out there, I was the only one who ever held the baby. When we sat, Sullivan would sometimes hold my hand for brief moments.

One afternoon on the lawn, Harding gave a sudden frown and patted at her chest.

"What is it?" I asked.

She lowered her voice, and I moved in close to hear her. "It's nearly time for Alby to nurse. Nothing is there. I fear my milk supply is drying up."

Harding had secretly fed Alby once or twice during the day to keep her supply going, but it was impossible for her to do so too often, or Mona would have become suspicious.

"It could run out during the night," she said, sounding nervous.

"If it does, we will use the idea the doctor gave us," I said. "With the milk and sugar. It will be fine."

Harding seemed unsettled but turned her attention back to Alby. It was one of those beautiful afternoons. Sun shone down through the trees, making them even more green than usual. We had a small red ball that Alby loved. We'd roll it to him, and he'd laugh in delight and kick his feet to let us know he wanted us to do it again.

I was startled to see Sullivan walk into the yard, looking clean shaven and fresh. He was so handsome and so kind. Getting to my feet, I smiled up at him.

"This is a nice surprise," I said.

"Well, it will be," he said. "I've come to walk Harding to town. She has some special items to acquire."

The sudden sense of betrayal made my vision blur. Even though I didn't want my future to be here, I'd taken comfort in the idea that it was a possibility. My pride struggled to think that Sullivan had been interested in Harding the entire time.

"Oh." I swallowed hard. "Well, I hope the two of you enjoy the day."

Sullivan smiled. "We'll be discussing you, so I can't think of anything nicer."

The two of them exchanged glances. Suddenly, I understood.

"Harding!" My mouth dropped open. "I told you not to make a fuss."

My nineteenth birthday was the next day. My parents had never seemed that interested in celebrating my birth, but back when I was a child, Fedelma had sometimes seen to it that I had the opportunity to eat cake. I'd once mentioned that to Harding during one of those spring nights where we'd discussed our lives. She was aghast that I'd never had a birthday party and insisted that this year, I'd have a full celebration.

It was shocking to me that, with everything that was going on, she had remembered. Harding squeezed my hands tightly.

"Take care of Alby while I'm gone," she said.

"Well, of course."

Harding gathered him up, kissing him until he giggled, then placed him in my arms. "Love you," she called, then set off across the yard with Sullivan.

I brought Alby to the main house. Even though Harding and I took most of our meals there, occasionally with my parents but mostly without, it often felt as though I'd been absent from my home for quite some time.

Walking in, I called, "Hello?"

I wasn't sure whether my parents were home or out. They were gearing up to travel soon, another trip to Argentina after I returned to university, so they'd been busy making preparations. It had been comforting to have them home for several weeks, and I hoped it wouldn't be too stressful when they left, with only Seamus and the cook to watch over us.

Mona bustled into the main area, wiping her hands on an apron. "I'll take the child," she said, with her friendly smile.

I handed him to her and looked out the front window. The day was getting to be hot, and I wondered what Sullivan and Harding were planning on their walk into town.

It concerned me to have Harding go out without me, but at the same time, Sullivan wouldn't let anything happen to her. I sat next to the window, threading a needle to finish darning a pair of socks. The string slipped through the eye on the first try, and I felt a sense of satisfaction as the needle flashed like a silverfish, binding the fabric with ease.

The clock in the hallway gave a deep and resonant chime. Mona returned with Alby, and I set down the socks to hold him close. He nestled into me, content and warm.

There was a sudden shout, and I jumped, startling Alby into tears. The front door banged shut, and through the window, I saw my father racing toward the motorcar shed.

My heart clutched with the thought that something had happened to Harding. My mother's voice rang through the house.

"Evie! Quickly, dear." She was running down the stairs as I emerged from the sitting room with Alby in my arms.

"What is it?" I asked.

The household staff rushed out from the back rooms, looking worried.

"Miss?" Seamus said.

My mother kept one eye on the window and spoke in a brisk tone. "There has been talk of an attack for months. My husband believes it is happening now. Go to your families, lock the doors, and be prepared to fight."

"Is it the Germans, miss?" Mona asked, her hand to her chest.

"No, the nationalists. Filled with fury and vinegar." My father pulled up in front of the house, and my mother moved to the door. "Evie, come. We must leave."

My breath caught. "We can't. Not without Harding."

My mother grabbed my elbow. Her strength surprised me as she guided me to the door. "We must get out quickly, or we might not get out at all."

"No." My voice came out as a strangled cry. "I can't—"

"Think of the child." My mother was firm in a way that I'd never seen. She didn't look scared, but incredibly focused. "We cannot put him at risk."

"Please," I begged.

My father leaped out and opened the car doors. I held Alby close and didn't want to get in. Not without Harding.

"I will not leave you here." My mother's gaze was hard as steel. "Get in."

"Let me leave a note," I begged. "I have to tell her where we've gone."

"There is no time," she said.

I heard a series of bangs in the distance, coming from the village. My father looked grim. "They're here."

I thought of my mother's words—about protecting Alby—and I got in. My father drove quickly. Smoke rose up from the direction of the village, and Alby began to cry once again. I thought of the early days in the cottage, the peace on Harding's face as she nursed him.

"We have to bring Mona," I gasped. "The baby can't eat."

My father said an unsavory word, then stopped the car and shouted for Mona. She hesitated but then waved him off as she rushed down the road. I knew she was thinking of her own children.

"It's all right," my mother said, leaning back against the seat. The lines around her eyes were tense. "We'll give him milk and sugar. He'll be all right."

My father drove fast and with surprising proficiency. I stared out the window, terrified for Harding, our village, and Sullivan.

"What do they want?" I asked. "Why are they here?"

"Members of the British aristocracy have quietly been buying up a section of land near the sea for years," my mother said. "Word got out, and there have been threats of riots, but this afternoon, your father received word that the homes built there would be attacked. Some burned down. The extreme sect of the nationalists will attack any institution affiliated with British rule."

"Like the church," my father said, his voice grim. "They're here to destroy it."

The Protestant church that overlooked the sea had been there as long as I could remember, but the majority of those in town were Catholic, like us, and attended Mass at Our Lady of the Sea.

"The danger is that once you have a mob intent to destroy, it will take anything that gets in its way," my mother said.

"Then why did we let them buy up that land?" I demanded. "It belongs to Ireland. It's no wonder the nationalists are angry, that there's unrest."

My mother looked at me in surprise. "There are diplomatic ways to solve disagreements that don't center on violence."

"I agree with you," I said. "But surely, the British must have seen that by doing this, the extremists would tear down everything in their way—"

"No one expects violence," my father said. "However, we must do our best to prepare for it."

I stared at him. "You expected it, though. Surely, you have people in place to protect the power grid. You should have warned me that this could have happened."

My parents exchanged glances but didn't speak. The conversation was over.

I held Alby close to my breast, breathing fast, determined to keep him protected. He nuzzled against me, looking for food. "He's hungry," I said, before realizing that Mona had recently fed him.

The responsibility of caring for Alby through this, while unable to tell Harding where we were, made me feel sick inside. I stared out the window, at the green grass blowing in the wind.

"How far will we travel?" I finally asked my father. "I'm truly worried for Harding. We shouldn't have left her there."

"We had no choice," my mother said. "Sullivan will see to it that she's safe."

"To Cork," my father said. "We'll stay with friends there."

He focused on the road in front of us. My mother was quiet and tense by my side. There were several wagons also headed out of town. I worried about hitting a barricade, whether it be sheep or rebels. I breathed in the strong scent of motor oil, and my head started to hurt. Alby snuggled deeper into my arms, and I slid my finger into his mouth, which he sucked gently.

I hoped that Harding could somehow hear my thoughts. Know that he was safe. I could only imagine the terror she must have felt being in the center of that, desperate to get back to the house, like that day in Dublin. Only this time, I was not by her side.

My mother's eyes were on me. "You're attached to him, aren't you?" she said, nodding at Alby.

"Yes." I pulled him close. "I sometimes feel as if he's my own."

The Gardas had the riot under control within hours, but my parents insisted on staying away for at least three days, to ensure that nothing additional would take place. I sent a telegram to let Harding know the time and date of our return but did not dare mention Alby for fear someone at the post office would catch on.

Harding replied back:

GOOD STOP ALL WELL HERE STOP

I could only imagine the grief she felt, and how much she missed holding her child. For me, our return could not happen soon enough, although Alby had done well. He had thrived on the milk mixture, slept well, and fussed little, but I couldn't shake the unease I felt with Harding on her own.

The morning of our return, Sullivan was waiting on the front porch when we pulled up. I was relieved to see him. My father stopped the car, and Sullivan came forward to open the doors and help us. Once I stepped out, though, his expression turned grave.

"What is it?" I asked.

Perhaps our home had been damaged. My father had said that a few of the places in town had broken windows and that the Protestant church had briefly been set on fire.

I looked down to adjust Alby's blanket, and my mother said, "Sullivan?" She seemed alarmed, and quickly, I looked up to find his chin was trembling.

My stomach dropped. "What is it?"

His eyes met mine, and I knew. In the sudden slowing of my heart, the sudden thickness of my thoughts. The loneliness that had haunted me since the moment I'd left her side.

My mouth felt too dry, and I pulled Alby close. Taking a step forward, I tried to whisper, but the words would barely come. "Sullivan, no."

So weak and pointless. My plea couldn't stop the rhythm of time, but I prayed I could find the right beat. That Sullivan's eyes would widen, and he'd be quick to tell me no, I'd misunderstood. That I should look up, the sun was still shining.

Instead, he cleared his throat. The shadows stretched long on the lawn.

"I'm so sorry. I know this will hurt you more than anyone." His eyes flicked to Alby, and my blood went cold.

"Please," I whispered. "No."

"It's Harding," he managed to say. "She's dead."

Chapter Eighteen

Ireland, present day

Once my grandmother had eaten dinner and gone to bed, I got on my computer and caught up on work. The evidence I'd submitted had resulted in approval for an expedited appeal, so now I was in the process of resubmitting all the necessary forms and coordinating a date with our intern to send out a new sample of the serum. Tia wouldn't even notice, as we sent out samples for testing all the time, so I felt optimistic that I'd have good news soon.

It was dark by the time I went back outside, and I walked to the edge of the bluff, breathing in the sea air. It left the slightest tinge of salt in my mouth, and I relished in the taste and the sensation of the cold air on my face. I headed over to the chair my grandmother had spent the day in and took a seat before dialing my mother.

I'd thought a lot about what Grady had said, about how I was here on her behalf, and I wanted to share what was going on. It was Saturday, so she didn't have classes and would have some time to talk.

"Hello?" She sounded slightly breathless.

"Hi," I said. "What are you doing? Playing tennis?"

"I just finished the biking trail at Frick. How's it going over there?"

I could imagine her drinking coconut water to rehydrate, then hooking her blue ten-speed to the back rack on her Subaru before heading home to shower. That had been her routine for years, so it surprised me when she said, "I'm here with Jake, so I can't talk for long."

"Jake?" I echoed. It took me a minute to remember where I'd heard that name. "Isn't that the guy who writes the signs in the break room?"

My mother laughed. "Turns out he's pretty funny. He likes to bike the trail on the weekends, too, so we decided to make a day of it."

Did she say "date" or "day"? I didn't mind either way; my grandmother and I had been telling her for years to get back out there, since my father had remarried right after their divorce. I just hadn't expected it to happen at this particular moment in time.

"Okay," I said. "Well, there's a lot going on, and it's pretty heavy." I half wished I'd grabbed a glass of wine on my way out. "Should I call you later to tell you about it?"

"Tell me now," she said. "He went to get us smoothies. It took forever the other day, so we should have time."

So, this was not a first date, which meant Jake might be able to offer emotional support if she needed it.

Letting out a breath, I said, "There's a lot. I'll start with the part that's a little disturbing—Grandma's parents were murdered after she left Ireland."

"What?" My mother sounded shocked. "Why?"

"I don't know yet." I stared at the outline of the sea, not quite knowing how to tell her about the money or the love letters. "I've heard a few rumors about some things—"

"Like what?"

I sighed. "One rumor is that Grandma took some money, and when the people came to get it, they murdered her parents."

My mother went silent.

"You still there?" I asked.

"Yes, I'm . . ." I could picture her shaking her head, trying to puzzle it out. "That doesn't sound like Grandma. I don't know what to say about that."

"I know," I said. "There's another part. Apparently, her parents helped a lot of people here in the village. Once her parents died, everyone had to fend for themselves. Some lost their farms, and others emigrated to England. So there's still some negative sentiment, like the whole thing was Grandma's fault, even though she'd moved to the States long before it happened."

A mosquito flew toward the light from my phone, and I brushed it away.

"What does Grandma say about it all?" my mother asked.

"I haven't talked to her about it yet," I said. "I will, but I also found the letters. They mean a lot to her. I read them to her earlier this afternoon."

"That was faster than we expected. Wait, hold on." I heard a voice in the background, and the phone rustled. My mom came back on the line and said, "Hey, I want to know more about all of this, but I need to run. Do you think I can go ahead and book your return flight? If you have the letters, you should bring her home. I don't like how this other stuff sounds. She doesn't need to deal with that, not at this point in her life."

"I know, but I think she wants to be here." I thought of how happy she'd been sitting in her old backyard. "Let me talk to her, okay? I'll call you when it's your morning."

My mother paused, and I realized she and Jake might be more serious than I thought.

"Why don't you call me?" I said, quickly. "We'll talk then."

"Tell her I love her."

Once we'd hung up, I sat in silence. The day had certainly gotten the best of me. So many emotions, and my body was still thrown off by the time change.

I decided to find that wine I'd been thinking about, in the hope that it would help me sleep, and headed inside. The kitchen was dark, but it was probably fine to poke through the icebox. My heart nearly stopped when I flipped on the lights to find Grady sitting on the blue-tiled island, sipping on what appeared to be whiskey. He still wore his green shirt, and his eyes smoldered in the low light.

"What are you doing?" I said, hand to my chest.

He squinted at the lights. "Turn those off, and I'll show you."

Curious, I flipped them off.

"Come here," he said.

Hearing his voice in the dark was much too appealing. I took careful steps, and when I got to him, his hand gently steadied my shoulder.

"Look," he said.

I wasn't quite sure what he meant, but then I saw it. Moths playing in the light from the gas lamp outside the window, leaving an ethereal glow in their wake. It was hypnotic and infinitely beautiful.

Ice clinked in Grady's glass as he took a drink, and the sultry notes of peat moss and vanilla wafted my way.

"How did it go with the letters?" he asked.

The sound of his voice was so easy. Rough and relaxed, with that beautiful lilt.

My eyes had adjusted, and I could see him in the darkness, studying me. "Good. I hope it gave her what she was looking for, but to me, it felt sad. The fact that they didn't end up together . . . I don't know why she'd want to relive all that, but maybe it was a door that she needed to close."

I watched the moths float near the light, their wings bright and fragile.

"There has to be something behind it," he agreed. "She wouldn't come all this way without a purpose."

I stood in silence, and he hopped down from the counter. "I'm being a terrible host. What do you need?"

"I'd like a glass of wine," I said. "White, if she has it."

The sauvignon blanc he poured was dry and crisp, exactly how I liked it. We clinked glasses, and he hopped back up on the counter.

The moths were still darting around, and I was entranced. I hoped he wouldn't mind if I stayed.

"Do you spend a lot of time here?" I asked.

"In the kitchen?"

"No, Aisling," I said, leaning against the edge of the counter.

"I live on the property," he said.

I thought of last night, when I'd gone out in a robe to call my mother. I was glad I hadn't bumped into him then.

"Do you help manage it or something?" I asked.

He grinned. "I'm the handyman."

That made sense, in some ways. Even though he was a nice guy, there was no reason for him to spend so much time helping his sister. It was also a little disappointing, because I'd half hoped he'd taken me to the storage unit because he was interested in me. Silly, but it was hard not to be attracted to someone as kind and intriguing as he was.

"Oh." I was unsure which direction to take the conversation. Away from personal things, since today was about him doing his job. "How long ago did she buy the property?"

He hesitated. "Well, Aisling went on the market about ten years ago. There was a family, the McDougals, who first bought it back in the late fifties. They lived here for years. This was always a place that Nora and I coveted, you know? Our family was poor and lived out in the country, so when we'd come into town, this was the house we wanted to own."

"And she did it," I said.

"The bed-and-breakfast thing was certainly her idea." His ice clinked again as he took a drink; then he set the glass on the counter. "I'd pictured it as a family home to raise tens of thousands of kids, but my wife wasn't interested, so it all worked out."

"You're married?"

The words came out disappointed, and I flushed.

"No," he said. "Not anymore."

I took a sip of wine. "What happened?" I held up my hand. "Sorry, that was rude. You don't have to—"

"It's fine." He studied the moths. "Do you want to join me up here?"

I'd been leaning against the counter, but at his invitation, I climbed up next to him, the tile cold through the thin fabric of my cargo pants. The view of the moths outside the window was even better than on the ground, and my shoulders relaxed for the first time all day.

He clinked his glass to mine.

"I got married right out of university," he said. "She was from a good family, one of those upper-crust types I'd wanted to be like my whole life." There wasn't a hint of bitterness in his tone, and I took another sip of wine, letting its cool sweetness linger on my tongue. "We stayed in Dublin, and her father connected me with a brilliant job in finance. I spent sixteen-hour days at the office, studying the markets, projecting where they were going to move, and advising clients from the United States to Tokyo about what to do with their money." He shrugged. "I was really good at it. I'm good with patterns and numbers, but it took over my life. I didn't have the time to be married. I wanted to give her that lifestyle she'd grown up with but missed the part where she wanted attention, more. She found someone who would give it to her."

"I'm sorry," I said.

"Yeah." He thought for a moment. "If we'd met now, I don't think we would have held each other's interest. We were too young. She's a good one, so I'm glad she found the right guy."

"That's when you moved back here?" I asked.

"No, that's when I became the vice president of the financial firm, worked day and night, and promptly had a heart attack."

The kitchen suddenly felt much too quiet.

"Didn't see that one coming," I said.

"You and me both." He took another drink. "It wasn't enough to kill me, but it scared the living piss out of me, and now, I'm on a self-imposed hiatus. Well, not *self*-imposed. The cardiologist explained that if I didn't completely change my lifestyle, I wouldn't make it to forty. Not exactly what you want to hear when you're at the peak of everything."

"Not what you'd want to hear ever." I took a sip of wine, trying to imagine that type of warning.

"To be honest, this is a pace I prefer. Because I'd like to make it to forty, fifty, sixty, seventy, and so on."

"You *are* good at numbers," I said, and he laughed. "That must have been hard, though."

In the dim light, his eyes met mine. "It was. Mainly because I was so used to the way I was living that I never thought to ask myself if I was happy. Not even when Shana left. I was so caught up in achieving." He grimaced. "Back then, I don't think I would have cared too much for this laid-back version of me."

"Do you now?" I asked.

"Tough question." He stared out the window, and I shifted my position on the counter to get a better look at him. "What about you?"

"I co-own a product research and development lab."

Grady nodded. "Do you enjoy that?"

"Tough question," I said, and he nodded.

It was, though. The past few years of my life felt like a mountain of stress, fear, and a promise that when I got to the finish line, everything would be all right. But what finish line? Once our product made it to market, then I'd have the work that came along with that, which had nothing to do with what I was interested in. Yes, I'd get back in the lab, but the facial serum would always be first.

Looking at Grady, I said, "I don't love what I do."

It was the first time I'd said it out loud, but I missed the science. I had moments where my mind actually filtered through the memory of what it felt like to examine slides under a microscope. The rhythmic documentation of information. Studying the discrepancies, patterns, or secrets waiting to be discovered. There was so much to uncover, so many worlds to explore.

"Science is my greatest passion," I told him. "It's only when I think of the actual business part that I feel overwhelmed. There was a time where I was so set on my career path. I knew exactly what I was going to do, but—"

"Which was what?" Grady asked.

"Lab work. I loved it. I could spend hours analyzing samples, comparing data, documenting it . . . before I knew it, the day was done."

"So why do the business?" he asked.

"It seemed smart at the time. So many companies were on a hiring freeze when I graduated, so it was a good opportunity. It's different now." I took a drink. "Tia's my best friend, and her father pushed her to start this company. She needed someone to partner with, so she picked me. Once I was committed, I was all in. To prove to her and her father that they'd made the right choice, I guess, because I've never really been all that interested in our product."

Disappointing but true. Tia and I had invested years into this business, and I didn't even like what we planned to sell. Why had I given away years of my life for something I didn't believe in?

"It's fine," I said, quickly. "I'll get back to the science part of it all, at some point."

He nodded. "If that's what you want, do it. Time moves fast. There's an ease for me, now that I've had to let it all go. The opportunity to take a breath. I do want to get back into the financial market in some capacity, because I love numbers, but until I can figure out how to keep a sense of moderation, I'm just going to sit out there with the sheep."

"You lost me," I said.

"I'm a sheep herder. That's what I do when I'm not hanging around this place."

"You mean, like . . . in a field?"

"Like, as in a shepherd."

I shook my head. "I sincerely hope you take me to meet your flock."

"They're Scottish Blackface. Their lambs are ridiculously cute."

"Sheep." I studied him. "So, with your aptitude for numbers, you're particularly good at . . . counting them?"

He burst out laughing. The next thing I knew, he'd cupped my chin in his hand and was giving me the sweetest kiss I'd ever had. Fire, whiskey, and fresh air seemed to cut through me, and I pulled him in close, running my hands over the hard lines of his upper body. We lingered together, foreheads touching.

He pulled back and moved off the counter. "Sorry." He held up his hands. "I shouldn't have done that."

"You absolutely should have done that," I said, still reeling from the kiss.

The smell of his cologne was on my cheeks, the taste of him in my mouth. I wanted him to sit back down and keep talking to me in that sweet, low lilt that had me intoxicated.

"No, I can't," he said. "You're a guest here."

He strode over and turned on the lights. I blinked like a mole in the sudden brightness. He stood at the door, looking disheveled and more attractive than ever. We stared at each other, and he rubbed a hand over his hair.

Taking cautious steps toward me, he said, "Listen, I promised my sister I'd never get involved with her guests."

"Do you need me to check out?" I asked. "I could, if that would help."

He gave me that heart-trembling smile.

I slid off the counter. More than anything, I wanted to make my way back to his arms. Instead, I rested my hand on the cool tiles to anchor my body. I did my best to think of anything but the way his lips had felt on mine.

We looked at each other for a long moment. Then he said, "I'll pop off, then, yeah? Have a good night."

He headed out, and I stood there in silence. Finally, I flipped the lights back off and climbed back up onto the counter to watch the moths. They were lost in uncertainty but somehow made the chaos look beautiful.

Chapter Nineteen

Ireland, 1950

Sullivan and I sat outside on the front porch in silence.

It was three days after Harding died, and my mind was still completely numb from the pain. Nothing felt real, least of all the patch of sun reflecting off the leather of my shoe. The world felt dark, and all I could do was stare at Alby, wondering if he knew she was gone.

Sullivan had called on me each day, but I'd been unable to get out of bed to see him. I finally did, because it was the only way for me to learn what had happened. No one in my house would speak of it, for fear of upsetting me even more.

"I need you to tell me what happened," I said.

"We'd made it to the village just as it all began." Sullivan plucked a piece of clover from the ground and put it between his teeth. He chewed it, his expression somber. "Harding wanted to return to Alby, of course. I tried to talk her out of it, but she wouldn't listen. She started to run back to the house, and we saw Mona. She told us you'd gone."

I shook my head. "I begged my parents to go find her before we left."

"Mona said that. She told us you didn't have a choice in leaving and that you'd find milk for Alby."

"Thank God Harding knew. I—" The words caught in my throat, and I squeezed my hands together tight.

"Right after she told us, there was smoke in the air and the sound of gunfire. Harding and I ran through the woods to my house. My parents . . ." Sullivan nodded, wiping his hand across his face. "They did me proud, Evie. They welcomed her into our home. They insisted that she stay with us until your family returned, and they did not say one word about what they knew about her work."

He shook his head, staring out at the field. After several minutes of silence, he said, "The chaos died down, but we were shaken. The whole town. It was all anyone could talk about, and we kept waiting for something more. People would come to the store and go straight back home. Harding stayed with me, reading and watching out the window, waiting for news of Alby." He stopped talking, and I looked at him.

"Please," I managed to say.

I closed my eyes and drew Alby close.

"That third day, she walked to the post office to send you a telegram. The Garda found her in the woods, near the shipping ports. Someone had shot her in the back. They said she died instantly. She might not have even known it was coming."

Oh, she knew. She had known for quite some time that this day would come.

My head hurt, and I covered my eyes to block out the sun.

"They thought it was because of the rebellion, the dodgy element lurking around," Sullivan said. "I doubt it was that." He looked like he felt responsible. Turning to me, he demanded, "Was she still involved with the trade?"

"No." I placed my hand to rest on the soft fuzz on Alby's head. "She was scared, though. Ever since the attack. She kept telling me that people were after the money she'd made, especially in these parts, close to the docks. She owed her partners money, but they had an arrangement, and she still had time to pay them."

Sullivan's jaw was tight with emotion. "If I'd have known, I would not have permitted her to leave my side."

Harding must have downplayed her concerns, or perhaps she'd been so desperate to hear word of Alby that she was willing to risk it. That, I could picture. The decision to go to the post office the moment the thought jumped into her head, instead of waiting for Sullivan to finish his time at the store and escort her there.

I couldn't quite grasp the idea that I'd lost her. That she was gone. The pain hovered somewhere in the distance, like a wave of heat that I couldn't hold on to. There were nights I sat waiting for the tears to come, to offer me some form of relief from the ache in my blood.

Being with Alby helped. He snuggled up against my breast, drank easily from his bottle, and wiggled his toes, reaching for them in wonder.

I worried if he longed for her. When his tiny face also twisted with grief, and his fists clenched with fury. Guilt washed through me, knowing that I had failed. If Harding could have put the ocean between her and her past, she would have been safe. I never should have allowed her to stay.

Getting to my feet, I nodded at Sullivan. "I have to go change him," I said. "We'll speak soon."

Once I walked inside, I made it up to my bedroom before sinking to the ground, still holding him tight.

"I miss her," I told Alby. He stared up at me with her eyes. "You do, too."

The tears finally came, in racking, full-body sobs. Alby joined in, and I couldn't help but think he understood. How could he not? His body had been a part of hers, and now, she was gone.

Reaching out my finger, I let him squeeze it tight, and I cried until I could barely breathe.

My voice was hoarse, but I got the words out. "From now on, it's you and me."

∼

My parents—my mother in particular—seemed to suffer alongside my grief. She joined me on long walks, spent time sewing next to me, and listened as I pounded my devastation into the piano.

I was back in the main house and refused to set foot inside the cottage. Seamus had quietly collected Harding's things, moved them to my bedroom, and didn't protest when I demanded they be moved back out once again. I had no plans to return to university anytime soon, and my parents had not mentioned it.

"This has been so hard for you," my mother said, one night at dinner. My father was hunting with some men from town, and Alby was already in bed, so it was the two of us again. The thing I'd wanted my whole life, and now, it didn't matter in the least.

"What can I do, Evie?" my mother asked. "I'd like to help you grieve the loss of your friend."

I looked down at my soup. "I don't think you can."

There were so many things I couldn't tell her. I certainly couldn't tell her the truth about Harding.

I'd considered it, especially in those first days, but anxiety held me back. I feared that my mother would insist on finding Alby a proper placement in a proper home. I was not about to lose him, in spite of the absolute terror that came with knowing I had to carry the weight of him on my own.

Losing Harding had made it hard to breathe. On some days, I felt like I'd forgotten something and couldn't figure out what it was. Sometimes, my mind took me to the woods where she'd been found, and I imagined what she'd thought and seen in her final moments. Whether she'd felt the bullet cut through her back. The pain turned my stomach, and I didn't know when or if it would ever end.

I couldn't tell my mother the truth because I couldn't risk losing Alby. I was certain that without him, I would not be able to go on at all.

~

My parents left for Argentina less than a month after Harding was killed. I stood outside, holding Alby tight, filled with rage that my mother would leave. The sun beat down on my head, burning it, but the discomfort seemed a million miles away. My parents were about to get into the car that would take them to port when I stepped forward.

"I want you to stay," I told my mother. "You asked what you could do to help me, and that's it. I need you to stay."

My mother wore a white dress, a pair of sunglasses, and a neckerchief. She looked fashionable and ready to mingle with the posh crowd whom she and my father spent their time with each time they went to Buenos Aires. At my words, she rested her hand on the top of the car.

"Darling, I—"

My father cut in: "Evie, your mother comes with me. There is no debate in that."

"Please." I held Alby close. "I'm frightened. I can't be here alone, I—"

"You are not alone," my father growled. "The entire staff is here." He looked to the porch where the three of them stood as if mortified they were witnessing this exchange.

"There could be more riots," I said. "What are we to do if—"

"Let's bring her." My mother lifted her sunglasses and regarded my father with clear eyes. "It would be a good experience for her to see Buenos Aires, to see another part of the world."

My father looked horrified. "You know we can't do that."

"Why not?" my mother demanded. "She'll miss a month or two more of university, then be back with a broader perspective of the world."

Insects trilled around us as we stood at the car, the sun beating down on us, and my father looked more impatient at each moment that passed. The house staff looked on with interest.

My father shrugged his shoulders. "Fine. We do need to make it to port. We'll have Seamus pack her wardrobe from university, along with some personals. I'll telegram ahead about the change, and we'll deal with any lodging issues when we arrive." He nodded at me. "Looks like you'll join us. Give the child to Mona, then, along with any necessary instructions."

I looked back and forth between my parents. They both seemed somewhat alarmed but vaguely pleased, as if they'd solved some big problem. It was baffling that they thought I could leave Alby behind. Now that I was a parent, I had to wonder how they had so easily left me. They'd said it was too dangerous to take me, but my father could have changed his career, or my mother could have stayed at home.

"Sorry, but that won't work," I said. "I have a child and cannot travel with you. I'm asking for my mother to stay home with me." Feeling my chest grow tight, I looked at her and said, "I've never once told you that I needed you. That wasn't allowed. So I'm telling you now. I can't do this alone. Please, this one time, stay."

My mother pressed her hand to her mouth and let out a muffled sound. It was impossible to see behind her sunglasses, but for a moment, it looked like she was crying.

"This is nonsense," my father practically shouted. "We must go. We will not miss the boat."

He ducked into the car and shut the door firmly behind him.

My mother walked over and gave me a firm hug. "Be brave, Evie." Her voice cracked slightly, and she gently touched my chin. Then she got into the car with my father and let him take her away.

The autumn days passed slowly. In the beginning, Fedelma attempted to live up to her responsibilities as a tutor, but I refused to do the work. It wasn't even so much as a refusal as an inability to do anything but stare straight ahead, with Alby on my lap. He was the only thing that could pull me out of my stupor, when he would smile, coo, or do something like try to roll over. Those were the moments that made it possible to make it through the day.

Fedelma was at our home often, perhaps because she was earning a wage, or perhaps because she felt a duty to watch over me. She sat in the corner of the room, darning socks, reading to me out loud, and offering suggestions about Alby. She told me to tie a red string to his crib, to keep away the faeries, and to rest a penny on the doorjamb above the nursery, to make him wealthy.

"That's what I did with you," she said.

The traditions charmed me, and I felt that Harding would have warmed to them, so I did what she said.

One afternoon, while we were sitting in the parlor, she eyed me over a pair of knitting needles. "It troubles me that you don't want to see to your studies. Perhaps you could make a memento for the child?"

"What do you mean?" I asked.

The energy that it would take to sew or knit him something was too much. Plus, the very idea of knitting brought back those days with Harding, which I refused to revisit in my mind. The time in the cozy cottage that belonged to her aunt, reading by the fire.

"Create a journal," Fedelma said, her thin shoulders bent in effort over a particularly complicated knot. "Do some writings, some poems. Document this time with him so that when he's older, he'll have the opportunity to remember you. The interest to see what you were all about."

Fedelma spoke of the moment my parents expected would happen at the start of the new semester. The time I'd return to university and board Alby to a family who would one day place him in an industrial school. Little did they know that I was not about to do that. I had no intention of returning to university at all. Instead, I planned to claim Alby as my son. He would simply not have a father, and I'd retell the story of how I'd found him to anyone who asked.

I'd never be able to marry, and I'd accepted that. Sullivan had visited repeatedly since Harding's death, offering his support as well as his devotion. I knew full well that he would care for Alby as his own, but I could not ask him to do that.

"I'd like to make a memory for him," I told Fedelma.

The idea made me feel a spark of motivation for the first time in weeks. Mainly because I had already forgotten so many of the little moments I'd shared with Alby, the day-to-day things he did that had captured my affection. The way he held the bottle or what songs I'd sing to him as he fell asleep at night. It might be nice to document those things to look back, later, and find the joy in this time instead of the darkness.

Fedelma got up and rummaged in her carpetbag. "Here." She handed me a pencil and several sheets of paper.

"Get it down on paper," she said. "Otherwise, time has a gift for washing those precious memories away."

Chapter Twenty

I was so caught up in the day that I never called Tia that night. I'd thought about her but hadn't managed to pick up the phone. The next morning, I dashed off a quick text, grateful to think she'd still be asleep when it went through.

> Time change makes it so complicated to connect. Grandma is doing well, it's beautiful here. Should be back in about ten days but we'll talk before then.

I stared at the message after I pressed "Send." It felt so . . . dishonest. There had been a time in my life where nothing would have stopped me from talking to my best friend. I would have sent text after text, trying to calculate the exact second we could call each other to maximize our time. The fact that I was sending evasive messages had to be raising red flags. Or maybe she assumed I was upset about my grandmother and needed time to work through it all.

That was true, but I missed my best friend. When I thought back to the night before, and the kiss I'd shared with Grady, it was frustrating to think I'd finally met someone and couldn't tell her all about it. I needed to hear her voice, as well as her advice, to handle my feelings about everything happening here.

Once I'd taken a shower and blow-dried my hair, thinking of when Grady had complimented it in the storage unit, I found my grandmother up and awake. She sat in the chair by the window, doing her best to read one of the letters on her own.

"Good morning," I said. "Do you want me to read that to you?"

Even though I really could have used a cup of coffee first, I was happy to see her being so self-reliant. It was a good sign to see that she'd gotten up on her own and was trying to reclaim a sense of independence.

"Good morning." She coughed and turned to me, smiling. "I was rather hoping you'd help me get into that thing," she said, pointing at the trunk. "I woke up this morning, and there it is, and once again, I . . ." She put her hand to her head. "It sat there before, you know."

"It did?" I said.

The trunk was over by the closet, out of the way but noticeable, since it looked like a giant wooden treasure box that had washed to the shore.

"It's so much older now. Worn. Like me." She touched the back of her hands, as if surprised the skin had changed. "I wouldn't mind seeing what's hidden inside."

"Gladly." If we searched through it together, there was a good chance she'd talk to me about the past.

"Let's move you closer," I said. "See what this is all about."

Once my grandmother was comfortably situated, she said, "This trunk belonged to a dear friend of mine. I had always thought it so glamorous, and I was delighted when my parents got me one for university. Eventually, I took it to America."

"I'd love to see it." I didn't want her to stop talking. "Do we still have it?"

"No, it got lost somewhere along the way. Sullivan made it, you know. He was good at woodwork. He wouldn't come with me, not without being married. The trunk felt a bit like having him by my side. It would have been wise to bring him, but not fair. It ended us."

This was the most my grandmother had spoken about her past, ever, and we hadn't even opened the trunk yet. I wondered once again if Sullivan was the man in the letters, but I didn't dare ask.

My grandmother tugged at the sleeves of her dressing gown. "Let's open this," she said, turning back to the trunk. "See what's inside."

"So this was similar to the trunk you traveled with," I said, considering it. "What was it like to move to a new country? I've always thought that was really brave."

It was so impressive to me that she'd moved to the United States on her own. I'd considered giving New Zealand a try for a gap year after high school but was too scared to do it. I'd regretted that decision many times.

"What was it like?" my grandmother repeated. "It was terrifying."

I sat in silence, waiting for her to say more. To my surprise, she did.

"I lied about my age," she said, giving a little laugh. "Pretended to be a widow. I only ate once a day, to avoid going to the dining room, and would sneak bread back to my room. It feels like a grand adventure now, but back then, it was a terror."

"Why did you pick the United States?" I asked.

She looked down at her hands. "I was chasing a dream that belonged to someone else. With time, I found my own dreams and grew to accept the ones I'd left behind. There's little that our family knows about my time here because I ran away from my life. I know you're curious and your mother is, too, but it's something I spent years trying to forget. It was hard on me."

My cheeks burned to think that she was aware of our speculation, but of course she must have known we were curious about the past. It felt important that she'd finally addressed that.

"Do you want to talk about it?" I asked. "Why did you run?"

"Well, why does anyone do anything?" She sat in silence for a moment. "I ran because the things that had happened here had caused me great pain."

"I'm proud of you for coming back," I told her. "To face it."

My grandmother put her hand to her head. "Let's open the trunk."

There was quite a bit inside. I knew it would be overwhelming to show her everything at once, so I started with the photo album. I'd wanted to look through it in the storage unit, but I'd been so focused on the letters, and then Grady, that I hadn't gotten the chance.

"Do you recognize this?" I asked, passing it to her. "Some of the stuff in here might not be yours. The family who bought the house from you put it in here."

My grandmother ran her hand over the cover. She opened it and sat silently. The first page held two large black-and-white photos—a man with a long, thin nose, a high forehead, and a twinkle in his eye, and a striking woman with eyes like mine. Her thick, smooth hair fell past her shoulders. They were both well dressed and seemed full of life. I knew who they were right away.

"These are my parents," she said, holding up the book.

Moving closer, I took in every detail. Her father resembled my mother. It wasn't one obvious feature that made me think that, but something about the shape of his face, the tilt of his head.

"Will you tell me about them?" I asked. "I'd love to know what they were like."

My mother would want to know. Like Grady had said, I was here to find out, so it might be uncomfortable to push, but it was important.

"Oh, goodness." My grandmother worried her sleeve with her fingers. "They weren't here too often. They traveled due to my father's work. He worked for the ESB, the Electricity Supply Board, for the government. He was in charge of heading up electricity for the town when he was quite young. Then, as he got older, he was often in charge of big projects, both here and abroad—it might be things like acquiring the necessary parts to build a power grid or learning ways to do it better—and when my parents were home, the house was filled with people. They had big parties, full of fun, until the Emergency."

I sat in silence, listening, trying to remember all the details. She turned the pages in the photo album slowly, lingering over a photograph of her parents standing next to a car, her father squinting into the sunlight. He appeared handsome and commanding, with his arm around my great-grandmother's waist. She must have enjoyed fashion because her outfit was bold and dramatic, with a sweeping skirt and a paneled organza blouse.

"Did they go out a lot?" I asked.

"Not at home," my grandmother said. "There was nowhere to go. Guests visited for weeks at a time, and Aisling became the place to be. It was quite lively." She traced her finger over her mother's face. "I kept out of the way."

I thought of my grandmother and the parties she'd enjoyed hosting. It was a piece from her past that we hadn't known about, something she'd seen growing up.

My grandmother continued to turn the pages, occasionally making a noise with her mouth. Then she stopped on a picture of her mother.

"She's beautiful," I said, and she nodded.

"My mother was very smart." Her voice was full of admiration. "My father, he was always at the center of everything. I do wish he'd deferred to my mother more, but that was not the way it was back then. I think I made a decision when I was young that I did not want to marry someone like him, which is how I ended up with a wonderful man like your grandfather."

"I feel like you showed me what to look for," I told her. "I remember Grandpa. The way he was with you."

"Ah." My grandmother pressed her lips together and lifted her chin. "Good. I wish . . ."

She stopped talking. I had a feeling she wanted to mention my parents, but she didn't. My mother and grandmother rarely spoke of my father in front of me, which I appreciated. He was a good guy, but he and my mother had gotten married right out of high school. They grew up and grew apart. I thought of what Grady had said, about the younger version of himself, and wondered what would have happened if my parents had met later in life. I probably wouldn't be around.

"Things happen as they should," I said.

"I don't know about that," my grandmother said. "I think sometimes, things just happen. Then it's up to us to deal with the aftermath." She looked back down at the album. "My parents would have liked your mother. I'd have liked for them to meet, but that was not to be."

"How did they die?" I asked.

Silence. I looked over at her, and she focused on the album.

"Look at that," she said. "It's hard to believe I was ever that young."

My grandmother had also been a stunning woman. Even without makeup or with her hair pulled back, it was impossible to look away from her dimpled, bright smile, the perfectly spaced cheekbones set in a pretty, round face, and deep brown eyes. She had Irish-cream skin, lightly dusted with freckles, and a hint of red in her hair.

"You look beautiful," I said. "You do now, too."

"Inside, I don't feel I've aged a bit. That's the strange thing about growing old. You'll see."

"I can only hope to be so lucky," I said, stretching out my legs.

Once we'd reached the last page, she closed the book. "Those are the only pictures. I brought one small photograph of my parents with me when I left. I often envied your mother's ability to take thousands of pictures and videos of you on her phone. Sometimes, I wonder if I'd have been less inclined to think so much of the past if I'd had the choice to have it laid out in front of me."

"Why didn't you bring this photo album?" I asked. "When you moved to America?"

"There was only so much room and so much time." She brushed her hands over a photograph of her as a baby, in the arms of her mother. "Plus, my mind was on other things, like how to survive on my own in a new country."

It must have been such a huge culture shock, moving to New York from a tiny place like this. Everything from the air that she breathed to the food she put in her body to the clothes she wore. What, exactly, was the dream she'd been chasing?

She gestured at the trunk. "What else is in there?"

I pulled out the first thing on the top. It was a brown folder with paperwork from the Department of Foreign Affairs. "This is pretty cool," I said, studying it. "Clearance letters and identification for your parents."

Behind the paperwork were badges printed with their names. I liked that her mother had been able to work during the war, and I wondered if she continued once it was all over.

"Did your mother stay on with Foreign Affairs after the Emergency?" I asked. "Or did she have to quit?"

My grandmother wrinkled her forehead. "No, she didn't work. She accompanied my father. That's most likely paperwork for them to go overseas, which he had to do a lot."

"Oh," I said, confused. The paperwork read like she was employed. "These must be guest passes or something, then. But . . ." One of the badges had a photograph with "Security Clearance" clearly stamped on it. "This looks formal," I said, holding it up. "She must have been cleared to go with him quite frequently?"

I passed it to my grandmother. "That's interesting," she said. "He did work on power grids, so certain parts of it must have been quite secretive."

While she looked at it, I studied the paperwork a bit more closely. According to the paperwork, her parents were both registered to work. I handed it to my grandmother and gave her a questioning look.

"Your mother was employed," I said. "I thought I'd read that women couldn't be if they were married. Is there any reason that they wouldn't tell you that she was working?"

Maybe it was a class issue. Or maybe, since married women weren't supposed to hold a job in certain areas, her employment was kept a secret.

My grandmother squinted at the paperwork. She paused and put a hand to her forehead, looking vaguely upset.

"What is it?" I asked.

"I begged her to stay home," she said, quietly. "There were a few men like my father who would come to stay with us, and their wives did not travel with them. They were home with their children, and I remember asking her why she didn't stay home with me. I'd assumed she preferred the company of my father. She couldn't have been working, though. You're right, she wasn't allowed. Not if she was married."

"Maybe they made an exception for her."

My grandmother seemed troubled, but then she closed her eyes. "I'd like for you to find that out. If it's true, that she was working, I'd be glad to know."

"I'll look into it," I promised.

Perhaps, if I contacted the Department of Foreign Affairs, I could find out whether she'd had some sort of job while traveling with her husband, or if the paperwork was a formality because she did, in fact, prefer to travel than to stay at home. Giving her a "job" might have made it easier for her at the border.

If it was the latter, I'd keep it to myself. Some truths didn't need to be told. The moment I had that thought, I wondered if that very philosophy was the reason behind my grandmother's secrecy.

"Thank you," she said. "I appreciate that." Her expression had been bright when she'd first asked to look at the trunk, but I could tell she was fading.

"Would you like to rest?" I asked. "We can look through this later."

"No, no." She gave an impatient wave of her hand. "What else is in there?"

"Some fun things." I handed her the pink velvet jewelry box, and when she opened it, her hand fluttered to her mouth.

"This belonged to my mother. I never thought I'd see these things again."

The box contained a small collection of necklaces and brooches. They were gold, with precious gemstones that still sparkled. I opened a gold locket and showed it to her.

"This has your picture inside."

My grandmother drew back. Then she reached for it with shaking hands. "Please, put this on me."

Once I'd fastened it to her neck, she went to the mirror and gazed at her reflection. I went back to the trunk and reached for a small cardboard box.

"I think this is from when you were little," I said, pulling it out.

It held a collection of baby items. I lifted out a small, crocheted white blanket to show to her first.

"Do you remember this?" I asked.

My grandmother moved more quickly than I'd seen in years, rushing across the room in her haste to hold it. She stumbled slightly, and I caught her, then helped her sit back down.

My eyes smarted to see that the blanket meant so much to her. It was incredible that a piece of her childhood had remained here, in a bed-and-breakfast across the world, and the owner had been kind enough to share it. I looked at my grandmother, expecting a sense of peace, and was startled to see she'd turned pale.

"Grandma?" I said, kneeling next to her.

Her pallor could have been from standing up too quickly, but I also should have insisted on ordering breakfast before we did all this. Quickly, I got her a glass of water. She didn't touch it, but slowly, the color returned to her cheeks. She seemed transfixed, holding the blanket tight.

"Here," I said. "Let me call for breakfast and—"

"What else is in that box?" she asked, quietly.

I pulled out the items and set them on the side table close to the chair: a silver rattle, a toy soldier doll made of cloth, a hardcover children's book that looked to be a collection of fairy tales, and a small dressing gown.

My grandmother stared at the items as if seeing a ghost. I was starting to feel uneasy, like I'd pushed her too far.

"It must feel strange to see all your old things," I said.

"These do not belong to me," she said.

"Oh," I said, relieved for some reason. "Nora said there might be some things in here that were from the other—"

"They belonged to my son."

"Grandma," I said, gently. "You don't have a—"

My grandmother looked up at me. The pain in her eyes was so raw that it cut me to the quick. I considered all the secrets that we kept close, to keep our hearts from shattering. My grandmother had lived a full life before she came to the States. Like my mother had said, there were things she didn't want to discuss.

"Did he die?" I said, quietly.

She squeezed my hand. "He was taken from me much too soon."

"Grandma, I'm so sorry."

Sea air rustled the curtains as we sat in silence, the pain hanging heavy between us. My grandmother gestured at the side table. I touched the objects, and she nodded when I got to the toy soldier doll.

I handed it to her. She studied it for a moment, running her fingers over its face, the brown yarn of its eyes. Her lips trembled.

Then she rested the doll against her cheek and wept.

Chapter
Twenty-One

Ireland, 1950–1952

I had expected it to be a battle to convince my parents to allow me to raise Alby. They had planned for me to return to university following Christmas, but once I made the decision that wouldn't happen, I sent them a telegram.

WILL RAISE ALBY. REFUSE TO BOARD HIM OUT. NOT ATTENDING UNI.

The telegram I received in reply was from my father. I'd fully expected him to threaten me and for us to engage in a battle over the wire. His response, much to my surprise, was neutral.

TAKE A YEAR OF REST.

It was an interesting tactic. I held the telegram tight, considering his words. Perhaps he assumed the monotony of raising a child would push me toward a different life, but there was not a moment when I'd found being with Alby dull. He was bright and funny and made me see the world in the way Harding had—full of wonder.

One night, I'd shown him the moon, and he squealed, clapped his hands, and grabbed my face, turning it back up toward the sky. We were on a blanket behind Aisling, lying in the grass. When I turned to look at Alby, the love I felt for him was brighter than the moon.

The year passed quickly. He grew and began to talk and walk. He became big almost overnight. Tall, strong, and curious. Our days were spent exploring the grass along the moor while pointing at birds, sheep, and butterflies, and my life had never felt so full. Whenever I had the time or the energy, I wrote him letters, like Fedelma had suggested, but I didn't write them in anticipation of being apart; I wrote them so that when he was older, I could hand them to him myself.

My parents were more accepting of the situation than I ever would have dreamed. At times I wondered if they'd pieced together the truth about his parentage or if it was simply that they were willing to give me the time I needed to heal, since they couldn't give of themselves. A year of rest quickly turned to two, and I delighted in my time with Alby.

But as he grew, I realized I could not stay at Aisling forever. That became clear one night when my parents allowed Alby to eat dinner with us. I was folding my fork into the soft skin of a potato as my father discussed what he'd read about the progression of the telephone cables being laid throughout Ireland.

Irritated with his meal, Alby plucked a carrot out of his stew and threw it across the table in dislike, hitting my father in the face. My mother laughed, but my father was furious.

"This will not stand at Aisling," he stormed, pounding his fists on the table. "We can no longer go on like this!"

Alby burst into tears, and I left the room with him. My mother shushed my father and, later, came to check on me. I was sitting in the nursery, rocking Alby to sleep.

She knocked on the door and entered, bringing in a waft of frankincense, the top note of her latest perfume. Elegant as ever, she perched on the windowsill, her ankles crossed. I took notice of her shoes, a fashionable pair of heels in a color Harding would have adored, and her necklace, made of gold, with a heart-shaped locket.

"We'll be leaving again next week," she said. "Upon our return, we plan to entertain guests."

I knew exactly where she was going with this. In the early summer, Aisling would be full of visitors, elegant dinners, and dancing. Lawn parties while the rain held. My parents wouldn't want the bother of a child underfoot, which meant Alby would be confined to the nursery. I hadn't minded the last time this happened, because he was small. Now, though, he was becoming a boy, and he needed the space to explore.

"I'd like to know how long you plan to care for Alby," she said. "This has gone on too long. Will you ever attend university? Marry? That child is nearly two. It pains me to see you giving your life away."

The mobile I had hung over Alby's bed, made of paper birds, fluttered in the breeze from the open window.

"Is that how you saw it?" I asked. "That having a child was giving your life away?"

The question was not meant to be combative. I was curious about my mother's take on motherhood, because I wanted to understand the choices she'd made, raising me the way she had. Instead of discussing it, she frowned.

"There are things you'll one day understand. I'm not free to explain them to you now."

"Why?" I asked.

Her dark eyes met mine. Then she looked down at Alby and changed the subject. "He's quite cozy, then, isn't he?"

He was also still awake, because he cracked an eye open and reached out a hand to her. My mother got to her feet and held his hand for a brief moment, then gave an uncomfortable laugh. "Your father intends to play a round of croquet. Would you like to join us when Alby's asleep?"

The switch in topic was jarring. My mother seemed interested in amusement, and not much else. Still, I took what I could get, so I nodded.

"Yes, it's a lovely night," I said. "I'll see you out there soon."

Once she left the room, I thought about her questions. I couldn't stay at Aisling with Alby forever, and as I watched the mobile flutter in the breeze, an idea began to take shape.

Perhaps it was time to do what Harding had planned all along—take him to America, to safety, and away from all this. My parents would no longer need to concern themselves with my unconventional choices, and I could find a new life, one where I wouldn't have to convince them that my plans held value, too.

It wouldn't be hard for me to leave. Certainly not to leave my parents. I still had moments when I thought of that time in the motorcar, when I begged them to go find Harding before we left, and they'd refused. I had no power here, no voice. The money Harding had hidden would give me the resources to leave it all behind.

The thought had hovered in the dark corners of my mind, and now that I'd brought it into the light, it frightened me. Yes, this money would mean freedom, but I didn't want anything to do with it. Harding had lived in fear because of this money; she'd died for it. Yes, she'd wanted to give Alby a secure and comfortable future, but I didn't want that shadow hanging over him or haunting me.

Yet it did. I had made Harding a promise that I'd take care of her son. That I'd be responsible for him. I wouldn't be able to give him much of a life without resources.

Perhaps I could ask my parents to bring him into our family?

It was an impossible thought. They would never agree to such a thing. I was living on borrowed time.

While I played croquet with my parents, I kept stealing glances at the gardener's cottage. I hadn't been in there since Harding passed, and to the best of my knowledge, no one had touched her things. In the beginning, I kept waiting for someone to break into the house, to search for answers, but when that didn't happen, I realized that whoever killed her must have believed the secret had died with her.

Yet another reason to stay far away from it all. Harding had given her life for that money. I'd have to find a way to care for Alby without it.

When night fell and my parents went to bed, the opposite argument remained as I tossed and turned in my sheets: Harding had given her life for that money, and it would honor her to use it as she'd wanted.

Perhaps I could see if she left me a way to find it. If she didn't, then there's nothing to decide.

Still reluctant, I tracked down a torch and took the back stairs to the door out to the lawn. The moon was bright, and the grass glistened in its silvery light. The tree branches were etched against the sky and creaked in the slight breeze.

Even though I knew I should feel afraid, I didn't. For the first time since the thought about the money had entered my head, I felt at peace, as though something were guiding me. That Harding was by my side.

Taking a deep breath, I let myself into the cottage. There, I held the back of a kitchen chair as my eyes swept the room, seeking out memories. It had been so long since I'd seen her. Someone had come in and placed her belongings in her trunk but her perfume still lingered, and I closed my eyes, remembering the way we'd laughed.

I brushed my hand over the oily wood of the table, turning my focus to the search and trying to figure out where to look. With tentative hands, I tried the inside of the cradle, the portable one we'd taken Alby outdoors in. My fingers touched on a paper pressed against the edge, and my pulse quickened, but it was only the paint beginning to peel. I stripped the small piece off and looked beneath, only to find nothing. I was frustrated that this endeavor felt hopeless.

Setting my jaw, I went through Harding's clothing, fighting back the lump that formed in my throat at the sudden memories, and the soft feel of the blankets she'd knitted for Alby. Harding hadn't kept a journal, and the only book she had was *Children's Tales*. I hesitated, then opened it.

Turning from page to page, I ran my hand over the words, waiting for something to stand out, but the only thing in there was the train ticket we'd used as a bookmark. Finally, when I flipped to the very end, I discovered a map of Ireland on the inside of the back cover that I'd always overlooked. It had a brief blurb about the history of the fairy tales on the left-hand side. I studied the map and noticed that, in faded pencil, someone had put a circle around a section of a small town to the north.

The text below also had faint circles around certain words and a few underlined letters. I found a piece of paper, wishing Harding were here to encourage me, and wrote out the words. Coupled with the underlined letters and words, it swiftly became a message:

Beneath the windmill by the creek, in a well.

I looked over to the chair that Harding had favored, half convinced that I'd see her there, laughing that she had put something like this together. Of course the chair was empty, and the shadows stretching across the floor were long.

I stared down at the words and then at the map, noting the circled area. It seemed impossible that I'd be able to find the exact location, but my father did have a detailed collection of maps in the library. I could study them and see what I could find. My attempts would likely end in failure, but Harding had always had a way of making the impossible seem possible.

Holding the paper close, I tucked the book under my arm. It didn't escape my attention that it was a book of fairy tales. Magical, filled with hope clouded by the threat of darkness, and, in some ways, so close to the life I was now living.

~

The preparations necessary to find the money gave me a sense of purpose that I'd lacked ever since Harding's death. First, I needed to figure out exactly where the location was, so I studied maps in my father's library until I was certain I had a good idea of where it was and how to get there. Then I realized I'd either need to hire a driver, have Sullivan help, or get there myself somehow.

It was too risky, I decided, to have a stranger bring me, and I did not want to implicate Sullivan. That left getting there myself. I decided to learn how to drive the motorcar when my parents were out of town. While Alby happily played on a blanket on the floor, I spent hours reading a book my father had in the library on driving. Then, once I understood it, I waited until the cook had gone to the market to gather supplies and Seamus had taken his walk into town to visit friends. Mona was up in the nursery with Alby, so I doubted she'd notice, and I knew she wouldn't say anything, even if she did, because she was grateful for the ease of her position.

It was less challenging than expected to start the car and bring it backward out of the carriage house, but I did not anticipate how quickly it could turn off the road and into the grass. The first time, it got stuck, and I worried I'd have to call on Sullivan to help, but I managed to push it back onto the road myself. That gave me the confidence I needed, and after three days of practice, I took a long ride into the country before stopping to get it filled up with petrol. If the attendant was startled to see me driving, he didn't say anything. I purchased an extra can of petrol to put in the back, carefully surrounding it with bricks that I'd brought to keep it steady before heading back home.

There, I took my time penning a letter to Sullivan to leave on my dresser in the event that something should happen to me. I was careful to keep it cryptic.

Dear Sullivan,

I have left to handle an issue that was important to Harding. If I do not return, please see to it that Alby receives the finest care. NO HOMES. Speak to my parents, in detail, and ensure he is in good hands.

Your friendship is important to me.

Always,

Evie

Finally, I sent for Mona. She had stopped feeding Alby but had stayed on to help care for him. I knew she had a soft spot for his bright-blond hair and eager smile, because no matter what toy he threw across the room, I'd never once heard her scold him.

"Good afternoon," I called as I walked into the nursery.

It was such a cozy room, with its striped wallpaper and small framed paintings of animals and balloons, left over from when I was a child. I wondered if Alby would miss it when we left.

"Mum," Alby cried, wobbling his way to me.

I scooped him up and spun him around before covering his face with kisses. He smelled like butter and bread, and he tried to catch my face in his chubby little hands.

"Hello, miss." Mona had watched him play while I had lunch at the pub in town with Sullivan. "Do you need him dressed?"

"No, I wanted to talk to you about something." I settled onto the ground and pulled Alby into my lap. "I have an obligation that I must tend to on Friday, and I cannot bring Alby with me. There is also a chance that I will be detained until Sunday and would require you to remain. Would it be possible for you to stay to care for him? I'm willing to pay three times your wage for each day."

While I spoke, I lifted Alby's arms up and made him clap, which made him squeal in delight.

"Aye, miss," Mona said, eagerly. "I can do that."

"Thank you." I held Alby tight, kissing the soft hair on his head. "I'm grateful."

Once everything was in place, I still was not convinced that the trip would be worthwhile or that I should have any part of it at all. Surely, someone else would have found the money by now, or the map she'd left for me wouldn't be as detailed as I needed it to be. But I owed it to Harding to try, in spite of my misgivings.

On Friday evening, I handed Alby to Mona, squared my shoulders, and took off in the motorcar. I followed the map as night fell, bugs smashing against the windscreen as I drove. I'd been hopeful that I'd be able to locate the windmill quickly, as the map my father had was detailed enough to show all the creeks that ran through the area, but I wouldn't know for sure until I was there.

I pulled into the small farming village, drove through the main street, and continued out to the woods. The town was inland, with minimal access to the ports where Harding had been involved with the trade. It was probably why she had chosen this area. It was remote.

My breath caught as I spotted the creek and then the windmill. I drew closer, slowing the car slightly, and sure enough, I spotted a well beneath the windmill. The property where it sat was quite large, with a small cottage off to the edge of the pastureland, as well as several barns to house the sheep and horses grazing the land. Small stone fences surrounded the perimeter, and I noted areas where the fence was crumbling, making it easy to access the yard.

I didn't see anyone there, but a trickle of gray smoke was coming up from the chimney. I drove forward into the woods, then hid the car in the brush and waited until everyone was likely in bed.

The mosquitoes buzzed and ferns brushed against my legs as I used the low light of the moon to find my way to the crumbled stones in the fence and then slowly move my body over them. The hairs on the back of my neck prickled, and I looked around, worried I'd been noticed. I heard a rustling sound in the brush, and I tensed before realizing that it must have been a small animal, perhaps a raccoon.

Clutching my torch tight, I moved toward the windmill and knelt down on the cold stone. I leaned over the edge and peered down into the well. Once I switched on the torch, I felt an all-consuming rush of disappointment to see that the only thing inside was a mossy stretch of rocks, with black water down below. Perhaps it was down deep, but the money wouldn't be there, or it would have been destroyed.

I tried to search for any loose stones in the construction of the well, my hands quickly tiring with the effort. Nothing. Then I shined the light up into the wooden structure above, hoping to see a reasonable hiding place.

"Can I help you find something?" a low voice said.

I turned to find myself staring down the barrel of a gun.

Chapter Twenty-Two

Ireland, present day

I rested my hands on my grandmother's knees. She was no longer crying, but she still held tightly to the doll, her cheeks damp with tears.

My mind moved too fast, trying to piece it all together. Did my mother know that at one point in her life, she'd had a brother? Half brother, I realized, and wondered who the father had been.

I would assume it was the man from the letters, which was part of the reason she'd chosen to not marry Sullivan. Perhaps she'd fled to America because she was pregnant, and she'd left the baby items behind.

"I'm so sorry," I said, softly. "It must be so painful for you to see these things again. If I'd known, I never would have—"

"I'm grateful," she said. "To speak of him. To hear the letters, to see his things. I have missed him every single day of my life. Every day."

"Was the man in the love letters his father?" I asked.

My grandmother gave me a baffled look. "What love letters?"

"The . . ." My voice trailed off.

I picked up one of the letters and quickly skimmed through it.

My precious darling,

God created a masterpiece when he created you. The sweet shadow of your lashes, the perfect bow on your mouth, the brilliant gleam in your eye. The sound of your laughter fills my soul, heals it. I never thought I could feel love again, but you have healed me. You have my heart, forever.

"These aren't love letters," I said, finally seeing it.

"No." She held the doll close, still wiping away tears. "They're letters to my son, something I wrote to give to him when he was older. So that he could see a piece of his life that he wouldn't remember. I never thought I'd be the one reading them to remember."

So he'd been born here, in Ireland. I'd have to look at them again to be sure, but I remembered that in one of them, he'd said "I love you" to her and had even written her a poem. Even if the poem was something silly, he'd lived to be old enough to rhyme things, which was devastating in itself.

"Would you like to talk about him?" I asked, quietly. "Because I'd love to hear about him."

"I don't know." She looked lost. "I think . . ."

Her voice faltered, and she fell silent. It was too much for her to face. The very thought left me fighting back tears.

"Let's get you back to bed," I said. "I'll go get some breakfast for us, and we'll talk when you're ready, okay?"

I'd half expected she would disagree and want to keep searching the trunk, but instead she nodded.

She brought both the doll and the baby blanket back to bed with her and requested to have the children's book and rattle on the bedside table next to the crystal from the chandelier. She was staring at the objects, holding the doll close, as I shut the bedroom door.

Out in the hallway, I sank to the ground and buried my head in my hands. Tears rushed out, and I tried to cry as silently as possible.

My grandmother's heartbreak was so painful. On top of that, I couldn't stop thinking about my mother.

She didn't know she'd once had a brother. Why had my grandmother kept that a secret? It was one thing to run away from bad memories but another to deliberately keep the people closest to you in the dark.

My grandmother had kept half of her life hidden from us. The memories were hard for her, I could see that, but these secrets affected us all. I couldn't help but be angry that she hadn't found the courage to face these things until now. Who was I to talk, though? These were major issues, not like the small ones holding me back with Tia, and I could barely face those.

There was a click as a door opened down the hallway.

Getting up, I wiped my face and walked toward the steps, moving faster until I was racing down them. Too quickly, as if running from something. I gripped the railing tight and took a deep breath, forcing myself to slow down.

I was here, and in spite of everything, I refused to run from the past.

～

Once I got to the kitchen, I asked Nora if she could send breakfast up to the room.

"Yes, I can have it up right away." She refilled the urn of coffee. "Is everything all right?"

My eyes must have looked puffy from crying, and I appreciated that she was giving me a choice in whether to address it.

"I'll be fine," I said. "Thank you."

"Bread always helps," she said, cutting me a slice. "Here, have a piece."

The Irish soda bread was as comforting as a hug. It was thick, warm, and spongy, with a sprinkling of oats on the top. A plate of salted butter rested on the counter, and Nora slid it over to me.

"Thank you," I told her.

Cradling it in a cloth napkin, I went outside in hopes of finding Grady before my breakfast was ready. I'd heard a saw buzzing earlier, and if he was the handyman, it might have been him. He'd served as a source of comfort ever since I arrived, and regardless of the kiss we'd shared the night before, I needed someone to talk to.

I followed the sound and felt relieved to find him at the edge of an arbor, cutting back some branches. Spotting me, he turned off the saw and lifted his protective goggles.

"Top of the morning to you," he said, with a grin. When I didn't smile back, he said, "Uh-oh. Are you here to tell me off because of the kiss? Look, I understand that it was out of—"

"They're not love letters," I said, coming to a stop in front of him. "They're letters she wrote to her son, a son that I had no idea she'd even had."

He set down the saw. "Bollocks. Really?"

"Yeah."

"Here, sit down." He led me over to a place behind the trees out of view of the house. It was a small clearing, with a wet log and a few wildflowers. "That's got to be a shock for you."

"It is." He sat next to me on the log, and I stared down at his boots. "It's such a mess. I can't get mad at her for not telling us, because she's here to mourn his loss, I guess, but what am I supposed to say to my mother?" I ran my hands over the wet bark. "I hate it that I'm stuck in the middle of all of this, but at the same time I'm grateful that I'm here, finally learning about my family and its messed-up history. You know, I haven't even broached the topic of my great-grandparents, which is a whole other topic, and . . ." I shook my head. "This is more than I bargained for."

"You handling it okay, though?" he asked.

"No, which is why I came to find you."

He nodded. For a moment, I thought he was going to put his arm around me, and I'd have been more than fine with that.

Instead, he said, "You're strong. I can see that about you. There's a reason your grandmother wanted you to be here with her. You can't change any of this. The best you can do is be there for her."

"I'm trying." I peeled back a piece of bark on the log. "It's just that she shuts down right after she starts to tell me these things, so I'm learning enough information to stress me out but not enough to take action."

"What kind of action do you want to take?" he asked.

"I don't know." I thought for a moment. "I want to help her deal with some of these things straight on. Like, she and Sullivan O'Leary were close, apparently. I want to reunite them, but without knowing the whole story, I don't know if that's appropriate."

Grady also broke off a piece of bark and fiddled with it. "If they truly cared for each other, it doesn't really matter what got between them, does it?"

"In theory," I said. "But I don't know how angry people are with her around here, and there's no way I'm going to send her off to battle. She's ninety-three."

"Mac would know," Grady said. "He would tell you flat out whether or not it would be a good idea for the two of them to meet. You should go talk to him."

"Thanks," I said. "Maybe I will." Brushing my hands off, I got to my feet to go retrieve my breakfast. "I'm sorry I bothered you. I—"

"There's no way you could bother me." He hesitated for a moment and glanced back toward the house. Then he said, "Enjoy your day."

Picking up the saw, he got back to work.

~

My grandmother wanted to rest after we'd eaten breakfast, so I went out for a walk along the moor. The sun was hot even with the clouds off in the distance, and the Celtic Sea looked so inviting that I walked to the edge to get a better view. There was a somewhat worn path, I noticed, that led down closer to the water, and it seemed to have better shade.

Carefully, I picked my way down it, stopping once or twice to remove a small stone from my shoe. The path curved down and around. I was just about to turn back, concerned that I'd suddenly step out too close to the sea, when I noticed the path led behind a section of exposed rock.

Stepping around it, I drew in a sharp breath at the sight of a bright-blue pool of water, isolated and still. It was so tranquil, roughly thirty feet wide, with a slow waterfall that must have formed from rainwater at the top of the rocks.

I walked to the edge of the pool and dipped my toe in. There was less sun here, because of the shield of the rocks, so the water was ice-cold. But it was clear, and it looked perfect for a quick dip. I could hardly remember the last time I'd taken the time to swim, and it was one of my favorite things to do. Hopefully, it would chase away the darkness in my thoughts.

"Hey!" A voice shattered my reverie. Grady thundered around the corner, looking panicked. He was breathing hard, like he'd been running. "What are you doing?"

"Where did you come from?" I called, surprised to see him again.

He made his way to me and stopped, still out of breath. I could smell his sweat and musk, and the combination was as inviting as the water.

"I was on the moor cutting back some bramble. But for the past five minutes, I've been running because I noticed you go down here. Didn't you read the visitors' information in the room?"

I gave him a blank look.

"This is completely off-limits, eh?" he said. "This pool."

"To who?" I demanded.

He crossed his arms. "Tourists."

"It's a law?" I asked.

"It's a recommendation. There's a gate that blocks the path, but it's been out for repairs for two weeks now. It'll be back up next week."

The pool didn't seem to belong to anyone but nature. That said, the restrictions might have been an environmental thing, not wanting everyone to traipse through it, which was fair.

I eyed the cool water. "Have you ever gone in?"

He shoved his hands in his pockets. "Well . . ."

"You have," I said, gently pushing his chest. It was so hard and muscular. Must have been all that cutting back bramble. "How deep is the water?"

"Ten feet, all around. Deeper in other spots. It's deceptive. There's an inlet that leads straight out to sea, and people underestimate the waves caused by the current."

"Got it. Any rocks at the bottom?"

"It's sand."

Giving him my most winning smile, I said, "Sounds good." I peeled off my sandals and my sun-shirt before he could blink. Then I darted to the edge, executed a perfect dive, and sliced into the icy water with the precision of an Olympic athlete. Once I broke the surface, I smoothed back my hair.

Grady stood at the edge of the water, actually looking scared. "I'm telling you, it's not safe, Rainey."

"I'm an AAAA swimmer," I called. "It means I swim better than the fish." Glancing around, I added, "If there's an inlet, there's the tide to consider, and I bet the waves come up quick, right?"

"Yes. It can be really dangerous."

"Guess we better be extra careful, then," I called.

He watched as I dove down, relishing in the icy water. When I broke the surface, he shook his head.

"You coming?" I called.

Without a word, he took off his shoes, emptied his pockets, and pulled off his shirt.

Grady executed an equally flawless dive and soon surfaced, the droplets of water gleaming in his ever-present five-o'clock shadow. He swam toward me with sure strokes, and when he was next to me, our eyes locked. I tried not to stare at his incredibly broad shoulders, but considering everything about him was gorgeous, I failed.

"Are you enjoying your stay?" he asked, and I laughed.

This was such a beautiful location, completely private, and I felt giddy to think I was in the water alone with one of the most attractive men I'd ever seen.

He pointed at the waterfall. "Race you there."

I let Grady get ahead for a few seconds to let him feel good, and then I cut through the water, easing up onto the rocks before him.

He climbed up, his tan arms strong and glistening, and he playfully flicked water at me. "I thought I had a chance."

"Well, you always have a chance," I said, lifting up my gaze to take in the mossy beauty of the waterfall. The next thing I knew, he'd pulled me to him, and we were kissing with more heat than the sun.

He laid me back against the wet rocks, and I ran my hands through his hair, the water rushing around us. His kiss was deep, passionate, and rhythmic. Everything felt like fire, and I practically expected to see steam rising up around us. I was lost in the moment; then he suddenly pulled back.

"Don't you dare tell me it's because I'm a guest," I gasped, pulling him back to me.

"No, I heard thunder."

Without a moment's hesitation, we both dove back into the water. The tranquility of the pool had already been broken, and waves had swelled up, creating a sudden and dangerous pull toward the inlet. Halfway across, Grady got stuck and I heard him shouting. I turned back to grab him and dragged him along with me. Once he'd recovered, we fought our way to the rocks and scrambled up.

With the sexiest grin I'd ever seen, he said, "Thanks for saving my life," and pulled me in for another kiss as the rain pelted down.

"Why is it always raining?" I said, laughing.

Grady pulled me back into his arms, sheltering my head from the onslaught with his hands. The waves in the pool ripped back and forth as we sat safe on the rocks, with the rain pouring down around us.

I climbed into his lap and buried my face into his shoulder. His body tensed, then relaxed, and he settled his face into my hair. We sat like that until the rain had subsided and then slowly drew apart.

Our eyes met, and he shook his head.

"My sister is not going to be happy with me," he said, and he pulled me in for another kiss.

$\sim$

Once the rain stopped, he headed back to the brambles, and I headed back to Aisling, but our hands lingered before we went our separate ways. I walked back, letting my hair dry off in the sun as I tried to process what had just happened.

It had probably been the best hour of my life. I couldn't stop thinking about that moment where we'd folded into each other in the rain. The warmth and safety I'd felt in his arms.

Back in the room, my grandmother was still sleeping, so I changed and went downstairs to find Nora. She was in the kitchen washing dishes, with jazz music playing from a Bluetooth speaker. Her cheeks were flushed, and she wore a brightly colored apron. Looking over her shoulder, she smiled at me.

"Can I help?" she asked.

"I wanted to say thanks for breakfast and ask for a favor. I was thinking about taking a walk into town. Would you mind checking on my grandmother every once in a while?"

"I'd be happy to," she said, scrubbing down a pan. Her movements were so efficient, and I thought about what Grady had told me the night before: how opening the bed-and-breakfast was her dream come true.

I also thought about the way he'd kissed me beneath the waterfall but quickly pushed that thought out of my head.

Glancing up at me, she said, "You headed out to explore?"

"No. I'm going to . . ." I lowered my voice, not that the Australian man lingering over the paper in the dining room had any interest in our conversation. "I was hoping to talk to Mac, the bartender who was at the pub the other night, when I had all the trouble. My grandmother knew his father, and I think it would make her happy to see him again."

"Sullivan?" Nora brightened. "Oh, he's the best old guy around. Still lives on his own in a sweet little house by the cliffs, which drives Mac bananas. He's always worried ol' Sullivan will wander off over the edge or something."

"Do you think Mac will be there this early?" I asked.

It was only ten-thirty in the morning, even though it felt like I'd been up for days.

"He owns the place." Nora rinsed the pan, then toweled off her hands and looked up at the clock. "His flat is upstairs from the pub. Ring the bell on the side of the building if you don't see him. Tell him I sent you."

"Thank you, Nora," I said.

"Of course." She smiled at me. "I want to see pictures from that reunion, when he's seeing your grandmother again."

~

Mac was already hard at work, washing the windows on the outside of the pub, when I walked up. Spotting me, he dropped his rag into the bucket.

"I've been waiting for you to come back," he said. "Come inside, then. There's lots to say."

He set us up at a table with a hard apple cider and a bowl of Taytos, then pulled out the chair across from me. It was too early to drink, but I appreciated the gesture and breathed in the crisp scent. It was reminiscent of a fall festival, but it also reminded me of the days when I used to bake apple pies with my grandmother.

She'd loved to bake, which was one of many things I used to love doing with her. She taught me how to roll out the dough and pinch the sides on the pan. My favorite part was cutting out the shape of something with a cookie cutter to lay on top. Typically, we'd cut out an apple, but other times, we'd do stars or little birds. The house would fill with the aroma of cinnamon and cloves as the pie cooked, and we'd sit playing cards while we waited for it to be ready.

"You need a coffee?" Mac asked with a nod toward my untouched drink.

I considered the cider. "No. Actually, this is perfect."

Picking it up, I took a drink. The cider was cold and tart on my tongue, and I was glad I'd decided to try it. Looking around the pub, I relished in the stone hearth fireplace and the four-paned windows looking out over tall bright-green grass shifting in the wind. Sitting here, it felt like what my grandmother had said about being transported to another time.

"So, how's Ireland been treating you?" he asked.

"It's a whole new world," I said. "She never spoke of her time here. We only came because she fell ill and . . ." I didn't want to share about the letters, not without her permission. "I'm learning so much about her life that I didn't know."

The lines in his face deepened as he nodded, the twinkle in his eye not as bright as it had been the night we met.

"My father was in love with her." Mac held his drink for a moment before taking a sip, then set it down on the thick wood of the table. "Those things Jimmy talked about at the door . . . My father, he thought it was his fault, you know. That her parents were killed. He's blamed himself for years."

"What?" I said, surprised. "Why would he think that?"

Perhaps I was naive or foolish, but it was hard for me to believe that something that had happened seventy years ago could still affect someone who lived here today.

"That's a question for him," Mac said. "It wasn't his fault, though. No matter what he might think."

"I have to say," I told him, shaking my head, "everyone's laying blame or taking blame, and I don't even know how my great-grandparents died."

"Someone shot them on their way into town."

I winced. "Oh."

"Yeah. They were left there by the side of the road. Their driver was killed, too. They'd all gotten out of the car. The Garda never figured out who did it. There was talk, of course. This is a small town. Everyone knows something. Pieces to the puzzle have been on the floor of the pub for years, but instead of picking them up and putting them together, time swept them away."

I sat with that for a minute. "Why did your father blame himself?"

Mac adjusted his watch. It looked old, with a leather strap and classic face. "He was crushed that Evie had left. One night, a couple weeks before it happened, he got pissed at the pub and told one of his buddies that she was running away because of this money she'd taken. Once the secret was out, it wasn't a secret anymore.

"The story got passed around, it built and built, until the idea that Evie was some sort of criminal became truth. The whole lot here was angry with her, but it wasn't out of some deep friendship with her parents. Evie's father was no better than what everyone railed against. The way he drove around in that car and cheating on the ration books—a lot of people around here wouldn't have minded seeing him dead, but once he was gone, the benefits of knowing him were, too. That's what all this is about."

"People expected him to take care of them," I said, remembering what Grady had told me.

"Yeah." Mac popped a few potato chips in his mouth, sending the smell of sunflower oil and salt my way. "Some of the families were forced to move—they couldn't survive here in pure poverty, not knowing when the next meal would come. Evie's father had been the one that kept this village going. He made sure the shipments got here, that we had the equipment we needed, the coal when no one else had it, but once he was gone, there were families that . . ."

"What?"

"Starved."

We sat in silence, and I watched the grass blowing outside. The sky was dark, and it looked like rain again.

"I'm confused about that," I admitted, also taking a chip. "How could the death of one man, who was barely here, make that big of a difference? If people were starving, they could have moved somewhere else, found a place with greater opportunity or some type of assistance."

"What opportunities do you think were there?" His eyes were lit with fury, but I knew it wasn't directed at me. "The whole country was in ruin. There were no jobs, and the families who've farmed this land, who've raised the sheep and tended the crops, have been doing it for decades. The petrol shortage killed the farming equipment, the weather wouldn't cooperate, and there was little food.

"It wasn't as if the farmers could easily walk away from the only thing they'd ever known, because unless they wanted to emigrate, the choices weren't that bright anywhere else. Evie's father made it possible for those people to stay here, because he helped sustain this village. It was for a price, though. That pretty house by the sea came from somewhere."

"Do you think he had enemies?" I asked.

He took a deep drink. "There's no question about that."

"Yet everyone still believes she was the reason her parents died."

"Not the folks from your generation," he said. "The world's kept turning, so there's a lot more of the younger folk than those of us who would have been around to hear about it. But there are angry people out there who believe your grandmother is the reason they lost their family farm."

"That's unfair."

He held up his hands. "Hey, when everything's gone to shite, you jump on the first person who comes to mind. Evie had the honor of giving them someone to blame."

He held out the bag of Taytos, and when I waved it away, he finished them off before crumpling up the bag.

"Is she in danger?" I asked. "To be back?"

It hadn't occurred to me until now, but if people really blamed her for the loss of their livelihoods, it was possible.

Mac shrugged. "Depends on what your definition of 'danger' is. If it has to do with getting your feelings hurt because people are going to say things about the past, then yeah. I doubt anyone's going to come around looking for the money, though. Don't see how anyone could lay much of a claim on that anymore. Besides, like with most things around here, it was a story. Doesn't mean it was actually true."

"Good point," I admitted. "I'm going to ask her, though. About the money."

"It couldn't have been that much. How would she have gotten it to America without someone asking questions?" he asked, scratching his chin.

I got the sense this was a question the men at the pub had puzzled about for years. It was another answer that I didn't know, but I was more than interested in finding out.

"Do you think your father would want to see her?" I took another drink of cider. "In spite of all this?"

Mac gave a quick nod. "Oh yes. They were close. Life has a way of testing friendships, but a true friend will be there forever."

There were so many uncertainties about her relationship with Sullivan, but I did know that every time she said his name, she said it with favor. It was a risk to set up a meeting without her approval, but I could always cancel if she didn't want to go.

"Let's do it in the next day or so," I said. "If that works for you. I'll still have to clear it with her, but based on everything I've heard, she'd be delighted to see him again."

"He'd love that." Mac smiled at me. "Isn't life a beautiful thing? Time never stops swinging back around."

~

On my walk back home, I thought about the things Mac had said, especially the part about friendship. It made me think of Tia and the truths I'd shared with Grady the night before. I hadn't realized how unhappy I'd been until I came here. The pressure of back home was too much, and it was not how I wanted to spend the rest of my life. I wanted to be more like Grady—taking the time to figure out what made me happy. Lying to my best friend was not a part of that.

I stopped right there on the edge of the road and dialed Tia's number. She liked to hit the gym first thing in the morning, so she wouldn't mind me calling so early. I'd spent all this time thinking I should focus on fixing the problems with the business, but the most important thing to fix was our relationship. It was time to tell her the truth about what I'd done.

"Hey," she said, picking right up. It was loud in the background, and it sounded like she was on the el train. "How's your grandmother?"

It felt so good to hear her voice. It meant so much that she hadn't started our conversation with something like, *Where have you been?* She started our conversation with care and concern about my family and me. She was such a good person, and our friendship meant so much to me that I couldn't believe I'd let things go so far.

"I've really missed you," I said. "My grandmother seems completely recovered, and it's beautiful here. Listen. I—"

"I'm on the train," Tia said. "You're breaking up."

"I have to tell you some things that are a little bit difficult. I understand if you're angry with me, but I—"

"I can't . . ." The signal was going in and out. "Me . . . later?"

"Yes, I'll call you later," I said. "You can't hear me?"

I heard more broken speech, so I said, "I do want you to know that I love you. You're the best friend I could ask for, and I'll talk to you soon, okay?"

The call had dropped, and I squeezed the phone tight, staring at the path that led to Aisling. I hoped she'd heard at least a little part of that. I started walking, and my text alert went off.

Love you, too.

My eyes smarted. It was going to be all right. Everything between us would be just fine.

Chapter
Twenty-Three

Ireland, 1952

The man with the gun gave me a steady smile. "I figured someone would return for that money."

When we were first out by the well, he'd told me his name was Jon. Now, we stood in the main room of his farmhouse. He wore old pants and an undershirt, and he was large, with an imposing frame and strong upper arms. He had a pleasant face, however, and did not seem intent on doing me any harm.

The house where he lived was cozy but poor. There was no sitting room, simply a kitchen table and a hearth, where a bowl of soup bubbled like a cauldron. It smelled of sour potatoes, and I hoped he wouldn't offer me something to eat.

Instead, he returned the gun to a back room and came back out with an oil lamp. He lit it, then struggled to place it in the window, moving it around several times until he found a good footing.

Turning a kitchen chair, he took a seat and gestured that I should do the same. His eyes were kind, if bright from drink. "I found it out there last spring. You could have knocked me over with a feather. I haven't touched a note. I'm honest."

"Much obliged," I said, for lack of anything better.

"I've kept armed, though." He ran his hand through his hair. "Not knowing what kind of person would come for it. I didn't expect it to be someone like you."

"I know." I looked down at my hands. "My family was forced to hide our possessions during the Emergency. When Plan W was drafted and it was rumored that the battle would move to our land, my father feared the soldiers would take everything we had. He had no choice but to hide it."

He frowned. "It took him some time to return, then."

Get out.

Harding's message seemed to pass through my brain. I thought of Alby, innocently sleeping back home.

"Thank you for being so honest." I got to my feet. "I really should be getting on."

"Well, I'd like to know your story," he said. "To see if there's anything I can do to help. My wife passed on a few years back, and I miss the company. Your family is still alive, then?"

"Yes." The steady way he looked at me was starting to make me nervous. "My parents and brothers, yet it's my father waiting in the woods, for fear I'd run into trouble. I'm worried that if I'm here too long, he'll mistake that for trouble."

The man studied me. "I've managed to avoid trouble for quite some time." Getting to his feet, he said, "Let me get it for you, then, and you can be on your way."

In the next room, I heard a thump. Harding had once told me the majority of the money had been £100 notes, wrapped in heavy plastic for safekeeping. He walked back into the room, the package held close in his arms like a child.

My heart pounded with a sense of triumph. For the first time since Harding died, I felt alive. Right or wrong, I had done what she'd asked me to do.

"Thank you," I breathed.

"I'd like for you to count it." The man glanced toward the window. "To ensure it's all there. After this, I don't want to see you or your family on my land again." He set the parcel on the table and waited. "How many people know about this?"

Something didn't feel right. That move with the lamp could have been signaling the Garda. Or maybe he wanted to see how many people knew about the money to find out if killing me would clear his path to keep it. The thought was chilling.

"I told you." When he didn't speak, I looked toward the window. "My father might end up joining us if I take much longer."

He gave me a little smirk. "The more the merrier. Yes?"

He knew I was lying. I'd been a fool to come here, to think that I could be as bold as Harding.

"Then let's count." I started to sit and then did my best to look embarrassed. "First, do you have a water shed?"

"Aye, it's out back." I headed out the front door with purpose, but when I was a few steps away, I stopped on the front porch and stood right outside the door.

The wooden floors creaked, and I looked through the window. Jon had left the main area, which meant he'd gone to the back room, maybe to get the gun. I darted inside, grabbed the bundle, and raced toward the shadows of the field.

I was halfway across when a cry of rage echoed through the night.

"Come back here!" he shouted, the front door banging shut behind him.

Slowing my steps, I focused on moving as quietly as possible. Crashing through the woods would lead him right to me, so once I reached the road, I walked slowly and quietly, the way I'd approached. Sweat poured down my face, making my dress cling to me and mosquitoes swarm around me, but I kept the same pace, listening carefully for his angry muttering. He was on the opposite side of the field, back over by the well.

The silhouette of the motorcar came into sight, and I started to move quickly. The sticks crackled as I did, the forest smelling like damp soil and mushrooms in the night. His steps paused, and then he changed course.

The door to the car creaked only slightly as I opened it and slid into the front seat, my legs shaking. The package safely in the front seat, I powered up the engine. Backing up, I turned the wheel, trying to get out of the woods and back onto the street. In the dim light, I saw the man scramble over the stone wall.

He howled, "Come back here or I'll kill you!"

My ears rang as a bullet shattered through the night, missing the car but cutting into a tree right next to me. My breath came in short, fast gasps, but my hands were steady, and my actions felt clear.

Turn the wheel. Don't hit the tree. Avoid the rut.

The man ran into the road and stood in front of the headlights, the rifle pointed right at the car. I pressed down on the pedal, saying a prayer that he'd have the common sense to move, because I was not about to let him kill me. He fired, and the windscreen shattered, spraying glass across my lap and my hands. The car sped up, and his eyes changed from hate to fear as he leaped out of the way and into a ditch.

I stared steadily at the road, flinching as gunfire rang out yet again, but it missed the motorcar entirely. I drove as fast as possible before finally checking to see if he was anywhere behind me. My skin was hot with blood. A large gash on my forehead bled down my face and into my eyes, stinging them. It made me think of the first time Harding and I met, and for whatever reason, I started laughing.

"It's all right," I kept saying out loud. "It's all right."

Even though I wanted to pull over and hide, I had to keep going. The man might have access to a car himself, and he would travel the road, looking for me. Stopping only once to use the spare can of petrol, I pulled into town before morning light and parked the motorcar back in the carriage house.

The windscreen was destroyed. Glass covered the black vinyl seats. I couldn't see any bullet holes or any other damage.

I wanted to sink down next to the car in exhaustion, but I needed to get cleaned up before anyone spotted me. Sneaking into the house, I dared look at my face in the mirror. The bleeding had stopped. It was only one small gash. The rest, tiny scrapes.

After locking the door of my bedroom and closing the shutters, I sank down to the floor with the package. It occurred to me that it might not be money at all, but a collection of blankets the man had used to trick me.

With firm hands, I peeled back the layers, and only then could I breathe. I held the money close and let my trembling overtake me.

"I did it, Harding," I whispered. "That was more than enough excitement for the rest of my life, but I did it."

~

The next morning, I slept until noon. When I finally awoke and took breakfast, the realization of what I'd done hit me. The money that I'd found, the money that was now here in this house, was the root of the reason Harding had been killed.

I'd known that before I got it, of course. I'd considered that thought again and again. Yet I always knew I had a choice, that I could still turn back.

Not anymore. The memory of staring down the barrel of that gun made my mouth taste like metal, and I took a deep breath to calm my nerves, but they wouldn't steady.

Having the money here, with Alby and me, felt too dangerous. I had nowhere to hide it. Seamus or the servants could find it, or anyone else who happened to pass through. I struggled to find a good place to put it before finally settling on my parents' room, in a tiny nook hidden within their closet.

The hiding space wasn't deliberate, like a safe, but the closet had a small pocket behind a set of shelves that was the perfect place to tuck things away. When I was a child, my mother had played "hide the teddy bear" with me, putting it in that hiding spot again and again while she dressed. It was one of my rare memories of actually playing with her. Now, I put the money there and tried to fight off the wave of nerves that came with having it at all.

Was this what Harding had felt like the summer she died? The worry must have weighed on her every moment, and I closed my eyes, sending her a brief prayer of peace. It was something I'd taken to doing, to try to feel anything other than sorrow when I thought of her.

It was late afternoon when I'd finished picking out each piece of glass from the seats of the motorcar. I'd brought Alby a blanket and a ball, letting him play on the ground while I cleaned. I had to stop working several times to sit down and take deep breaths to stop my nerves from getting the best of me. Those moments, I held Alby and sang to him, grateful for his sweet smile.

Finally, after the car was free of glass, I walked into town to seek out the advice of Sullivan. He was just closing the shop and invited me to the pub for an early dinner. Once we'd eaten and he'd ordered a pint, I settled Alby in my lap with a bottle. Then, in a low tone, I told him about the money. His eyes became wider with every word.

"Why?" he said, aghast. "Didn't you understand what happened to her?"

His admonition didn't help. I'd been hoping for comfort, not condemnation, because I was completely terrified by what I'd done.

"I know," I said. "It fills me with fear to have it here."

The thought made my mouth go dry once again, and I took a drink of water, looking around the pub. It was busy, filled with the locals and their families, as well as a few men from the docks. Everyone was eating, laughing, and having a good time, such a far cry from what I'd experienced the night before.

We sat in silence, and Sullivan took a long drink. I ran my hand along the edge of the table, waiting for another wave of panic to pass. Alby was starting to doze off in my lap, clutching my finger tight.

"There's so much I don't know about her," I admitted. "About who she was and all she was doing, but I promised her that I would get this for him, for his future."

Sullivan's eyes were wide. "Why would you risk that?"

"Trust me, it wasn't a decision that was made lightly." My hands were shaking, and my breath felt shallow. "I regret it, yes. But it's done."

"You need to put it back," Sullivan said.

I shook my head. "I'm never setting foot on that property again. The man shot at me. It's mine now, and I'll use it for Alby, to give him everything that's good and right."

"Evie." Sullivan looked at me like I was a stranger. "This is wrong. If you keep it, you're just like her. You've become a thief, too."

I drew back. "What right do you have to say that?"

The fact that Sullivan kept speaking to my darkest fears did not endear me to him. I could not face his judgment alongside my own.

The idea that I'd committed a crime had haunted me from the moment I pulled into the garage with the glass shattered across the seats like bullets. I couldn't change it, though. It was done, and it was much too dangerous to return.

"You're right," Sullivan said. "I'm sorry. It's not what I meant."

"It *is* what you meant." My eyes filled with tears. "You have no idea how this feels. I've come to you as a friend, seeking support, and the only thing you're worried about is whether or not I've committed a *crime*? I think the greatest crime is not standing beside the people who matter to you."

It wasn't a fair assessment, because Sullivan had stood by me since Harding died. Still, taking this money had terrified me, and I'd come to him for reassurance, something he refused to give.

"I need you to stand by me, Sullivan."

"I can't do that if you're willing to put everyone you care for at risk," he told me. "That's what she did."

I stared at him in disbelief. "I've been tormented by this. Tormented." Emotion made me stop talking. I was completely alone, and I hated him for it. "You know, it's pretty obvious Harding was the only person in this world who cared a bit about me. Now she's gone, and the only thing you can offer is judgment. Thanks for the warning. Harding was right—life with you would have been a prison."

I regretted the words immediately, but it was too late to take them back. Sullivan got to his feet and gave me a polite nod, like he would with a customer.

"I best be going, then," he said.

"Sullivan." I held Alby tight. "I'm sorry. I . . ."

"No, I'm sorry." The pub was still as animated as ever, but silence had fallen over the two of us. "You know, Evie, there was a moment where I'd thought we'd have a life together, but a moment can pass, as easy as the clouds. You need to put the money back."

"I can't."

"Then you're on your own. Standing beside you is not a risk I can take."

His words gutted me. I fought back tears, holding Alby tight while I watched the one person who had been through all of it walk away.

On the way home, the sky was blue with powder-puff clouds, and the grass waved around me in the breeze. Sullivan's words echoed in my mind, about putting everyone around me at risk. It was still possible that wasn't true.

The farmer had no way of finding me. He did not know my name or where I was from, and he hadn't followed me. In spite of all that had happened, I had absolutely no reason to think I was in danger at all.

That is, until I walked up the path to Aisling and discovered an unknown black motorcar waiting for me in the drive.

Chapter Twenty-Four

Ireland, present day

My grandmother was awake when I returned from the pub, and she was looking through the children's book I'd set on her nightstand. She seemed tired and emotionally drained. I decided to wait until I had a set time with Sullivan before telling her about the plan, because it might be too much at the moment.

I settled in next to her on the bed. "Can I read to you?"

"Please," she said, handing me the book.

The cover was faded red leather embossed with gold, and it said *Children's Tales*. The inside front cover was inscribed with a name, and I wondered if someone had passed it down to her family.

"It's so nice to see this again," she said. "I must've read it a thousand times. So many moments well spent."

I read to her, and she considered the pictures. The book was a work of art, with vibrant, detailed drawings of animals and vivid fancies that would have captured my imagination all hours of the day.

"Do you have a favorite story in here?" I asked.

"Yes. I can't remember, but it's something about the land of dreams, where the sea stood guard against the night." My grandmother took the book and flipped through it in silence. She stopped at a page with stars glittering brightly over a stretch of water. The bottom-left corner of the page had a picture of a cat, and her hand brushed over it, as if petting it. "I spent so many hours reading this story." Her eyes met mine. "No one's ever read it to me before."

"Not even your parents?" I asked.

"No. This was a book I used to read to Alby."

My grandmother seemed to brighten from saying his name out loud.

Alby.

"That was his name?" I asked.

"Yes. I've thought about him many times, especially that playful smile on his face." She sighed and studied the pages. "He loved this storybook, Rainey. Thank you for reading it to me."

If the baby had loved the book, that meant he'd been alive long enough for her to read it to him.

"Grandma, how old was he?" I asked. "When you lost him?"

"Nearly two." She traced the silver drawing of the moon. "It's funny how such a short period of time can change the rest of your life."

She settled back into her pillows, indicating the conversation was over. I opened the book and began to read, trying to not think about how fragile and vulnerable she seemed.

How she was now the one like a child.

That afternoon, my grandmother was sleeping soundly, and I visited the website of the Department of Foreign Affairs in hopes of finding some more information about my great-grandmother. I clicked through until I decided that my best bet was to call them directly.

I spoke to a man who was as kind as could be and left him my contact information, as well as my question of whether my great-grandmother had been an employee. The man on the phone was pleasant, but I doubted anyone would call me back with any sort of efficiency. I got the impression that I'd have to visit the office. It was located in Dublin, and a trip there wasn't on the roster anytime soon.

My grandmother opened her eyes. "Sweet girl," she said. "Why are you on that computer once again?"

"Sorry," I said, closing it and getting to my feet. "Did I wake you?"

"Oh, I've slept long enough." My grandmother eased herself up and considered the items on the bed. "I'd like to sit out on the lawn. Get some fresh air."

"I'll join you," I said.

"No. I'd like for you to go out and explore. See Ireland." My grandmother reached up and touched the locket. "I need some time to think, my darling. To look out at the sea. I used to do that a lot, you know. When I was younger. Like the answers could be found in the waves."

"I'll help you get set up, then."

"That you could do."

Once my grandmother was settled in her favorite chair in the backyard with some tea and soda bread, I debated on how to spend this time. I was getting sleepy, but a walk would be better than a nap, so I decided to head out to the moor.

I'd checked the status of the appeal right before my grandmother woke up, and it hadn't moved forward, which made me feel a little nervous. I still planned to tell Tia the truth the moment she called me back, but it would've been nice to do that with some better news.

I was walking out front to find the path to the moor when my favorite Irish voice called out: "Hey."

I smiled to see Grady walking out to the driveway, toward his bike.

"Where are you headed?" I asked. "Back to the water?"

"The sheep." He ran his hand through his hair. "Would you like to join me?"

It was so tempting, but his smile was taking up too much space in my brain. Not to mention the memory of our adventure in the watering hole. Even though everything about him made my heart beat a little bit faster, it wouldn't be smart to waste my time and energy getting emotionally invested in this guy.

"I'd like to see the sheep," I said, slowly. "It's just that . . . I do want to be clear about where we're at. We're friends, right? Leaving it at that? I mean, I'm sure there are women passing through here each week. So I appreciate you not putting me in that position."

He hesitated. "What position, exactly?"

"The tourist romance. Or whatever." My cheeks colored. "The 'bed' in bed-and-breakfast."

He laughed. "Why do you insist on cracking me up every single time we talk?"

"I'm being serious," I said, but I couldn't fight back a smile.

"Well, I'll tell you something." He took a step closer to me. "I've never dated one of my sister's guests. I've actually . . ." He shoved his hands into his pockets, looking uncomfortable. "I haven't dated much since the divorce. Once or twice, but not lately. If that eases your mind."

"It does," I said. "Thanks."

We both stood in silence, looking at each other. The trees made shadows on the ground around us.

"My flight leaves in a week," I said.

He nodded. "I should hurry and get your helmet, then."

"We won't be gone long, will we?" I asked, thinking of my grandmother.

"I can bring you back whenever. Sheep are surprisingly bad at keeping me up to ninety."

"I don't even know what that means."

He tapped his watch. "Meet you back here in five."

∼

The Scottish Blackface sheep stared up at me. Their sweet faces matched their legs, like fancy ladies in white coats and black tights. I didn't know the difference between a ram and an ewe, but I was mesmerized by the deep and soulful way they stared me down.

"They are the cutest things I've ever seen," I said.

"Told you," Grady said, cheerfully. "Here, pet him."

I hesitated, then rested my hand on its back. The wool fell in neat curls and looked as soft as a featherbed but felt thick and coarse, almost oily. My hand barely sank down as I petted the sheep, but I liked the feeling.

Grady's flock was on the edge of a hill that went straight up, with smaller, rolling hills all around us and a view of the water in the distance. The grass was tall and scratched against the top of my boots. The open field made me feel like I'd stepped into another time.

Grady took a seat on a section of shorter grass and pulled on a burnt-orange newsboy cap that brought out a hint of gold in his eyes. I settled in next to him, and the sheep grazed alongside us.

He plucked a piece of clover from the ground and put it between his lips. I watched, curious how clover tasted. I plucked my own piece and bit down. It was surprisingly sweet.

His gaze dropped to my lips. "What do you think?"

I took it out. "It reminds me of the green juice I'd get right after this particularly vicious spinning class I used to take. There's an injustice in this place, you know."

"How's that?" he asked.

I'd worked so hard on a bike in a gym, sweating and grunting, while Grady was out here, breathing in cool fresh air. Walking the hills and building his muscles better than I'd been building my own. It wasn't like we didn't have nature back home, but it wasn't like this.

"I don't know," I said. "I've spent my whole life trying to survive, pay bills, staring at the inside of an office, while these sheep were over here living like kings."

He tugged at the grass. "If it makes you feel any better, there's been so many times I've stared out at these hills wondering what it would be like to be anywhere else. The grass is always greener."

"Especially in Ireland." I thought of my grandmother and the grief she was facing. "I feel like I'm running into the same problems here that I do back home. I feel more stress than I should, I think, because I'm trying to . . ."

Grady looked at me. "What?"

"Orchestrate things. Fix things. That's what science is all about for me, and I love it—figuring out how to do something, gathering evidence to support my theory, and finding a way to make it work. I've gotten really good at making things go how I want them to."

"Like when you set those boundaries."

"No." My cheeks colored again. "I'm talking about with my grandmother. It hurts me to see her cry, and I'm frustrated because I can't stop her pain or save her from the past."

"Maybe you don't have to," he said.

I twirled the clover between my fingers. "But I want to be supportive."

"Why do you think being supportive means fixing things?" he asked.

A memory of my mother came to mind, right after she and my father had divorced. I'd walked past the door of the den and was startled to see her sobbing into a box of tissues, her students' papers in a mess all around the room. I'd organized the papers, and picked up the tissues. My mother stopped crying and lay in silence on the couch with a cold compress on her head. It had felt good to help her through that, to stop her pain. In some ways, I'd been trying to do the same for everybody ever since.

"I don't know," I said. "I don't want people to feel sad."

"I get that," he said. "But if I learned anything from my divorce, it's that it's important to feel your feelings. Move through them, even if it's hard. Then you can let them go."

Part of the reason I'd tried to help my mother was because I didn't know how to handle losing my father, either. He and I found a new relationship with time, but it still hurt when I thought about what it had meant to watch my family fall apart.

"Your grandmother is stronger than you think," he said. "Let her talk about her time here, her feelings. Let her know you'll be right by her side. That's all you can do. Life is full of sorrow. It doesn't do us a bit of good to run from it."

My eyes settled on his lips, and I thought about what he'd said about boundaries. Yes, I was trying to orchestrate the situation with him, too. To stop the hurt of losing him before it even happened.

I took in the view of the grass and the hills and the sheep grazing beneath the perfect pale-blue sky. Finally I said, "It's easy to believe there's no such thing as heartbreak in a place as beautiful as this."

"Don't be fooled." He looked out over the land. "It hides in the shadows, waiting to take what it can. It lives here, too, and has for much too long."

"The history of Ireland is complicated, isn't it?" I asked. "I'd love to learn about it."

Grady leaned back on his hands and started talking. Weaving stories about the past, explaining the British rule, the Irish Free State, the difference between the Republic of Ireland and Northern Ireland, and sharing his thoughts on all the politics in between. It was fascinating to receive such an in-depth history lesson, and to hear his thoughts on it all, and the future. I hung on his every word, watching the way his mouth moved and the spark in his eyes.

He was as beautiful as the landscape, and I could have listened to him until the sun went down. I was absolutely fascinated with him, and that was a problem, but for once, it was one I didn't feel the need to solve.

～

Grady brought me back to Aisling around four. We stood in the driveway, near the flowers and English ivy. The bees buzzed around, and I didn't want the day to end.

"I have to go back to the sheep," he said. "What do you think, though, about letting me take you out Friday night for some good old-fashioned Irish fun?"

"You want to take me out?" I said, and I could swear he blushed.

"No," he said, quickly. "You were clear about things. I just meant out in the world. To experience Ireland."

"Right." My mind instantly jumped to the motorbike, the way it had felt to rest my cheek against his back for the duration of the ride. "Doing what?"

"It's a surprise. You don't have to dress."

"Sorry?"

"Dress up."

"Got it," I said.

He grinned. "I sort of regret explaining it."

This time, it was my turn to blush.

∾

I was headed up the stairs to my room when the phone rang. Tia. This time, I didn't hesitate to pick up the call. I missed her, I wanted to talk to her, and I didn't want my mistake standing in the way. I just wanted to hear her voice.

"Hi." Eagerly, I took a seat in one of the chairs in the upper hall that provided a nice view of the water. "Thank you for being so patient with me. I've wanted to talk to you so badly. You wouldn't believe what just—"

"You're right, I wouldn't believe it." Tia's voice was low and measured. "Because apparently, the one thing you excel at is telling lies."

Chapter Twenty-Five

Ireland, 1952

The black motorcar sat in the drive, waiting for me. I drew back, debating whether or not to run. Before I could, Seamus appeared on the front porch and beckoned, a tense expression on his face. He seemed concerned rather than fearful, and I wondered if my parents had fallen ill.

Rushing up the drive with Alby in my arms, I called, "Is everything all right?"

Two people stepped out of the car, a well-dressed man and a fashionable woman wearing a large hat and satin gloves. I started before coming to a stop. The woman looked exactly like Harding.

It must be her aunt. My parents had asked if I knew of any existing family back when Harding passed. I'd given her the name of the town where we'd stayed, but I couldn't think of her aunt's name. My parents had sent a general telegram but had never heard back. Now, I held Alby tight.

I had nothing to fear, though. My mother did not know that he belonged to Harding, and the doctor who was there that night had given us his word that he would keep the birth confidential. Perhaps the aunt had finally come to collect Harding's personal items. Or perhaps she wanted to have a brief remembrance for her niece.

Squaring my shoulders against a sudden rush of emotion, I called, "Hello, I'm Evie. You must be Harding's aunt?"

The woman wrinkled her brow. "I'm seeking a young woman named Flannery. I received word from my sister that she passed away some time ago. She was my daughter."

Harding was an orphan. That conversation was as fresh in my mind as the argument I'd had with Sullivan at dinner.

Now that I was closer, I realized the woman had green eyes, but she didn't look that much like Harding. Her expression was tight and condescending, so different from the open beauty of my best friend.

"I'm so sorry." I set down Alby, who instantly took a seat on the driveway and started playing with a rock. "I don't know who that is."

Even though speaking with Harding's family would have been emotional, I was disappointed that I couldn't do that. I missed her every day, and it would have been nice to talk with someone about her.

"You're welcome to ask around in town to see if anyone knows Flannery," I added. "The pub would be a good place."

The man stepped forward, pulling a photograph out of a leather folder. "This is her when she was younger."

He handed me a black-and-white photograph, and my mouth went dry. Harding wore a haughty secondary school uniform, sitting on grand steps, while sharing a wry smile with the camera.

"Where did you get this?" I demanded.

This could not be her. This image did not fit with the childhood she'd described to me, living out on the farm, toiling in the hot sun, surrounded by brothers and sisters. Fighting for every mouthful of food.

"You recognize her?" the man said.

I pushed away the photograph. "No, I . . ." Suddenly, I felt nervous. What did these people want? Who were they, really? The woman did resemble her, but what if someone had discovered who Alby belonged to and had come for him out of vengeance?

I picked him up and held him close. Shaking my head at the photo, I said, "I don't know who that is."

The couple exchanged glances.

"The girl in the photograph is our daughter," the woman said.

I felt like she had punched me. Or that Harding had slapped me across the face. *I, Harding Keelin McGovern, am an orphan.* The words were as clear in my memory as if she stood beside me now.

I stood there, sweat suddenly hot on my body. If she'd lied about being an orphan, she could have lied about anything. The money . . . it might not even belong to her.

The realization made it hard to breathe. I forced in some air and held Alby tight. He smiled at the woman. His green eyes seemed brighter than ever in the sunlight, his face as peaceful as an angel.

"It is quite disgusting that Flannery's lies led to this . . ." She eyed Alby like a sin, a black mark on her daughter's chastity. "However, he's family and will be raised as such. With the ideals and principles that seem to have escaped his mother."

Barely able to feel my legs, I practically ran with Alby to the house. The couple followed, and I thrust him at Seamus.

"Take him inside," I said. "Tell Mona not to leave the nursery."

Seamus ushered him indoors. The couple had followed me up the steps, and they stood there on the porch, staring at me.

"I cannot be of help to you," I said, crossing my arms.

The woman seemed amused. "Well, we do intend to leave here with our grandchild."

The more the woman spoke, the more I knew that she was, indeed, Harding's mother. They had the same eyes, the same tilt to their chin. I would have almost preferred this woman to be one of Harding's adversaries, if only for the knowledge that my friend hadn't been raised by someone so awful.

"I'm sorry," I said. "I can't help you."

The woman stared me down. "Regardless of the mistakes Flannery made, the boy is our family. We can't blame him for the things she's done."

Even though I wanted to scream that his mother was like a sister to me, in spite of all her lies, I was not about to confirm Alby's identity.

"I do apologize," I said. "I wish you luck in finding news of your daughter; however, it's time for me to tend to my son."

"Don't leave, or I'll be forced to fetch the Garda." Harding's mother dabbed at the moisture on her face with a silk cloth, her voice as cool as ice. "Personally, I don't understand your loyalty to my daughter when you didn't even know her first name. Typical Flannery. She's always been a liar."

My blood chilled. Perhaps Harding had lied to me about her name and the way she'd been raised, but she'd also run from these people. She didn't want to claim them as her family. Which meant I could not give them her son.

Seamus returned just then with water in a heavy crystal glass. I drank it in silence, then set it on the decorative side table.

"The child isn't the boy you're seeking," I told her. "I found him by the side of the road."

Seamus stepped forward. "I can confirm that, madame. I was here the day Evie arrived with him. He was found. Her friend didn't come for several days later. She was quite slow to warm to him, I might add."

It was the most I'd heard Seamus speak ever on my behalf. It must have been out of respect to my father, but I was grateful all the same.

"The doctor will identify him," she said. "The boy has a small red mark on the back of his arm."

I swallowed hard. The doctor had betrayed us, after all. Still, I was not about to give in.

"I will repeat myself," I said, getting to my feet. "I don't know a Flannery. You cannot arrive here without warning and attempt to take my child. Now, I will kindly ask you to leave."

I'd expected the mother to argue with me. Or perhaps, to see me with new respect and understand that I was protecting her daughter's interests. Instead, she gave her husband a pointed look.

He nodded. "I'll fetch the Garda."

The woman took a seat in the other chair on the front porch as he drove away. She folded her gloves and stared out at the grass in silence. Seamus stood nearby, looking as stunned as I felt.

My breath came quick as I tried to figure out what to do. Surely, Perry wouldn't order me to hand over Alby. He'd been there those first few days when strangers tried to claim the baby, and he wouldn't let these people do the same. But Perry had also seen Harding, and he would recognize her in the picture.

My mind raced, desperate to find a solution.

Her mother and I sat in silence until two sets of headlights illuminated the path. Once they'd parked, Harding's father finished some story that made Perry laugh, a sure sign that they'd gotten on.

Slowly, I got to my feet. "I need to change and feed him. Seamus, please let our visitors into the parlor."

His eyes met mine. "I shall prepare a tea."

Quick as lightning, I fetched a bottle, two liters of milk, and a small bucket of ice. Then I listened at the parlor door. The three spoke in low tones, laughing at yet another story.

Seamus appeared from the shadows. I expected him to lecture me. Instead, he gave me the keys to the motorcar and a gun.

"Go now," he said, with a nod. "Run."

My eyes filled with tears. With a nod of thanks, I held Alby close and stole out the back door, headed for the garage. Then I remembered the money.

Carefully, I set Alby in the black vinyl seat next to mine, put the milk on the floor in the back, and hid the gun high up on a shelf in the garage. I ran back inside and crept up the staircase.

Once I had the money, I raced down the stairs. Too quickly, as if running from something. Gripping the railing tight, I took a deep breath and forced myself to slow down.

I returned to the car with the money wrapped in a blanket. I tucked the gun under my seat and fired up the motorcar. Cringing at the sudden sound, I put my hand on Alby's leg and sped off into the ether of the evening.

Both the Garda and Harding's parents had cars in greater working order than mine, so I took a gamble and turned to the road that led into the forest, to the path Sullivan had used to carry Harding on the day of the attack. Alby was crying now, probably frightened to feel the wind on his face and the hard bumps on the ground.

"It's okay," I told him. "We'll be there soon."

Once I'd parked beneath a weeping willow, I covered the car in heavy vines while he looked on with big eyes, holding a handful of leaves. It was impossible to carry everything, so I found another tree and buried the money beneath sticks and branches. No one would find it even if they did know to look, and I had little choice but to leave it.

Rushing through the woods, I held Alby tight in my arms. The room above the stables had remained vacant since Harding's stay, and the doors didn't have locks. My plan was to hide up there and return for the money at the first light of dawn. Then I'd take Alby to the ports and sail for America.

It was starting to get dark, but the horses were not yet in from the stable. No one was around.

"We have to be quiet as a mouse," I whispered. "Quiet as can be."

He giggled and made shushing noises.

"Shh," I begged. "Please."

Once he nodded, I picked him up and darted across the yard and to the barn, the wooden steps echoing in the night.

There, I sank down to the floor. I was trapped but safe. We didn't have food or water, but Alby had milk and I had a gun. The plan would work—it had to. I'd have no time to say goodbye to my parents or anyone else I cared for, but that was a small price to pay when the alternative was to lose my son forever.

It was hot, but I didn't dare crack the windows. I'd do it once it was completely dark outside. In the meantime, I kept Alby cool with the ice for the milk, which made him laugh.

I had thought to grab him a small wooden car. Now, I handed it to him and relished in the joy on his face, his mind whirring with possibility at what he could play. The simplicity of his heart made mine swell, then ache, as I considered how complicated it had all become.

One thought that plagued me was the idea that Harding had not trusted me enough to tell me the truth about her parents. She'd had so many opportunities to come clean, but she never had. Which made me question, once again, whether her claims about the money were true. What if the money I'd taken was something she'd wanted to steal from one of her former partners, or someone she'd worked with? She'd already told me she'd cheated them. What if she'd taken it one step further, as payback beyond the grave?

The thought made my body tremble. We had to leave; we had to get out of here. The morning couldn't come quickly enough.

Once night fell, the insects singing in the evening, I opened the windows and laid Alby in the bed. He gripped his toy tightly.

"Sleep well." I tried to keep my voice steady and strong. "Tomorrow's going to be a big, big day."

Exhaustion sent me into a fitful sleep right at his side. I dreamed of freedom, of Alby's face smiling at me, with the ocean out beyond. Then I saw a ship with a bright light coming straight at us. Too bright, and I awoke to find a torch shining straight in my face.

~

The stable hand had heard footsteps while putting the horses away for the night. He'd crept up the stairs and saw me, then informed the Hannigans they had a vagrant. Now, Mrs. Hannigan was nearly in tears at the confusion.

"There's no problem here," she told Perry, who'd been summoned earlier. "You know I've known Evie since she was a little girl."

We all stood in the parlor: Mr. and Mrs. Hannigan, Harding's parents, Alby and me. I held him tight, my teeth clenched against the violent trembling of my fear.

"You're always welcome to stay," Mrs. Hannigan told me. Turning to Perry, she said, "The girl needed a rest. She used our barn, and that's fine. Let's let this whole thing go."

"She tried to steal our child." Harding's father's voice was deep and resonated in the small space. "She deserves to be punished."

Mrs. Hannigan stood up to her full height. "Excuse me, sir. Do not come into my home and presume that you're the one to make those decisions. Evie has been caring for that child. To be quite frank, if you're the one who abandoned him by the side of the road, the Garda should consider whether you should be allowed to be near him at all."

"Now, now." Perry held up his hands. "Let's not fight. We need to come to a resolution. I have received a telegram from the doctor confirming there is indeed a birthmark behind the child's arm. If it is there, Evie must hand him over. I don't want any more trouble."

Alby watched the scene unfold with wide eyes. The one thing I could not bear was to have him suffer the indignity of being searched, considering I knew full well he had the birthmark.

"There's no need," I said quietly. "This is Harding's son."

Mrs. Hannigan put her hand to her mouth. "What?"

Images of Harding's face flashed through my mind. That time we spent waiting for Alby to come, the smell of turf on the fire, and the coziness of our quiet conversations. The terror in her eyes when I left to fetch the doctor. The screams she gave as he was born, and the sudden, sweet realization that there were now three of us in our home.

I'd been there since the moment Alby took his first breath. This child was mine, almost as much as he'd belonged to her. I loved him with every part of me. How could I let these people take him away, to live a life that his mother had so clearly run from?

I'd given Harding my word that I'd protect him, but I was trapped. The only way to keep him from them would be to keep running. There was no way to do that, though. The Garda would stop me. They would say he wasn't mine.

I held Alby tight, my mind running through the options. I rested my lips on his head, breathing in his sweet warmth, the smell of yeast and milk and that precious, sour scent that was only him.

"Help me," I said to Mrs. Hannigan. "I told Harding I'd protect him. She does not want him to be anywhere else but with me."

"Oh, my dear." If Mrs. Hannigan was scandalized, she didn't show it. Instead, she turned to Perry. "Clearly, there's a misunderstanding here. This child . . ."

"There is no misunderstanding." Harding's father's voice boomed. "He's our grandchild. There is no further debate."

Perry nodded. "Let's get on with it, then."

I held Alby as tight as I could. Letting him go would mean letting go of Harding, because she still lived on in him. The flash of his smile, the gleam in his eye. I loved them with everything in me, and I couldn't lose them both.

Perry seemed to hesitate as he watched me grip him so tight. For a moment, I felt like I might have some hope. Then he set his jaw and reached forward.

I nearly jerked Alby away. I could make it to the front door or through the front window in time. In between the sudden flash of courage was the cut of reality. If I resisted, Alby could get hurt. Nothing was worth that risk.

In a swift moment, the Garda removed him from my arms. The warmth and the weight of my son left, and the moment we felt it, Alby's face twisted in outrage.

"Mum," he said, then wailed it, reaching for me. "Mumma!" He started to scream and kick, tears rolling down his cheeks. I began to shiver, my eyes locked onto his.

"I love you." I rushed forward and gripped his hands tight. "I love you, I love you. Be brave. You will always be right here. Right here inside my heart." I hit my chest to show him, and Alby reached out his hand to touch my heart as Perry handed him to Harding's mother.

The woman barely held him, looking irritated at his cries.

"Please," I begged, my body already aching with grief. "You don't want to raise another child. Let me care for him as his governess. Please. You will not pay me. I just need to be with him."

"That's not possible," Harding's mother said. "He belongs with us."

"Mumma," Alby cried again, reaching for me.

Her husband opened the door, and they stepped out.

It clicked shut behind them, and I ran for it, but the Garda blocked my way. I collapsed to the floor, sobbing, and Mrs. Hannigan pulled me to my feet. She held me tight against her chest, as if she were my mother. The type of mother I'd wished to have. The type of mother Alby had lost.

I could see so clearly that he would be raised as a scar on the family, instead of celebrated for the beautiful soul that he was. I stared straight ahead, unable to move, my heart filled with a despair so deep that I wondered if I could ever move past it. There was nothing left, nowhere to go.

"There, there, child," Mrs. Hannigan whispered. She led me to the couch and sat by my side, her hand patting mine. "I know," she whispered, quietly. "I know."

Chapter Twenty-Six

Ireland, present day

Tia waited in furious silence on the other end of the line. My entire body went hot and then cold with embarrassment. This was what I'd dreaded, feared, the moment the lie had first come out of my mouth.

"I was going to tell you," I said.

"Do you know how humiliating this is?" she demanded. "When I logged on to find out an exact date that we'd have our approval, I was informed our password had been changed."

My stomach dropped. "Tia, I can—"

"Then, when I called to find out what on earth was going on, I was informed that our facial serum's undergoing an 'appeal' process. What's going on?"

I still had a chance to dig myself out of this, to get her to understand, but the very idea of that was exhausting.

Maybe you don't need to fix it.

I stared out at the sea through the window, trying to find the right words.

"The levels showed heavy metals were in the sample," I said. "It failed."

"What?" she roared. "Why didn't you tell me?"

"Because I was in a panic the night we got the news because of my grandmother," I said. "I knew something wasn't right, because we'd tested the serum so extensively before we sent it, and I wanted the time to figure out what had happened. I should have just told you. I'm sorry."

"You found out the night that you *left*?" she demanded. "You told me that letter said our report was delayed."

"I'm so sorry, I—"

"'Sorry' isn't going to cut it." Tia's voice was shaking. "My father's going to pull our funding! We won't be able to finish this. Do you know who called them first and found out there was a problem? *He* did. You know what that has done to my credibility? To *yours*?"

My cheeks turned hot. "I understand you're angry . . ."

"'Angry' doesn't even begin to describe it. I'm in disbelief. I thought I could trust you like family, that I'd pick up this phone and prove to my father there'd been some sort of a mistake. The only mistake was partnering with you."

I gripped the edge of the window, fighting the pain coursing through me. "Please, I need you to understand. I really thought I could fix it, but I've realized that I don't always need to—"

"There are two of us! Why did you think it had to be on you?" she demanded. "You made me look like a complete fool."

"That was not my inten—"

"You're no longer with our company."

The words hit me hard. Then anger set in. I'd made one mistake, in all our years of working together. Yes, it was a big one, but that's all it took?

"I don't even know what to say to that," I told her. "I've worked day and night for the past five years of my life, and for what? So you could impress your father?"

"How dare you." Her voice was like ice.

"I'm sorry," I said, already regretting the words. "If anything, I was the one trying to impress your father, and that's not how it should have been."

She was silent for a long moment. Then she said, "Just so you know, my father wanted to sue you to recoup the costs of the past few weeks. I talked him out of that. You're welcome. I never want to hear from you again."

With a click, she hung up.

Time felt frozen. I stared out the window, surprised to see the water still moving in the wind and the clouds drifting by.

Tia had every right to be angry at me. I'd lied that night because I feared her father would lose faith in us. He'd never believed in me, not really, and I'd accepted that because I hadn't been brave enough to believe in myself.

If I could do it over, I would have come clean. Collaborated on solutions and worked together as a team, but I hadn't trusted Tia to handle the situation. My fault, my insecurity—and it had cost me the best friend I'd ever had. I was so caught up in the idea that I was the one who always had to fix things, or the world would fall apart. Well, sometimes the word fell apart anyway. It was time I learned to accept that.

Slowly, I walked back downstairs. I found my grandmother in her chair by the water, chatting with an older Englishwoman.

"This must be your granddaughter." The woman adjusted her straw hat and smiled at me. "Your grandmother is so proud of you."

Would my grandmother be proud to learn that I'd just lost my job? Or, more important, that I'd lost my best friend?

My smile was shaky, but it kept the tears from coming. "Yes. Thank you."

"I'll leave you two to enjoy the evening." The woman got to her feet. "Let's speak again soon."

Instead of sitting in the chair, I settled into the soft grass as the woman walked away. I didn't dare look up at my grandmother, for fear she'd see that I was upset.

"You've been making friends," I said.

The words felt hollow, but my grandmother gave a cheerful nod.

"Yes, we've been talking. People are so interesting, Rainey. Everyone has a story, if you're lucky enough to hear it."

I yanked at the grass. "I'd like to hear your story. If you'd be willing to tell it."

It might be hard and it might be painful, but I could listen. If I could just be strong enough to sit through her pain, I could listen.

To my surprise, she reached for my hand. "Let's order a high tea. There are indeed some things you deserve to know about my past."

~

The sun's rays were long by the time my grandmother told me about Harding, her son, and the money that she'd hidden away. My stomach twisted and turned when I heard the anguish that she'd gone through.

I was stunned to learn that Alby had not died but had been taken from her, even though she loved him as if he were her own. The idea that my grandmother had lost her friend—no, the idea that my grandmother's best friend had been murdered, like her parents—was hard to wrap my mind around. No wonder she'd run from this place. There was more than just beauty here; there was something so much darker, a grit beneath the roots.

My grandmother looked out at the water and set down her cup of tea. "It feels like all of this happened a moment ago, but it's been a lifetime." She held up her hands, as though confused that they were wrinkled. "You asked me earlier what it felt like to move to a new country on my own, and I've thought about that ever since. When I first moved to the States, I had days of agony, but also immense freedom. My shame at running was coupled with a feeling of incredible power that I'd managed to survive. There were times I shouldn't have made it, but it felt as though Harding was protecting me. Or maybe it was my parents."

My grandmother touched the locket as she spoke. Her words were slow, but I hung on each one of them.

"My parents spent so much of my life traveling, and then tucking me away during important moments. They had guests in our home that were worldly and glamorous, and they gave me the sense that I didn't belong there. That I was an unwelcome distraction. That hurt." Her face clouded. "A part of me pined for my mother and worried that I'd put my family in danger. It took me three years to build up the courage to reach out to them, after I'd left. I was afraid that, if they communicated with me, it would cause trouble."

My grandmother went quiet, and I took her hand. Taking in a breath to fight back my emotion, I focused on the scenery.

"I wrote to my parents with shaking hands," she said. "The solicitor was the one who wrote back, to tell me what had happened. I was shattered to think that I . . ."

"It wasn't your fault," I said.

"I can still imagine them here." She looked back at the house, as if hopeful her parents would still be standing there in the yard. "I didn't see them often, but I loved them, and I felt responsible. I feel responsible. The people that came after Harding came for me. They took my parents instead."

"You don't know that for sure," I said. "They could have had enemies. From what I understand, your father had a big hand in running this town, so there could have been bad blood from somebody he'd dealt with. Or it could have been random." Bowing my head, I admitted, "I heard about it down at the pub."

She gave a slow nod. "Do people think I'm to blame?"

I was careful with my answer. "Your generation is not around. The thing that matters is if you blame yourself."

"I blame myself for being too much of a coward to say goodbye. I hadn't planned to leave without telling my parents. Once I'd taken that money, I knew I was in danger, and I was scared. That's when they took Alby from me. I couldn't do anything but leave. There were memories everywhere I looked, and I had no way to find him. So I packed up, and with Sullivan's help, I was gone."

The breeze was cool on my arms. I took a final bite from a tea sandwich.

"You don't sound angry with her," I said.

"With who?" my grandmother asked.

"Harding."

"Oh." My grandmother fidgeted with her hands. "No. Harding changed my life for the better. She pushed me to try things that I wouldn't have done." My grandmother gave a little laugh. "I remember the time we sneaked down to the swimming hole. It was not allowed, because we could have been swept away or smashed against the rocks. In spite of the danger, I tasted freedom."

My mouth dropped open. "You went in the swimming hole? It's really dangerous."

Her face brightened. "Yes, it was dangerous, and that alone was a gift. She taught me that my life did not have to be how my parents had prescribed it. That I only needed to become the person that I wanted to be."

And to think I'd only thought of my time in the water as a way to see Grady with his shirt off.

"Harding was the proof that it was possible to take charge of my life," my grandmother said, "in spite of the time we lived in. Some people would say she was a troublemaker, but that was because she wasn't willing to settle for the life she had been born into. Yes, I was angry at some of the things that she did, but I wouldn't be who I am today if I had not met her."

Tia flashed through my mind. Meeting me at the airport in Chicago and helping me find an apartment, and the night we stood together at the top of one of the tallest buildings, looking out over the city. Because of her, I'd believed I could achieve great things.

"Good friends can show you a whole new world," my grandmother said. "Harding also gave me the gift of Alby. Such a wonderful boy. So happy, so curious. I never thought I could love anyone like that. Until your mother came along, of course, but Alby was first. I loved him like my own."

Knowing that Alby was not her biological son made things less complicated. It wasn't as if my mother could have learned the secret by accident, on some ancestry site, long after her mother was gone.

"Would you like me to help track him down?" I asked. "Would you like to see him again?"

Her shoulders tensed. "I don't know if it's possible. I . . . I've never been brave enough to look for him. They have all these resources now that can help with that sort of thing, and I considered it so many times. But I wasn't certain that was my intent, coming here. I just wanted to read the letters and remember, and then decide if I should try to share them with him."

"I think you should," I said.

My grandmother stared up at the clouds. The rims of her eyes turned red, and she blinked several times. "What if he doesn't want to see me?" she whispered. "He won't remember who I am. Why would he care at this point?"

"You're a piece of his history. Even if he doesn't remember you, you're still the connection to his mother."

Just like he was the connection to Harding. Now that I understood the story, I knew she wanted the opportunity to catch a glimpse of Harding in him. To hear her in his laugh, see her in his smile. If that was what would bring her peace in her final days, I was willing to scour the ends of the earth to find this guy in order to give my grandmother that gift.

"We could find him." I plucked at the grass, thinking. "The technology that exists for this sort of thing is pretty advanced."

"It won't be easy," she said. "I don't know who Harding really was. I only know her first name was Flannery."

"What about her aunt?" I asked.

My grandmother took a sip of tea. "I can't remember her name. I'm also not sure what village she lived in. It was so long ago."

That was an obstacle. We didn't have any pictures of Alby, either, so I couldn't use facial recognition software. But I was glad my grandmother had been brave enough to tell me what she wanted so that I could do everything in my power to accomplish it for her. It wouldn't replace the despair from all those years without him, but it might give her closure. Help her heal.

"If we find him," she said, "I'd also like to give him that money. It's what Harding wanted."

I paused. It was one thing to search for this man because my grandmother wanted to reunite, but I didn't want my focus to be on finding him to repay some debt.

"You don't owe that to her," I said. "She—"

My grandmother held up her hand. "She might have lied and cheated and all of that, but she had her reasons. We went through a time together that can't be explained or re-created."

"Have you thought about giving it to Mom?" I asked.

My grandmother shook her head. "It's not mine. I didn't earn it, and I didn't die for it. Harding, I believe that she did."

"What if we don't find him? I mean, we're going to try, but . . ."

"I've left it to Helping Hearts in my will, but it's not too late to change that," my grandmother said. "It's in a separate bank account from my regular savings in the States. It took years to deposit it all because I didn't declare it when I came to the country."

My mouth dropped open. "You smuggled it?"

"I was a young girl traveling alone with nearly five thousand pounds. That was equivalent to almost twice the average salary back then. I kept it hidden, then put it in the bank."

"How on earth did you smuggle in that much?" I asked.

Five thousand pounds would have been a cumbersome bit of cash, even if it was divided up into £100 notes.

"Sullivan put a false bottom in the steamer trunk. He and I made amends before I left. I also sewed some into the lining of my jacket. I figured that if they discovered my trunk, I'd have the backup funds in my coat."

I stared at her and then burst out laughing. She seemed surprised, but the more I laughed, she started in, too.

"I didn't realize you'd lived such an exciting life." I tried to picture my sweet grandmother laden with a trunk—and coat—full of questionably earned cash. Never in a billion years would I have suspected that to be her story.

My grandmother's expression became troubled. "It was exciting from the outside, perhaps. Like something out of a movie. Back then, it was one heartache after another."

"Did Grandpa know?" I asked.

"He respected my privacy."

"But . . ." I felt guilty that she'd carried this weight on her own. "Why wouldn't you talk to him about it? Or us? We're your family. We could have helped."

"Some things are too painful to say out loud." She held her necklace tight. "Until you don't have any other choice."

I considered the lush green lawn. The view of the sea, the sight of the hills and the cliffs, and the stunning property that was Aisling. Everywhere she looked, there had to be shadows of the past.

"It must be hard," I said. "To be back here."

She shook her head. "It's wonderful. I'm home."

Chapter Twenty-Seven

Ireland, present day

The next morning, the first thing I thought when I woke up was that my best friend never wanted to speak to me again. The words had tormented me through the night, mixed in with the emotion of my grandmother's story, and the pain was right there waiting for me in the morning.

My grandmother was sleeping comfortably as I headed into the shower, and I blasted myself with water as cold as I could handle to bring down the swelling in my eyes and face. I'd cried into my pillow for half the night. My grandmother had been through so much worse, I knew that, but it was a hard truth to swallow that I was the one to blame for making a mess of my life.

It took every ounce of energy I had in me to pick up the phone and place a breakfast order with Nora.

"Are you sick?" she asked after hearing my scratchy voice.

"No, I think the jet lag finally caught up to me."

"Ah," she said. "I'll bring you an extra-large coffee, then."

My grandmother woke up right before breakfast and settled in at the table by the window. Once Nora had dropped off our plates and the heavenly aroma of the extra-large coffee mingled with the cool breeze from the window, I pushed aside my grief and focused on what needed to be done to find Alby.

Picking up a yellow pad, I said, "Okay. I need to get some information. Did Harding ever tell you where she was from?"

My grandmother took a bite of her eggs. "Dublin. But who knows? There were so many things about Harding that she kept close to her chest. Other than the things that she lied about, of course."

"Where did you meet her again?" I asked.

"The Declee. It was a big, fancy hotel in Dublin. My parents took me on the last day of the Emergency. They didn't know the Emergency was about to end, of course. It had been spoken of for some time, so there was no telling. Harding was never a guest at the hotel, but she did business there." My grandmother gave me a wry smile. "I met her standing out front."

I pulled out my phone to take a look at the place she was talking about. "Wow. There's some history there."

"Yes." My grandmother gazed out the window, across the yard. "It feels odd now to think that I was there during the riots. That trip to Dublin was the first time I saw true poverty. The first time I witnessed violence." She picked up her fork. "I learned about loyalty that day. A man attacked me in the crowd; he hit me across the face. In spite of the danger, Harding didn't leave my side. She got me safely back to the hotel. I never forgot that."

The plate of food blurred in front of me. It only added to my misery to discover that, even with all her lies, Harding had been a more loyal friend than I'd been.

I took another sip of coffee. "What about her death certificate—was it filed here?"

"Under the wrong name, surely. No one knew who she was until her parents came along."

"How did they find out she died?" I asked, trying a bite of colcannon. It had really grown on me, with its mixture of kale and butter and a hint of onions on top.

My grandmother frowned. "I think my parents sent a telegram to her aunt."

I paused. "You didn't know her name. How did they find her?"

"I imagine they sent the telegram to the town where she lived with word to pass it along. Town gossip did its job, there."

"It must have been a small town," I said, noting that. "You don't have any idea where it was?"

"It was a train ride away from university, but I can't remember its name." My grandmother went back to eating. She thought for a few bites, then shook her head. "There are so many of those little towns. I just don't know."

"What about Alby's birth certificate?" I tried.

"I checked with the Civil Registration Service right after your grandfather died. I don't know what pushed me to do that, maybe the grief for your grandfather. I was always afraid the people who'd come after Harding would figure out that she had a son, and I prayed that wouldn't be so. I found out she didn't register him, probably for that very reason. She wanted to keep him a secret."

I nodded, looking at my notes. We had no leads. Harding hadn't wanted to be found back then, which made it even harder to find her now.

Pointing at the trunk, I said, "That belonged to her, right? I can search to see if it has a return address."

It still sat in the corner of the room. We'd looked through all the items in it but had never taken the time to look for any type of markings.

My grandmother squinted at it. "It's very possible her home address is hidden somewhere in there. I never thought to look. Some of the biggest secrets are kept in plain sight." She shook her head. "I'll never forget how easily the town accepted the claim that I'd found a baby. They never questioned it. They were genuinely shocked when Harding's parents came along to take him. A lot of babies were abandoned back then, but goodness. Why didn't anyone doubt it?"

"Probably because no one would expect you to lie."

I got to my feet and searched the trunk from top to bottom. There were no indicating marks on the wood, no address, nothing that could lead me to the source of where it had been made or purchased, or who it had belonged to. I sat back on my heels, staring at it.

There had to be something. Some sort of clue about who Harding was and how we could find her parents. They had to be long gone by now, but that path would lead us to Alby. Time was running out.

Returning to the table, I crossed "trunk" off the list, then wrote down "any possessions?"

"How about searching for him on social media?" I suggested, sitting back down. "Have you done that? It would be as easy as typing in his name and seeing how many Albys came up."

My grandmother took a drink of water. "Yes. There's too many."

I pulled up one of the main social media sites, typed in "Alby," and found a huge list of names. I held up my phone and showed my grandmother the pictures, scrolling through them. She shook her head.

While I was on there, it occurred to me to see if Tia was still a part of my account. She had completely disappeared, which meant she'd blocked me. Mouth dry, I shut the app.

I looked down at our list. I saw a few things I could pursue, like if the telegram office had any archives. If I could track down the telegram my great-grandparents had sent about Harding's death, then we might be able to find the aunt, even without a name.

"Wait," I said, thinking of something.

My grandmother's book of fairy tales rested on her bedside table. Wasn't there a name inside the front cover? I rushed over and took a look. Sure enough, it read *Grace Delany*.

"You said you found this book at Harding's aunt's house," I said, holding it up. "Is this her name?"

My grandmother peered at the signature. "Maybe. How would we know?"

I typed the name into the search engine, but again, countless options came up. Without the town or any other information, I couldn't do a thing with it.

"I don't know yet," I said. "Either way, it's a step in the right direction."

"I can't tell you how much your help means to me, Rainey. I've felt so alone in this. For years."

Fighting back a wave of emotion, I gripped her hand tight.

"Don't worry," I said. "I'll be right by your side."

I spent the day doing everything possible to find Alby, while my grandmother rested on the lawn, listening to an audiobook and making friends with the older couples who liked to sit there, too.

By late afternoon, I'd made countless phone calls and had spent so much time searching the web that I thought my head would explode. Finally, I got dressed to go out and take a walk.

It had rained, making it a bit chilly out, so I pulled on a pair of wellies and a heavy Aran-wool sweater that Nora had available for guests. The wool was soft and a little bit scratchy, but so oversize and snuggly that it felt like a blanket. It was comforting, which was exactly what I needed right now.

I caught a glimpse of myself in the mirror in the hallway and stopped in surprise. My hair—I hadn't paid attention to it at all. It just fell to my shoulders in loose waves and looked so different from the tightly held-back version I used to wear into work. Now it was tinged with the salt from the sea air, my skin was ruddy and chapped from the wind, and the only makeup I'd thought to put on was ChapStick.

I felt like a different person from who I was in Chicago. I'd worked so hard there, at all hours of the day. It was a grind, really, and even though so much of the visit here had been emotional, it had helped me find a sense of peace, too.

Heading down the stairs, I considered that. I needed to start searching for a new job the moment I returned to Chicago. When I did, I'd find something that would give me the time and space to do more than work. To focus on things I liked to do and spend time with friends and family. Because as my grandmother had shown me, those were the only things that mattered in the end.

∾

Mac called later that day, when I was about to join my grandmother in the library to see an Irish folk singer perform. I stepped out to the back lawn to talk to him.

"Sullivan plans to come in the morning," he said, getting right to it. "You should have seen his face when he heard the news that Evie was here. Does she still want to see him?"

"I'm sure she will," I said, feeling grateful. "I can't wait to meet him."

In the library, the performance had not yet started. The singer was chatting with some guests, while Nora finished setting up his equipment. I shared the news about Sullivan with my grandmother in a hushed whisper.

Her eyes went wide. "I didn't expect that." She leaned on the back-support pillow on the couch, holding her locket tight.

I hoped I hadn't crossed a line. "You want to see him, though, right?"

"Oh yes." She gave a firm nod. "There is no question about that."

∾

The next morning, I waited for Sullivan in the lobby, fascinated to meet the man who'd played an integral part in my grandmother's story.

I don't know what I'd imagined him to be, but the moment he walked through the door, he checked all the boxes.

Kind face. Brown wool sweater with a white T-shirt shirt beneath it, along with a plaid newsboy hat. A perfect, dentured smile and intelligent eyes. I liked him right away, which matched with the estimation I'd received from every person who'd spoken about him.

He considered the entryway of the bed-and-breakfast, taking it all in. Then he spotted me. His smile got even brighter, and he took confident steps toward me with his cane.

"You're Evie's granddaughter. I'd have picked you out in the middle of a crowd at the Senior Football Championship."

I held out my arms to give him a big hug. "Why do I already feel like we know each other?"

"I feel the same." He chuckled and took a seat in one of the lobby chairs. "Now, where is my Evie?"

"Resting at the moment." I hoped he didn't mind. "She really wanted to see you today, so I figured we could chat until she wakes up." I looked at my watch. "She's been asleep for a bit, so it should be any moment."

I'd left her a note in the room. She knew Sullivan was coming, so she'd woken up too early because she was so excited. That put her back to sleep right around the time he was scheduled to come by.

His eyes twinkled. "I might nod off myself for a few, but that seems to happen a lot these days."

"My grandmother had wonderful things to say about you," I said. "I know that there was some tension right before she left for America but that you two made up. She didn't get in touch because she was so distressed by everything that had happened. She never stopped caring for you, though. I wanted to get all that out of the way right now, before she comes down."

His face went serious. "I was planning to tell her this, and I still will, but you should know it, too. I was married and had four children—you've met my son, Mac. It's been a really good life, and I loved my wife immensely, even after she'd taken her last breath. In spite of it all, there was always a spot in my heart for Evie." He took off his hat and ran a hand over his short white hair. "I wondered what it would have been like if she'd stayed. If we would have had

257

a family together. I've found peace with it, but I'm not afraid to tell you that she was the love of my life."

I reached out and squeezed his arm. It made me grateful to think that, in spite of all the heartache she'd left behind, an enormous amount of love had remained.

"Can you tell me about Harding?" I asked.

He frowned. "How much do you know?"

"I know about Alby," I said. "I'd like to try and track him down, but I can't do it unless I know more about this girl."

"Well, Harding was something." Sullivan put his hat back on. "I can't say that I liked her very much in the beginning, but that was because she came in and changed things. For years, I thought I'd marry your grandmother, but then our relationship became about cleaning up the messes Harding left behind."

"Did Alby ever come looking for her?" I asked.

It was possible that, in spite of being a young child, he'd remembered his time with my grandmother and was curious about her.

"No, I've never heard that. Alby was little, you see. Probably doesn't remember much about his time here, and I bet the people who took him never said hide nor hair about it." He frowned. "I've thought about it a lot, over the years. That little boy meant everything to Evie."

"I wonder if—"

I was about to ask about phone records, whether there'd be any from that time, or if anyone had communicated with Harding's aunt by phone, but then I heard my grandmother say, "Sullivan O'Leary."

"Evie Campbell." That little old man hopped to his feet faster than I could blink. "Someone tell my children I love them, because I'm standing at the gates of heaven."

My grandmother walked to him, and he held out his arms. The two held each other tight. Then, right there in what was once the main entrance of my grandmother's home, Sullivan O'Leary swept her up in a kiss, and she kissed him right back.

Chapter Twenty-Eight

Ireland, present day

My grandmother and Sullivan seemed to forget about everything as they sat on the lawn and talked for hours. I kept going to see her, suggesting that perhaps she should rest, but she waved me away. Hint taken, I went back to my search for Alby.

I had no luck and went back down to check on her. Nora had just delivered them lunch. After I finally met her husband, Shane, a cheerful ob-gyn headed out to deliver another baby, she and I stood in the shade by the house, watching my grandmother and Sullivan as they shared their meal.

"This is absolutely darling," she said. "Every time I look over there, I just want to burst into applause. I knew they were friends but didn't know it was a love long lost."

"I know," I said. "It's adorable."

Each moment they looked at each other, the history they shared passed like a current between them. It was interesting that they'd lived full lives, completely separate from one another. Then, the moment they reunited, it was like they'd never been apart.

Nora wiped her hands on her apron. "I have a feeling Sullivan will not leave her side."

"I have a feeling that will be perfectly fine with her," I said. "Do you need help with anything?"

Spending so much time alone this morning had me thinking too much about the problems with Tia. I needed to find some company and focus on something else.

Nora brightened. "Sure! I'd love some help. I'm making biscuits. They're a little over the top, but everyone always loves them."

We both washed our hands in the big farmer's sink; then Nora sprinkled some flour on the silicone mats she'd laid out across the blue countertops.

"The dough should be ready . . ." She uncovered some bowls that had been sitting in a patch of sunshine. "Here we are." She set out four balls and handed me a rolling pin. "Let's do it."

The cookie dough smelled like spun sugar, and I got to work, rolling it out.

"It's nice to have a spare set of hands," Nora said. "I'm starting to get a little tired, these days."

"Well, I'm sure you get up at the crack of dawn."

She smiled. "Well, it's more that Shane and I are about to move into the next phase in our lives. It all moves pretty fast, doesn't it?"

"You're pregnant?" I looked down at Nora's stomach, surprised to realize that beneath that apron she always wore was a small bump. "Congratulations! That's wonderful news."

"Yes, we're excited. We've had the whiskey cake in the freezer for ages, so I told him we'd better get on it."

"Whiskey cake?" I echoed.

"It's the top part of the wedding cake. It's fruit, nuts, and whiskey. Spiced, you know. We had some bites on our first anniversary but saved the rest for the christening. I told Shane we couldn't let the cake go bad, so it was time to make it happen. We're having a little girl."

"That's wonderful," I said. "You must be delighted."

"Thrilled. And he's been around all these babies for years, so he's ecstatic to have one of his own. Kids are the greatest blessing." She set some shamrock-shaped cookie cutters on the counter. "We just found out the sex last week."

"Was Grady excited?" She looked at me, and I blushed. "I mean, he'll be a really good uncle."

"He'll be a good father, too. He's just as obsessed about it as we are."

"What's it like to raise a child here?" I asked.

Leaning against the counter, Nora told me all about the Irish traditions for the little ones, then all about their progression through school. She talked about the dresses she'd already collected, where she wanted the playroom to be, and the design ideas she'd had for the nursery. I'd never heard her say so much at one time, and finally, she beamed at me.

"I'm a little excited, as you can see," she said. "I keep thinking that it will be such an interesting life for her, being raised here."

"Aisling is so beautiful," I said. "She'll love it."

I thought of my grandmother as a little girl. Growing up in this house, running through the tall grass. Lying on the ground and staring up at the sky. Then the time she'd shared with Alby. Taking walks. Playing with him in the backyard.

The thought made me look out the back window to check on her. Sullivan was right by her side. They were both fast asleep in their chairs, their hands touching.

"That is a picture," Nora said, and she snapped it on her phone.

"It's wonderful," I agreed. "Those two were good friends even when they were little. Kind of wild to think about all that."

"Do you have anyone special at home?" she asked.

I wanted to tell her that I'd had a best friend, and in some ways, that had been more important than a man. Tia and I had spent every moment together, working, bingeing our way through the occasional Netflix marathon, and talking for hours over takeout. It was going to be hard to get used to life without her.

"No." Pressing down the dough, I admitted, "I've been single forever because I work too much. My best friend and I were business partners, and things fell apart. On Sunday, actually." I set down the rolling pin. "I'm a little broken up about it, to be honest."

"I'm so very sorry." Nora gave me a sympathetic look. "I've been there. The times I've fought with my best friend, it was like the world was ending."

"It doesn't feel like a fight." I thought of the things she'd said. "This was something different. I made a mistake, and I don't know if it's something she'll be able to forgive."

The more I thought about it, the more I realized how in the wrong I'd been. I should have been honest. I should have trusted her enough to talk about it all.

"People make mistakes," Nora said. "It's part of being human. It's how we choose to handle those mistakes that shapes our lives."

I thought of my grandmother and how she'd handled the situation with Harding, and the money. With Sullivan. Even though she blamed herself for running away, she'd been honest. Plus, she was still interested in finding Alby because she'd made a promise to Harding and wanted to see it through.

"I need to tell my grandmother how brave I think she is," I said. "The thing that you just said, about how you handle those mistakes. I think my grandmother believes she didn't handle things well when she lived here, but I think she did the best anyone could have with that mess. As for me . . ." I shook my head. "I could learn from her."

"How?" Nora asked, passing me a cookie cutter in the shape of a shamrock. "What could you do to make the situation with your friend better?"

I thought for a moment, then pressed the cutter into the dough. "Apologize. Send a note explaining why I did what I did. Let her know how much she matters to me, and then . . ." I moved the cookie cutter across the dough in steady succession, creating a row of perfect luck. "Give it time, I guess."

"Time heals," Nora said. "It's the best balm on the market." She admired the cutouts I'd been making, then handed me a jar of green sprinkles. "You do the honors. Even in the darkest times, there's still fun to be had."

Fun. The feeling seemed so far away.

I focused on shaking the jar of green sparkles over the shamrocks. The cookies looked pretty and, somehow, hopeful.

"It was nice, helping you with this," I told her.

Nora nodded. "I do think you should go upstairs and dash off that note to your friend. Time does heal, but a good apology note always seems to make it happen faster." She smiled at me. "Let me know if you need anything. If all else fails, I can always send my brother up for a chat."

My cheeks flushed. "I don't know what you're talking about."

She winked. "Don't you, though?"

Chapter
Twenty-Nine

Ireland, present day

Friday night arrived before I knew it, and it was time for my big night out with Grady. I nearly canceled, since I hadn't been able to shake my depression, but my grandmother talked me into going.

"Life is shorter than you think," she said. "Do you want to look back on your time in Ireland and think all you did was spend time with your grandmother instead of that handsome young man?"

"Considering that's what we're here for, yes," I said, but I decided to keep the plans.

Since an outing with Grady could mean anything from sheep shearing to mountain climbing, I had no idea what to wear. I settled on something simple: a flouncy pink shirt, jeans, and a casual sweater.

My grandmother opted for an early dinner with Sullivan, so before getting ready, I took advantage of the quiet to write that apology note. It ended up being two pages, on the stationery from Aisling. I used my neatest cursive writing, and I poured out my heart until my hand hurt.

I explained how much her friendship had meant to me over the years. How much I cared for her and didn't want to lose her from my life. Then I talked about what I'd learned about letting life move forward instead of trying to hang on. I told her I didn't want my job back, but the one thing I did not want to lose was her.

I finished the letter by saying:

> With time, I hope that you can forgive me for the mistakes I made and believe me when I say that the lie I told was a misguided attempt to keep this idyllic time we've had together alive. I will always be grateful for the business we built, the experiences we shared, but most of all, that I have been so lucky to call you my best friend.

It felt like something that should be mailed, but it would take some time to get there. So I took a picture to send by text and email, hoping she hadn't blocked me there, too. I hesitated, then pressed "Send."

If she didn't want to respond, I'd understand. It would hurt, but I was proud I'd been brave enough to take that risk.

∼

I headed downstairs to meet Grady and found my grandmother settled in to watch the piano player in the library with Sullivan. The guests were drinking, and there was a festive feeling in the air.

Once I'd kissed her good night, Sullivan leaned in and said, "Grady has always been one of my favorites. I think you're making a good choice with him."

My cheeks flushed. "How did you know I was going out with Grady?" I whispered, giving a nervous look around.

Sullivan chuckled. "In this village, you might as well bet that I know what you had for breakfast."

My grandmother laughed, and the two of them waved Nora down as she circled the room with a tray of drinks. I kept an eye out to make sure that my grandmother reached for sparkling water instead of whiskey.

Nora noticed, and she winked. "Have fun," she said as the piano player began to play. "I'll keep an eye on the kids."

"Thank you," I said. "Call if she needs anything at all."

Nora smiled at my grandmother, who was already mesmerized by the music. "I've got her. And don't let my brother take advantage of you."

"Of course not," I scoffed, as if the very idea of even being attracted to him was the most ridiculous thing in the world.

But the moment I stepped outside and spotted him waiting by his motorbike, there was no sugarcoating it—Grady was hot. His strong jaw was peppered with dark stubble, and he wore a cream-colored wool sweater with a collar that went up to his chin, framing him like a perfect photograph.

He held out a helmet. "You look beautiful. Thanks for not dressing."

I laughed and secured the straps around my chin. I'd been looking forward to another opportunity to get back on the bike, if only for the chance to wrap my arms around him again.

We set out along the coast, and for the first time all day, the tension in my shoulders started to fade. My worries about Tia relaxed, too. Instead, I focused on taking in the most breathtaking view I'd ever experienced as the sun started to dip in the sky and the hills loomed high above us.

This time, we were on the road for only fifteen minutes before Grady pulled into a small village. This one had a local pub made of stone, with the Irish flag hanging above its hand-carved wooden sign. Once we were inside, the pulse of the music and the buzz of conversation instantly swept me up into its joyful vibe.

"Would you like some wine?" Grady asked.

I looked around the bar. Everyone seemed to be drinking either whiskey or what looked like Guinness.

"I might try some whiskey," I said.

"When in Ireland . . . ," he said.

Once the bartender had poured two small glasses of liquid gold, I threw it back, waiting for the burn. Sure enough, my throat felt like it was on fire as it spread its warmth through me.

He rested his hand on mine. "Come on."

I tried to fight against the extra jolt of heat that came with his touch as he led me toward some stone steps in the back that could have been built in the Dark Ages. As we headed up, a hanging light illuminated our shadows on the wall in a way that felt both mysterious and romantic.

"Where are you taking me?" I could hear faded music coming through a door, and a smile cut across my face. "Real Irish music!"

"Finally, right?" He gave me that enticing grin and pushed open the door.

The entire room was in motion, a kaleidoscope of dancing to the bright tunes of an Irish violin. The band stood up on a small stage, a group of three women nearly as old as my mother, playing an up-tempo jig that had everyone on their feet.

"Shall we?" Grady asked.

I looked around. The dancing didn't seem to be anything too complicated, except it was all in the lower body. One girl was not moving her upper body at all, instead kicking up her legs and feet with gusto.

"Explain that to me," I said, leaning close to him to be heard.

He returned the favor, giving me chills. "Dancing was outlawed. So, back in the day, the Irish only used their legs so the Garda couldn't see them dancing through the window. Women held brooms to make it look like they were doing some vigorous housework. Look." He pointed over to the side of the dance floor, at a collection of brooms. "Those will be coming out later, when people have had plenty to drink, and they're not for sweeping."

"Let's try it," I said, and he led me into the boisterous crowd of people.

His dark hair fell in tendrils around his ears, and I couldn't stop thinking about our kiss by the water. Maybe my eyes said as much, because he grabbed my hand and gently pulled me close up against him. His sweater smelled so good, its wool soft but rough against my cheek, and I breathed in his spicy scent as our feet moved in time to the music.

The trio played song after song, some fast, some slow. The old wooden floorboards were thick beneath my feet, ancient and worn. The floor had seen so many generations of people walk over it, and it creaked and groaned but held strong. The bones of this building were firmly intact, and I wondered how long it had been standing, and how much it had seen. So many tears shed, so many loves shared, and so many moments of laughter, joy, and passion.

Grady went to the bar by the back windows to get us water. We kept dancing, the room spinning, and he smiled at me, as bright as the stars.

Leaning forward, he pressed his lips against my ear. "Follow me."

It was something I'd be happy to do again and again. He led me out to a large wooden balcony. It was dark by now, but I thought it overlooked a field. The cold air chilled my hot face, and I breathed it in. Several people were outside, but no one paid attention to us.

"Nora told me to not let you take advantage of me," I said. "I know that we also said that we were going to be friends and all of that. But . . ."

That smile that had caught my heart stretched across his face. Leaning in, I made a move to kiss him, but he stopped me, then pulled me into a back corner of the balcony where no one could see. I pressed up against him, his arms tight around me. I ran my hands up and under the back of his sweater, tracing the firm muscles in his back and relishing in the heat between us, stronger than the warmth of the whiskey.

My phone started to buzz in my pocket, and I pulled it out to turn it off. It was an Irish number, and I hesitated before holding it up.

"That's Nora," he said.

"Hello?" I said, picking up. "Is everything all right?"

I'd been in a different world here at the pub with Grady. The motorbike ride, the whiskey, the dancing . . .

Looking at the time, I realized it was getting late. We'd already been out for nearly three hours.

"How close are you to Aisling?" Nora asked.

Her tone was calm, but instantly, I knew something was wrong.

"Is she okay?" I asked. "We're probably fifteen minutes away. We—"

"She's fine, but she has a fever. It's up to 101."

My shoulders tensed. "Coughing?" I asked.

"Yes, a bit. It sounds deep, like it's hollow in her chest. I've contacted the doctor, and he's on the way, but I need to give her some aspirin. Is that safe for her?"

The first twinges of panic set in. This was exactly the thing that I'd been afraid of. That we would get here, and my grandmother would fall ill again. The idea that it had happened in a moment where everything had finally felt so good and peaceful was jarring, like a crystal glass that had shattered without warning.

"Yes." Mentally, I ran through the instructions my mother had given me. "Aspirin won't interfere with her other medications. We'll head back right away."

Grady took my hand to lead me back into the pub. The music rang out, too loud for me now, but I could still hear Nora.

"I won't be leaving her side," she said.

"Thank you." I felt a sudden catch in my throat. "Can I talk to her?"

"She's asleep. I'll have to give her the medicine, though. Would you like me to call you then?"

"Let her rest, and we'll be there soon."

I followed Grady down the staircase. It was the same type of phone call I'd received in Chicago, with its tall buildings, but now, I was here, with dark hills looming all around me.

"Are you okay?" Grady asked.

I held my helmet, letting it dangle by the strap. "Yeah. One thing I have to start being honest with myself about is the idea that maybe, my grandmother came here to die."

Grady squeezed my hand. "Then we'd better hurry."

Chapter Thirty

Ireland, present day

The thing I'd never considered about living in the country was how dark it could get. The moon put out its soothing light, and the stars poked through like specks of glitter. There were no lights to compete, to take away from the splendor of the sky.

I turned away from the window and looked at my grandmother. She was fast asleep in the bed, and Grady sat in the chair in the corner.

I walked over and knelt down on the floor next to him. He got to his feet to give me the chair. I tried to wave him away, but he insisted, so I sank into it.

"I can't believe she won't go to the hospital," I said.

The doctor had been here when we arrived. He'd informed me that yes, my grandmother had relapsed into double pneumonia and needed to be admitted to the hospital. Of course, she'd refused.

Now, she stirred in her bed. "I'm not leaving Aisling." Her voice was so weak I could barely hear it; then she drifted back off to sleep.

"I don't know what to do," I whispered to Grady.

My grandmother needed to be in the hospital, not here. Still, I could empathize. She had traveled across the world to return home. I didn't want to force her to leave. The situation alone was upsetting, but in the center of it was the reality that my grandmother was going to die.

I couldn't wrap my mind around the idea. My grandmother had always been there. Dressed in her brushed wool coat with the brass buttons, stomping snow off her boots and holding tight to a to-go coffee. Showing me how to check a cake to see if it was done without making its sweet center collapse. Magically appearing when I had a sore throat, with a new stuffed animal and the brand of unhealthy Popsicles my mother refused to buy.

Grady held my hand. "Have you got a hold of your mother yet?" he asked, keeping his voice low.

"Yes. It'll take her some time to get here."

I'd had the main office at the university send an assistant to tell her to call me, since she kept her phone off during classes. She was devastated, heartbroken to think this was how it was going to end. I booked her a flight, but it didn't leave for seven hours.

"If your grandmother wants to stay, I think we should put her in my house," Grady said. "That would give the two of you more space, and the nurses would have better access. She could be there until the end, if that's what it comes to."

It was such an incredible kindness, but I didn't want him to give up his house. But I also didn't want Nora to have doctors and nurses traipsing through the hallways at all hours. Still, I hesitated.

"I can't do that," I said. "Where would you live?"

"Nora will give me a room." He shrugged. "It's really no bother."

The situation was such that I did not waste my breath with niceties. "Yes." I gripped his hand tight. "Thank you."

∽

Grady lived in the old gardener's cottage, located next to the clearing in the woods where we'd sat on Sunday. It was small on the outside, with two front windows, a door, and a chimney in the center for the fireplace. The ivy had been cut back, and it had a clean, simple stone facade with a small pathway that led to the front door.

I went down with him to make sure moving her would be a good solution, and when we walked in, I marveled at the open floor plan. The cozy living area had plenty of bookshelves and a large fireplace. Everything was tidy. Not a dish in the sink, and all the blankets were neatly folded.

Grady stood at the door, thinking. "We could clear out this main area where the couch is and put the bed in the living room," he said, indicating the open area. "That way, she can have a view of the main house and the sea while she's lying in bed. The nurses will have an easy in and out, and you and your mum can sleep in the bedroom or in a cot out here. I know that Nora has at least one that we could transfer out."

"I think it's all a great idea," I told him.

We worked together to move the furniture. Grady propped the couch up against the wall, and once we'd transferred his bed into the main room, he moved it into his bedroom. He had a sweet collection of photos on his dresser—of himself, his friends, and his family—captured in a variety of silly moments. The idea that I'd have him around, in a sense, was oddly comforting.

Once or twice, my mind managed to revisit the moment where we'd kissed. I couldn't help but think of what could have happened between us in the next few days if life had taken a different turn. Rides on the motorbike, stolen kisses in wooden doorways, and the fun of a brief romance. Instead, we'd quickly stepped into much deeper territory.

Grady and I barely knew each other. Yet he was about to witness one of the most painful moments of my life. I didn't know him well enough to feel comfortable letting him in, but he was already there, and I didn't know what to do with that feeling.

Once the bed was set up in the living room, he packed his things in a leather shoulder bag. "Let's go." We headed back up to the main house, and he shined a flashlight to guide our path.

When we reached the front door, I stopped walking and said, "Everything is about to change, so before it does, I need to tell you one thing. This time with you has meant a lot to me."

He held my gaze. "Me too."

"I totally get it if you step back for a while. You're not obligated to be here, you know, just because you asked me out on a date. I—"

"Rainey." He took my hands and ran his thumb over mine, maintaining eye contact. "I'll stand with you. You do not have to face this alone."

Nora opened the front door. I fought back tears as she said in a hushed tone, "The nurses are ready to transfer her to the wheelchair."

The two nurses were strong, with large arms and a no-nonsense attitude, but they had kind faces. Once they'd seated my grandmother in the chair and wrapped her tightly in a blanket, they wheeled her into the elevator.

Outside, Grady shined his flashlight on the path, and the stockier nurse shook her head. "She'd get right jostled with that route."

My grandmother had already fallen back to sleep. She looked smaller and much more frail than she had only that morning.

"I can carry her," Grady said. "Rainey, shine the torch, okay?"

The nurse nodded. "I'll hold the oxygen. On three . . ."

Grady lifted her easily out of the chair. Her eyes fluttered open briefly but closed again as we walked. Once we got to the cottage and Grady had lowered her into the bed, she opened her eyes.

She fingered the locket at her neck. "Alby? Is he here?" She fought for breath. "We stayed here." She gestured at the room. "When he was young."

My eyes filled with tears. "Then it's the perfect place for you to be."

Her eyes were bright with fever. "Please, bring him to me."

I had to step outside. These were my grandmother's final days, maybe her final moments, and the only thing she could think about was what she'd lost. Not the wonderful life she'd lived or my mother, but the thing that had ripped her heart to shreds.

It hurt so much that I could hardly breathe. She had lived a life that had brought joy to so many, especially me. More than anything, I wanted to help her move past this heartache.

I thought of the Christmas a few months after my grandfather had died. My grandmother had upheld the traditions, and that night, like every year, she sat at the piano for her holiday playlist. The silver tinsel on the tree danced in the white lights of the tree; her hair was swept up in a silver chignon. My parents sipped their eggnog as she lifted her hands to play. Then she stopped, her hands frozen above the keys.

My parents were confused, but I knew the problem. My grandmother had always performed "Jingle Bells" with my grandfather. So I plunked myself onto the piano bench and whispered to her, "I'll be by your side."

I played the first chords, and we were off. Her look of gratitude warmed me as much as the cinnamon on the eggnog.

Now, I squeezed my eyes tightly shut, fighting back tears. After walking back into the cottage, I knelt by the bed and took her hand.

"It's okay," I told her. "I'll be by your side."

The nurses left detailed instructions. They planned to return in eight-hour cycles, to check her vitals and determine whether hospice was required. They also left a series of phone numbers, in the event I needed to reach one of them directly.

Even though my grandmother would receive better care in the hospital, I was grateful for this solution. My grandmother could remain in her beloved home, as she wanted, and I had the necessary support to keep her safe and as comfortable as possible.

Once one of the nurses had left and the other sat in a corner of the room to keep watch, Grady gathered his things, and I walked him outside. It was nearly one in the morning.

"We need to find the man she came here to see," Grady said. "Quick."

The fact that he'd said "we" meant more to me than it should have, and I pulled him close. He rested his chin on my head as the sounds of the night settled around us.

"I need to talk to Sullivan," I said. "Find out more about who Flannery was. Harding. What do I even call her?"

"Harding. That's how your grandmother knew her."

I nodded. "Do you think it will be possible to find this guy in time? I worry that if it could be done, my grandmother would have done it."

"Well, she avoided Ireland for years," he said. "It's not as if she's tried before, has she?"

I shook my head. "No."

"Then it's not going to be easy, but it's possible. Someone will have the information we need." He kissed my head, then stepped back, his eyes searching mine.

"Thank you for everything," I said. "Truly."

He hesitated, then gave me a quick nod. He started to walk across the lawn to the main house, but then he turned back. "Do you need me to stay? If you want me to be there, I can sleep on the couch in the next room."

Normally, I would have said no, that I could handle things on my own. But I'd spent too long trying to fix everything on my own, and now someone I cared about was right in front me, extending a helping hand.

"I'd be grateful."

We walked back inside together. I lay down next to my grandmother in the bed in the living room, where I could keep watch while listening to the sounds of her labored breaths. In the next room, the couch creaked as Grady settled in.

"Riley?" my grandmother whispered.

My mother. She was asking for my mother.

"Mom is on her way," I said, through the lump in my throat. "Rest now, and dream of the ones you love."

My grandmother fell back to sleep. The tears I'd held in all night streamed down my cheeks. I was so grateful to hear her asking for my mother. It had felt as though my mother had gotten pushed aside, somehow, in the midst of all this. It gave me such comfort to know she was in the center of my grandmother's heart.

I stared out the window. Outside, I could see parts of the sea. It frothed and roiled in the distance under the moonlight, keeping watch.

Chapter
Thirty-One

Ireland, present day

The next morning, I woke with the sun. It was bright in the cottage, but my grandmother was still fast asleep. I peeked into the bedroom and saw that Grady was sleeping, too.

My phone rang, and quickly, I silenced it. I didn't recognize the number, but it might have been one of the nurses, so I stepped outside to answer.

"Hello?" I whispered. There were already guests out on the lawn, so I stepped across the wet dew of the grass into a nearby grove of trees.

I stood listening to the man on the other end of the line speak. Emotions flooded through me. Bewilderment. Disbelief. Then gratitude.

Grady happened to walk out from the cottage just then, headed toward the main house. He looked rumpled and half-asleep, but when he saw me, he headed my way.

"Thank you," I said into the phone. "Thank you so much."

I hung up and stared at him.

"What was that all about?" he said. "You look . . ."

"Amazed? I am." I took in the bright-green lawn, the leaves blowing in the breeze overhead, and the sound of laughter from the guests in the chairs by the sea. Then I shook my head. "Turns out, there's no excuse for me to not use my intelligence to figure out how to find Alby. Because apparently, finding information is in my blood."

Grady raised an eyebrow. "You lost me."

"My great-grandmother!" I gestured at the house. "The one who never stayed home. The one who left my grandmother wondering why she followed her husband around instead of giving her daughter the love that she needed . . ." I blinked fast, fighting off tears. "The one who was murdered, without any leads?"

"Yes?" Grady prompted.

"Well, there was a reason for all that," I told him. "My great-grandmother was a spy."

~

Grady and I headed up to the house, talking a mile a minute. The news was so interesting, and I was relieved the man had called me today, while I still had time to share it with my grandmother.

"Your mother will be fascinated, too," Grady said. "How close is she?"

I checked the flight tracker on my phone. My mother had just left. She'd be here by dinner, and although my grandmother's breath had been ragged while she slept, I knew there was still time.

Grady and I planned to get coffee and breakfast and bring it all back. Enough for three, in case my grandmother woke to discover the doctor was wrong: this wasn't pneumonia but some simple, passing virus she'd caught on the plane.

Grady led us through the back door and into the kitchen. We stopped, startled, to find Sullivan already seated on a chair in the lobby, reading the *Irish Times*.

The heartbreak on his face made me hug him tight. He smelled like wool and butterscotch.

"I refuse to be sad about all the time we wasted." He folded up the paper. "Instead, I'm going to make use of every second I still have her in my life."

"Have you eaten?" I asked.

"Not yet," he said. "I figured I could get something here. This is a bed-and-breakfast, isn't it?"

I linked my arm in his. "Well, then, Sullivan O'Leary, let's get you something to eat."

With Nora's help, I got breakfast for four set up at the dining room table down at the gardener's cottage, right next to my grandmother's bed.

"I should tell her now, right?" I asked Grady, and he nodded.

My grandmother needed her rest. I knew that. I also knew that the question about her mother, and her seeming lack of interest, had troubled my grandmother her entire life. I was not willing to risk letting her go to her grave without hearing the truth.

Kneeling down next to her bed, I whispered, "Grandma, I need to tell you something." Her eyes fluttered open, and once they'd focused, I said, "I just learned something you'll want to know."

Sullivan helped her take a drink of water out of a cup with a straw, which the nurses had recommended, then I continued.

"I contacted the Department of Foreign Affairs to find out whether or not your mother had a job. Well, a man called me back. He wasn't allowed to reveal much, but ultimately, he told me that your mother did indeed work for them. She traveled with your father, and well . . ." I paused, and my grandmother gave a nod, as if to say, *Go on.*

"Grandma, your mother was responsible for gaining information about the areas they traveled to. The man wouldn't go so far as to tell me that she was a spy, but that's what it was, and it's something no one would have expected. Most people assumed she was just a woman traveling with her husband. She never wanted to leave you, Grandma, but probably felt she had no choice. She was duty bound."

My grandmother stared up at the ceiling. The words sank in, and her brown eyes pooled with tears.

"It's okay, my darling," Sullivan said, reaching for her hand.

"I know these questions have plagued you," I said. "But the Department of Foreign Affairs—they knew of the death of your parents and quietly investigated it in the years that followed. Their murders were orchestrated by a radical in Northern Ireland who your mother had fought to bring down. She's a hero, Grandma. The man who killed them was caught and put behind bars. He's still serving his sentence."

Sullivan looked furious. "Why didn't they inform her?"

"Because her parents had listed her as deceased," I said. "They made the change in your file shortly after you went to America."

Confusion crossed her face. "Why would they do that?"

"For your safety," I said. "You see, the man who'd killed them had once worked with your mother. He had access to everyone's file and was slowly coming after those he could get information on. If you'd not left for America, you would have been killed, too. The fact that you were gone kept you safe. It gave your parents a sense of peace, to know that you'd be protected."

My grandmother's eyes filled with tears. She clutched her locket and raised her eyes to the heavens.

"They were always watching out for you," I told her. "Even when they were away."

"I never dreamed . . ." She coughed.

"Rest," I said, but she grabbed my hand tight.

"My parents received justice. Knowing that is a gift I'd not expected," she whispered. "Thank you."

The lump in my throat made it hard to speak. "They loved you."

I sat back in the chair, and Sullivan gave me a smile of gratitude.

"May I?" he asked, and I nodded as he reached for her hands.

"You deserve all good things, Evie," he told my grandmother. "I've known that about you for years."

The nurses traded shifts in the morning and early afternoon. The shadows were long in the room when the latest one arrived. Grady had gone out to tend to the sheep, while I sat with my grandmother and Sullivan napped in a chair.

"How does she look?" I asked the nurse.

I'd been holding my grandmother's hand and reading quietly to her, even though she was fast asleep.

"Stable," the nurse said as she bustled around. "Pneumonia can be hard on the young and healthy, so it can be especially brutal for someone her age."

"Do you think she'll make it through the day?" I asked.

The nurse's hands were busy adjusting the oxygen flow, and they paused. "There's no true predicting, my dear."

I held my grandmother's hand a little tighter on that one.

My mother arrived that evening with a stoic expression and her typical no-nonsense air. Her computer bag was tucked under one arm, she wore a sensible two-piece brown suit, and she had her hair pulled back into a tortoiseshell clip. I hugged her tight, and then she stared at Aisling through a pair of sunglasses, her chin jutting out as she took it all in.

"It's much more imposing than in the pictures."

"You think?" I said, letting her adjust.

My mother had spent the whole flight alone with her grief, and I wanted to give her the space she needed. There were so many things to show her, to tell her, but they could wait.

She stood in silence, staring up at the house. "I thought that coming here, something would click about my mother." Her voice sounded hoarse, perhaps from the long flight or from crying. "That I'd see this place, and I'd see a piece of her that would explain it all. So far, being here feels like the start of a pretty vacation, but I know that's not the case."

"There's a lot that she's talked about here," I told my mother. "Lots that I can show you. Sullivan is here, too." We'd talked about him briefly on the phone. "He had a front-row seat for all of it, so he'll have plenty to say. There's also a photo album of your grandparents. Your grandfather looks like you." I let her sit with that for a moment. "What do you think? Do you want to go see her?"

My mother scratched her nose. "I'm scared." Her voice was quiet.

The words made me push back my nerves. I was young when my grandfather died. My mother and grandmother had grieved his loss together, while I spent my time riding my bike. Now, I needed to be there for her.

I pulled her into another hug. "We're going to miss her, aren't we?"

Her shoulders shook as I held her tight. "I know that everyone *dies*, but she's my mother. She's . . . her. She's not someone who just gets sick and *dies*. The woman never even had a cough drop or a Tylenol when I was growing up. I . . ." She went silent. "I don't want this to be the end."

"I know." We took a step apart and stood in the shadow of the house. "Let's sit out back by the water until you're ready. It's her favorite spot."

Through the window, I noticed Nora bustle through the front room with an armful of ironed napkins. She'd decided my mother should have the room in the house to recover from the flight or if she simply needed space, because Nora thought of those things. Of course, she refused to let me pay.

I guided my mother around the house to the back lawn.

"It is so beautiful here," she said. "I can see why people—"

She came to a sudden halt and took off her sunglasses.

"It's nice, isn't it?" I said, taking in the view of the sea.

"This is her yard at home," my mother said. "The layout. It's an exact replica."

I stopped in confusion. This entire time, that detail had escaped me, but now I saw it. The rose garden to the left. The wildflowers to the right. The small arbor of trees, next to the spot where my grandmother had built a small, charming shed. Even the stone pathways. The only thing missing was the sea.

"I never noticed," I said, quietly. "You're right, though. This is where she's spent most of her time."

Instead of sitting down in the chair by the water, my mother squared her shoulders and headed straight for the gardener's cottage. I walked beside her, still careful to let her move at her own pace.

~

Since I'd made my way through my list of ideas to find Alby, I headed to the main house to search through the items in the trunk. The sun's rays were getting longer, and most of the guests had moved indoors to prepare for dinner.

My phone rang. Tia, on video.

The person I'd have called the moment all this started, if I hadn't made such a big mistake. I wondered if she'd read my apology letter. It seemed like years, now, since I'd sent it.

Sinking down next to the stone wall of the house, I answered. "Hi."

Tia sat in a blue chair in her apartment, her curls backlit from the window. On the sill sat a blooming cactus I'd gotten her, one that had survived three winters.

"It's great to see you," I said.

Her face was so familiar. The curls, the glasses, the intensity.

"I was on my way to the airport," she said. "To come see you."

My shoulders tensed. "Really?"

"Yeah. But then I realized I don't have a passport."

I laughed, and my eyes filled with tears.

"Thank you for the letter," she said. "It's not your fault. I made so many mistakes, too. I made you feel that you didn't have a voice in our partnership, because I let my father run the show."

Tears streamed down my face. The past few days had been so hard, and it was such a relief to hear these words from someone I loved like a sister.

"You have no idea how much you mean to me," she said, chin trembling. "I'm not willing to lose you over this."

The tears turned into sobs, and I buried my head in my hands.

"Rainey," I heard her say. "It's okay. You're okay."

I waved my hand. So much emotion had built up inside me that there was really nothing else I could do. When I got it together, I wiped my eyes and blew my nose.

"I need you in my life," I told her. "It's not the same without you."

"Same for me." Tia took off her glasses and dried them on her shirt. "Well, since we're already crying, I might as well say it all. I would have paid for the flight over there with my signing bonus."

I nodded, the tears still coming. "You took the job?"

"Yes. I did."

I sat with that a moment, unsure how it made me feel. Fine, actually. Happy for her.

"It was a different one, though, one where my dad didn't get me the interview. I got it myself."

"That's so great," I said.

She smiled. "He was annoyed."

We both started laughing. When we got serious again, she said, "I'm ready to start living life on my own terms. Running that company with you was one of the greatest things I've ever done, but at night, when I'd lay down to go to sleep, I felt trapped. My decisions weren't my own. I'd rather work for a company and be honest about who's running the darn thing, instead of having it handed to me. I deserve so much more than waiting for someone else to make my dreams come true. You taught me that, you know."

"By lying?" I said, my cheeks burning.

"No, by taking charge. By taking matters into your own hands. You believed in us, in our product, instead of letting it go. Few people would have been strong enough to fight so hard for us in spite of an error. You didn't want my dad to jump in and put a stop to it all, so you handled it on your own." She smiled. "The serum passed, Rainey. It can go to market."

"Really?" I said, delighted.

"Yeah." Her cat jumped into her lap, poking its face into the computer screen. "Such good news. But then, my father decided it would be best to sell the company. My knee-jerk reaction was to disagree, but then I realized it's the best choice. I want to do research. Not this."

It felt anticlimactic to get this far, only to pass the finished product on to someone else, but I felt the same as she did.

"The only thing I liked about running the business was doing it with you," I admitted. "Congratulations. I'm happy for you."

The sale of the product would bring in a lot of money. Not a fortune, but enough to give Tia freedom from her father for quite some time.

Tia stretched. "Well, if something good comes out of it, which it should, I'd like to remind you that your contract had it written in that regardless of circumstance, you'd receive half the sale proceeds."

We smiled at each other.

"I don't deserve you after all this," I told her.

"I've never deserved *you*," she said. "I love you, though. It's really as simple as that."

∽

Tia stayed on the phone with me as I went up to search through the trunk, listening to every detail of my grandmother's story and my time with Grady. I searched the trunk from top to bottom for some sort of address that could lead me to Alby. There was nothing. Exhausted, I collapsed on the bed.

"I'm so sorry you're going through all this," Tia said.

I surveyed the bedroom where my grandmother and I had shared so many moments laughing over breakfast, looking through the photo album, or simply staring out at the sea. "I keep trying to remind myself that death is a part of life," I said. "That doesn't make it easier to say goodbye."

"Well, your grandmother shaped who you are," Tia said. "Losing her is like losing a piece of yourself. A blueprint of your heart."

I squeezed my eyes shut tight on that one, to keep the tears from coming. "I'd love to think that I'm like her," I said, "but she's a thousand times stronger. She lived through one of the most difficult periods in history, survived the death of her best friend and the loss of a child, not to mention fleeing to America, only to learn her parents had been killed and then worry that it was her fault. I mean, Tia . . . this woman baked elaborate cakes for my birthday and shooed away any boy who looked at me twice . . . and in the midst of all that, I never understood what was under the surface, all the things that had shaped her, until I came here."

"You are exactly like her," Tia insisted. "You're brave. You were brave to go there with her, and you're brave to see it out until the end. I know you're going to find this man, and help her find the peace she's looking for."

After we'd ended the call, I headed back to the cottage with her words ringing in my ear. I was halfway to the house, watching a few guests in the thick of a game of croquet, when I spotted Grady. He was coming from the area with the toolshed, looking gorgeous in a pair of rugged blue jeans and a blue plaid shirt.

"That jumper looks good on you," he called.

I'd borrowed one of his sweaters, a deep cream–colored Irish wool with patches of navy on the elbows. The sleeves were so long that my hands nestled inside them, like mittens.

Holding them up, I called, "It's big but cozy."

"I never knew it could look so good." He strode across the grass and came to a stop. Considering the guests on the lawn, he winked and said, "Let's take a walk."

My pulse quickened as he gently steered me toward the woods. Once we were hidden in the grove of trees, he leaned down and kissed me.

"I'm sorry if this isn't appropriate," he said, pulling me close. "It's just that I've been thinking about that all day."

I splayed my fingers with his as the birds chirped overhead. "If I've learned anything from my grandmother, it's to celebrate life while you have the chance."

"I have to tell you," he said, taking a seat on the log we'd talked on the other day. "Sullivan got to me."

"What do you mean?" I said, joining him.

"Well, I'm watching him sit by the bed of the woman he's loved from the beginning, in what could be the last days of her life, and all I can think about is how they missed out on so much time." He looked at me. "I know she loved your grandfather, and Sullivan loved his family, but still. Rainey, I can't stand the idea that once you leave, I might not see you again until I'm ninety. It's breaking me up inside. You're one of the few people that . . ."

His voice trailed off, and then he cleared his throat.

"Divorce is hard," he said. "It makes you question yourself and your ability to love and to be loved, and I have been very careful to stay at an arm's length from all of that, but then you came along and . . ." He turned to look at me again, a lock of hair falling over his eye. "There's something between us. I feel a connection with you that goes beyond what I can understand. Like I've known you much longer than I have, and I don't want to be away from you again. I can't put much sense behind it, but there. Now you know."

My mouth went dry. He'd put into words exactly what I'd been thinking.

"That's how I feel," I whispered. "When I look ahead to a few days from now or weeks or whenever it's time to go, it feels a little harder to breathe. To think you won't be there."

He took my hands. "What if you stayed for a while, so we could figure this out? Or I could come there and see where it goes. Is that at all the direction you're thinking, or am I completely misreading this?"

"I think we're more than on the same page."

Grady's eyes met mine, and then he leaned forward to kiss me. Deep and gentle, the type of kiss that I could have lived in forever.

I pulled him close, and we sank down to the leaves, the damp of the soil and the scent of the fresh grass rich in the afternoon. The heat between us built, and I was lost in the pattern of the sun shining through the trees and the softness of his hair beneath my hands.

Laughter from the croquet game on the lawn made us break apart, and we looked at each other. Grady's hair was rumpled, and he helped me up, gently brushing leaves off my clothes. It was everything I could do to not pull him back down to the ground once again.

"Where are you headed?" I asked, still trying to catch my breath.

"The sheep."

"Tell them I said hi."

"I'll go out first, so the guests don't think we were up to something, okay?"

"Oh, they'll know," I said, cheerfully. "If anyone takes one look at the absolute glee on my face, they'll know in an instant."

Grady shot me a wink before strolling across the grass toward the house. His shoulders were broad, like some hero in a painting: a work of art that could have kept me fascinated forever.

Chapter
Thirty-Two

Ireland, present day

The joy I'd felt in Grady's arms left the moment I walked into the cottage and heard my grandmother cough. My mother's eyes met mine. I took a seat next to her, by the bed, and we sat in silence.

My grandmother's condition continued to deteriorate through the night. It was as if, once my mother arrived, she'd given herself permission for a more rapid decline. We all slept in the cottage, with the exception of Sullivan, but he was back with us at six o'clock in the morning.

Nora brought us breakfast, but I barely had an appetite and only managed to pick at the fried potatoes. My mother read to my grandmother from the book of fairy tales. The words were soothing, and I stared out the window at the greenery of the trees, sipping on my coffee as Grady rustled the paper.

My mother finished my grandmother's favorite story and then flipped through the book to find a new one. When she did, a piece of paper fluttered to the floor.

"You dropped something," Sullivan said, reaching for it. "Well, isn't that something. It's part of a . . ." He hesitated, studying it. "Will you hand me that book for a minute?"

He flipped through the pages. "There it is." He peeled something off and matched it with the paper he'd picked up. "It's an old train ticket. April 1950. It must have been stuck to this page, sitting in this book for years."

"Can I see it?" I studied the damaged pieces. "This has to be the ticket she used to travel to the aunt's house. When Harding had the baby."

"Where is it, then?" my mother said quickly, peering over my shoulder. "Where's the village?"

I handed her the train ticket, and she peered through her reading glasses. Looking at Sullivan, she said, "Linwood."

"That's one hour north of here."

Silence fell over the room.

I opened my laptop and typed "Linwood" into the search engine, along with the woman's name we'd found in the book. The woman had died, but next to her obituary was a picture of a small, tidy house.

I knelt by my grandmother's bedside and gently touched her shoulder. When her eyes fluttered open, I showed her the picture. "Is this the house where you stayed with Harding? When she had her baby?"

My grandmother squinted at it. "Oh," she said, surprised. "That tree got much bigger." She stared at it for a moment, and her eyes closed again.

I nodded at my mother. "It's her."

~

The obituary for Harding's aunt led us straight to Harding's mother. She had passed, several years back. I pulled up her obituary and then saw his name.

Alby Murphy.

"I've got him," I whispered.

A collective hush fell over the room.

Quickly, with shaking hands, I typed his name into the search engine, along with the name of their town. His professional profile came up first, and I clicked on it to see the picture. Alby was in his midsixties, had a kind face with bright-green eyes, and worked as a project manager for a technology company. He looked friendly, like a person who might actually be willing to travel across the country to see an old friend.

"He lives nearby." I pointed at the name. "Isn't that about an hour?"

Sullivan scratched his head. "Depends on if you plan to be coming by bus or car—"

"Car," my mother said, quickly.

"Two hours," he said. "Depending."

"What do we do? Email him?" I said, glancing at my grandmother. She was fast asleep, nestled into her pillow with her mouth open. She looked as vulnerable as a child. "I mean . . . it's a little awkward, isn't it? To do this?"

We had been so intent on finding Alby that it had never occurred to me that it would be delicate to approach him. How did you reach out to someone you'd never met and ask them to come to the bedside of a woman who was dying?

"I'd think it was a hoax," Sullivan said, adjusting his plaid cap. "Plain and simple. You could not convince me to come down here to meet with strangers for anything in the world."

My mother nodded. "I agree."

I looked over at Grady. He hesitated, then nodded. Nora had just walked in with a plate of sausages for us all, and when we ran it by her, she agreed.

Even though I was frustrated with their response, I had to admit I felt the same.

Nora set down the plate of sausages, the smell of the smoked meat permeating the room like peat smoke. "I'd suggest taking your grandmother to him," she said, "but I don't think that would be safe at this point."

"Plus, such a huge part of this happened at Aisling," my mother pointed out.

"What does your grandmother want from it all?" Grady asked me, resting his hand on the table.

"To give Alby the letters," I said. "The opportunity to remember. She wants to see him, but I think it's more about having the opportunity to share her memories about his mother, to give him the chance to learn about Harding."

My mother settled in front of the computer to read his profile. "He sounds kind. He's involved with several charities."

Grady chewed on a sausage, thinking. "We might want to send an email first, and explain the situation. Give him about twenty-four hours to digest it all and then give him a call. If he picks up, he might be willing to come."

My mother leaned closer to the computer, rereading something. "He stopped working three years ago. He's a little young . . . Hold on." She clicked back to the search engine and scrolled down.

We both saw it at the same time.

In loving memory . . .

It took a moment for me to process what I was reading. To accept it. Because in spite of my desire to grant my grandmother her final wish, it was impossible.

Alby was already gone.

~

My mother and I held hands, with Sullivan, Grady, and Nora gathered at the computer behind us. It felt strange to cry for a man I'd never met, but that didn't stop the tears. He had shaped every breath of my grandmother's life, from the moment he was born.

When I agreed to bring her to Ireland, I'd had no idea why we were coming. To find the letters, yes, but I had no idea about the story that lived within them. Now, I knew the heartbreak that had chased her away and the power of the love that had brought her back.

That love wasn't only for Alby. It was for Harding. My grandmother had hoped to look into his eyes and catch a glimpse of her dear friend. To hear the timbre of her voice in his. To travel back in time and sit with the ones who had given her life such meaning.

My throat tightened at the thought, and I looked over at Grady. The things that mattered moved past so quickly. Often, they were gone before we could embrace them, or even be grateful for them, because they were always meant to fade away.

Grady walked over and stood next to me.

"I wish we could have met him," my mother said. "He went through his whole life not knowing there was someone out there who loved him like she did." My mother read through his obituary once again. Looking up at me, she said, "Cancer. Survived by two children. One day, we should talk to them."

"I'd like that," I said.

My mother closed the computer and got to her feet. "We need to tell her. In case she's waiting for him."

The thought made me lean in close to Grady, and he put his arm around me.

"I feel I should be the one," Sullivan said. "Nora, do you think you could print out the picture of him up at the house? Maybe even some things about him that I could share?"

"Of course," she said. "I'll be right back."

Sullivan nodded and took off his hat. He walked outside and stood in silence, staring out at the sea.

I sat down next to my mother in a chair at the table. Grady put his hand on my shoulder. I rested my cheek against it, watching my grandmother sleep.

Too many memories rushed through my head. My mind settled on one of the countless images of her greeting me at the bus stop, her smile lit with joy and the simple promise of a fun afternoon.

My grandmother had been one of the most significant people in my life, an Irish angel with a heart of gold. I'd do my best to live up to what she'd expected of me, to honor her legacy. More than anything, though, I would miss her. I would miss her with every breath. The thought made my eyes sting with tears.

I took in the sight of the cottage, picturing its storied history. The past was all around, mingled with the present, holding my grandmother like a warm hug.

My mother knelt by the bed.

"The letters," my grandmother whispered.

I winced, wishing she would talk of something—anything—else.

"Yes," my mother said, quietly. "I—"

"Each word brought me back," my grandmother said. "To—"

My mother's eyes filled with tears. "Mom, I—"

"To *you*." The words came out strong, and my grandmother fought to catch her breath. "Look in your dresser at home. There are ones at home to you. Keep them close, so you'll know how much I love you."

Tears streamed down my mother's cheeks. She went to her bag and returned with a collection of papers tied with red string.

"I do know," she whispered. "I know."

My mother cradled my grandmother close, gently kissing the top of her head, before helping her lie back against the pillow. My grandmother sank into it, fighting for breath, and closed her eyes. She coughed, deep and hollow, as vast as the sea.

The sound brought Sullivan in. He stood at her bedside and quietly took her hand.

My grandmother's eyes opened, and she gazed up at him. Then she drew in a sharp breath and stared at the foot of the bed. "Alby," she whispered.

She must have heard us talking about him earlier. Kneeling down, I said, "We love you, Grandma. We're here."

My grandmother smiled at me, then caressed Sullivan's face before grasping my mother's hand. Then she reached out her other arm and closed her fist tight.

Her voice was so quiet that I had to lean in. "I can hear it. I can hear the rain."

I took in a slow breath, feeling the weight of the history here. The strength of the love.

The rain had begun, and it fell outside the window, as steady as time. Our small group stood together in silence, listening.

Acknowledgments

Alicia Clancy, thank you from the bottom of my heart for this book! You encouraged me to step into new territory, and writing this story was such a delight. There's a reason you're a star.

Melissa Valentine, what a joy to have you join the party! Thanks for the perfect balance of encouragement and guidance. I loved working with you on this.

Brent Taylor, super-agent . . . book ten?! A milestone, and you've been there from the beginning. I'll always be grateful for that book signing at Carmichael's!

Lake Union, I continue to be astonished at your ability to put books into the hands of readers.

You're innovative, passionate, and I am beyond lucky to be one of your authors. A loud shout-out to the incredible publicity team—you're amazing. Heartfelt thanks also goes to the entire team that worked on this book, especially the additional editors, copyeditors, sales team, and audio team.

Stephanie Parkin, Jennifer Mattox, and Frankie Wolf, thank you so much for your early enthusiasm about this one. Stephanie, I will never forget that one breakthrough coffee. That talk, that moment, helped me suddenly see this book. That's the magic of our writers' group.

While writing this book, I thought a lot about friendship—in particular, the strong, beautiful, vibrant women I've been lucky enough to know through each season of my life. "Good friends can show you a whole new world." My life has been so much richer because of you.

Love to the Rice and Ellingsen families! And, Mom, I want to thank you and Dad for investing in my dreams. Theater training, encouragement to write, making sure I had books on hand . . . as parents, you led me to the path that was right for me. That's love, and I appreciate it.

Finally, to my family: Ryan, Hudson, and Hazel. Thank you for each moment, each beautiful second we've shared, and all the memories yet to come. I love you.

About the Author

Photo © 2010 Brian McConkey

Cynthia Ellingsen is the Amazon Charts bestselling author of *A Play for Revenge*, *A Bittersweet Surprise*, *The Winemaker's Secret*, and *The Lighthouse Keeper* in the Starlight Cover series as well as the stand-alone novels *When We Were Sisters* and *The Choice I Made*. She is a Michigan native and currently lives in Lexington, Kentucky, with her family. For more information visit www.cynthiaellingsen.com.